PENGUIN BOOKS

THE PENGUIN BOOK OF
RUSSIAN SHORT STORIES

David Richards, who is a Reader in Russian at Exeter University, was educated in Bournemouth, in the Royal Navy, at Oxford and at Eton, where he later taught modern languages. His publications include *Zamyatin—A Soviet Heretic* (1962), an edition of Lermontov's *A Hero of Our Time* (1962 and 1965), *Soviet Chess—Chess and Communism in the USSR* (1965) and *Russian Views of Pushkin* (1976).

The Penguin Book of
Russian Short Stories

EDITED BY
DAVID RICHARDS

PENGUIN BOOKS

PENGUIN BOOKS

Published by the Penguin Group
27 Wrights Lane, London w8 5TZ, England
Viking Penguin Inc., 40 West 23rd Street, New York, New York 10010, USA
Penguin Books Australia Ltd, Ringwood, Victoria, Australia
Penguin Books Canada Ltd, 2801 John Street, Markham, Ontario, Canada L3R 1B4
Penguin Books (NZ) Ltd, 182–190 Wairau Road, Auckland 10, New Zealand

Penguin Books Ltd, Registered Offices: Harmondsworth, Middlesex, England

First published 1981
Reprinted 1986, 1987, 1988

Printed and bound in Great Britain by
Cox & Wyman Ltd, Reading
Set in Monotype Garamond

CONTENTS

INTRODUCTION

VIEWED simply as a brief narrative in prose, the short story is one of the oldest types of literary art known to man, but in its more complex modern form it is a child of the nineteenth century, engendered simultaneously in France, Germany, Russia and the United States and reaching full maturity with the work of Chekhov and Maupassant.

The fluid modern short story is more easily described than defined. It must be concise – H. G. Wells suggested that no short story should take longer than half an hour to read – it usually conveys a distinct unity of impression, and, however relaxed and artless its narration may appear to the casual reader, it has to be carefully shaped and balanced. Much more than the novelist, the short-story writer relies for his effects on the apt selection of significant detail, on suggestion and the creation of atmosphere, and on presenting the truth about his characters or situations through sudden revelations rather than continuous development; furthermore, since the short-story writer normally hints rather than expounds, his readers must always be prepared to make active efforts of imagination.

The Russian short story, like so much modern Russian literature, began with Pushkin. Whereas almost all Russian prose written before him now seems laboured and antiquated, Pushkin's stories, most notably *The Tales of Belkin* and *The Queen of Spades*, still remain models of concise, polished and energetic Russian. Gogol too exercised a powerful formative influence, but his complex prose and grotesque imagination pointed in directions quite different from Pushkin's classical restraint.

The great Russian nineteenth-century novelists, Turgenev, Tolstoy and Dostoevsky, all wrote remarkable short stories, as did the later Gorky, Nabokov and Solzhenitsyn. A number of other Russian men of letters, however, such as

7

Garshin and Chekhov in the last century or Bunin, Babel and Kazakov in this, devoted their efforts almost exclusively to the short story itself. Beyond doubt the greatest mastery of the genre was achieved by Chekhov, to whom all subsequent Russian, and many foreign, short-story writers owe an immense debt.

The impressive standards set by Russian nineteenth- and early twentieth-century short-story writers have been maintained since the 1917 revolution, both by Soviet literary men and, perhaps more strikingly, by cultivated émigrés like Bunin and Nabokov. Indeed, the contribution to the modern short story made by Russian writers from about 1830 to the present day can hardly be paralleled in any other national literature.

In selecting items for inclusion in this volume I was guided by four principles. In the first place, to qualify for consideration a work had to be something English readers would recognize as a short story, no matter what its Russian author might have called it – for Russian writers are notoriously inconsistent in their employment of the terms *rasskaz* (short story), *povest* (short novel) and *roman* (novel). In the event, all but five of the selected items proved to be works classified by their authors as *rasskazy*; the stories by Pushkin, Lermontov and Gogol, however, are designated *povesti*; 'Bezhin Lea' is one of Turgenev's *zapiski* (sketches), while Gorky oddly sub-titled his 'Twenty-six Men and a Girl' *poema* (a narrative poem). Secondly, it goes almost without saying, I looked for stories of the highest literary quality; thirdly, I wanted each story to be typical of its author's work in general; and finally, by including works produced at various times from 1830 onwards, I hoped to give some impression of the development of the Russian short story over the past century and a half. To this end the stories in the present volume are arranged in chronological order, by date of first publication.

Thirteen of these stories have been newly translated for

this collection, while the remaining translations were all produced within the last few years, except for Raymond Rosenthal and Waclaw Solski's 'Guy de Maupassant' which first appeared in 1950, and Constance Garnett's rendering of Chekhov's 'The Party' which was published in 1917. The only Russian author who is also his own translator is the inimitable Nabokov.

D.R.
Exeter, 1979

ACKNOWLEDGEMENTS

Acknowledgement is due to the following for permission to reprint the stories specified:

The Bodley Head and Farrar, Straus & Giroux, Inc., for 'Zakhar-the-Pouch' by Alexander Solzhenitsyn from *Stories and Prose Poems* translated by Michael Glenny

The translator's literary estate, Chatto & Windus and Macmillan (New York), Inc., for 'The Party' by Anton Chekhov translated by Constance Garnett

William Heinemann Ltd and Doubleday & Co., Inc., for 'Spring in Fialta' by Vladimir Nabokov from *Nabokov's Dozen* translated by Vladimir Nabokov

Methuen & Co and S. G. Phillips, Inc., for 'Guy de Maupassant' by Isaac Babel from *Collected Stories* translated by Raymond Rosenthal and Waclaw Solski

Penguin Books Ltd for 'The Nose' by Nikolay Gogol from *The Diary of a Madman and Other Stories* translated by Ronald Wilks; 'Taman' by Mikhail Lermontov from *A Hero of Our Time* translated by Paul Foote; 'Bezhin Lea' by Ivan Turgenev from *Sketches from a Hunter's Album* translated by Richard Freeborn

VAAP for permission to translate 'Ida' by Ivan Bunin; 'Twenty-Six Men and a Girl' by Maxim Gorky; 'On the Island' by Yury Kazakov; 'The Winter Oak' by Yury Nagibin; 'Streams Where Trout Play' by Konstantin Paustovsky; 'The Third Son' by Andrey Platonov; 'The Lion' by Evgeny Zamyatin.

PUSHKIN

ALEXANDER PUSHKIN is one of the most attractive nineteenth-century Russian writers. In his brief career – cut short when he was killed in a duel – he forged much of the modern literary language and established an unsurpassed aesthetic standard. Russians regard him as their national poet, but his cool elegance and light touch are more reminiscent of the French eighteenth century than of any previous or subsequent Russian literary achievements. 'The Shot' is one of the five *Tales of Belkin* which Pushkin wrote in the autumn of 1830. In it the author's crisp and energetic prose style shows to great advantage.

THE SHOT

Translated by David Richards

A duel we fought. (Baratynsky)

I vowed to put a bullet through him in
accordance with the duelling code — he
still owed me my shot.
(*An Evening in Bivouac*)

I

WE were stationed in the little town of X. The life of an
ordinary officer is well known: in the morning drill and
riding practice; then dinner with the colonel or at a Jew's
inn; and in the evening, punch and cards. In X there was
not one open house or marriageable girl; we would gather
at each other's quarters, where, apart from our uniforms,
we saw nothing.

Only one man belonged to our group without being an
army officer. He was about thirty-five years old and consequently we considered him an old man. Experience gave
him many advantages over us; moreover his habitually
sombre air, austere disposition and sharp tongue had a
powerful influence on our young minds. A certain mysteri-
ousness shrouded his fate; he seemed to be Russian, but
bore a foreign name. At one time he had served in the
Hussars and indeed with success; no one knew what had
caused him to retire and settle in this poor little town where
he lived simultaneously both poorly and extravagantly; he
always went on foot, dressed in a threadbare, black frock-
coat, but he kept an open table for all the officers of our
regiment. True, dinner would consist of two or three dishes
prepared by a retired soldier, but champagne withal flowed
like water. No one knew the extent of either his capital or

his income, and no one took the liberty of asking him about them. There were books in his house, for the most part on military matters, but also a few novels. He willingly lent them, never requesting their return; but then he never returned to its owner any book he himself borrowed. His chief regular occupation consisted in pistol-shooting. The walls of his room were riddled with bullets and full of holes like a honey-comb. An expensive collection of pistols was the sole luxury in the little thatched clay house where he lived. The degree of skill he had achieved was incredible, and if he had offered to shoot a pear off anyone's cap, no one in the regiment would have hesitated over exposing his head to the shot. Our conversation often touched on duelling, but Silvio (as I shall call him) never joined in. When asked if he had ever chanced to fight a duel, he dryly replied that he had, but would not go into any details, and it was evident that he found such questions distasteful. We assumed that he had on his conscience some unfortunate victim of his fearsome skill. At the same time it never even entered our heads to suspect him of anything like lack of confidence. There are men whose appearance alone banishes all such suspicions. However, a certain chance incident amazed us all.

One day some ten of our officers were dining at Silvio's. We had been drinking as usual, that is a great deal; after dinner we began to urge our host to put up the bank for us in a gambling game. For a long time he declined, for he rarely gambled, but in the end he ordered some cards to be brought, tipped fifty ten-rouble coins on to the table and sat down to deal. We grouped ourselves round him, and play began. It was Silvio's habit to maintain complete silence while playing, never to argue and never to offer explanations. If one of the players happened to miscalculate, he would immediately either pay out the surplus money or chalk up the remainder. We knew this well enough and never interfered with his running things in his own way;

but on this occasion we had with us an officer who had only recently been transferred to the regiment. He was also playing and absent-mindedly doubled his stake in error. Silvio picked up the chalk and adjusted the score in his usual way. Thinking that Silvio had made a mistake, the officer launched into explanations. Silvio silently continued dealing. Then the officer lost his patience, picked up the duster and rubbed out what seemed to him to have been wrongly chalked up. Silvio picked up the chalk and wrote it again. The officer, excited by the wine, the gambling and the laughter of his comrades, decided that he had been grossly insulted; in a fury he snatched a brass candlestick off the table and hurled it at Silvio, who only just managed to avoid being hit. We were all taken aback. Silvio stood up, white with rage, and with flashing eyes pronounced:

'My dear sir, have the goodness to leave, and thank God that this happened in my house.'

We had no doubt about the consequences and counted our new comrade already dead. The officer left, saying he was prepared to answer for the offence in whatever way the banker might choose. Play continued for a few more minutes but, sensing that our host was in no mood for the game, we stood down one after the other and dispersed to our quarters, talking about the impending vacancy.

The next day at riding practice we were just asking whether the poor lieutenant was still alive when he himself appeared among us; we put the same question to him. He replied that he had not yet received any communication from Silvio. This astonished us. We went to Silvio and found him in the yard, sending bullet after bullet into an ace which was glued on to the gate. He received us in his usual way, without saying a word about the previous evening's occurrence. Three days passed, and the lieutenant was still alive. Surely Silvio's going to fight? we asked in astonishment. But Silvio did not fight. He contented himself with a very mild apology and made his peace.

This came close to doing him immense damage in the esteem of the young officers. Lack of courage is the last thing to be excused by young men, who usually regard bravery as the acme of human virtue and an excuse for all manner of vices. However, gradually all was forgotten, and Silvio regained his former influence.

I alone was quite unable to feel close to him again. Possessing a naturally romantic imagination, I had previously been more strongly attached than all the others to this man whose life was an enigma and who seemed to me like the hero of some mysterious tale. He was fond of me; at least, it was only with me that he abandoned his customary biting sarcasm and spoke about various topics in a straightforward and uncommonly agreeable manner. But after that unfortunate evening the thought that his honour had been sullied, and by his own fault left uncleared, that thought would not leave me and prevented me from behaving towards him as I had previously; I felt ashamed when I looked at him. Silvio was too intelligent and too experienced not to notice this and not to guess the reason for it. This appeared to distress him; at least, I noticed a couple of times a desire on his part to explain things to me; but I evaded these opportunities and Silvio gave up the attempt. After that I saw Silvio only when my comrades were also there, and our former open conversations ceased.

The distracted inhabitants of the capital have no conception of many emotions which are very familiar to the inhabitants of villages and small towns, such as for instance looking forward to post day: on Tuesdays and Fridays our regimental office would be full of officers, some expecting money, some a letter, some newspapers. Post was usually opened on the spot, news would be announced, and the office would present a most animated picture. Silvio's letters were also addressed to our regiment and he would usually be there too. One day he was handed a letter whose seal he tore open with an expression of the greatest impatience on his face. As he ran through the letter his eyes flashed. The officers, all occupied with their own letters, noticed nothing.

'Gentlemen,' Silvio said to them, 'circumstances demand my immediate departure; I shall travel this very night. I hope you will not refuse to dine with me for the last time. I expect you too,' he continued, turning to me. 'I expect you without fail.'

With these words he hurried out, and having agreed to gather at Silvio's, we went our separate ways.

I arrived at Silvio's at the appointed time and found almost the entire regiment in his house. All his goods had already been packed, and there remained only the bare, riddled walls. We sat down at the table; our host was in an extremely good mood and soon his cheerfulness became general; corks popped every other minute, glasses foamed and hissed unceasingly, and with the utmost zeal we wished our departing friend a pleasant journey and all good fortune. It was already late in the evening when we got up from the table. As we sorted out our caps Silvio, who was bidding everyone farewell, took me by the arm and stopped me just as I was about to leave.

'I must have a word with you,' he said quietly.

I stayed behind.

The guests had all gone, leaving the two of us alone together; we sat down opposite one another and silently lit our pipes. Silvio was preoccupied; every trace of his convulsive cheerfulness had gone. His sombre pallor, his flashing eyes and the thick smoke issuing from his mouth gave him a truly diabolical appearance. After a few minutes Silvio broke the silence.

'Perhaps we shall never see each other again,' he said to me. 'Before we part I wanted to explain things to you. You may have noticed that I have little respect for others' opinions, but I'm fond of you and understand your feelings; I would find it painful to leave an unjust impression in your mind.'

He paused and began to refill his pipe, which had gone out; I remained silent, staring at the floor.

'You found it strange,' he continued, 'when I failed to demand satisfaction from that drunken fool, R. You will agree that since I had the right to choose weapons his life was in my hands, while my own was in hardly any danger. I could ascribe my restraint simply to magnanimity, but I do not want to lie. If I could have punished R. without risking my own life in the slightest, then nothing would have persuaded me to forgive him.'

I looked at Silvio in amazement. His declaration had taken me aback.

'Yes, precisely,' Silvio continued, 'I do not have the right to expose myself to the risk of death. Six years ago I received an insult and my enemy is still alive.'

My curiosity was greatly excited.

'Did you not fight with him?' I asked. 'I suppose circumstances kept you apart?'

'I did fight with him,' replied Silvio. 'And here is a souvenir of our duel.'

He got up and took out of a cardboard box a red hat with braid and a gold tassel – the sort which the French call *bonnet de police*; he put it on; there was a hole through it less than two inches above his forehead.

'You know,' continued Silvio, 'that I used to serve in a certain Hussar regiment. My character is familiar to you: I am used to taking the leading role in any company, but in my youth that was my ruling passion. In our day daredevilry was all the rage and I was the army's leading daredevil. We used to boast of our drinking bouts – once I outdrank the famous Burtsov who is celebrated by Denis Davydov. Duels were constantly being fought in our regiment, and I was either a witness or a participant in all of them. My comrades worshipped me, and our commanding officers, who were continually being replaced, regarded me as a necessary evil.

'I was quietly (or noisily) enjoying my reputation when

we were joined by a young man from a rich and noble family – I don't want to name him. Never in my life had I met anyone of such brilliance and good fortune. Picture to yourself youth, intelligence, beauty, the most furious gaiety, the most carefree courage, a famous name and money, which he kept no account of but which never ran out, and imagine the effect he was bound to produce among us. My supremacy was in the balance. Captivated by my reputation, he was on the point of seeking my friendship, but I met him coldly, and without the slightest regret he moved away from me. I conceived a hatred for him. His successes in the regiment and in women's company brought me to complete despair. I began to seek quarrels with him; to my epigrams he responded with his own, which always seemed to me more spontaneous and sharper than mine and which were naturally incomparably more amusing, for he jested, while I indulged my malice. At last, at a ball given one day by a Polish landowner, seeing him the centre of attention of all the ladies, and especially of the hostess herself with whom I enjoyed a liaison, I whispered some unsubtle rude remark in his ear. He flared up and slapped my face. We rushed for our sabres; the ladies swooned; we were dragged away from each other, but that very night we rode out to fight.

'The duel took place at dawn. I was standing at the appointed place with my three seconds, awaiting my opponent with indescribable impatience. The spring sun had risen and the heat was beginning to make itself felt. I caught sight of him in the distance. He was coming on foot in full uniform with sabre and accompanied by a single second. We walked towards him. He approached, carrying his cap which was full of cherries. The seconds measured out twelve paces for us. I was supposed to shoot first, but my fury made me so agitated that I felt I couldn't count on my hand being steady and, so as to give myself time to calm down, I ceded the first shot to him; my opponent would not agree. It was decided that we should cast lots, and the winning number went to

him, eternal darling of the gods. He took aim and his shot
went through my hat. Now it was my turn. His life was at
last in my hands; I scrutinized him avidly, endeavouring to
detect just the faintest flicker of anxiety. He stood in front of
my pistol, selecting ripe cherries from his cap and spitting
out the stones which flew right to where I was standing. His
indifference infuriated me. What's the point, I suddenly
thought, of depriving him of his life, when he doesn't value
it at all? A malicious thought flashed through my mind. I
lowered my pistol.

'"It appears, you are now in no mood to die," I said to
him. "You wish to breakfast; I have no desire to disturb
you."

'"You are not disturbing me in the least," he retorted.
"Be so kind as to fire – or just as you please; you may keep
your shot, I am always at your service."

'I turned to my seconds, announcing that I had no intention of firing that day, and with that our duel finished.

'I retired from the army and withdrew to this little town.
From that time not a single day has passed without my
thinking of revenge. Today the moment has come . . .'

Silvio took out of his pocket the letter he had received
that morning and gave it to me to read. Someone–apparently
his business agent – had written to him from Moscow that a
certain individual was soon to enter into marriage with a
young and beautiful girl.

'You can guess who this certain individual is,' said Silvio.
'I am going to Moscow. We shall see whether he greets
death just as nonchalantly on the eve of his wedding as he
once awaited it with his cherries!'

With these words Silvio stood up, threw his cap on to the
floor and began to pace up and down the room, like a tiger
in its cage. I listened to him without moving; strange con-
flicting emotions stirred within me.

A servant came in and announced that the horses were
ready. Silvio clasped my hand firmly and we embraced. He

climbed into a small cart in which two cases were lying, one containing his pistols and the other his effects. We bade each other farewell once more, and the horses galloped off.

II

Several years passed and domestic circumstances obliged me to settle in a poor hamlet in the district of N. Busying myself with my farming, I never ceased to sigh quietly for my former boisterous and carefree life. The most difficult thing for me to get used to was spending the autumn and winter evenings in complete solitude. I managed somehow to drag out the time up to dinner, talking with the village headman, riding around to inspect the work or visiting new developments; but as soon as it began to grow dark I did not know what to do with myself. The few books which I had found under cupboards or in the store-room I had read until I knew them by heart. All the tales which my housekeeper, Kirilovna, could possibly remember had been told to me over and over again; the peasant women's songs bored me to death. I almost took to rough spirits, but they made my head ache; I must admit I was afraid of becoming a drunkard from *hard luck*, that is the most *hardened* type of drunkard, of which I saw numerous examples in our district. I had no close neighbours near by apart from two or three *hardened* ones whose conversation consisted for the most part of hiccups and sighs. Solitude was more bearable.

About three miles away from me was a rich estate belonging to a Countess B., but only her steward lived there, the countess herself having visited the estate only once, in the first year of her marriage – and then she had stayed for less than a month. However, during the second spring of my seclusion the rumour circulated that the countess and her husband were coming to their village for the summer. And indeed they arrived at the beginning of June.

The arrival of a rich neighbour is an important epoch in the life of country folk. The landowners and their servants talk about it for a couple of months beforehand and for some three years afterwards. As far as I was concerned, I must confess, the news of the advent of a young and pretty neighbour had a strong effect on me; I burned with impatience to see her and so the first Sunday after their arrival I set off after dinner to introduce myself to their excellencies as their nearest neighbour and most humble servant.

A footman took me to the count's study and went off to announce my presence. The spacious study was appointed with the utmost luxury; the walls were lined with bookcases, on each of which stood a bronze bust; above the marble fireplace was a wide mirror; the floor was covered with a green cloth and several carpets. Having grown unaccustomed to luxury in my poor corner and not having seen anyone else's riches for a long time, I found my confidence waning and I awaited the count with some trepidation, as a petitioner from the provinces waits for a minister's appearance. The doors opened and in came a most handsome man of about thirty-two. The count came up to me with an open and friendly air; I tried to regain my assurance and was just about to introduce myself when he forestalled me. We sat down. His conversation, easy and amiable, soon dispelled my unsociable bashfulness; I was just beginning to recover my normal state when suddenly the countess came in and I was overcome with confusion worse than before. She was indeed beautiful. The count introduced me; I strove to appear at ease but, the more I tried to assume an air of naturalness, the more awkward I felt. In order to give me time to compose myself and get used to new acquaintances, they began to talk to each other, treating me as an old neighbour and without any ceremony. Meanwhile I began to walk up and down, examining the books and the pictures. I am no expert on pictures but one drew my attention. It depicted some Swiss scene, but what struck me was not the painting itself, but the circumstance that in the picture were two bullet-holes, one on top of the other.

'That's a good shot,' I said, turning to the count.

'Yes,' he replied, 'a most remarkable shot. And do you shoot well?' he continued.

'Quite well,' I replied, cheered that the conversation had at last touched on a subject dear to my heart. 'I won't miss a card at thirty paces – that is of course with pistols I'm used to.'

'Really?' said the countess with a most attentive expression on her face. 'And would *you* hit a card at thirty paces, my dear?'

'One day we shall try it,' answered the count. 'In my time I wasn't a bad shot, but it's four years now since I last handled a pistol.'

'Well,' I remarked, 'in that case I wager your excellency won't hit a card even at twenty paces; pistol-shooting needs daily practice. I know that from my own experience. I was considered one of the best marksmen in our regiment. Once I happened not to touch a pistol for a whole month – mine were being mended – and would you believe it, your excellency, the first time I tried shooting after that I missed a bottle four times in a row at twenty-five paces. We had a cavalry captain who was a wit and an amusing chap; he happened to be there and said to me: "You see, my friend, your hand refuses to do violence to a bottle." No, your excellency, you mustn't neglect to practise, otherwise you'll immediately lose the knack. The best marksman I ever met used to shoot every day, at least three times before dinner. It was as much part of his routine as a glass of vodka.'

The count and countess were glad that I had begun to talk more freely.

'But how did he practise?' the count asked me.

'Well, in this way, your excellency: he would see a fly land on the wall. You laugh, countess? Honestly, it's the truth. He would see a fly and shout, "Kuzka, bring my pistol!"

Kuzka brings him a loaded pistol. Bang – and the fly is squashed into the wall!'

'That's amazing!' said the count. 'And what was his name?'

'Silvio, your excellency.'

'Silvio!' exclaimed the count, leaping up from his seat. 'You knew Silvio?'

'I certainly did, your excellency. We were friends. He was accepted in the regiment as one of us. But it must be five years now since I last heard anything of him. So your excellency must have known him too?'

'Yes, I knew him very well. Did he never tell you about a certain very strange incident?'

'You don't mean the slap, your excellency, which he was given at a ball by some scoundrel?'

'And did he tell you this scoundrel's name?'

'No, your excellency, he didn't. Oh, your excellency,' I continued, realizing the truth, 'forgive me . . . I didn't know . . . It can't have been you?'

'It was I,' answered the count, with an extremely agitated air, 'and that picture with the bullet-holes is a souvenir of our last meeting . . .'

'Oh, my darling,' said the countess, 'for Heaven's sake don't tell that story; I shall be frightened, listening to it.'

'No,' said the count, 'I will tell it; he knows how I insulted his friend; let him now learn how Silvio avenged himself on me.'

The count moved up an armchair for me, and with the most intense curiosity I heard the following story.

'Five years ago I got married. The first month – what the English call "the honeymoon" – I spent here in this village. To this house I owe the happiest moments of my life and one of my most painful memories.

'One evening we went out for a ride together; my wife's horse for some reason started refusing, she became frightened, handed the reins to me and set off home on foot. I rode

23

on ahead. In the courtyard I saw a travelling waggon and was told that waiting in my study was a man who had declined to give his name, saying simply that he had business with me. I came into this room and in the darkness made out a man who was covered in dust and wearing several days' growth of beard; he was standing here by the fireplace. I went up to him, trying to recall his face.

'"You don't recognize me, count?" he said in a trembling voice.

'"Silvio!" I exclaimed, and I must confess I felt my hair standing on end.

'"Precisely," he continued. "A shot is owing to me; I have come to discharge my pistol. Are you ready?"

'A pistol was protruding from one of his side pockets. I measured out twelve paces and stood over there in the corner, begging him to shoot quickly, before my wife returned. He lingered and asked for more light. Candles were brought in. I shut the door firmly, ordered that everyone should keep out and again asked him to shoot. He took out his pistol and aimed . . . I counted the seconds . . . I thought about her . . . A terrible minute went by. Then Silvio lowered his arm.

'"I am sorry," he said, "that my pistol is not loaded with cherry stones – the bullet is heavy. I keep thinking that I am engaging in a murder rather than a duel: I am not accustomed to aiming at an unarmed man. Let us begin afresh. We shall cast lots to see who is to fire first."

'My head was spinning . . . I think at first I didn't agree . . . Finally we loaded another pistol; we screwed up two pieces of paper; he put them in the cap which I had once shot my bullet through; again I drew the first number.

'"You, count, are diabolically lucky," he said with a mocking smile which I shall never forget.

'I don't understand what came over me and how he managed to force me into it, but . . . I fired and hit that picture.'

The count pointed at the picture with the bullet-holes. His

face glowed like fire; the countess was paler than her own kerchief. I could not restrain an exclamation.

'I fired,' continued the count, 'and, thank God, I missed; then Silvio – at that moment he was in truth terrible – Silvio began to take aim at me. Suddenly the doors flew open and Masha runs in, screams and throws her arms round my neck. Her presence restored my courage.

'"Darling," I told her, "can't you see we're joking? How frightened you were! Go and drink a glass of water, then come back to us and I will introduce to you an old friend and comrade."

'Masha still found it hard to believe.

'"Tell me, is my husband speaking the truth?" she asked, turning to the menacing Silvio. "Is it true that you're both joking?"

'"He is always joking, countess," replied Silvio. "Once, as a joke, he gave me a slap, as a joke he shot a bullet through this hat of mine; as a joke he has just missed me; now I feel I would like to play a little joke myself."

'With this he began to take aim at me – in her presence! Masha threw herself at his feet.

'"Get up, Masha, you should be ashamed!" I shouted in a fury. "And you, sir, will you stop mocking a poor woman. Are you going to shoot or not?"

'"I am not," replied Silvio. "I am satisfied. I have seen your confusion and your lack of confidence; I have forced you to shoot at me; that's enough for me. You will remember me. I leave you to your conscience."

'Then, just as he was on the point of leaving, he stopped in the doorway, glanced back at the picture my shot had passed through, fired at it, almost without taking aim, and disappeared. My wife lay in a swoon; the servants did not dare to stop him and watched him with horror; he went out on to the porch, called his coachman and drove off before I had time to collect myself.'

The count fell silent. Thus I heard the end of the tale

whose beginning had earlier made such an impression on me. The hero of it I never saw again. Rumour has it that at the time of the Alexander Ypsilanti rising Silvio commanded a detachment of Hetairists and was killed at the Battle of Sculeni.

GOGOL

IN his own day Nikolay Gogol was generally
regarded as a realist, set on denouncing contemporary social evils. Modern readers and
critics, however, see him more clearly as a
fantasist, projecting his subconscious fears
and anxieties on to the world around him.
Gogol is best known for his strange comedy,
The Inspector General and his grotesque novel,
Dead Souls, but his shorter prose works like
'The Nose' provide equally striking examples of his bizarre imagination at work. If
Turgenev, Tolstoy and Chekhov may be seen
as followers of Pushkin, Gogol's influence is
manifest in Dostoevsky. 'The Nose' was
first published in Pushkin's journal, the
Contemporary, in 1836.

THE NOSE

Translated by Ronald Wilks

I

AN extraordinarily strange thing happened in St Petersburg on 25 March. Ivan Yakovlevich, a barber who lived on Voznesensky Avenue (his surname has got lost and all that his shop-front signboard shows is a gentleman with a lathered cheek and the inscription 'We also let blood'), woke up rather early one morning and smelt hot bread. As he sat up in bed he saw his wife, who was a quite respectable lady and a great coffee-drinker, taking some freshly baked rolls out of the oven.

'I don't want any coffee today, Praskovya Osipovna,' said Ivan Yakovlevich, 'I'll make do with some hot rolls and onion instead.' (Here I must explain that Ivan Yakovlevich would really have liked to have had some coffee as well, but knew it was quite out of the question to expect both coffee *and* rolls, since Praskovya Osipovna did not take very kindly to these whims of his.) 'Let the old fool have his bread, I don't mind,' she thought. 'That means extra coffee for me!' And she threw a roll on to the table.

Ivan pulled his frock-coat over his nightshirt for decency's sake, sat down at the table, poured out some salt, peeled two onions, took a knife and with a determined expression on his face started cutting one of the rolls.

When he had sliced the roll in two, he peered into the middle and was amazed to see something white there. Ivan carefully picked at it with his knife, and felt it with his finger. 'Quite thick,' he said to himself. 'What on earth can it be?'

He poked two fingers in and pulled out – a nose!

He flopped back in his chair, and began rubbing his eyes

and feeling around in the roll again. Yes, it was a nose all right, no mistake about that. And, what's more, it seemed a very familiar nose. His face filled with horror. But this horror was nothing compared with his wife's indignation.

'You beast, whose nose is *that* you've cut off?' she cried furiously. 'You scoundrel! You drunkard! I'll report it to the police myself, I will. You thief! Come to think of it, I've heard three customers say that when they come in for a shave you start pulling their noses about so much it's a wonder they stay on at all!'

But Ivan felt more dead than alive. He knew that the nose belonged to none other than Collegiate Assessor Kovalyov, whom he shaved on Wednesdays and Sundays.

'Wait a minute, Praskovya! I'll wrap it up in a piece of cloth and dump it in the corner. Let's leave it there for a bit then I'll try and get rid of it.'

'I don't want to know! Do you think I'm going to let a sawn-off nose lie around in *my* room . . . you fathead! All you can do is strop that blasted razor of yours and let everything else go to pot. Layabout! Night-bird! And you expect me to cover up for you with the police! You filthy pig! Blockhead! Get that nose out of here, out! Do what you like with it, but I don't want that thing hanging around here a minute longer!'

Ivan Yakovlevich was absolutely stunned. He thought and thought, but just didn't know what to make of it.

'I'm damned if I know what's happened!' he said at last, scratching the back of his ear. 'I can't say for certain if I came home drunk or not last night. All I know is, it's crazy. After all, bread is baked in an oven, and you don't get noses in bakeries. Can't make head or tail of it! . . .'

Ivan Yakovlevich lapsed into silence. The thought that the police might search the place, find the nose and afterwards bring a charge against him, very nearly sent him out of his mind. Already he could see that scarlet collar beautifully embroidered with silver, that sword . . . and he began shaking all over. Finally he put on his scruffy old trousers and shoes and with Praskovya Osipovna's vigorous invective ringing in his ears, wrapped the nose up in a piece of cloth and went out into the street.

All he wanted was to stuff it away somewhere, either hiding it between two curb-stones by someone's front door or else 'accidentally' dropping it and slinking off down a side street. But, as luck would have it, he kept bumping into friends, who would insist on asking: 'Where are *you* off to?' or 'It's a bit early for shaving customers, isn't it?' with the result that he didn't have a chance to get rid of it. Once he *did* manage to drop it, but a policeman pointed with his halberd and said: 'Pick that up! Can't you see you dropped something!' And Ivan Yakovlevich had to pick it up and hide it in his pocket. Despair gripped him, especially as the streets were getting more and more crowded now as the shops and stalls began to open.

He decided to make his way to St Isaac's Bridge and see if he could throw the nose into the River Neva without anyone seeing him. But here I am rather at fault for not telling you before something about Ivan Yakovlevich, who in many ways was a man you could respect.

Ivan Yakovlevich, like any honest Russian working man, was a terrible drunkard. And although he spent all day shaving other people's beards, he never touched his own. His· frock-coat (Ivan Yakovlevich never wore a dress-coat) could best be described as piebald: that is to say, it was black, but with brownish-yellow and grey spots all over it. His collar was very shiny, and three loosely hanging threads showed that some buttons had once been there. Ivan Yakovlevich was a very phlegmatic character and, whenever Kovalyov the collegiate assessor said 'Your hands always stink!' while he was being shaved, Ivan Yakovlevich would say: 'But why *should* they stink?' The collegiate assessor used to reply: 'Don't ask me, my dear chap. All I know is, they *stink*.' Ivan Yakovlevich would answer by taking a pinch of snuff and then, by way of retaliation, lather all over

Kovalyov's cheeks, under his nose, behind the ears and beneath his beard – in short, wherever he felt like covering him with soap.

By now this respectable citizen of ours had already reached St Isaac's Bridge. First of all he had a good look round. Then he leant over the rails, trying to pretend he was looking under the bridge to see if there were many fish there, and furtively threw the packet into the water. He felt as if a couple of hundredweight had been lifted from his shoulders and he even managed to produce a smile.

Instead of going off to shave civil servants' chins, he headed for a shop bearing the sign 'Hot Meals and Tea' for a glass of punch. Suddenly he saw a policeman at one end of the bridge, in a very smart uniform, with broad whiskers, a three-cornered hat and a sword. He went cold all over as the policeman beckoned to him and said: 'Come here, my friend!'

Recognizing the uniform, Ivan Yakovlevich took his cap off before he had taken half a dozen steps, tripped up to him and greeted him with: 'Good morning, Your Excellency!'

'No, no, my dear chap, none of your "Excellencies". Just tell me what you were up to on the bridge?'

'Honest, officer, I was on my way to shave a customer and stopped to see how fast the current was.'

'You're lying. You really can't expect me to believe that! You'd better come clean at once!'

'I'll give Your Excellency a free shave twice, even three times a week, honest I will,' answered Ivan Yakovlevich.

'No, no, my friend, that won't do. Three barbers look after me already, and it's an *honour* for them to shave me. Will you please tell me what you were up to?'

Ivan Yakovlevich turned pale . . . But at this point everything became so completely enveloped in mist it is really impossible to say what happened afterwards.

Collegiate Assessor Kovalyov woke up rather early and made a 'brring' noise with his lips. He always did this when he woke up, though, if you asked him why, he could not give any good reason. Kovalyov stretched himself and asked for the small mirror that stood on the table to be brought over to him. He wanted to have a look at a pimple that had made its appearance on his nose the previous evening, but to his extreme astonishment found that instead of a nose there was nothing but an absolutely flat surface! In a terrible panic Kovalyov asked for some water and rubbed his eyes with a towel. No mistake about it: his nose had gone. He began pinching himself to make sure he was not sleeping, but to all intents and purposes he was wide awake. Collegiate Assessor Kovalyov sprang out of bed and shook himself; still no nose. He asked for his clothes and off he dashed straight to the head of police.

In the meantime, however, a few words should be said about Kovalyov, so that the reader may see what kind of collegiate assessor this man was. You really cannot compare those collegiate assessors who acquire office through testimonials with the variety appointed in the Caucasus. The two species are quite distinct. Collegiate assessors with diplomas from learned bodies ... But Russia is such an amazing country, that if you pass any remark about *one* collegiate assessor, every assessor from Riga to Kamchatka will take it personally. And the same goes for all people holding titles and government ranks. Kovalyov belonged to the Caucasian variety.

He had been a collegiate assessor for only two years and therefore could not forget it for a single minute. To make himself sound more important and to give more weight to his status he never called himself collegiate assessor, but 'Major'. If he met a woman in the street selling shirt fronts he would say: 'Listen dear, come and see me at home. My

flat's in Sadovaya Street. All you have to do is ask if Major
Kovalyov lives there and anyone will show you the way.'
And if the woman was at all pretty he would whisper some
secret instructions and then say: 'Just ask for Major Kovalyov, my dear.' Therefore, throughout this story, we will
call this collegiate assessor 'Major'. Major Kovalyov was in
the habit of taking a daily stroll along the Nevsky Prospekt.
His shirt collar was always immaculately clean and well
starched. His whiskers were the kind you usually find among
provincial surveyors, architects and regimental surgeons,
among people who have some sort of connection with the
police, on anyone in fact who has full rosy cheeks and plays a
good hand at whist. These whiskers grew right from the
middle of his cheeks up to his nostrils. Major Kovalyov
always carried plenty of seals with him – seals bearing coats
of arms or engraved with the words: 'Wednesday, Thursday,
Monday,' and so on. Major Kovalyov had come to St
Petersburg with the set purpose of finding a position in
keeping with his rank. If he was lucky, he would get a vice-
governorship, but, failing that, a job as an administrative
clerk in some important government department would
have to do, Major Kovalyov was not averse to marriage, as
long as his bride happened to be worth 200,000 roubles. And
now the reader can judge for himself how this major felt
when, instead of a fairly presentable and reasonably sized
nose, all he saw was an absolutely preposterous smooth flat
space.

As if this were not bad enough, there was not a cab in
sight, and he had to walk home, keeping himself huddled up
in his cloak and with a handkerchief over his face to make
people think he was bleeding. 'But perhaps I dreamt it!
How could I be so stupid as to go and lose my nose?' With
these thoughts he dropped into a coffee-house to take a look
at himself in a mirror. Fortunately the shop was empty, except for some waiters sweeping up and tidying the chairs. A
few of them, rather bleary-eyed, were carrying trays laden

with hot pies. Yesterday's newspapers, covered in coffee stains, lay scattered on the tables and chairs. 'Well, thank God there's no one about,' he said. 'Now I can have a look.' He approached the mirror rather gingerly and peered into it. 'Damn it! What kind of trick is this?' he cried, spitting on the floor. 'If only there were *something* to take its place, but there's nothing!'

He bit his lips in annoyance, left the coffee-house and decided not to smile or look at anyone, which was not like him at all. Suddenly he stood rooted to the spot near the front door of some house and witnessed a most incredible sight. A carriage drew up at the entrance porch. The doors flew open and out jumped a uniformed, stooping gentleman who dashed up the steps. The feeling of horror and amazement that gripped Kovalyov when he recognized his own nose defies description! After this extraordinary sight everything went topsy-turvy. He could hardly keep to his feet, but decided at all costs to wait until the nose returned to the carriage, although he was shaking all over and felt quite feverish.

About two minutes later a nose really did come out. It was wearing a gold-braided uniform with a high stand-up collar and chamois trousers, and had a sword at its side. From the plumes on its hat one could tell that it held the exalted rank of state councillor.* And it was abundantly clear that the nose was going to visit someone. It looked right, then left, shouted to the coachman 'Let's go!' climbed in and drove off.

Poor Kovalyov nearly went out of his mind. He did not know what to make of it. How, in fact, could a nose, which only yesterday was in the middle of his face, and which could not possibly walk around or drive in a carriage, suddenly

---

*A state councillor held the fifth of the fourteen ranks in the civil service hierarchy. A collegiate assessor was three grades lower. (Translator's note.)

turn up in a uniform! He ran after the carriage, which fortunately did not travel very far and came to a halt outside
Kazan Cathedral.* Kovalyov rushed into the cathedral
square, elbowed his way through a crowd of beggar women
who always used to make him laugh because of the way they
covered their faces, leaving only slits for the eyes, and made
his way in. Only a few people were at prayer, all of them
standing by the entrance. Kovalyov felt so distraught that he
was in no condition for praying, and his eyes searched every
nook and cranny for the nose in uniform. At length he
spotted it standing by one of the walls to the side. The nose's
face was completely hidden by the high collar and it was
praying with an expression of profound piety.

'What's the best way of approaching it?' thought Kovalyov. 'Judging by its uniform, its hat, and its whole appearance, it must be a state councillor. But I'm damned if I know!'

He tried to attract its attention by coughing, but the nose
did not interrupt its devotions for one second and continued
bowing towards the altar.

'My dear sir,' Kovalyov said, summoning up his courage,
'my dear sir . . .'

'What do you want?' replied the nose, turning round.

'I don't know how best to put it, sir, but it strikes me as
very peculiar . . . Don't you know where you belong? And
where do I find you? In church, of all places! I'm sure you'll
agree that . . .'

'Please forgive me, but would you mind telling me what
you're talking about? . . . Explain yourself.'

'How can I make myself clear?' Kovalyov wondered.
Nerving himself once more he said: 'Of course, I am, as it
happens, a major. You will agree that it's not done for some
one in my position to walk around minus a nose. It's all right
for some old woman selling peeled oranges on the Voskre-

*Such was the severity and idiocy of the censorship in Gogol's day,
that in the original version Kazan Cathedral had to be replaced by a
shopping arcade, on the grounds of 'blasphemy'. (Translator's note.)

sensky Bridge to go around without one. But as I'm hoping
to be promoted soon . . . Besides, as I'm acquainted with
several highly placed ladies: Madame Chekhtarev, for
example, a state councillor's wife . . . you can judge for yourself . . . I really don't know what to say, my dear sir . . . (He
shrugged his shoulders as he said this.) Forgive me, but you
must look upon this as a matter of honour and principle.
You can see for yourself . . .'

'I can't see anything,' the nose replied. 'Please come to the
point.'

'My dear sir,' continued Kovalyov in a smug voice, 'I
really don't know what you mean by that. It's plain enough
for anyone to see . . . Unless you want . . . Don't you realize
you are *my own nose*!'

The nose looked at the major and frowned a little.

'My dear fellow, you are mistaken. I am a person in my
own right. Furthermore, I don't see that we can have anything in common. Judging from your uniform buttons, I
should say you're from another government department.'

With these words the nose turned away and continued its
prayers.

Kovalyov was so confused he did not know what to do or
think. At that moment he heard the pleasant rustling of a
woman's dress, and an elderly lady, bedecked with lace,
came by, accompanied by a slim girl wearing a white dress,
which showed her shapely figure to very good advantage,
and a pale yellow hat as light as pastry. A tall footman, with
enormous whiskers and what seemed to be a dozen collars,
stationed himself behind them and opened his snuff-box.
Kovalyov went closer, pulled the linen collar of his shirt
front up high, straightened the seals hanging on his gold
watch-chain and, smiling all over his face, turned his attention to the slim girl, who bent over to pray like a spring
flower and kept lifting her little white hand with its almost
transparent fingers to her forehead.

The smile on Kovalyov's face grew even more expansive

when he saw, beneath her hat, a little rounded chin of dazzling white, and cheeks flushed with the colour of the first rose of spring.

But suddenly he jumped backwards as though he had been burnt: he remembered that instead of a nose he had nothing and tears streamed from his eyes. He turned round to tell the nose in uniform straight out that it was only masquerading as a state councillor, that it was an impostor and a scoundrel, and really nothing else than his own private property, *his* nose . . . But the nose had already gone: it had managed to slip off unseen, probably to pay somebody a visit.

This reduced Kovalyov to absolute despair. He went out, and stood for a minute or so under the colonnade, carefully looking around him in the hope of spotting the nose. He remembered quite distinctly that it was wearing a plumed hat and a gold-embroidered uniform. But he had not noticed what its greatcoat was like, or the colour of its carriage, or its horses, or even if there was a liveried footman at the back. What's more, there were so many carriages careering to and fro, so fast, that it was practically impossible to recognize any of them, and even if he could, there was no way of making them stop.

It was a beautiful sunny day. Nevsky Prospekt was packed. From the Police Headquarters right down to the Anichkov Bridge people flowed along the pavements in a cascade of colour. Not far off he could see that court councillor whom he referred to as Lieutenant-Colonel,* especially if there happened to be other people around. And over there was Yaygin, a head clerk in the senate, and a very close friend of his who always lost at whist when he played in a party of eight. Another major, a collegiate assessor, of the Caucasian variety, waved to him to come over and have a chat.

'Blast and damn!' said Kovalyov, hailing a drozhky. 'Driver, take me straight to the chief of police.'

* The civil service ranks had their corresponding ranks in the army. (Translator's note.)

37

He climbed into the drozhky and shouted: 'Drive like the devil!'

'Is the police commissioner in?' he said as soon as he entered the hall.

'No, he's not, sir,' said the porter. 'He left only a few minutes ago.'

'This really *is* my day.'

'Yes,' added the porter, 'you've only just missed him. A minute ago you'd have caught him.'

Kovalyov, his handkerchief still pressed to his face, climbed into the drozhky again and cried out in a despairing voice: 'Let's go!'

'Where?' asked the driver.

'Straight on!'

'Straight on? But it's a dead-end here – you can only go right or left.'

This last question made Kovalyov stop and think. In his position the best thing to do was to go first to the city security office, not because it was directly connected with the police, but because things got done there much quicker than in any other government department. There was no sense in going direct to the head of the department where the nose claimed to work since anyone could see from the answers he had got before that the nose considered nothing holy and would have no difficulty in convincing its superiors by its brazen lying that it had never set eyes on Kovalyov before.

So, just as Kovalyov was about to tell the driver to go straight to the security office, it struck him that the scoundrel and impostor who had behaved so shamelessly could quite easily take advantage of the delay and slip out of the city, in which event all his efforts to find it would be futile and might even drag on for another month, God forbid. Finally inspiration came from above. He decided to go straight to the newspaper offices and publish an advertisement, giving such a detailed description of the nose that anyone who happened to meet it would at once turn it over to Kovalyov, or at least tell him where he could find it. Deciding this was the best course of action, he ordered the driver to go straight to the newspaper offices and throughout the whole journey never once stopped pummelling the driver in the back with his fist and shouting: 'Faster, damn you, faster!'

'But sir . . .' the driver retorted as he shook his head and flicked his reins at his horse, which had a coat as long as a spaniel's. Finally the drozhky came to a halt and the breathless Kovalyov tore into a small waiting-room where a grey-haired bespectacled clerk in an old frock-coat was sitting at a table with his pen between his teeth, counting out copper coins.

'Who sees to advertisements here?' Kovalyov shouted. 'Ah, good morning.'

'Good morning,' replied the grey-haired clerk, raising his eyes for one second, then looking down again at the little piles of money spread out on the table.

'I want to publish an advertisement.'

'Just one moment, if you don't mind,' the clerk answered, as he wrote down a figure with one hand and moved two beads on his abacus with the other.

A footman who, judging by his gold-braided livery and generally very smart appearance, obviously worked in some noble house, was standing by the table holding a piece of paper and, just to show he could hob-nob with high and low, started rattling away:

'Believe me, that nasty little dog just isn't worth eighty kopecks. I wouldn't give more than sixteen for it. But the countess dotes on it, and that's why she makes no bones about offering a hundred roubles to the person who finds it. If we're going to be honest with one another, I'll tell you quite openly, there's no accounting for taste. I can understand a fancier paying anything up to five hundred, even a thousand for a deerhound or a poodle, as long as it's a good dog.'

The elderly clerk listened to him solemnly while he carried

on totting up the words in the advertisement. The room was crowded with old women, shopkeepers, and house-porters, all holding advertisements. In one of these a coachman of 'sober disposition' was seeking employment; in another a carriage, hardly used, and brought from Paris in 1814, was up for sale; in another a nineteen-year-old servant-girl, with laundry experience, and prepared to do *other* work, was looking for a job. Other advertisements offered a drozhky for sale – in good condition apart from one missing spring; a 'young' and spirited dapple-grey colt seventeen years old; radish and turnip seeds only just arrived from London; a country house, with every modern convenience, including stabling for two horses and enough land for planting an excellent birch or fir forest. And one invited prospective buyers of old boot soles to attend certain auction rooms between the hours of eight and three daily. The room into which all these people were crammed was small and extremely stuffy. But collegiate assessor Kovalyov could not smell anything as he had covered his face with a handkerchief – and he could not have smelt anything anyway, as his nose had disappeared God knows where.

'My dear sir, will you take the details down now, *please*. I really can't wait any longer,' he said, beginning to lose patience.

'Just a minute, if you *don't* mind! Two roubles forty-three kopecks. Nearly ready. One rouble sixty-four kopecks,' the grey-haired clerk muttered as he shoved pieces of paper at the old ladies and servants standing around. Finally he turned to Kovalyov and said: 'What do you want?'

'I want ...' Kovalyov began. 'Something very fishy's been going on, whether it's some nasty practical joke or a plain case of fraud I can't say as yet. All I want you to do is to offer a substantial reward for the first person to find the blackguard ...'

'Name, please.'

'Why do you need that? I can't tell you. Too many people

know me – Mrs Chekhtarev, for example, who's married to
a state councillor, Mrs Palageya Podtochin, a staff officer's
wife . . . they'd find out who it was at once, God forbid! Just
put "Collegiate Assessor", or even better, "Major".'
        'And the missing person was a household serf of yours?'
        'Household serf? The crime wouldn't be half as serious!
It's my *nose* that's disappeared.'
        'H'm, strange name. And did this Mr Nose steal much?'
        '*My* nose, I'm trying to say. You don't understand! It's my
own nose that's disappeared. It's a diabolical practical joke
someone's played on me.'
        'How did it disappear? I don't follow.'
        'I can't tell you how. But please understand, my nose is
travelling at this very moment all over the town, calling
itself a state councillor. That's why I'm asking you to print
this advertisement announcing the first person who catches
it should return the nose to its rightful owner as soon as
possible. Imagine what it's like being without such a con-
spicuous part of your body! If it were just a small toe, then
I could put my shoe on and no one would be any the wiser.
On Thursdays I go to Mrs Chekhtarev's (she's married to a
state councillor) and Mrs Podtochin, who has a staff officer
for a husband – and a very pretty little daughter as well.
They're all very close friends of mine, so just imagine what
it would be like . . . In *my* state how can I visit any of
them?'
        The clerk's tightly pressed lips showed he was deep in
thought. 'I can't print an advertisement like that in our
paper,' he said after a long silence.
        'What? Why not?'
        'I'll tell you. A paper can get a bad name. If everyone
started announcing his nose had run away, I don't know
how it would all end. And enough false reports and rumours
get past editorial already . . .'
        'But why does it strike you as so absurd? *I* certainly don't
think so.'

'That's what *you* think. But only last week there was a similar case. A clerk came here with an advertisement, just like you. It cost him two roubles seventy-three kopecks, and all he wanted to advertise was a runaway black poodle. And what do you think he was up to really? In the end we had a libel case on our hands: the poodle was meant as a satire on a government cashier – I can't remember what ministry he came from.'

'But I want to publish an advertisement about my nose, not a poodle, and that's as near myself as dammit!'

'No, I can't accept that kind of advertisement.'

'But I've lost my *nose*!'

'Then you'd better see a doctor about it. I've heard there's a certain kind of specialist who can fix you up with any kind of nose you like. Anyway, you seem a cheery sort, and I can see you like to have your little joke.'

'By all that's holy, I swear I'm telling you the truth. If you really want me to, I'll *show* you what I mean.'

'I shouldn't bother if I were you,' the clerk continued, taking a pinch of snuff. 'However, if it's *really* no trouble,' he added, leaning forward out of curiosity, 'then I shouldn't mind having a quick look.'

The collegiate assessor removed his handkerchief.

'Well, how very peculiar! It's quite flat, just like a freshly cooked pancake. Incredibly flat.'

'So much for your objections! Now you've seen it with your own eyes and you can't possibly refuse. I will be particularly grateful for this little favour, and it's been a real pleasure meeting you.'

The major, evidently, had decided that flattery might do the trick.

'Of course, it's no problem *printing* the advertisement,' the clerk said. 'But I can't see what you can stand to gain by it. If you like, why not give it to someone with a flair for journalism, then he can write it up as a very rare freak of nature and have it published in *The Northern Bee** (here he took another pinch of snuff) so that young people might benefit from it (here he wiped his nose). Or else, as something of interest to the general public.'

The collegiate assessor's hopes vanished completely. He looked down at the bottom of the page at the theatre guide. The name of a rather pretty actress almost brought a smile to his face, and he reached down to his pocket to see if he had a five-rouble note, since in his opinion staff officers should sit only in the stalls. But then he remembered his nose, and knew he could not possibly think of going to the theatre.

Apparently even the clerk was touched by Kovalyov's terrible predicament and thought it would not hurt to cheer him up with a few words of sympathy.

'Really, I can't say how sorry I am at what's happened. How about a pinch of snuff? It's very good for headaches – and puts fresh heart into you. It even cures piles.'

With these words he offered Kovalyov his snuff-box, deftly flipping back the lid which bore a portrait of some lady in a hat.

This unintentionally thoughtless action made Kovalyov lose patience altogether.

'I don't understand how you can joke at a time like this,' he said angrily. 'Are you so blind you can't see that I've nothing to smell with? You know what you can do with your snuff! I can't bear to look at it, and anyway you might at least offer me some real French rapée, not that filthy Berezinsky brand.'

After this declaration he strode furiously out of the newspaper office and went off to the local inspector of police (a fanatical lover of sugar, whose hall and dining-room were crammed full of sugar-cubes presented by merchants who wanted to keep well in with him). Kovalyov arrived just

*A reactionary St Petersburg periodical notorious for its vicious attacks on writers of talent, including Gogol. (Translator's note.)

when he was having a good stretch, grunting, and saying, 'Now for a nice two hours' nap.' Our collegiate assessor had clearly chosen a very bad time for his visit.

The inspector was a great patron of the arts and industry, but most of all he loved government banknotes. 'There's nothing finer than banknotes,' he used to say. 'They don't need feeding, take up very little room and slip nicely into the pocket. And they don't break if you drop them.'

The inspector gave Kovalyov a rather cold welcome and said that after dinner wasn't at all the time to start investigations, that nature herself had decreed a rest after meals (from this our collegiate assessor concluded the inspector was well versed in the wisdom of antiquity), that *respectable* men do not get their noses ripped off, and that there were no end of majors knocking around who were not too fussy about their underwear and who were in the habit of visiting the most disreputable places.

These few home truths stung Kovalyov to the quick. Here I must point out that Kovalyov was an extremely sensitive man. He did not so much mind people making personal remarks about him, but it was a different matter when aspersions were cast on his rank or social standing.

As far as he was concerned they could say what they liked about subalterns on the stage, but staff officers should be exempt from attack.

The reception given him by the inspector startled him so much that he shook his head, threw out his arms and said in a dignified voice, 'To be frank, after these remarks of yours, which I find very offensive, I have nothing more to say . . .' and walked out. He arrived home hardly able to feel his feet beneath him. It was already getting dark. After his fruitless inquiries his flat seemed extremely dismal and depressing. As he entered the hall he saw his footman Ivan lying on a soiled leather couch spitting at the ceiling, managing to hit the same spot with a fair degree of success. The nonchalance of the man infuriated him and Kovalyov hit him across the

forehead with his hat and said: 'You fat pig! Haven't you
anything better to do!'

Ivan promptly jumped up and rushed to take off Kovalyov's coat. Tired and depressed, the major went to his
room, threw himself into an armchair and after a few sighs
said:

'My God, my God! What have I done to deserve this? If
I'd lost an arm or a leg it wouldn't be so bad. Even without
any *ears* things wouldn't be very pleasant, but it wouldn't be
the end of the world. A man without a nose, though, is God
knows what, neither fish nor fowl. Just something to be
thrown out of the window. If my nose had been lopped off
during the war, or in a duel, at least I might have had some
say in the matter. But to lose it for no reason at all and with
nothing to show for it, not even a kopeck! No, it's absolutely
impossible . . . It can't have gone just like that! Never! Must
have been a dream, or perhaps I drank some of that vodka I
use for rubbing down my beard after shaving instead of
water: that idiot Ivan couldn't have put it back in the cup-
board.'

To prove to himself he was not drunk the Major pinched
himself so hard that he cried out in pain, which really did
convince him he was awake and in full possession of his
senses. He stealthily crept over to the mirror and screwed up
his eyes in the hope that his nose would reappear in its
proper place, but at once he jumped back, exclaiming:

'That ridiculous blank space again!'

It was absolutely incomprehensible. If a button, or a silver
spoon, or his watch, or something of that sort had been
missing, that would have been understandable. But for his
nose to disappear from his own flat . . . Major Kovalyov
weighed up all the evidence and decided that the most likely
explanation of all was that Mrs Podtochin, the staff officer's
wife, who wanted to marry off her daughter to him, was to
blame, and no one else. In fact he liked chasing after her, but
never came to proposing. And when the staff officer's wife

used to tell him straight out that she was offering him her daughter's hand, he would politely withdraw, excusing himself on the grounds that he was still a young man, and that he wanted to devote another five years to the service, by which time he would be just forty-two. So, to get her revenge, the staff officer's wife must have hired some witches to spirit it away, and this was the only way his nose could possibly have been cut off – no one had visited him in his flat, his barber Ivan Yakovlevich had shaved him only last Wednesday, and the rest of that day and the whole of Thursday his nose had been intact. All this he remembered quite clearly. Moreover he would have been in pain and the wound could not have healed as smooth as a pancake in such a short time. He began planning what to do: either he would sue the staff officer's wife for damages, or he would go and see her personally and accuse her point blank.

But he was distracted from these thoughts by the sight of some chinks of light in the door, which meant Ivan had lit a candle in the hall. Soon afterwards Ivan appeared in person, holding the candle in front of him, so that it brightened up the whole room. Kovalyov's first reaction was to seize his handkerchief and cover up the bare place where only yesterday his nose had been, to prevent that stupid idiot from standing there gaping at him. No sooner had Ivan left than a strange voice was heard in the hall:

'Does Collegiate Assessor Kovalyov live here?'

'Please come in. The major's home,' said Kovalyov, springing to his feet and opening the door.

A smart-looking police officer, with plump cheeks and whiskers that were neither too light nor too dark – the same police officer who had stood on St Isaac's Bridge at the beginning of our story – made his entrance.

'Are you the gentleman who has lost his nose?'

'Yes, that's me.'

'It's been found.'

'What did you say?' cried Major Kovalyov. He could

hardly speak for joy. He looked wide-eyed at the police officer, the candle-light flickering on his fat cheeks and thick lips.

'How did you find it?'

'Very strange. We caught it just as it was about to drive off in the Riga stagecoach. Its passport was made out in the name of some civil servant. Strangely enough, I mistook it for a gentleman at first. Fortunately I had my spectacles with me so I could see it was really a nose. I'm very short-sighted, and if you happen to stand just in front of me, I can only make out your face, but not your nose, or beard, or anything else in fact. My mother-in-law (that's to say, on my *wife's* side) suffers from the same complaint.'

Kovalyov was beside himself.

'Where is it? I'll go right away to claim it.'

'Don't excite yourself, sir. I knew how much you wanted it back, so I've brought it with me. Very strange, but the main culprit in this little affair seems to be that swindler of a barber from Voznesensky Street: he's down at the station now. I've had my eyes on him a long time on suspicion of drunkenness and larceny, and only three days ago he was found stealing a dozen buttons from a shop. You'll find your nose just as it was when you lost it.'

And the police officer dipped into his pocket and pulled out the nose wrapped up in a piece of paper.

'That's it!' cried Kovalyov, 'no mistake! You *must* stay and have a cup of tea.'

'I'd like to, but I'm expected back at the prison . . . The price of food has rocketed . . . My mother-in-law (on my *wife's* side) is living with me, and all the children as well; the eldest boy seems very promising, very bright, but we haven't the money to send him to school . . .'

Kovalyov guessed what he was after and took a note from the table and pressed it into the officer's hands. The police officer bowed very low and went out into the street, where Kovalyov could hear him telling some stupid peasant who had driven his cart up on the pavement what he thought of him.

When the police officer had gone, our collegiate assessor felt rather bemused and only after a few minutes did he come to his senses at all, so intense was his joy. He carefully took the nose in his cupped hands and once more subjected it to close scrutiny.

'Yes, that's it, that's it!' Major Kovalyov said, 'and there's the pimple that came up yesterday on the left-hand side.' The major almost laughed with joy.

But nothing is lasting in this world. Even joy begins to fade after only one minute. Two minutes later, and it is weaker still, until finally it is swallowed up in our everyday, prosaic state of mind, just as a ripple made by a pebble gradually merges with the smooth surface of the water. After some thought Kovalyov concluded that all was not right again yet and there still remained the problem of putting the nose back in place.

'What if it doesn't stick?'

With a feeling of inexpressible horror he rushed to the table, and pulled the mirror nearer, as he was afraid that he might stick the nose on crooked. His hands trembled. With great care and caution he pushed it into place. But oh! the nose just would not stick. He warmed it a little by pressing it to his mouth and breathing on it, and then pressed it again to the smooth space between his cheeks. But try as he might the nose would not stay on.

'Stay on, you fool!' he said. But the nose seemed to be made of wood and fell on to the table with a strange cork-like sound. The major's face quivered convulsively. 'Perhaps I can graft it,' he said apprehensively. But no matter how many times he tried to put it back, all his efforts were futile.

He called Ivan and told him to fetch the doctor, who happened to live in the same block, in one of the best flats on the first floor.

This doctor was a handsome man with fine whiskers as black as pitch, and a fresh-looking, healthy wife. Every morning he used to eat apples and was terribly meticulous about keeping his mouth clean, spending at least three quarters of an hour rinsing it out every day and using five different varieties of toothbrush. He came right away. When he had asked the major if he had had this trouble for very long the doctor pushed back Kovalyov's chin and prodded him with his thumb in the spot once occupied by his nose – so sharply that the major hit the wall very hard with the back of his head. The doctor told him not to worry and made him stand a little way from the wall and lean his head first to the right. Pinching the place where his nose had been the doctor said 'Hm!' Then he ordered him to move his head to the left and produced another 'Hm!' Finally he prodded him again, making Kovalyov's head twitch like a horse having its teeth inspected.

After this examination the doctor shook his head and said: 'It's no good. It's best to stay as you are, otherwise you'll only make it worse. Of course, it's possible to have it stuck on, and I could do this for you quite easily. But I assure you it would look terrible.'

'That's *marvellous*, that is! How can I carry on without a nose?' said Kovalyov. '*Whatever* you do it couldn't look any worse; and God knows, that's bad enough! How can I go around looking like a freak? I mix with nice people. I'm expected at two soirées today. I know nearly all the best people – Mrs Chekhtarev, a state councillor's wife, Mrs Podtochin, a staff officer's wife ... after the way *she's* behaved I won't have any more to do with *her*, except when I get the police on her trail.' Kovalyov went on pleading: 'Please do me this one favour – isn't there any way? Even if you only get it to hold on, it wouldn't be so bad, and if there were any risk of it falling off, I could keep it there with my hand. I don't dance, which is a help, because any violent movement might make it drop off. And you may rest assured

I wouldn't be slow in showing my appreciation – as far as my pocket will allow of course . . .'

The doctor then said in a voice which could not be called loud, or even soft, but persuasive and arresting: 'I never practise my art from purely mercenary motives. That is contrary to my code of conduct and all professional ethics. True, I make a charge for private visits, but only so as not to offend patients by refusing to take their money. Of course, I could put your nose back if I wanted to. But I give you my word of honour, if you know what's good for you, it would be far worse if I tried. Let nature take its course. Wash the area as much as you can with cold water and believe me you'll feel just as good as when you had a nose. Now, as far as the nose is concerned, put it in a jar of alcohol; better still, soak it in two tablespoonsful of sour vodka and warmed-up vinegar, and you'll get good money for it. I'll take it myself if you don't want it.'

'No! I wouldn't sell it for anything,' Kovalyov cried desperately. 'I'd rather lose it again.'

'Then I'm sorry,' replied the doctor, bowing himself out. 'I wanted to help you . . . at least I've tried hard enough.'

With these words the doctor made a very dignified exit. Kovalyov did not even look at his face, and felt so dazed that all he could make out were the doctor's snowy-white cuffs sticking out from the sleeves of his black dress-coat.

The very next day he decided – before going to the police – to write to the staff officer's wife to ask her to put back in its proper place what belonged to him without further ado. The letter read as follows:

Dear Mrs Alexandra Grigorevna,

I cannot understand this strange behaviour on your part. You can be sure, though, that it won't get you anywhere and you certainly won't force me to marry your daughter. Moreover, you can rest assured that, regarding my nose, I am familiar with the whole history of this affair from the very beginning, and I also know that you, and no one else, are the prime instigator. Its sudden detachment from its rightful place, its subsequent flight, its masquerading as a civil servant and then its re-appearance in its natural state, are nothing else than the result of black magic carried out by yourself or by those practising the same very honourable art. I consider it my duty to warn you that if the above-mentioned nose is not back in its proper place by today, then I shall be compelled to ask for the law's protection.

I remain, dear madam,

Your very faithful servant,
Platon Kovalyov.

Dear Mr Kovalyov,

I was simply staggered by your letter. To be honest, I never expected anything of this kind from you, particularly those remarks which are quite uncalled-for. I would have you know I have never received that civil servant mentioned by you in my house, whether disguised or not. True, Philip Ivanovich Potanchikov used to call. Although he wanted to ask for my daughter's hand, and despite the fact that he was a very sober, respectable and learned gentleman, I never gave him any cause for hope. And then you go on to mention your nose. If by this you mean to say I wanted to make you look foolish,* that is, to put you off with a formal refusal, then all I can say is that I am very surprised that you can talk like this, as you know well enough my feelings on the matter are quite different. And if you care to make an official proposal to my daughter, I will gladly give my consent, for this has always been my dearest wish, and in this hope I remain at your disposal.

Yours sincerely,
Alexandra Podtochin.

'No,' said Kovalyov when he had read the letter. 'She's not to blame. Impossible! A guilty person could never write a letter like that.' The collegiate assessor knew what he was talking about in this case as he had been sent to the Caucasus several times to carry out legal inquiries. 'How on earth did this happen then? It's impossible to make head or tail of it!' he said, letting his arms drop to his side.

* Russian is rich in idioms referring to the nose, most of which have a derogatory meaning, for example to make a fool of. (Translator's note.)

Meanwhile rumours about the strange occurrence had spread throughout the capital, not, need we say, without a few embellishments. At the time everyone seemed very preoccupied with the supernatural: only a short time before, some experiments in magnetism had been all the rage. Besides, the story of the dancing chairs in Konyushenny Street* was still fresh in people's minds, so no one was particularly surprised to hear about Collegiate Assessor Kovalyov's nose taking a regular stroll along the Nevsky Prospekt at exactly three o'clock every afternoon. Every day crowds of inquisitive people flocked there. Someone said they had seen the nose in Junker's Store and this produced such a crush outside that the police had to be called.

One fairly respectable-looking, bewhiskered character, who sold stale cakes outside the theatre, knocked together some solid-looking wooden benches, and hired them out at eighty kopecks a time for people to stand on.

One retired colonel left home especially early one morning and after a great struggle managed to barge his way through to the front. But to his great annoyance, instead of a nose in the shop window, all he could see was an ordinary woollen jersey and a lithograph showing a girl adjusting her stocking while a dandy with a small beard and cutaway waistcoat peered out at her from behind a tree – a picture which had hung there in that identical spot for more than ten years. He left feeling very cross and was heard to say: 'Misleading the public with such ridiculous and far-fetched stories shouldn't be allowed.'

Afterwards it was rumoured that Major Kovalyov's nose was no longer to be seen strolling along the Nevsky Prospekt but was in the habit of walking in Tavrichesky Park, and that it had been doing this for a long time. When Khozrov-

*An entry in Pushkin's diary for 17 December 1833 mentions furniture jumping about in one of the houses attached to the Royal Stables. In 1832 a certain lady called Tatarinova was exiled from St Petersburg for deceiving people into thinking she could will objects to move. (Translator's note.)

Mirza* lived there, he was astonished at this freak of nature. Some of the students from the College of Surgeons went to have a look. One well-known, very respectable lady wrote specially to the head park-keeper, asking him to show her children this very rare phenomenon and, if possible, give them an instructive and edifying commentary at the same time.

These events came as a blessing to those socialites (indispensable for any successful party) who loved amusing the ladies and whose stock of stories was completely exhausted at the time.

A few respectable and high-minded citizens were very upset. One indignant gentleman said that he was at a loss to understand how such absurd cock-and-bull stories could gain currency in the present enlightened century, and that the complete indifference shown by the authorities was past comprehension. Clearly this gentleman was the type who likes to make the government responsible for everything, even their daily quarrels with their wives. And afterwards ... but here again the whole incident becomes enveloped in mist and what happened later remains a complete mystery.

III

This world is full of the most outrageous nonsense. Sometimes things happen which you would hardly think possible: that very same nose, which had paraded itself as a state councillor and created such an uproar in the city, suddenly turned up, as if nothing had happened, plonk where it had been before, that is right between Major Kovalyov's two cheeks. This was on 7 April. He woke up and happened to glance at the mirror – there was his nose! He grabbed it with his hand to make sure – but there was no doubt this time. 'Aha!' cried

*A Persian prince who had come with official apologies for the murder of the famous playwright A. S. Griboedov, in Tehran, in 1829. (Griboedov had gone to Tehran to negotiate with the shah regarding the Peace of Turkmenchai.) (Translator's note.)

Kovalyov, and, if Ivan hadn't come in at that very moment, he would have joyfully danced a trepak round the room in his bare feet.

He ordered some soap and water, and as he washed himself looked into the mirror again: the nose was there. He had another look as he dried himself – yes, the nose was still there!

'Look, Ivan, I think I've got a pimple on my nose.'

Kovalyov thought: 'God, supposing he replies: "Not only is there no pimple, but no nose either!"' But Ivan answered: 'Your nose is quite all right, sir, I can't see any pimple.'

'Thank God for that,' the major said to himself and clicked his fingers.

At this moment Ivan Yakovlevich the barber poked his head round the corner, but timidly this time, like a cat which had just been beaten for stealing fat.

'Before you start, are your hands clean?' Kovalyov shouted from the other side of the room.

'Perfectly clean.'

'You're lying.'

'On my life, sir, they're clean!'

'Hm, let's have a look then!'

Kovalyov sat down. Ivan Yakovlevich covered him with a towel and in a twinkling had transformed his whole beard and part of his cheeks into the kind of cream served up at merchants' birthday parties.

'Well, I'll be damned,' Ivan Yakovlevich muttered to himself, staring at the nose. He bent Kovalyov's head to one side and looked at him from a different angle. 'That's *it* all right! You'd never credit it . . .' he continued and contemplated the nose for a long time. Finally, ever so gently, with a delicacy that the reader can best imagine, he lifted two fingers to hold the nose by its tip. This was how Ivan Yakovlevich normally shaved his customers.

'Come on now, and mind my nose!' shouted Kovalyov. Ivan Yakovlevich let his arms fall to his side and stood there more frightened and embarrassed than he had ever been in his life. At last he started tickling Kovalyov carefully under the chin with his razor. And, although it was awkward for him, and not holding the olfactory organ made shaving very difficult, by planting his rough, wrinkled thumb on his cheek and lower gum (in this way gaining some sort of leverage) he managed to shave him.

When everything was ready, Kovalyov rushed to get dressed and took a cab straight to the café. He had hardly got inside before he shouted, 'Waiter, a cup of chocolate,' and went straight up to the mirror. Yes, his nose was there! Gaily he turned round, screwed up his eyes and looked superciliously at two soldiers, one of whom had a nose no bigger than a *waistcoat* button. Then he went off to the ministerial department where he was petitioning for a vice-governorship. (Failing this he was going to try for an administrative post.) As he crossed the entrance hall he had another look in the mirror: his nose was still there!

Then he went to see another collegiate assessor (or major), a great wag whose sly digs Kovalyov used to counter by saying: 'I'm used to your quips by now, you old niggler!'

On the way he thought: 'If the major doesn't split his sides when he sees me, that's a sure sign everything is in its proper place.' But the collegiate assessor did not pass any remarks. 'That's all right then, dammit!' thought Kovalyov. In the street he met Mrs Podtochin, the staff officer's wife, who was with her daughter, and they replied to his bow with delighted exclamations: clearly, he had suffered no lasting injury. He had a long chat with them, made a point of taking out his snuff-box, and stood there for ages ostentatiously stuffing both nostrils as he murmured to himself: 'That'll teach you, you old hens! And I'm not going to marry your daughter, simply *par amour*, as they say! If you *don't* mind!'

And from that time onwards Major Kovalyov was able to stroll along the Nevsky Prospekt, visit the theatre, in fact go everywhere as though absolutely nothing had happened.

And, as though absolutely nothing *had* happened, his nose stayed in the middle of his face and showed no signs of wandering off. After that he was in perpetual high spirits, always smiling, chasing all the pretty girls, and on one occasion even stopping at a small shop in the Gostiny Dvor* to buy ribbon for some medal, no one knows why, as he did not belong to any order of knighthood.

And all this took place in the northern capital of our vast empire! Only now, after much reflection, can we see that there is a great deal that is very far-fetched in this story. Apart from the fact that it's *highly* unlikely for a nose to disappear in such a fantastic way and then reappear in various parts of the town dressed as a state councillor, it is hard to believe that Kovalyov was so ignorant as to think newspapers would accept advertisements about noses. I'm not saying I consider such an advertisement too expensive and a waste of money: that's nonsense, and what's more, I don't think I'm a mercenary person. But it's all very nasty, not quite the thing at all, and it makes me feel very awkward! And, come to think of it, how *did* the nose manage to turn up in a loaf of bread, and how *did* Ivan Yakovlevich . . .? No, I don't understand it, not one bit! But the strangest, most incredible thing of all is that authors should write about such things. That, I confess, is beyond my comprehension. It's just . . . no, no, I don't understand it at all! Firstly, it's no use to the country whatsoever; secondly, it's no use . . . I simply don't know *what* one can make of it . . . However, when all is said and done, one can concede this point or the other and perhaps you can even find . . . well then you won't find much that *isn't* on the absurd side, will you?

And yet, if you stop to think for a moment, there's a grain of truth in it. Whatever you may say, these things do happen – rarely, I admit, but they do happen.

* The same shopping arcade substituted by the censorship for Kazan Cathedral in the original version. It was built in the eighteenth century and opened off the Nevsky Prospekt. (Translator's note.)

LERMONTOV

MIKHAIL LERMONTOV burst into literary prominence with an ireful elegy on the death of Pushkin and was quickly recognized as his hero's poetic successor. Army officer, aristocratic rake and cruel wit as well as sensitive dreamer, Lermontov himself was killed in a duel fought on the slopes of Mount Mashuk in the Caucasus. Lermontov's writing is more exuberant than Pushkin's, but his best work in both prose and verse is marked by a wonderfully controlled sense of linguistic pitch and balance. 'Taman', which Chekhov regarded as a model short story, is one episode from Lermontov's vigorous prose masterpiece, *A Hero of Our Time* – the first Russian psychological novel – which appeared in 1840, a year before the writer's death.

TAMAN

Translated by Paul Foote

TAMAN is the foulest hole among all the sea-coast towns of
Russia. I practically starved to death there, then on top of
that someone tried to drown me. I arrived there late one
night by stage. The driver pulled up the weary troika by the
gate of the one stone house in the place, just at the entrance
to the town. Hearing the harness-bell, a Black Sea Cossack
sentry gave a wild yell, half-asleep: 'Who goes there?' A
Cossack sergeant and corporal came out. I explained I was
an officer travelling on duty to my unit at the front and
wanted a billet for the night. The corporal took us round the
town. Every house we stopped at was full. I'd had no sleep
for three nights and was tired and cold. I began to lose my
temper. 'Take me anywhere, damn you!' I shouted. 'To the
devil himself, as long as it's a place to sleep.' The corporal
scratched the back of his head. 'There is one other place, sir,
but you wouldn't fancy it. Unwholesome, it is.'

I didn't know what he meant by this last remark and told
him to lead the way. We passed through a lot of filthy back-
streets, seeing nothing but ramshackle fences, till finally we
drove up to a small hut right on the edge of the sea.

A full moon shone on the thatched roof and white walls of
my new abode. The yard had a rubble wall round it, and in
the yard was another tumbledown shack, smaller and more
ancient than the first. Almost at the foot of its walls there was
a sheer drop to the sea, with dark blue waves splashing and
murmuring unceasingly below. The moon looked calmly
down on the turbulent element it ruled. Some way offshore I
could make out two ships in the moonlight, their black
rigging motionless, silhouetted like a spider's web against

the pale outline of the horizon. There are ships at the quay, so I can leave for Gelenjik tomorrow, I thought.

My batman was a Cossack from one of the frontier regiments. I told him to get my valise down and dismiss the driver, then called for the master of the house. There was no answer. I knocked, and still there was no answer. What did it mean?

In the end a boy of about fourteen came out from the porch.

'Where's the master?' I asked.

'No master here,' answered the boy in Ukrainian.

'You mean there isn't a master at all?'

'That's right.'

'Well, where's the mistress?'

'Gone to the village.'

'Who'll open the door for me then?' I asked, giving it a kick. The door opened by itself, and a dank smell came from within. I lit a sulphur match and held it up to the boy's face. Its light showed a pair of wall-eyes: the boy was totally blind, and had been since birth. He stood before me without moving, and I had a good look at his face.

I confess I'm strongly prejudiced against the blind, one-eyed, deaf, dumb, legless, armless, hunch-backed, and so on. I've noticed there's always some odd link between a person's outward appearance and his inner self, as though when a man loses a limb he loses some inner feeling as well.

So I studied the blind boy's face. But what can you expect to see in a face without eyes? I took a long look at him, and couldn't help feeling sorry for him, when suddenly the ghost of a smile flitted across his thin lips. For some reason this struck me very unpleasantly. I had an idea that this blind boy might not be so blind as he seemed. I told myself that there was no way of faking wall-eyes, and anyway why should he want to? But it was no good – prejudice often takes me this way.

In the end I said:

'You the son of the house?'

'No.'

'Who are you then?'

'A poor orphan.'

'Has the woman got any children?'

'No. She had a daughter, but she went off with a Tatar. Over the sea.'

'Who was this Tatar?'

'I don't know. A Crimean Tatar he was, a boatman from Kerch.'

I went into the hut. There was no furniture apart from a table, a couple of benches and a huge chest by the stove. There wasn't a single ikon on the walls – a bad sign. The sea wind blew through a broken window-pane.

I took a stump of candle from my valise, lit it and unpacked. I stood my sabre and gun in the corner, laid my pistols on the table and spread my cape out on one of the benches, while my Cossack did the same on the other. Ten minutes later he was snoring, but I couldn't get to sleep. I kept seeing the wall-eyed boy before me in the darkness.

An hour or so passed. The moonlight shining through the window played on the mud floor of the hut. Suddenly a shadow flitted across the patch of moonlight on the floor. I sat up and looked at the window. Once more someone ran past it and vanished. I couldn't imagine that this person had run on down the vertical drop to the sea, but there was nowhere else he could have gone.

I got up, put on my beshmet, fastened my belt and dagger and crept silently out of the hut. Coming towards me was the blind boy. I hid by the fence and he walked past me, his step cautious, but sure. He had a bundle under his arm. Turning towards the quay, he started down the steep and narrow pathway. Then shall the dumb sing and the blind see, I thought, and went after him, keeping close enough to have him in sight.

By now the moon was clouding over. A mist lay over the

sea, and the stern lantern of the nearest ship glimmered faintly through it. Foaming breakers gleamed along the shore, threatening every minute to overwhelm it.

I made my way with difficulty down the steep slope and saw the blind boy pause at the bottom and turn right along the foot of the cliff. He walked very close to the water's edge and looked every moment as though he would be swept away by a wave. But judging by the sureness with which he jumped from rock to rock, avoiding the hollows, it was clearly not the first time he had taken this walk.

In the end he stopped and sat down on the beach, placing his bundle beside him and apparently listening for something. I watched his movements from behind a protruding rock. In a few minutes a white figure appeared from the other direction. It came up to the blind boy and sat down beside him. The wind brought me snatches of their conversation.

'What do you think, blind boy?' said a woman's voice. 'It's very rough. Yanko won't come.'

'Yanko's not afraid of storms,' said the blind boy.

'The mist's thickening,' said the woman, a note of sadness in her voice.

'It's easier to slip past the coastguards when it's misty,' replied the boy.

'And what if he's drowned?'

'What if he is? You'll go to church on Sunday without a new ribbon.'

There was silence. One thing had struck me, though – when the blind boy had talked to me he had spoken Ukrainian, but now he spoke pure Russian.

'There, I was right,' said the blind boy, clapping his hands. 'Yanko's not afraid of sea or wind or mist or coastguards. Listen! That's not the sea splashing – it's Yanko's long oars. You can't fool me.'

The woman leapt up and peered anxiously out to sea.

'Rubbish,' she said. 'I can't see anything.'

I looked hard out to sea, but I must say I could see nothing like a boat. Ten minutes went by, then, suddenly, a black speck appeared among the mountainous waves. One moment it grew bigger, the next smaller, rising slowly on the crests and dropping swiftly into the troughs of the waves. It was a boat coming in to shore. It was a bold sailor indeed who ventured out across the fifteen miles of the straits on such a night. And he must have some very special reason for doing it.

Turning this over in my mind, I watched with bated breath as the frail little craft dived like a duck into the abyss, then, beating its oars like wings, rose up again in a shower of spray. Next I thought it was going to be dashed to pieces on the shore, but it deftly turned broadside and slipped unscathed into the tiny bay.

Out of it stepped a man of middle height, wearing a Tatar sheepskin cap. He waved his hand and all three began lugging something out of the boat that was so heavy that I can't think why the boat hadn't sunk. They all took a bundle on their shoulders and set off along the shore. I soon lost sight of them. I had to get back, but I was very concerned by these weird doings, I don't mind saying, and impatiently waited for morning to come.

When my Cossack woke up he was very surprised to find me fully dressed, but I didn't tell him the reason for it. I spent some time at the window admiring the view. The blue sky was dotted with scattered clouds, the far Crimean shore was a mauve streak on the horizon, ending in a cliff topped by the white tower of a lighthouse. I set out for the fort of Phanagoria to find out from the commandant when I could leave for Gelenjik. But, alas, the commandant couldn't give a definite answer. All the ships at the quay were either coast-guard vessels or merchantmen that had still to take on cargo.

'There might be a packet boat in three or four days,' he said. 'We'll see about it then.'

I went back to my lodging, depressed and annoyed, to be met at the door by my Cossack, who looked scared.

'It looks bad, sir,' he said.

'Yes,' I answered. 'Heaven alone knows when we'll get out of here.'

At this he grew even more agitated and, leaning towards me, whispered:

'This place – it's unwholesome. I met up with a Black Sea Cossack I know today, a sergeant – he was in my unit a year back. When I told him where we were, he said the place was unwholesome and the people a bad lot. And he's right, too. What can you make of that blind boy? He goes everywhere on his own, fetches the water, goes down to the market for bread. Everybody here seems to take it for granted.'

'Well, what of it? Has the woman come back?'

'Yes, she came while you were out. She's brought her daughter.'

'Daughter? She hasn't got one.'

'Well, I don't know who it can be if it's not her daughter. Anyway, the old woman's in there in the hut now.'

I went into the hovel. The stove was going full blast and the meal being cooked on it looked rather lavish for poor folk. All my questions to the old woman met with the reply that she was deaf and couldn't hear. There was no point in going on, so I turned to the blind boy, who sat in front of the stove, putting sticks on the fire. I took hold of his ear.

'Now then, you blind imp,' I said. 'Where were you going with that bundle last night, eh?'

The boy suddenly burst into tears, bawling and whining.

'Where to?' he said (once more in Ukrainian). 'I didn't go anywhere. Bundle? What bundle?'

This time the old woman heard.

'Making things up,' she grumbled, 'and blaming it on a poor afflicted boy. What are you getting on to him for? What's he done to you?'

I'd had enough of this and went out, determined to get to the bottom of this mystery.

Pulling my cape around me, I sat down on a stone by the fence and gazed into the distance. Before me lay the sea, still rough after last night's storm, its monotonous din like the murmur of a town as it falls asleep. It reminded me of the old days and took my mind back to our cold northern capital. Stirred by these memories, I sat lost in thought.

An hour had gone by, perhaps more, when I suddenly heard what sounded like a song. Yes, it was a song, sung by the young, clear voice of a woman. But where was it coming from? I listened. It was an odd tune, slow and melancholy, then quick and lively. I looked around, but there was nobody about. I listened again. The sound seemed to come from the sky. I looked up and there, standing on the roof of my hut, was a girl in a striped dress, her hair flowing loose like a mermaid's. She was gazing out to sea, shielding her eyes from the sun with her hand. One moment she laughed, talking to herself, then she would start singing again. I can remember every word of it.

> Tall ships sail o'er the deep green ocean,
> White sails set on the billowy wave.
> My little boat sails there with the tall ships,
> Sails has she none, just her two good oars.
> Storm winds will blow, and the old tall ships
> Will lift their wings and fly over the sea.
> Then I'll curtsey and beg so humbly:
> 'Have pity on my boat, oh wicked sea.
> 'Precious are the goods that my boat carries,
> 'Bold is the heart that steers her through the night.'

I couldn't help thinking that I'd heard this voice the night before. I thought for a moment, and when I next looked at the roof the girl was gone. Suddenly, she darted past me, humming a different tune and snapping her fingers, and ran inside to the old woman. There was an argument, the old woman speaking angrily, the girl laughing loudly. Then again

I saw my sprite skipping towards me. She stopped as she reached me and stared me in the eye, as though surprised at my being there, then nonchalantly turned away and walked slowly off towards the quay.

That wasn't the end of it, though, because she hung around my quarters all day, singing and skipping. She was a strange creature. There were no signs of madness in her face – in fact, when she looked at me, her eyes were bright and penetrating. They appeared to have some magnetic power and seemed always to be expecting some question, but as soon as I spoke, she would run off with a crafty smile.

I had never seen a woman like her before. She wasn't at all beautiful, though I have my prejudices on the subject of beauty too. She had plenty of breeding, and breeding in a woman, as in a horse, means a lot – a discovery first made by *la jeune France*. It (breeding, that is, not *la jeune France*) comes out chiefly in a woman's walk, in her hands and feet, the nose being specially significant. In Russia a well-shaped nose is rarer than a tiny foot.

My singer appeared to be no older than eighteen. I was enchanted by the extraordinary suppleness of her figure, the special tilt she gave to her head, the golden tint of her lightly tanned neck and shoulders, her long auburn hair, and, above all, her well-shaped nose. True, there was something wild and suspicious about her sidelong glances, and an elusive quality in the way she smiled, but such is the power of prejudice that my head was completely turned by her regular nose. I thought I had lighted on Goethe's Mignon, that fabulous product of his German imagination. Indeed, they had much in common – the same sudden changes of mood, from restless activity to complete inertia, the same enigmatic speeches, the same skipping, the same strange songs.

Late in the afternoon I stopped her in the doorway and we had the following conversation.

'Tell me, my pretty one,' I said. 'What were you doing up on the roof today?'

'Looking to see which way the wind blew.'

'And why did you want to know that?'

'Happiness comes the way the wind blows.'

'Was your song meant to bring you happiness then?'

'Happiness goes with a song.'

'And what if your song brings you to grief?'

'What if it does? If things don't get better, they get worse, and it's a short road that leads from bad to good.'

'Who taught you that song?'

'Nobody taught me. I sing whatever comes into my head. It'll be heard by the one it's meant for, and you won't understand if you're not meant to hear.'

'And what's your name, my songstress?'

'Ask the man who christened me.'

'And who was he?'

'How should I know?'

'We are mysterious, aren't we,' I said. 'Well, there's something I do know about you.' There was no change in her expression, not even a flicker of her lips – I might have been talking of someone else. 'I know you went down to the shore last night.'

And I gave her a very solemn account of all that I had seen, expecting to confuse her, but not on your life! She just gave a loud laugh.

'It's plenty you saw, but little you know,' she said. 'And what you do know, you'd better keep to yourself.'

'And supposing, for instance, I decided to report it to the commandant?' I said, looking extremely solemn, even severe.

With a sudden hop, however, she burst into song and vanished like a bird startled from a bush. My final words were inopportune. I had no idea of their importance at the time, but later had occasion to regret them.

As soon as it was dark, I told my Cossack to heat up the teapot camp-style, then lit a candle and sat down at the table, taking an occasional puff at my travelling pipe. I was just finishing my second glass of tea when the door creaked and I heard footsteps and the light rustle of a dress behind me. I gave a start and turned round. It was my mermaid. She quietly sat down opposite me, saying nothing, but gazing at me with a look that seemed wonderfully tender. It reminded me of those looks that had played such havoc with my life in the old days. She appeared to expect some question, but for some reason I was filled with embarrassment and said nothing. You could tell she was excited from the dull pallor of her face, and I noticed a faint tremor in her hand as it strayed aimlessly over the table. One moment her bosom heaved, the next she seemed to be holding her breath. I was beginning to feel I'd had enough of this comedy and was on the point of putting a highly prosaic end to the silence – by offering her a glass of tea – when she suddenly leapt up, threw her arms round my neck and a moist, passionate kiss sounded on my lips. It went black before my eyes, my head swam, and I embraced her with all the force of youthful passion. But, with a whispered command to go to the beach that night when all were asleep, she slid snakelike through my arms and darted from the room. In the hallway she knocked over the teapot and a candle that stood on the floor.

'She-devil!' yelled my Cossack, who had settled down on some straw, intending to warm himself with what was left of the tea. Only then did I come down to earth.

Two hours later, when all was quiet on the quay, I roused my Cossack.

'If I fire my pistol, run down to the beach,' I said.

His eyes bulged, and he replied automatically, 'Very good, sir.' I stuck a pistol in my belt and went out.

She was waiting for me at the edge of the cliff. Her clothing was scant, to say the least, with a light shawl round her supple waist.

'This way,' she said. She took my hand and we began the descent. I still don't know how I escaped breaking my neck. At the bottom we turned to the right and took the path along which I had followed the blind boy the night before. The moon was not yet up, and two solitary stars shone like warning lights in the deep blue sky. The ponderous waves came in with steady rhythmic beat, barely lifting the lone boat that lay moored by the shore.

'Let's get into the boat,' said my companion.

I hesitated. I'm not at all keen on sentimental boat-trips, but this was no time for holding back, so I followed her into the boat, and before I realized what was happening we were afloat.

'What's this all about?' I asked angrily.

'This is what it's about,' she said, pushing me on to the seat and putting her arms around me. 'I love you.'

Her cheek pressed against mine, and I felt her fiery breath upon my face. Suddenly there was a loud splash as something fell into the water. I grabbed for my belt – and found my pistol gone. I suddenly had a horrible suspicion. The blood surged in my head. I looked round – we were a hundred yards from shore and I couldn't swim! I tried to push her away, but she clung to my clothes like a cat, and with a sudden push nearly had me in the sea. The boat rocked, but I steadied myself, and a desperate struggle began. My fury gave me extra strength, but I saw I was no match for my opponent when it came to agility.

'What is it you want?' I cried, squeezing her tiny hands till the bones crunched. But with her serpentlike nature she bore the pain and made no cry.

'You saw,' she said. 'You'll tell on us.'

Then, with a superhuman effort, she hurled me across the gunwale, and we both hung over the side of the boat, with her hair touching the water. It was a critical moment. Bracing my knee against the bottom of the boat, I seized her hair with one hand and her throat with the other. She let go of my clothes, and in an instant I pushed her into the sea. It was quite dark now. I glimpsed her head a couple of times in the spray, and that was all.

I found half an old oar in the bottom of the boat and after much labour somehow reached the quay. As I made my way back to the hut along the shore I automatically looked towards the place where the blind boy had awaited the nocturnal sailor the night before. The moon was up now and I fancied I saw someone in white sitting on the beach. Filled with curiosity, I crept nearer and dropped down in the grass above the cliff. By raising my head slightly I had a good view of all that was going on below and was not very surprised, in fact I was almost glad, to see that it was my mermaid. She was wringing the spray from her long hair, and her wet frock showed the outline of her supple waist and high bosom.

A boat soon appeared in the distance. It came swiftly in to shore and a man got out, as on the previous night. He wore a Tatar cap, though his head was shaved like a Cossack, and he had a large knife sticking from his belt.

'Yanko,' said the girl. 'Everything's ruined.'

They went on talking, but so quietly that I couldn't make out what they were saying.

'Where's the blind boy?' asked Yanko at last in a louder voice.

'I've sent him for the things,' said the girl.

He appeared a few minutes later carrying a sack on his back, which was stowed in the boat.

'Listen you, blind boy,' said Yanko. 'Keep an eye on the place... you know where, don't you. There's valuable stuff there. Tell (I didn't catch the name) that I've finished taking orders from him. Things are going wrong, and this is the last he'll see of me. It's too dangerous. I'll go and look for a job somewhere else. He won't find another daredevil chap like me, and you tell him that I'd never have left him if he'd paid better. But I go where I please, wherever the wind blows and the sea roars.' There was a pause, then Yanko said: 'She's going with me. She can't stay here now. And tell the old woman it's time she died. She's lived too long, she's had her time. She won't see us again.'

'What about me?' asked the blind boy plaintively.

'You're no concern of mine,' said Yanko.

Meanwhile my mermaid had jumped into the boat and waved to her companion. Yanko put something in the blind boy's hand and said:

'Here, buy yourself some gingerbread.'

'Is that all I get?' asked the blind boy.

'There's another then,' said Yanko, and I heard the ring of a coin falling on the rocks. The blind boy didn't pick it up.

Yanko got into the boat and, hoisting a small sail, they sailed swiftly away before the offshore wind. For a long time the white sail could be seen in the moonlight, bobbing among the dark waves. The blind boy still sat on the shore, and I heard what sounded like sobbing. He was crying. He cried and cried.

I felt sad. Why did fate toss me into the peaceful midst of these *honest smugglers*? I had shattered their calm, like a stone thrown into a still pool – and like a stone, too, I had nearly gone to the bottom.

I went back to my lodging. The guttering candle flickered on a wooden platter in the hallway. Despite my orders, my Cossack was sleeping like a log, with his gun in his hands. I didn't disturb him, but took the candle and went inside the hut. To my dismay I found my box, silver-mounted sabre and Daghestan dagger (the gift of a friend) had all vanished. Now I knew what that damned boy had been carrying! I roused my Cossack with a none too friendly shove and cursed him angrily. But there was nothing I could do. I could hardly go and complain to the authorities that I'd been robbed by a blind boy and very nearly drowned by a girl of eighteen.

Next morning there was a ship, thank God, and I left Taman. I've no idea what became of the old woman and the poor blind boy. And, anyway, the joys and tribulations of mankind are of no concern to me, an itinerant officer with a travel warrant in my pocket.

TURGENEV

IVAN TURGENEV, the most western of the
great Russian writers, is best known for his
series of polished novels depicting the lives
of the nineteenth-century gentry and intelli-
gentsia, but he also wrote poetry, plays and
numerous shorter prose pieces. His literary
reputation was first made during the years
1847–52 with some twenty evocative verbal
vignettes of the Russian countryside which
were collected together and issued at the end
of that period under the title *A Huntsman's
Sketches* – a book which is popularly believed
to have helped dispose the future Tsar Alexander II in favour of emancipating the serfs.
One of the most famous of the sketches is
'Bezhin Lea', in which sensitive descriptions
of nature are combined with affectionate portraits of a group of peasant boys recounting
their superstitious beliefs.

BEZHIN LEA

Translated by Richard Freeborn

It was a beautiful July day, one of those days which occur
only when the weather has been unchanged for a long time.
From early morning the sky is clear and the sunrise does not
so much flare up like a fire as spread like a mild pinkness. The
sun – not fiery, not molten, as it is during a period of torrid
drought, not murkily crimson as it is before a storm, but
bright and invitingly radiant – peacefully drifts up beneath
a long, thin cloud, sends fresh gleams through it and is
immersed in its lilac haze. The delicate upper edge of the
long line of cloud erupts in snaky glints of light: their gleam
resembles the gleam of beaten silver. But then again the
playful rays break out – and as if taking wing the mighty sun
rises gaily and magnificently. About midday a mass of high
round clouds appear, golden-grey, with soft white edges.
They move hardly at all, like islands cast down on the infinite
expanses of a flooding river which flows round them in
deeply pellucid streams of level blue; away towards the
horizon they cluster together and merge so that there is no
blue sky to be seen between them; but they have themselves
become as azure-coloured as the sky and are pervaded
through and through with light and warmth. The light, pale-
lilac colour of the heavens remains the same throughout the
day and in all parts of the sky; there is no darkening anywhere, no thickening as for a storm, though here and there
pale-blue columns may stretch downwards, bringing a
hardly noticeable sprinkling of rain. Towards evening these
clouds disappear. The last of them, darkling and vague as
smoke, lie down in rosy mistiness before the sinking sun. At
the point where the sun has set just as calmly as it rose into
the sky, a crimson glow lingers for a short time over the

darkened earth, and, softly winking, the evening star burns upon the glow like a carefully carried candle. On such days all the colours are softened; they are bright without being gaudy; everything bears the mark of some poignant timidity. On such days the heat is sometimes very strong and occasionally even 'simmers' along the slopes of the fields. But the wind drives away and disperses the accumulated heat, and whirling dust storms – a sure sign of settled weather – travel in tall white columns along roads through the ploughland. The dry pure air is scented with wormwood, harvested rye and buckwheat. Even an hour before nightfall you can feel no dampness. It is just such weather that the farmer wants for harvesting his grain.

It was on precisely such a day that I once went out grouse-shooting in Chernsk county in the province of Tula. I found, and bagged, a fair number of birds. My full game-pouch cut mercilessly at my shoulder. But I did not finally decide to make my way home until the evening glow had already died away and chill shadows began to thicken and proliferate in air that was still bright, though no longer illumined by the rays of the sunset. With brisk steps I crossed a long 'plaza' of bushy undergrowth, clambered up a hillock and, instead of the expected familiar moor with a little oak wood to the right of it and a low-walled white church in the distance, I saw completely different places which were unknown to me. At my feet there stretched a narrow valley; directly ahead of me rose, like a steep wall, a dense aspen wood. I stopped in bewilderment and looked around. 'Ah-ha!' I thought. 'I'm certainly not where I should be: I've swerved too much to the right' – and, surprised at my mistake, I quickly descended from the hillock. I was at once surrounded by an unpleasant, motionless damp, just as if I had entered a cellar. The tall, thick grass on the floor of the valley was all wet and shone white like a smooth tablecloth; it felt clammy and horrible to walk through. As quickly as possible I scrambled across to the other side and, keeping to the left, made my way along beside the aspen wood. Bats already flitted above its sleeping tree-tops, mysteriously circling and quivering against the dull paleness of the sky; a young hawk, out late, flew by high up, taking a direct, keen course in hurrying back to its nest. 'Now then, as soon as I reach that corner,' I said to myself, 'that's where the road'll be, so what I've done is to make a detour of about three quarters of a mile!'

I made my way finally to the corner of the wood, but there was no road there, only some low, unkempt bushes spread out widely in front of me and beyond them, in the far distance, an expanse of deserted field. Again I stopped. 'What's all this about? Where am I?' I tried to recall where I had been during the day. 'Ah, these must be the Parakhin bushes!' I exclaimed eventually. 'That's it! And that must be the Sindeev wood. . . . How on earth did I get as far as this? It's very odd! Now I must go to the right again.'

I turned to the right, through the bushes. Meanwhile night was approaching and rose around me like a thunder cloud; it was as if, in company with the evening mists, darkness rose on every side and even poured down from the sky. I discovered a rough, overgrown track and followed it, carefully peering ahead of me. Everything quickly grew silent and dark; only quail gave occasional cries. A small night bird, which hurried low and soundlessly along on its soft wings, almost collided with me and plunged off in terror. I emerged from the bushes and wandered along the boundary of a field. It was only with difficulty that I could make out distant objects. All around me the field glimmered faintly; beyond it, coming closer each moment, the sullen murk loomed in huge clouds. My footsteps sounded muffled in the thickening air. The sky which had earlier grown pale once again began to shine blue, but it was the blue of the night. Tiny stars began to flicker and shimmer.

What I thought was a wood had turned out to be a dark, round knoll. 'Where on earth am I?' I repeated again out loud, stopping for a third time and looking questioningly at

my yellow and white English dog, Diana, who was by far
the most intelligent of all four-legged creatures. But this
most intelligent of four-legged creatures only wagged her
small tail, dejectedly blinked her tired little eyes and offered
me no practical help. I felt ill at ease in front of her and
strode wildly forward, as if I had suddenly realized which
way to go, circled the knoll and found myself in a shallow
hollow which had been ploughed over. A strange feeling
took possession of me. The hollow had the almost exact
appearance of a cauldron with sloping sides. Several large
upright stones stood in the floor of the hollow – it seemed as
if they had crept down to that spot for some mysterious con-
sultation – and the hollow itself was so still and silent, the
sky above it so flat and dismal that my heart shrank within
me. A small animal of some kind or other squeaked weakly
and piteously among the stones. I hurried to climb back on
to the knoll. Up to that point I had not given up hope of
finding a way home, but now I was at last convinced that I
had completely lost my way and, no longer making any
effort to recognize my surroundings, which were almost
totally obliterated by the darkness, I walked straight ahead
of me, following the stars and hoping for the best . . . For
about half an hour I walked on in this way, with difficulty,
dragging one foot after another. Never in my life, it seemed,
had I been in such waste places: not a single light burnt
anywhere, not a single sound could be heard: one low hillock
followed another, field stretched after endless field and
bushes suddenly rose out of the earth under my very nose.
I went on walking and was on the point of finding a place to
lie down until morning, when suddenly I reached the edge
of a fearful abyss.

I hastily drew back my outstretched leg and, through the
barely transparent night-time murk, saw far below me an
enormous plain. A broad river skirted it, curving away from
me in a semi-circle; steely gleams of water, sparkling with
occasional faint flashes, denoted its course. The hill on which

I was standing fell away sharply like an almost vertical precipice. Its vast outlines could be distinguished by their blackness from the blue emptiness of the air and directly below me in the angle formed by the precipice and the plain, beside the river, which at that point was a dark, unmoving mirror under the steep rise of the hill, two fires smoked and flared redly side by side. Figures clustered round them, shadows flickered and now and then the front half of a small curly head would appear in the bright light.

At last I knew the place I had reached. This meadowland is known in our region as Bezhin Lea. There was now no chance of returning home, especially at night; moreover, my legs were collapsing under me from fatigue. I decided to make my way down to the fires and to await the dawn in the company of the people below me, whom I took to be drovers. I made my descent safely, but had hardly let go of my last handhold when suddenly two large, ragged, white dogs hurled themselves at me with angry barks. Shrill childish voices came from the fires and two or three boys jumped up. I answered their shouted questions. They ran towards me, at once calling off the dogs who had been astonished by the appearance of my Diana, and I walked towards them.

I had been mistaken in assuming that the people sitting round the fires were drovers. They were simply peasant boys from the neighbouring villages keeping guard over the horses. During hot summer weather it is customary in our region to drive the horses out at night to graze in the field, for by day the flies would give them no peace. Driving the horses out before nightfall and back again at first light is a great treat for the peasant boys. Bareheaded, dressed in tattered sheepskin jackets and riding the friskiest ponies, they race out with gay whoops and shouts, their arms and legs flapping as they bob up and down on the horses' backs and roar with laughter. Clouds of fine sandy dust are churned up along the roadway; a steady beating of hooves spreads far and wide as the horses prick up their ears and start running; and in front of them all, with tail high and continuously changing his pace, gallops a shaggy chestnut stallion with burrs in his untidy mane.

I told the boys that I had lost my way and sat down among them. They asked me where I was from and fell silent for a while in awe of me. We talked a little about this and that. I lay down beside a bush from which all the foliage had been nibbled and looked around me. It was a marvellous sight: a reddish circular reflection throbbed round the fires and seemed to fade as it leaned against the darkness; a flame, in flaring up, would occasionally cast rapid flashes of light beyond the limit of the reflection; a fine tongue of light would lick the bare boughs of the willows and instantly vanish; and long sharp shadows, momentarily breaking in, would rush right up to the fires as if the darkness were at war with the light. Sometimes, when the flames grew weaker and the circle of light contracted, there would suddenly emerge from the encroaching dark the head of a horse, reddish brown, with sinuous markings, or completely white, and regard us attentively and gravely, while rapidly chewing some long grass and then, when again lowered, would at once disappear. All that was left was the sound as it continued to chew and snort. From the area of the light it was difficult to discern what was happening in the outer darkness, and therefore at close quarters, everything seemed to be screened from view by an almost totally black curtain; but off towards the horizon hills and woods were faintly visible, like long blurs. The immaculate dark sky rose solemnly and endlessly high above us in all its mysterious magnificence. My lungs melted with the sweet pleasure of inhaling that special, languorous and fresh perfume which is the scent of a Russian summer night. Hardly a sound was audible around us . . . Now and then a large fish would make a resounding splash in the near-by river and the reeds by the bank would faintly echo the noise as they were stirred by the out-spreading waves . . . Now and then the fires would emit a soft crackling.

Around the fires sat the boys, as did the two dogs who had been so keen to eat me. They were still unreconciled to my presence and, while sleepily narrowing their eyes and glancing towards the fire, would sometimes growl with a special sense of their personal dignity; to start with these were only growls, but later they became faint yelps, as if the dogs regretted their inability to satisfy their appetite for me. There were five boys in all: Fedya, Pavlusha, Ilyusha, Kostya and Vanya. (I learnt their names from their conversation and I now intend to acquaint the reader with each of them.)

The first of them, Fedya, the eldest, would probably have been fourteen. He was a sturdy boy, with handsome and delicate, slightly shallow features, curly fair hair, bright eyes and a permanent smile which was a mixture of gaiety and absent-mindedness. To judge from his appearance, he belonged to a well-off family and had ridden out into the fields not from necessity but simply for the fun of it. He was dressed in a colourful cotton shirt with yellow edging; a small cloth overcoat, recently made, hung open somewhat precariously on his small narrow shoulders and a comb hung from his pale-blue belt. His ankle-high boots were his own, not his father's. The second boy, Pavlusha, had dishevelled black hair, grey eyes, broad cheekbones, a pale, pock-marked complexion, a large but well-formed mouth, an enormous head – as big as a barrel, as they say – and a thick-set, ungainly body. Hardly a prepossessing figure – there's no denying that! – but I nonetheless took a liking to him: he had direct, very intelligent eyes and a voice with the ring of strength in it. His clothes gave him no chance of showing off: they consisted of no more than a simple linen shirt and much-patched trousers. The face of the third boy, Ilyusha, was not very striking: hook-nosed, long, myopic, it wore an expression of obtuse, morbid anxiety. His tightly closed lips never moved, his frowning brows never relaxed; all the while he screwed up his eyes at the fire. His yellow, almost white, hair stuck out in sharp little tufts from under the small felt cap which he was continually pressing down about his ears with both hands. He had new bast shoes and foot cloths; a thick rope wound three times round his waist drew smartly tight his neat black top-coat. Both he and Pavlusha appeared to be no more than twelve years old. The fourth, Kostya, a boy of about ten, aroused my curiosity by his sad and medi-tative gaze. His face was small, thin and freckled, and pointed like a squirrel's; one could hardly see his lips. His large, dark, moistly glittering eyes produced a strange impression, as if they wanted to convey something which no tongue – at least not his tongue – had the power to express. He was small in stature, of puny build and rather badly dressed. The last boy, Vanya, I hardly noticed at first: he lay on the ground quietly curled up under some angular matting and only rarely poked out from under it his head of curly brown hair. This boy was only seven.

So it was that I lay down apart from them, beside the bush, and from time to time looked in their direction. A small pot hung over one of the fires, in which 'taters' were being cooked. Pavlusha looked after them and, kneeling down, poked the bubbling water with a small sliver of wood. Fedya lay, leaning on one elbow, his sheepskin spread round him. Ilyusha sat next to Kostya and continually, in his tense way, screwed up his eyes. Kostya, with his head slightly lowered, stared off somewhere into the distance. Vanya did not stir beneath his matting. I pretended to be asleep. After a short while the boys renewed their talk.

To start with, they gossiped about this and that – to-morrow's work or the horses. But suddenly Fedya turned to Ilyusha and, as if taking up from where they had left off their interrupted conversation, asked him:

'So you actually did see one of them little people, did you?'

'No, I didn't see him, and you can't really see him at all,' answered Ilyusha in a weak, croaky voice which exactly

suited the expression on his face, 'but I heard him, I did. And
I wasn't the only one.'

'Then where does he live around your parts?' asked
Pavlusha.

'In the old rolling-room.'*

'D'you mean you work in the factory?'

'Of course we do. Me and Avdyushka, my brother, we
work as glazers.'

'Cor! So you're factory workers!'

'Well, so how did you hear him?' asked Fedya.

'It was this way. My brother, see, Avdyushka, and Fyodor
Mikheevsky, and Ivashka Kosoy, and the other Ivashka
from Redwold, and Ivashka Sukhorukov as well, and there
were some other kids as well, about ten of us in all, the whole
shift, see – well, so we had to spend the whole night in the
rolling-room, or it wasn't that we had to, but that Nazarov,
the overseer, he wouldn't let us off, he said: "Seeing as
you've got a lot of work here tomorrow, my lads, you'd best
stay here; there's no point in the lot o' you traipsing off
home." Well, so we stayed and all lay down together, and
then Avdyushka started up saying something about "Well,
boys, suppose that goblin comes?" and he didn't have a
chance, Avdey didn't, to go on saying anything when all of
a sudden over our heads someone comes in, but we were
lying down below, see, and he was up there, by the wheel.
We listen, and there he goes walking about, and the floorboards really bending under him and really creaking. Then
he walked right over our heads and the water all of a sudden
starts rushing, rushing through the wheel, and the wheel
goes clatter, clatter and starts turning, but them gates of the
Keep† are all lowered. So we start wondering who'd raise

*'Rolling-rooms' or 'dipping-rooms' are terms used in paper fac-
tories to describe the place where the papers are baled out in the vats.
It is situated right by the mill, under the mill-wheel. (Author's note.)

†'The Keep' is the name used in our region for the place where the
water runs over the wheel. (Author's note.)

them so as to let the water through. Yet the wheel turned and
turned, and then stopped. Whoever he was, he went back to
the door upstairs and began coming down the stairway, and
down he came, taking his time about it, and the stairs under
him really groaning from his weight . . . Well, so he came
right up to our door, and then waited, and then waited a bit
more – and then that door suddenly burst open, it did. Our
eyes were poppin' out of our heads, and we watch – and
there's nothing there . . . And suddenly at one of the tubs the
form* started moving, rose, dipped itself and went to and
fro just like that in the air like someone was using it for
swilling, and then back again it went to its place. Then at
another tub the hook was lifted from its nail and put back on
the nail again. Then it was as if someone moved to the door
and started to cough all sudden-like, like he'd got a tickle,
and it sounded just like a sheep bleating . . . We all fell flat on
the floor at that and tried to climb under each other – bloody
terrified we were at that moment!'

'Cor!' said Pavlusha. 'And why did he cough like that?'
'Search me. Maybe it was the damp.'
They all fell silent.
'Are them taters done yet?' Fedya asked.
Pavlusha felt them.
'Nope, they're not done yet . . . Cor, that one splashed,'
he added, turning his face towards the river, 'likely it was a
pike . . . And see that little falling star up there.'

'No, mates, I've really got something to tell you,' Kostya
began in a reedy voice. 'Just you listen to what my dad was
talkin' about when I was there.'

'Well, so we're listening,' said Fedya with a condescending air.

'You know that Gavrila, the carpenter in the settlement?'
'Sure we know him.'
'But d'you know why he's always so gloomy, why he
never says nothing, d'you know that? Well, here's why. He

* The net with which the paper is scooped out. (Author's note.)

went out once, my dad said – he went out, mates, into the forest to find some nuts. So he'd gone into the forest after nuts and he lost his way. He got somewhere, but God knows where it was. He'd been walkin', mates, and no! he couldn't find a road of any kind, and already it was night all around. So he sat down under a tree and said to himself he'd wait there till mornin' – and he sat down and started to snooze. So he was snoozin' and suddenly he hears someone callin' him. He looks around – there's no one there. Again he snoozes off – and again they're callin' him. So he looks and looks, and then he sees right in front of him a water-fairy sittin' on a branch, swingin' on it she is and callin' to him, and she's just killin' herself laughin' ... Then that moon shines real strong, so strong and obvious the moon shines it shows up everythin', mates. So there she is callin' his name, and she herself's all shiny, sittin' there all white on the branch, like she was some little minnow or gudgeon, or maybe like a carp that's all whitish all over, all silver ... And Gavrila the carpenter was just frightened to death, mates, and she went on laughin' at him, you know, and wavin' to him to come closer. Gavrila was just goin' to get up and obey the water-fairy, when, mates, the Lord God gave him the idea to cross hisself ... An' it was terrible difficult, mates, he said it was terrible difficult to make the sign of the cross 'cos his arm was like stone, he said, and wouldn't move, the darned thing wouldn't! But soon as he'd managed to cross himself, mates, that water-fairy stopped laughin' and started in to cry ... An' she cried, mates, an' wiped her eyes with her hair that was green and heavy as hemp. So Gavrila kept on lookin' and lookin' at her, and then he started askin' her, "What's it you're cryin' for, you forest hussy, you?" And that water-fairy starts sayin' to him, "If you hadn't crossed yourself, human being that you are, you could've lived with me in joy and happiness to the end of your days an' I'm cryin' and dyin' of grief over what that you crossed yourself, an' it isn't only me that'll be dyin' of grief but you'll also waste away with grievin' till the end of your born days." Then, mates, she vanished, and Gavrila at once comprehended-like – how to get out of the wood, that is; but from that day on he goes around everywhere all gloomy.'

'Phew!' exclaimed Fedya after a short silence. 'But how could that evil forest spirit infect a Christian soul – you said he didn't obey her, didn't you?'

'You wouldn't believe it, but that's how it was!' said Kostya. 'Gavrila claimed she had a tiny, tiny, voice, thin and croaky like a toad's.'

'Your father told that himself?' Fedya continued.

'He did. I was lyin' on my bunk an' I heard it all.'

'What a fantastic business! But why's he got to be gloomy? She must've liked him, because she called to him.'

'Of course she liked him!' Ilyusha interrupted. 'Why not? She wanted to start tickling him, that's what she wanted. That's what they do, those water-fairies.'

'Surely there'll be water-fairies here,' Fedya remarked.

'No,' Kostya answered, 'this is a clean place here, it's free. 'Cept the river's close.'

They all grew quiet. Suddenly, somewhere in the distance, a protracted, resonant, almost wailing sound broke the silence – one of those incomprehensible nocturnal sounds which arise in the deep surrounding hush, fly up, hang in the air and slowly disperse at last as if dying away. You listen intently – it's as though there's nothing there, but it still goes on ringing. This time it seemed that someone gave a series of long, loud shouts on the very horizon and someone else answered him from the forest with sharp high-pitched laughter and a thin, hissing whistle which sped across the river. The boys looked at each other and shuddered.

'The power of the holy cross be with us!' whispered Ilyusha.

'Oh, you idiots!' Pavlusha cried. 'What's got into you? Look, the taters are done.' (They all drew close to the little pot and began to eat the steaming potatoes; Vanya was the only one who made no move.) 'What's wrong with you?' Pavlusha asked.

But Vanya did not crawl out from beneath his matting. The little pot was soon completely empty.

'Boys, have you heard,' Ilyusha began saying, 'what happened to us in Varnavitsy just recently?'

'On that dam, you mean?' Fedya asked.

'Ay, on that dam, the one that's broken. That's a real unclean place, real nasty and empty it is. Round there is all them gullies and ravines, and in the ravines there's masses of snakes.'

'Well, what happened? Let's hear.'

'This is what happened. Maybe you don't know it, Fedya, but that's the place where one of our drowned men is buried. And he drowned a long time back when the pond was still deep. Now only his gravestone can be seen, only there's not much of it – it's just a small mound . . . Anyhow, a day or so ago, the bailiff calls Yermil the dog-keeper and says to him: "Off with you and fetch the mail." Yermil's always the one who goes to fetch the mail 'cos he's done all his dogs in – they just don't somehow seem to live when he's around, and never did have much of a life no-how, though he's a good man with dogs and took to it in every way. Anyhow, Yermil went for the mail, and then he mucked about in the town and set off home real drunk. And it's night-time, a bright night, with the moon shining . . . So he's riding back across the dam, 'cos that's where his route came out. And he's riding along, this dog-keeper Yermil, and he sees a little lamb on the drowned man's grave, all white and curly and pretty, and it's walking about, and Yermil thinks: "I'll pick it up, I will, 'cos there's no point in letting it get lost here," and so he gets off his horse and picks it up in his arms – and the lamb doesn't turn a hair. So Yermil walks back to the horse, but the horse backs away from him, snorts and shakes its head. So, when he's quieted it, he sits on it with the lamb and starts off again holding the lamb in front of him. He looks at the lamb, he does, and the lamb looks right back at him right in the eyes. Then that Yermil the dog-keeper got frightened: "I don't recall," he thought, "no lambs looking me in the eye like that afore." Anyhow, it didn't seem nothing, so he starts stroking its wool and saying "Sssh, there, sssh!" And that lamb bares its teeth at him sudden-like and says back to him: "Sssh, there, sssh!..."'

The narrator had hardly uttered this last sound when the dogs sprang up and with convulsive barks dashed from the fire, disappearing into the night. The boys were terrified. Vanya even jumped out from beneath his mat. Shouting, Pavlusha followed in hot pursuit of the dogs. Their barking quickly retreated into the distance. There was a noisy and restless scurrying of hooves among the startled horses. Pavlusha gave loud calls: 'Grey! Beetle!' After a few seconds the barking ceased and Pavlusha's voice sounded far away. There followed another short pause, while the boys exchanged puzzled looks as if anticipating something new. Suddenly a horse could be heard racing towards them: it stopped sharply at the very edge of the fire and Pavlusha, clutching hold by the reins, sprang agilely from its back. Both dogs also leapt into the circle of light and at once sat down, their red tongues hanging out.

'What's there? What is it?' the boys asked.

'Nothing,' Pavlusha answered waving away the horse. 'The dogs caught a scent. I thought,' he added in a casual tone of voice, his chest heaving rapidly, 'it might have been a wolf.'

I found myself full of admiration for Pavlusha. He was very fine at that moment. His very ordinary face, enlivened by the swift ride, shone with bold courageousness and a resolute firmness. Without a stick in his hand to control the horse and in total darkness, without even so much as blinking an eye, he had galloped all by himself after a wolf . . . 'What a marvellous boy!' was my thought, as I looked at him.

'And you saw them, did you, those wolves?' asked the cowardly Kostya.

'There's plenty of them round here,' answered Pavlusha, 'but they're only on the prowl in the winter.'

He again settled himself in front of the fire. As he sat down he let a hand fall on the shaggy neck of one of the dogs and the delighted animal kept its head still for a long while as it directed sideward looks of grateful pride at Pavlusha.

Vanya once again disappeared under his mat.

'What a lot of horrible things you've been telling us, Ilyusha,' Fedya began. As the son of a rich peasant, it was incumbent upon him to play the role of leader (though for his own part he talked little, as if for fear of losing face). 'And it could've been some darned thing of the sort that started the dogs barking . . . But it's true, so I've heard, that you've got unclean spirits where you live.'

'In Varnavitsy, you mean? That's for sure! It's a really creepy place! More than once they say they've seen there the old squire, the one who's dead. They say he goes about in a coat hanging down to his heels, and all the time he makes a groaning sound, like he's searching for something on the earth. Once grandfather Trofimych met him and asked him: "What's it you are searching for on the earth, good master Ivan Ivanych?"'

'He actually asked him that?' broke in the astonished Fedya.

'He asked him that.'

'Well, good for Trofimych after that! So what did the other say?'

'"Split-grass," he says. "That's what I'm looking for." And he talks in such a hollow, hoarse voice: "Split-grass. And what, good master Ivan Ivanych, do you want split-grass for?" "Oh, my grave weighs so heavy," he says, "weighs so heavy on me, Trofimych, and I want to get out, I want to get away . . ."'

'So that's what it was!' Fedya said. 'He'd had too short a life, that means.'

'Cor, stone me!' Kostya pronounced. 'I thought you could only see dead people on Parents' Sunday.'

'You can see dead people at any time,' Ilyusha declared with confidence. So far as I could judge, he was better versed in village lore than the others. 'But on Parents' Sunday you can also see the people who're going to die that year. All you've got to do is to sit down at night in the porch of the church and keep your eyes on the road. They'll all go past you along the road – them who're going to die that year, I mean. Last year, Grandma Ulyana went to the church porch in our village.'

'Well, did she see anyone?' Kostya asked him with curiosity.

'Sure she did. To start with she just sat there a long, long time, and didn't see no one and didn't hear nothing. Only there was all the time a sound like a dog starting to bark somewhere. Then suddenly she sees there's someone coming along the road – it's a little boy in nothing but a shirt. She looked close and she saw it was Ivashka Fedoseev walking along.'

'Is that the boy who died in the spring!' Fedya broke in.

'That's the one. He walks along and doesn't even raise his head. But Ulyana recognized him. But then she looks again and sees a woman walking along, and she peers and peers and – God help us! – it's she herself, Ulyana herself, walking along.'

'Was it really her?' asked Fedya.

'God's truth. It was her.'

'But she hasn't died yet, has she?'

'No, but the year's not over yet either. You take a close look at her and then ask yourself what sort of a body she's got to carry her soul around in.'

Again they all grew quiet. Pavlusha threw a handful of dry sticks on the fire. They blackened in sharp outline against

the instantly leaping flames, and began to crackle and smoke
and bend, curling up their burned tips. The reflections from
the light, shuddering convulsively, struck out in all directions, but particularly upwards. Suddenly, from God knows
where, a small white pigeon flew directly into the reflections,
fluttered around in terror, bathed by the fierce light, and
then vanished with a clapping of its wings.

'Likely it's lost its way home,' Pavlusha remarked. 'Now
it'll fly until it meets up with something, and when it finds it,
that's where it'll spend the night till dawn.'

'Look, Pavlusha,' said Kostya, 'mightn't that be the soul
of some good person flying up to heaven, eh?'

Pavlusha threw another handful of sticks on the fire.

'Maybe,' he said after a pause.

'Pavlusha, tell us, will you,' Fedya began, 'were you able
to see that heavenly foreboding* in Shalamavo?'

'You mean, when you couldn't see the sun that time?
Sure.'

'Didn't you get frightened, then?'

'Sure, and we weren't the only ones. Our squire, tho' he
lets us know beforehand that "Well, there'll be a foreboding
for you," but soon as it gets dark they say he got real scared.
And in the servants' hut, that old granny, the cook, well –
soon as it's dark, listen, she ups and smashes all the pots in
the oven with a pair of tongs. "Whose going to need to eat
now it's the end of the world," she says. The cabbage soup
ran out all over everywhere. And, boy! What rumours there
were going about in our village, such as there'd be white
wolves and birds of prey coming to eat people, and there'd
be Trishka† himself for all to see.'

'What's this Trishka?' asked Kostya.

*The name given by the local peasants to an eclipse of the sun.
(Author's note.)

† The superstition about 'Trishka' probably contains an echo of the
legend about Antichrist. (Author's note.)

'Don't you know about Trishka?' Ilyusha started up heatedly. 'You're a dumb cluck, mate, if you don't know who Trishka is. It's just dunces you've got in your village, nothing but dunces! Trishka – he'll be a real astonishing person, who'll be coming, and he'll be coming when the last times are near. And he'll be the sort of astonishing person you won't be able to catch hold of, you won't be able to do nothing to him: that's the sort of astonishing person he'll be. The peasants, say, will want to try to catch him, and they'll go out after him with sticks and surround him, but what he'll do is lead their eyes astray – he'll lead their eyes astray so that they start beating each other. Say they put him in prison and he asks for some water in a ladle; they'll bring him the ladle and he'll jump right into it and vanish clean away, all trace of him. Say they put chains on him, he'll just clap his palms together and they'll fall right off him. So then this Trishka'll go walking through the villages and the towns; and this smart fellow, this Trishka, he'll tempt all Christian folk . . . but there won't be a thing you can do to him . . . That's the sort of astonishing, real cunning person he'll be.'

'Yes, that's the one,' Pavlusha continued in his unhurried way. 'He was the one that we were all waiting for. The old men said that soon as the heavenly foreboding begins, Trishka'll be coming. So the foreboding began, and everyone poured out into the street and into the field to see what'll happen. As you know, our place is high up and open so you can see all around. Everyone's looking – and suddenly down from the settlement on the mountain there's a man coming, strange-looking, with an astonishing big head . . . Everyone starts shouting: "Oy, oy, it's Trishka coming! Oy, oy, it's Trishka!" and they all raced for hiding, this way and that! The elder of our village, he crawled into a ditch and his wife got stuck in a gate and let out such a howling noise that she fair terrified her own watch-dog, and it broke its chain, rushed through the fence and into the wood. And Kuzka's

father, Dorofeich, jumped in among the oats, squatted down
there and began to make cries like a quail, all 'cos he thought
to himself: "For sure that soul-destroying enemy of mankind'll spare a poor wee birdie!" Such a commotion they
were all in! . . . But all the time that man who was coming
was simply our barrel-maker Vavila, who'd bought himself
a new can and was walking along with that empty can per-
ched on his head.'

All the boys burst out laughing and then once again fell
quiet for an instant, as people talking'out in the open air
frequently do. I looked around me: the night stood guard in
solemn majesty; the raw freshness of late evening had been
replaced by midnight's dry mildness, and it still had a long
time to lie like a soft quilt over the dreaming fields; there was
still a long time to wait until the first murmur, the first
rustlings and stirrings of morning, the first dew-beads
of dawn. There was no moon in the sky: at that season
it rose late. Myriads of golden stars, it seemed, were
all quietly flowing in glittering rivalry along the Milky
Way, and in truth, while looking at them, one sensed
vaguely the unwavering, unstoppable racing of the earth
beneath . . .

A strange, sharp, sickening cry resounded twice in quick
succession across the river, and, after a few moments, was
repeated farther off . . .

Kostya shuddered: 'What was that?'

'That was a heron's cry,' Pavlusha answered calmly.

'A heron,' Kostya repeated. 'Then what was it, Pavlusha,
I heard yesterday evening?' he added after a brief pause.
'Perhaps you know.'

'What did you hear?'

'This is what I heard. I was walkin' from Stone Ridge to
Shashkino, and at first I went all the way along by our nut
trees, but afterwards I went through that meadow – you
know, by the place where it comes out like a narrow file,*

---

* A 'narrow file' is a sharp turn in a ravine. (Author's note.)

where there's a tarn.* You know it, the one that's all over-grown with reeds. So, mates, I walked past this tarn an' suddenly someone starts makin' a groanin' sound from right inside it, so piteous, like: Oooh – oooh ... oooh – oooh! I was terrified, mates. It was late an' that voice sounded like somebody really sick. It was like I was goin' to start cryin' myself ... What would that have been, eh?'

'In the summer before last, thieves drowned Akim the forester in that tarn,' Pavlusha remarked. 'So it may have been his soul complaining.'

'Well, it might be that, mates,' rejoined Kostya, widening his already enormous eyes. 'I didn't know that Akim had been drowned in that tarn. If I'd known, I wouldn't have got so terrified.'

'But they do say,' continued Pavlusha, 'there's a kind of little frog makes a piteous noise like that.'

'Frogs? No, that wasn't frogs ... what sort of ...' (The heron again gave its cry over the river.) 'Listen to it!' Kostya could not refrain from saying. 'It makes a noise like a wood-demon.'

'Wood-demons don't make a cry, they're dumb,' Ilyusha inserted. 'They just clap their hands and chatter ...'

'So you've seen one of them, a wood-demon, have you?' Fedya interrupted him scornfully.

'No, I haven't, and God preserve that I should see one. But other people have seen one. Just a few days ago one such overtook one of our peasants and was leading him all over the place through the wood and round and round some clearing or other ... He only just managed to get home before it was light.'

'Well, did he see him?'

'He saw him. Big as big he was, he said, and dark, all wrapped up, just like he was behind a tree so you couldn't

---

* A 'tarn' is a deep hole filled with spring water remaining after the spring torrents, which does not dry up even in summer. (Author's note.)

see him clearly, or like he was hiding from the moon, and looking all the time, peering with his wicked eyes, and winking them, winking . . .'

'That's enough!' exclaimed Fedya, shuddering slightly and convulsively hunching his shoulders, 'Phew!'

'Why should this devilish thing be around in the world?' commented Pavlusha. 'I don't understand it at all!'

'Don't you scold it! It'll hear you, you'll see,' Ilyusha said. Again a silence ensued.

'Look up there, look up there, all of you!' the childish voice of Vanya suddenly cried. 'Look at the little stars of God, all swarming like bees!'

He had stuck his small, fresh-complexioned face out from beneath the matting, was leaning on one little fist and slowly looking up with his large, placid eyes. The boys all raised their eyes to the sky, and did not lower them until quite a while had passed.

'Tell me, Vanya,' Fedya began to say in a gentle voice, 'is your sister Anyutka well?'

'She's well,' Vanya answered, with a faint lisp.

'You tell her she ought to come and see us. Why doesn't she?'

'I don't know.'

'Tell her that she ought to come.'

'I'll tell her.'

'Tell her that I'll give her a present.'

'And you'll give one to me, too?'

'I'll give one to you, too.'

Vanya sighed. 'No, there's no need to give me one. Better you give it to her, she's so good to us.'

And once more Vanya laid his head on the ground. Pavlusha rose and picked up the little pot, now empty.

'Where are you going?' Fedya asked him.

'To the river, to get some water. I'd like a drink.'

The dogs got up and followed him.

'See you don't fall in the river!' Ilyusha called after him.

'Why should he fall?' asked Fedya. 'He'll be careful.'

'All right, so he'll be careful. Anything can happen, though. Say he bends down, starting to dip up the water, but then a water-sprite grabs him by the hand and pulls him down below. They'll start saying afterwards that, poor boy, he fell in the water . . . But what sort of a fall is that? Listen, listen, he's in the reeds,' he added, pricking up his ears.

The reeds were in fact moving, 'hushing', as they say in our parts.

'Is it true,' asked Kostya, 'that that ugly woman, Akulina, has been wrong in the head ever since she went in the water?'

'Ever since then . . . And look at her now! They say she used to be real good-looking before. The water-sprite did for her. Likely he didn't expect they'd drag her out so soon. He corrupted her down there, down in his own place at the bottom of the water.'

(I had come across this Akulina more than once. Covered with tatters, fearsomely thin, with a face as black as coal, a vacant gaze and permanently bared teeth, she used to stamp about on the same spot for hours at a time, at some point on the road, firmly hugging her bony hands to her breast and slowly shifting her weight from one foot to the other just like a wild animal in a cage. She would give no sign of understanding, no matter what was said to her, save that from time to time she would break into convulsions of laughter.)

'They do say,' Kostya went on, 'that Akulina threw herself in the river because her lover deceived her.'

'Because of that very thing.'

'But do you remember Vasya?' Kostya added sadly.

'What Vasya?' asked Fedya.

'The one who drowned,' Kostya answered, 'in this very river. He was a grand lad, a really grand lad! That mother of his, Feklista, how she loved him, how she used to love Vasya! And she sort of sensed, Feklista did, that ruin would come to him on account of water. That Vasya used to come with us boys in the summer when we went down to the river

93

to bathe – and she'd be all bothered, his mother would. The other women wouldn't care, going waddling by with their wash-tubs, but Feklista would put her tub down on the ground and start calling to him: "Come back, come back, light of my life! O come back, my little falcon!" And how he came to drown, God alone knows. He was playing on the bank, and his mother was there, raking hay, and suddenly she heard a sound like someone blowing bubbles in the water – she looks, and there's nothing there 'cept Vasya's little cap floating on the water. From then on, you know, Feklista's been out of her mind: she goes and lies down at that place where he drowned, and she lies down, mates, and starts singing this song – you remember the song Vasya used to sing all the time – that's the one she sings, plaintive-like, and she cries and cries, and complains bitterly to God . . .'

'Here's Pavlusha coming,' Fedya said.

Pavlusha came up to the fire with a full pot in his hand.

'Well, boys,' he began after a pause, 'things aren't good.'

'What's happened?' Kostya quickly asked.

'I heard Vasya's voice.'

They all shuddered.

'What's that you're saying? What's it all about?' Kostya babbled.

'It's God's truth. I was just bending down to the water and suddenly I hear someone calling me in Vasya's voice, and it was just like it was coming from under the water: "Pavlusha, hey, Pavlusha!" I listen, and again it calls: "Pavlusha, come down here!" I came away. But I managed to get some water.'

'God preserve us! God preserve us!' the boys said, crossing themselves.

'It was a water-sprite for sure calling you, Pavlusha,' Fedya added. 'And we were only just talking about him, about that Vasya.'

'Oh, it's a real, bad omen,' said Ilyusha, giving due weight to each word.

'It's nothing, forget it!' Pavlusha declared resolutely and again sat down. 'Your own fate you can't escape.'

The boys grew quiet. It was clear that Pavlusha's words had made a profound impression on them. They began to lie down before the fire, as if preparing to go to sleep.

'What was that?' Kostya suddenly asked, raising his head. Pavlusha listened.

'It's some snipe in flight, whistling as they fly.'

'Where would they be flying?'

'To a place where there's never any winter, that's what they say.'

'There isn't such a land, is there?'

'There is.'

'Is it far away?'

'Far, far away, on the other side of the warm seas.'

Kostya sighed and closed his eyes.

More than three hours had already flowed by since I joined the boys. Eventually the moon rose. I failed to notice it immediately because it was so small and thin. This faintly moonlit night, it seemed, was just as magnificent as it had been previously. But many stars which had only recently stood high in the sky were beginning to tilt towards its dark edge; all around absolute quiet descended, as usually happens only just before morning: everything slept the deep, still sleep of the pre-dawn hours. The air was not so strongly scented, and once again it seemed to be permeated with a raw dampness. O brief summer nights! The boys' talk died away along with the dying of the fires. Even the dogs dozed; and the horses, so far as I could make out by the vaguely glittering feeble flux of the starlight, were also lying down with their heads bowed. A sweet oblivion descended on me and I fell into a doze.

A current of fresh air brushed my face. I opened my eyes to see that morning was beginning. As yet there was no sign of dawn's pinkness, but in the east it had begun to grow light. The surrounding scene became visible, if only dimly.

The pale-grey sky shone bright and cold and tinged with blue; stars either winked their faint light or faded; the ground was damp and leaves were covered with the sweat of dew, here and there sounds of life, voices could be heard, and a faint, light wind of early morning began its wandering and fleet-footed journey across the earth. My body responded to it with a mild, joyful shivering. I got briskly to my feet and walked over to the boys. They slept the sleep of the dead about the embers of the fire; only Pavlusha raised himself half-way and glanced intently at me.

I nodded my head at him and set off to find my way home along the bank of the river, shrouded with smoky mist. I had hardly gone more than a mile when sunlight streamed all around me down the length of the wide damp lea, and ahead of me – across the freshly green hills, from forest to woodland, and behind me along the far, dusty track, over the glistening blood-red bushes and across the river which now shone a modest blue under the thinning mist – flowed torrents of young, hot sunlight, crimson at first and later brilliantly red, brilliantly golden. Everything began quivering into life, awakening, singing, resounding, chattering. Everywhere, large drops of dew began to glow like radiant diamonds. There carried to me, pure and crystal-clear as if also washed clean by the freshness of the morning's atmosphere, the sound of a bell. And suddenly I was overtaken by the racing drove of horses, refreshed after the night, and chased along by my acquaintances, the boys.

I have, unfortunately, to add that in that same year Pavlusha died. He did not drown; he was killed in falling from a horse. A pity, for he was a fine lad!

DOSTOEVSKY

FYODOR DOSTOEVSKY, one of the most powerful and most influential writers in European literature, is best known for his four great novels, *Crime and Punishment*, *The Idiot*, *The Devils* and *The Brothers Karamazov*, in all of which he undertakes a profound and intricate analysis of human nature. Like Solzhenitsyn a century later, Dostoevsky drew much of his strength and many of his insights from a period of imprisonment and exile to which he was condemned for a minor political offence. Dostoevsky's shorter works are generally inferior, but 'A Strange Man's Dream', written towards the end of his life, shares with the novels both a passionate concern for moral and religious truth and an involved prose style which reflects the author's complex reasoning.

A STRANGE MAN'S DREAM
A FANTASTIC STORY

Translated by Malcolm Jones

I

I'M a strange person. Now people are beginning to say that
I'm mad, and this might be regarded as a sort of promotion
if they didn't still think me just as strange as ever. But I don't
get upset about it any more. Now I like them all, even when
they laugh at me. In fact for some reason I particularly like
them when they laugh at me. Indeed I would happily join in
the laughter myself – not at my own expense but because I
love them – if it didn't make me so sad to look at them. The
sad thing is that they don't know the truth and I do. Oh,
what a burden it is to be the only person who knows the
truth! But they won't understand it. No, they won't understand it.

I used to get very upset at the thought that I appeared so
strange. Not appeared, in fact, but was. I have always been
strange and it's possible that I have always been aware of it.
Maybe I already knew at the age of seven that I was strange.
Then I went to school, then to the university, and the more
I studied, lo and behold, the more I learnt that I was strange.
Indeed in the last analysis all my university studies seem to
have had the sole purpose of revealing and explaining my
strangeness to me, and the more knowledgeable I became,
the more I became aware of it. As with knowledge, so with
real life. With every passing year my consciousness that I
appeared strange from every conceivable point of view continued to grow. Everybody laughed at me all the time. But
no one knew, indeed no one even guessed, that nobody was
more conscious of the situation than I, and it was all the more

humiliating just because they didn't know. But I was to blame for that. I was always so proud that I would never have admitted it for anything in the world. My pride increased over the years and if I had ever actually come to the point of admitting to someone that I was strange I think I should have gone straight home that very evening and put a bullet through my brain.

Oh, what torments I suffered as an adolescent, for fear that I would let the cat out of the bag in some way or other and suddenly reveal everything to my acquaintances. But when I became an adult, in spite of the fact that I continued to learn more and more about my awful affliction with each passing year, I for some reason grew a little calmer. I say 'fo some reason' advisedly, because I still cannot explain why. Perhaps it was because of the terrible anguish which arose in my soul and which had its origin in something infinitely greater than me: namely, in the conviction that overcame me that in this world *nothing matters* anywhere. I had a presentiment about this a very long time ago, but I suddenly became fully convinced last year. I suddenly felt that *it did not matter to me* whether the world existed or if there was nothing anywhere. I began to sense, and then to feel with my entire being, that *so far as I was concerned there was nothing*. To begin with it seemed that a lot of things had existed for me in the past, but later on I came to realize that in the past too there had actually been nothing. There had just seemed to be something. Gradually I became convinced that there never would be anything. Then I suddenly stopped getting angry with people and almost stopped noticing them altogether. It's true that this came out in the most trivial ways. For instance, I would bump into people as I was walking along the street. Not because I was immersed in my own thoughts, for what was there for me to think about? I had completely stopped thinking by then: nothing mattered to me. And it would have been different if I had solved any problems, but no, I didn't solve a single problem, many as there were to solve. *Nothing mattered to me* and the problems evaporated. And it was after this that I discovered the truth. I discovered the truth last November, the 3rd of November to be exact, and since then I can remember every moment of my life. It was on a gloomy evening, the gloomiest evening imaginable. I was returning home between ten and eleven at night and I had actually thought, I remember, that no night could conceivably be gloomier. Even physically speaking. It had been raining all day and the rain was cold, gloomy and menacing, displaying, I recall, an undisguised hostility towards humanity. Then suddenly, between ten and eleven, it stopped, and a horrible dampness set in. It was even damper and colder than when it had been raining, and a kind of steam was rising from everything, from every stone in the street and from the recesses of each alleyway as one glanced into its depths. It suddenly struck me that if the gas went out everywhere it would be less disagreeable, since everything seems even more oppressive by gaslight. I had had almost nothing to eat that day and from early evening I had been visiting an engineer who had a couple of other friends there as well. I was silent and I think they got fed up with me. They were talking about some controversial matter and suddenly flared up. But it didn't really matter to them, I could tell, and there was no particular reason for them to flare up. I suddenly told them so:

'Gentlemen, this doesn't really matter to you one way or the other.'

They weren't put off, but all laughed at me, since I said it without implying any criticism of them, but just because it was a matter of complete indifference to me. They noticed this and cheered up.

When I had had the thought about the gas as I was walking along the street, I had looked up at the sky. The sky was horribly dark, but it was possible to distinguish patches of fathomless blackness between the rifts in the clouds. Suddenly I noticed in one of these patches a tiny star, and I

began to stare fixedly at it. The tiny star had given me an idea.
I should kill myself that night. I had firmly decided on the
measure two months previously and, poor as I was, I had
bought a beautiful revolver and loaded it that very day. Two
months had now passed and it still lay in the drawer. But the
whole thing was of so little consequence to me that I decided
to choose a moment when it did matter – I don't know why.
So every night for these two months, as I walked home, I
thought of shooting myself. I was still waiting for the right
moment. And now that tiny star gave me the idea and I
decided that *without fail* I should do it that night. Why the
tiny star gave me that idea I don't know at all.

And then, as I was looking at the sky, I was suddenly
seized by the elbow by this little girl. The street was already
empty and there was virtually no one about. In the distance
a cabby was asleep on a droshky. The little girl was about
eight, with no more than a headscarf and a light dress to
protect her. She was wet through and I particularly noticed
her tattered, wet shoes. They particularly caught my attention and I remember them still. She suddenly started to tug
at my elbow and to call me. She wasn't weeping, but she was
trembling all over with a chill and couldn't pronounce her
words properly, so that they came out in a jerky fashion. She
was in terror of something and shrieked in desperation:
'Mummy, mummy!' I nearly turned to her. However, I said
not a word and continued on my way. She still ran and
tugged at me and in her voice was the sound of a terrified
child in despair. I know that sound. Although she failed to
complete a single word I understood that her mother was
dying somewhere or other or that something had happened
to them there, and that she had run out to call someone, to
find someone to help her mother. But I didn't follow her.
Quite the contrary, I considered driving her away. First of
all I told her to find a policeman. But she suddenly clasped
her hands together, and, sobbing and panting for breath,
she went on running at my side and would not let me go. I

stamped at her and shouted, but she just shouted back: 'Sir, sir!' Then suddenly she abandoned me and ran headlong across the street. Some other passer-by had appeared there and she had evidently transferred her attentions from me to him.

I ascended to my fifth-floor flat. I rent a flat in my landlord's house and we all have separate rooms. My room is poor and small, with a semi-circular attic window. I have an oil-cloth divan, a table with books on it, two upright chairs and an easy chair, which although extremely ancient is a Voltairean chair. I sat down, struck a match and began to think. In the next room to mine, behind a partition, there was absolute bedlam. It had been going on for two whole days. A retired captain lived there and he had six guests from the dregs of the city who were drinking vodka and playing stoss with old cards. The night before there had been a fight and I know that two of them were pulling each other by the hair. The landlady would have complained but she is terribly afraid of the captain. The only other lodger in our rooms is a little, thin lady from a military family with three little children who have all fallen ill since coming to live in the flat. She and the children are also mortally afraid of the captain and tremble and cross themselves all night. The smallest of them was so frightened that he had some sort of fit. This captain, I know for a fact, sometimes stops passers-by on the Nevsky Prospekt and begs for alms. He can't get a job in government service, but strangely enough – and I mention it for this very reason – this captain has, for the whole month he has lived with us, failed to arouse the slightest irritation in me. I have of course from the outset avoided his company, and indeed he lost interest in me from our first encounter. But, however much shouting there is behind the partition and however many of them there are, it doesn't bother me. I can sit there the whole night, quite oblivious to them, and not hear a thing. Indeed I stay awake every night until daybreak, and have done so for a year. I sit

the whole night in my armchair at my table and do nothing.
I read books only during the day. I sit there and do not even
think. It is rather that vague thoughts flit about in my head
and I let them go. In the course of a night my candle burns
away completely. I sat down at the table quietly, took out
the revolver and placed it in front of me. When I put it
there, I recall, I asked myself: 'Now?' and answered myself
in the affirmative, 'Now'. That is, I should shoot myself
now. I knew that I should shoot myself that night without
fail, but how long I should sit at the table first was a different
matter. And I certainly should have shot myself had it not
been for that little girl.

II

But you see, although nothing mattered to me any more, I
could, for example, still feel pain. If someone had hit me, I
would have felt the pain. And it was just the same in the
moral sphere. If something were to happen to arouse my
pity, I would have felt pity in just the same way as I had in
that period of my life before nothing mattered any more. And
I had felt pity recently. I could certainly have helped that
child. Why didn't I help that little girl? Because of a thought
that occurred to me: when she was tugging and appealing
to me, there suddenly arose in my mind a question which I
could not answer. It was an idle question, but it annoyed me.
I was annoyed because I had come to the conclusion that, if I
had already decided to put an end to my life that night, then,
now more than ever, nothing ought to matter any more.
Why did I suddenly feel that something did matter and why
did I feel pity for the little girl? I remember feeling very
sorry for her indeed. It pained me in a strange, quite improbable way, considering my position. It's true that I don't
know how to convey my fleeting sensation of the moment

very well, but the sensation continued at home when I sat down at the table, and I was very cross, more than I had been for a long time. One line of reasoning succeeded another. It became clear to me that if I was a human being and not yet a nothing, and until such time as I became a nothing, I remained alive and was capable of suffering, getting angry and feeling shame for my deeds. Very well then. But if I was going to kill myself in two hours' time, let's say, then why should I worry about the little girl and shame and anything else on this earth? I should be nothing, absolutely. And was it possible that my consciousness of the fact that I would *completely* cease to exist – and consequently that everything would cease to exist – should not have some slight influence on my feeling of pity for the little girl and my feeling of shame for my meanness to her? No doubt the reason I stamped and shouted so wildly at the unhappy child was that 'not only did I feel no pity but, if I were to commit some mean and inhuman act, there would be nothing to stop me since in two hours' time everything would be extinguished'. Can you believe that that was the reason why I shouted at her? I am now almost convinced of it. It dawned on me that life and the world, in a manner of speaking, now depended on me. One could put it even more strongly: the world was, so to speak, made exclusively for me. If I were to shoot myself, the world would not exist any more, for me at least. Not to mention the possibility that after my death nothing would exist for anybody and that the whole world, the moment my consciousness was extinguished, would itself be instantly extinguished, like a phantom, as the property of my own consciousness, and would be destroyed, for perhaps this whole world and all these people do not exist without me. I remember that as I sat and pondered I turned over in my mind all these new questions which crowded in one after the other in a new way, and I thought up some completely novel ideas. For example, there was one strange idea which suddenly occurred to me. If I had previously lived on the moon or Mars and had committed there the most shameful and dishonourable deed imaginable, and was cursed and disgraced in a manner which one associates with the occasional dream or nightmare rather than real life, and if I then found myself on earth and continued to retain the consciousness of what I had done on this other planet, and, in addition, knew that there was not the remotest chance of my ever returning there, would it matter to me, as I looked up from the earth to the moon, or not? Such questions were vain and gratuitous, since the revolver was already lying there in front of me and I knew with my whole being that *that* would undoubtedly take place. But the questions irritated me and I was furious. It seemed that I couldn't die now, leaving an unsolved problem. In a word, that little girl saved me, because I fended off the bullet with questions.

Meanwhile things had quietened down at the captain's too. They had finished playing cards, were settling down to sleep and at the same time grumbling and swearing at each other in a desultory fashion. Then I suddenly fell asleep, which had never happened to me before when I was sitting in the armchair in front of the table. I fell asleep completely without noticing it. Dreams, as everyone knows, are extremely strange things. One thing will present itself with terrifying clarity, with the minute and intricate detail of the decoration on a piece of jewellery, and yet you may leap through time and space, for instance, without apparently being aware of it. Dreams, it would seem, are impelled not by reason but by desire, not by the head, but by the heart, but all the same what subtle operations my reason has sometimes performed in dreams! Quite unfathomable things take place in dreams. For example, my brother died five years ago and I sometimes see him in dreams. He takes an active interest in my affairs and we have mutual concerns, but nevertheless I am fully aware throughout the entire dream that my brother is dead and buried. Why am I not surprised by the fact that although he is dead there he is beside me and doing things with me? Why does my mind permit such things? But that is enough of that. I will pass on to my dream. Yes, indeed, that was when I had my dream, my dream of the 3rd of November. They mock me now and tell me it was only a dream. But surely it doesn't matter whether it was a dream or not, if that dream proclaimed the truth to me. If you've once beheld the truth and recognized it, then you know it is the truth, that there is and can be no other, and that whether you are asleep or awake is irrelevant. Very well, it was a dream, but that real life which you so extol was precisely what I was about to extinguish by my suicide, whereas my dream, oh, it proclaimed to me a new, great, regenerated, powerful, life.

Now listen.

III

I said that I fell asleep imperceptibly and while still continuing to ponder these matters. I suddenly dreamed that I was picking up the revolver and, still seated, pointing it straight at my heart – at my heart, not my head. I had previously definitely decided to shoot myself in the head, in the right temple to be exact. Aiming at my breast, I waited a second or two and my candle, the table and the wall before me suddenly began to move and sway. Without further delay, I fired.

In dreams you sometimes fall from a great height, or you have your throat cut or are beaten, but you never feel pain, unless you somehow or other actually knock yourself on the bedstead. Then you feel pain and it almost always wakes you up. In my dream too I felt no pain, but it seemed as if with the shot everything in me shook and suddenly went dark, and around me all became terribly dark. It was as though I had been struck blind and dumb and was stretched out on my back, lying on something firm, seeing nothing and unable to make the slightest movement. All around people are walking and shouting, the captain in his bass voice, the landlady in her shrill voice. Then suddenly another lull, and then they are carrying me in a closed coffin. And I can feel the coffin swaying and am thinking about it and suddenly the thought occurs to me that I am dead, completely dead. I know, and do not question it. I cannot see or move, but I still feel and think. But I soon get used to this and as usual in dreams I accept reality without argument.

Now they are burying me in the ground. They all depart and I am alone, utterly alone. I cannot move. Before, when I was awake and imagined what it would be like to be buried in my grave, I always associated it with a sensation of dampness and cold and nothing more. Now too I felt very cold, especially the end of my toes, but felt no other sensation.

I lay there and, strangely, I expected nothing, accepting without argument that there is nothing for a dead man to expect. But it was damp. I don't know how much time passed, an hour or several days. Then suddenly there fell on my left closed eye a drop of water which had trickled through the lid of the coffin, and, then, a minute later, came another, then another minute passed and there came a third and so on and so on, each following the last at intervals of a minute. A profound indignation suddenly flared up in my heart and suddenly I felt a physical pain there. 'That is my wound,' I thought. 'It's the shot, the bullet . . .' And the drops kept on dripping, minute by minute, on my closed eye. And suddenly I appealed, not with my voice for I could not move, but with my entire being, to the lord and master of all that was happening to me:

'Whoever you are, if only you are, and if there exists something more rational than what is happening now, then let it come to pass here. If you are exacting vengeance on me for my irrational suicide by the ugliness and absurdity of being in the hereafter, then know that never, though my torments persist for millions of years, shall any torment that may afflict me compare with my silent scorn.'

I made my appeal and fell silent. The profound silence continued for almost a minute, and one more drop of water fell, but I knew, I knew and believed unreservedly and unshakably that everything would now certainly change. And then suddenly my grave opened wide. Actually I don't know whether it was dug and opened up, but I was taken by some dark and unfamiliar being and we found ourselves in space. I suddenly saw clearly: it was deep night and never, never was there such profound darkness. We sped on in space far from the earth. I asked no questions of him who bore me on, but proudly waited. I told myself that I was not afraid, and grew faint from excitement at the very thought. I cannot remember how long we travelled and I cannot describe it. Everything happened the way it does in dreams when you are leaping through space and time and the laws of being and reason, and you alight only where your heart prompts you to. I recall that in the darkness I suddenly saw a tiny star.

'Is that Sirius?' I asked, suddenly unable to contain myself any longer (for I had resolved not to inquire about anything).

'No, it is the star which you saw through the clouds as you were walking home,' the being answered, bearing me on.

I knew that its form was like that of a human. Strangely enough, I didn't like this being; indeed I actually felt a deep loathing for it. I was expecting complete oblivion and it was in this expectation that I had shot myself. And now I was in the hands of a being who was of course not human, but who *was*, who existed.

'That means there is life beyond the grave!' I reflected with that strange illogicality characteristic of dreams. But the promptings of my heart continued to press themselves on me in all their fullness.

'If I have to *be* all over again,' I thought, 'and live again according to some inalienable will, then I do not want to be defeated and humiliated!'

'You know that I am afraid of you and despise me for it,' I said suddenly to my companion, unable to restrain any longer the humiliating question which underlay this confession, and feeling my humiliation like a stab in my heart. He did not answer my question, but I suddenly felt that I was not the object of his scorn and laughter or even pity and that our journey had an unknown, mysterious destination which concerned me alone. Fear rose in my heart. Something was silently, painfully communicated to me from my silent companion and penetrated my heart. We sped on through dark and uncharted space. I had long ceased to recognize the constellations we passed. I knew that there were stars in the heavens whose light took thousands and millions of years to reach the earth. Perhaps we had already flown beyond these regions. I was waiting for something and a terrifying anguish tormented my heart. Suddenly I was shaken by a familiar and very welcoming sensation. I suddenly saw our sun! I knew that it could not be *our* sun, which had given birth to *our* earth and I knew that we were at an infinite distance from our sun, but I somehow or other comprehended with my entire being that this was exactly the same sort of sun as ours, a recurrence of it, its double. A sweet, rapturous, seductive feeling awoke in my soul: the native strength of that world, that very world which had given birth to me, resounded in my heart and resurrected it, and I sensed life, my former life, for the first time since the grave.

'But if that is the sun, if that is exactly the same kind of sun as ours,' I cried, 'where is the earth?' And my companion pointed to a little star sparkling in the darkness with an emerald sheen. We soared on towards it.

'Is it possible for such recurrences to take place in the universe, is that the law of nature? And if that is the earth there, then can it possibly be the same sort of earth as ours, exactly the same, unhappy, poor, but precious and eternally beloved, inspiring the same tormenting love for itself in its ungrateful children?' I exclaimed, shaking with uncontrollable, rapturous love for that native earth which I had abandoned. The image of the poor little girl whom I had wronged passed before my eyes.

'You will see all,' answered my companion, and a certain sadness was discernible in his voice. But we were quickly drawing nearer to the planet. It grew larger before my very eyes. I could already pick out the ocean, the outlines of Europe, and suddenly a strange feeling of exalted, sacred fervour flared up in my heart.

'How and why is such a recurrence possible? I love, I can love only that earth which I have left, on which drops of my blood remain in the place where they fell, when I, ungrateful wretch that I am, extinguished my life with a bullet in the heart. But never, never have I stopped loving that earth and even that night when I took my leave of it my love for it perhaps caused me greater torment than ever. Are there torments on this new earth? On our earth we can truly love only in torments and through torments. We know no other way of loving and no other kind of love. I want torment in order to love. I want, I thirst to kiss that earth which I have left this very moment, and wash it with my tears, and I do not want, I do not accept, life on any other planet.'

But my companion had already left me. Suddenly, hardly noticing it myself, I arrived on that other earth in the bright light of a sunny, heavenly day. I stood, apparently, on one of those islands which form the Greek archipelago on our earth, or somewhere on the shore of the mainland alongside the archipelago. Everything was exactly the same as on our earth, except that it was as if everywhere there was the glow of some festival and some great holy, final triumph. A gentle, emerald sea softly splashed the shores and kissed them with an evident, almost conscious love. The tall, beautiful trees stood in all the splendour of their colour, and their innumerable little leaves, I am convinced, greeted me with a soft, gentle sound and seemed to speak words of love. The grass was on fire with bright, fragrant flowers. Little birds flew over the sky in flocks and, unafraid of me, sat on my shoulders and arms and joyfully flapped their gentle, trembling little wings. And finally I saw and recognized the people of this happy earth. They approached me themselves, surrounded me and kissed me. Children of the sun, children of their own sun, oh, how beautiful they were! Never did I perceive such beauty in human beings on our earth. Just possibly one might find some distant, pale reflection of this beauty in our children in their earliest years. Their faces shone with intelligence and a kind of serene consciousness, but their faces were joyful; a childlike joy sounded in their words and voices. Oh, I immediately understood everything from my first glance at their faces. This was the earth untarnished by the Fall, on which there lived a people who had never sinned, living in the same sort of paradise in which our ancestors had lived according to the universal traditions of mankind, with the exception that the whole earth here was an undivided paradise. These people crowded round me laughing joyfully and caressed and comforted me. They took me to their homes and each of them tried to calm me. Oh, they asked me nothing; they seemed to know everything already and wanted to chase the suffering from my face as soon as possible.

IV

You see the point once again: suppose it was just a dream? But my sensation of love in these innocent and beautiful people has remained with me permanently, and I still feel that their love pours over me from their planet. I saw them myself, knew them and was won over. I loved them and later I suffered for them. Oh, I realized immediately, even then, that there was much about them I should never understand. It seemed inexplicable to me, as a modern Russian progressive, a vile native of St Petersburg, that they should, for example, know so much and yet not be in possession of modern science. But I soon understood that their knowledge was suffused with and nourished by other convictions than ours on earth and that their aspirations were quite different. They wanted nothing and were at peace. They did not aspire to an understanding of life as we strive to understand it, because their life was complete. But their knowledge was more profound and higher than that of our sciences. For our sciences seek to explain what life is and strive to understand it so as to teach others how to live. They knew how to live without science and, though I understood this, I could not fathom their knowledge.

They drew my attention to their trees and I couldn't understand how they could look at them with so much love: it was as if they were conversing with creatures like themselves. And, you know, I am possibly right in saying that they conversed with them! Yes, they discovered their language and I am convinced that the trees understood them. That was how they regarded the whole of nature – the animals who lived at peace with them did not attack them but loved them, won over by their love. They directed my attention to the stars and spoke to me about them concerning something I couldn't understand, but I am convinced that they were in some way in touch with the stars in the heavens, not by thought processes alone, but by means of some living contact. Oh, these people did not succeed in making me understand them; they loved me without that, but I knew nevertheless that they in their turn would never understand me and for that reason I hardly ever spoke to them about our earth. In their presence I simply kissed that earth on which they lived and silently worshipped them, and they saw this and permitted themselves to be worshipped without embarrassment, because they too loved greatly. They did not suffer for me when I sometimes kissed their feet in tears, joyfully aware in my heart of the force of love with which they would respond. Sometimes I would ask myself in astonishment how they could fail to offend someone like me and not once arouse in me feelings of jealousy and envy. Many times I asked myself how I, a braggart and liar, could refrain from speaking of my knowledge, about which, of course, they had no inkling, and not seek to astound them with it, even if only out of love for them.

They were playful and happy like children. They wandered in their beautiful groves and woods, they sang their beautiful songs, they fed themselves on light fare, the fruits of their trees, the honey from their woodlands and milk from the animals they loved. For their food and their clothing they engaged in only a little light work. They experienced love and gave birth to children, but I never noticed in them the slightest impulse of that *cruel* sensuality which affects almost everybody on our earth, each and every one of us, and is the unique source of almost all the sins of mankind. They rejoiced in their children as they appeared among them, as new participants in their bliss. There were no quarrels and there was no jealousy among them and they did not even understand what these words meant. Their children were the children of all, because they all constituted a single family. There was hardly any illness among them, although there was death; but their old folk died peacefully, as though they were falling asleep, surrounded by people who were there to take leave of them, blessing them, smiling at them and themselves bidding them farewell with happy smiles. I saw no grief or tears on such occasions, only love which rose to the point of rapture – a rapture which was calm, full and contemplative. One might have supposed that they remained in contact with their departed brethren even after death and that the earthly union between them was not severed. They barely understood me when I questioned them about eternal life, but were obviously so instinctively convinced of it that it did not constitute a problem for them.

They had no churches but they possessed a vital, living and uninterrupted union with the Totality of the universe; they had no faith, but they did have firm knowledge that when their earthly joy had reached the limits of earthly nature, then there would dawn for them, both living and dead, a still wider contact with the Totality of the universe. They awaited that moment with joy, but with patience and without suffering, as though they already possessed it in the presentiments of their hearts and communicated with each other about it. In the evenings, when preparing for sleep, they loved to compose harmonious and well-balanced choruses. In these songs they expressed all the sensations which the departing day had given them, they sang its praises and bade it farewell. They liked to compose songs one after another and praised each other like children; they were the simplest songs, but they flowed from the heart and penetrated it. And it was not only in songs; it was as if they spent their whole lives in admiration of each other. There was a sort of general, universal infatuation of each with all. Other songs which they sang, triumphant and ecstatic, I hardly understood at all. Though I comprehended the words, I could never plumb their full significance. They remained somehow inaccessible to my mind, while my heart seemed unwittingly to absorb them more and more.

I often said to them that I had had a presentiment of all this long ago, that all this joy and glory was made known to me when I was still on our earth in a deep yearning which sometimes reached a pitch of unbearable grief, that I had had a presentiment of them all and their glory in my dreams and fantasies and that on our earth I often could not look at the setting sun without tears; that in my hatred for people on our earth there was always an element of anguish. Why could I not hate them without loving them? Why did I feel constrained to forgive them whilst at the same time there was such anguish in my love for them? Why could I not love them without hating them? They listened to me and I saw that they had no conception of what I was talking about, but I was not sorry that I had told them. I knew that they understood all the force of my yearning for those I had left. Indeed, when they looked at me with their kindly, loving eyes, when I felt that in their presence my heart became as innocent and righteous as theirs, I had no regrets at not understanding them. I was overwhelmed by a sense of the fullness of life and I silently worshipped them.

Oh, now everyone laughs in my face and assures me that it is impossible to see in a dream the sort of detail which I am describing, and that in my dream all I saw or felt was a sensation generated by my feverish heart, and that I made up the details myself on waking. And when I told them that that might be perfectly true, good God, how they laughed in my face and what merriment I provoked! Yes, of course I was overcome by the sensation of the dream and that was all that had survived in my deeply wounded heart. But nevertheless the actual forms and images of my dream, the ones, that is, which I actually experienced when I was dreaming, were brought to such a pitch of harmony, were so seductive, so beautiful and so full of truth that, on waking, I was naturally unable to express them in our inadequate words, and the inevitable result was that they receded into the background of my mind and perhaps I did have to compose the details afterwards myself, no doubt distorting them in my passionate desire to pass them on as soon as possible in some small degree. How could I not believe that all this actually took place? Perhaps it was a thousand times better, more radiant and joyful than in my retelling. Even if it was a dream, it had to be true. Look here, I'll tell you a secret: it's possible that it wasn't a dream at all. For something happened, something so terrifyingly true that it couldn't have been just a dream. Even if it was my heart that generated it, is it really conceivable that my heart alone could have generated the terrifying truth which subsequently occurred? How could I have invented it or dreamt it in my heart, unaided? Surely my shallow heart and my capricious, petty mind could not have risen to such a revelation of truth. Judge for yourself. So far I have withheld the sequel, but now I'll tell the whole truth. The fact is I corrupted them all.

V

Yes. In the end I corrupted them all! How this could have happened I don't know, but I remember it distinctly. In my dream thousands of years flew by and left me with just the sensation of the whole. I know only that I was the cause of the Fall. Like a nasty parasite, like a plague virus infecting whole nations, I infected that happy earth which until my advent had been without sin. They learnt how to lie and came to love the lie and to know its beauty. Oh, no doubt it all began *innocently enough*, with a joke, a flirtation, an amorous intrigue. In fact perhaps it began with a mere particle of a lie, but that particle worked its way into their hearts and they liked it. Thereafter sensuality quickly developed, sensuality gave birth to jealousy, and jealousy to cruelty. Oh, I don't know, I don't remember, but very, very soon the first blood was spilt. They were amazed and terrified, and began to move apart and live separately from each other. Groups appeared, but now they were ranged against each other. Reproaches and reproofs were heard. They experienced shame, and shame gave rise to the idea of virtue. There arose the concept of honour and each group raised its own banner. They began to torment animals, and animals fled from them into the forests and became their enemies. They opened the struggle for separateness, isolation, individuality, for mine and thine. They began to speak different tongues. They came to know grief and to love it, they thirsted for torment and said that truth is attained only through torment. Then knowledge arose among them. As soon as they became evil, they began to talk of brotherhood and humaneness and understood these ideas. When they became criminal, they discovered justice, and for the preservation of justice they prescribed whole legal codes, and to back up their legal codes they instituted the guillotine. They could only just remember what they had lost, and didn't even care to believe that once they had been innocent and happy. They even laughed at the possibility of their former happiness and called it a dream. They couldn't even imagine it in forms and images but, strange and wonderful as it may seem, the moment they had completely lost faith in their former happiness and had classified it as a fairytale, they so badly wanted to be innocent and happy again that they fell down before the desires of their hearts like children, worshipped this desire, raised temples and began to pray to their idea, to their 'desire', and at the same time believed in its complete unrealizability and impracticality, while continuing to worship it and bow down before it in tears. However, if they could have returned to that innocent and happy condition which they had lost, and if someone had suddenly showed it to them again and asked them if they wished to return to it, they would certainly have refused. They answered me:

'Though we are deceitful, wicked and unjust, we *know* it and bewail it, and torment ourselves for it, and we exact harsher punishments perhaps than that merciful judge who will ultimately judge us and whose name is unknown to us. But we have science and with it we shall discover the truth again, but we shall acquire it consciously. Knowledge is superior to feeling, consciousness of life superior to life. Science will give us wisdom, wisdom will reveal laws, and knowledge of the laws of happiness is superior to happiness.'

That is what they said, and delivering themselves of these words each of them loved himself most of all, and indeed had no alternative. Each of them became so jealous of his own individuality that he tried with all his might to degrade and disparage that of others, and devoted his life to this task. Slavery arose, including voluntary slavery: the weak willingly subjugated themselves to the strongest, solely to secure assistance in suppressing those even weaker than themselves. There appeared righteous men, who went to these people with tears and spoke to them about their pride, about their loss of measure and harmony, about their loss of shame. But people laughed at them and stoned them. Sacred blood flowed on the threshold of the temples. Then people began to appear who started to consider how to bring everyone together again in such a way that each individual might continue to love himself most of all, and at the same time interfere with no one, thus permitting everybody to live together as if in a harmonious society. Wars arose as a result of this idea. All the combatants firmly believed all the while that the sciences, wisdom and a feeling of self-preservation would finally compel men to come together into a harmonious and rational society and therefore in the meantime, in order to accelerate the process, the 'initiated' attempted to eliminate with all possible speed the 'uninitiated' who did not understand their idea, so that they should not impede its eventual triumph. But the feeling of self-preservation soon began to weaken; there appeared proud men and sensualists who unceremoniously demanded everything or nothing. In order to secure everything, they had recourse to villainy and, when they were unsuccessful, to suicide. There appeared religions based on a cult of non-being and self-destruction for the sake of eternal peace in oblivion. Finally these people grew weary of their senseless labours, and suffering appeared on their faces. They proclaimed that suffering is beauty, for thought is only to be found in suffering. They praised suffering in their songs. I walked among them, wringing my hands, and wept over them, but I loved them even more perhaps than before when there was no suffering on their faces and when they were innocent and so beautiful. I came to love their profaned earth more than when it had been a paradise, simply because grief had appeared on it. Alas, I always loved sorrow and grief, but only for myself, and I wept for them and pitied them. I stretched out my hands to them and in my despair I accused, cursed and despised myself. I told them that I had done it all, I alone; that it was I who had brought vice, plague and lies among them! I implored them to crucify me, I taught them how to make a cross. I could not kill myself, I lacked the strength to do it, but I wanted to relieve them of their torments, I yearned for torments, yearned for my own blood to be spilt to the last drop while I suffered torments. But they just laughed at me and in the end started to regard me as a holy fool. They vindicated me, saying that they had got only what they wanted themselves, and that everything that now existed was inevitable. In the end they announced to me that I was becoming dangerous to them and that they would put me in an asylum if I didn't hold my peace. Then grief entered my soul with such force that my heart contracted and I felt that I was dying and then, then I awoke.

It was already morning or, rather, dawn had not broken but it was between five and six o'clock. I awoke in the same armchair, my candle had completely burnt away. They were asleep at the captain's and all round there was a stillness rare in my apartment. Straightaway I leapt up in utter amazement; nothing of the sort – down to the most trivial detail – had ever happened to me before. Never before, for instance, had I fallen asleep in my armchair. Then suddenly, while I stood there and recovered my senses, suddenly my revolver caught my eye, ready, loaded. But in a single instant I had thrust it away from me! Oh, now there would be life without end! I raised my hands and appealed to eternal truth, though not so much appealed as burst into tears. Rapture, a boundless rapture, lifted my whole being. Yes, to live and – to preach! About preaching I had come to a decision in a trice and, of course, it would be for the rest of my life. I should go forth and preach, I wanted to preach – but what? The truth, for I had seen the truth, seen it with my own eyes, in all its glory!

And since then I have been preaching! Apart from that, I love people, and love those who laugh at me most of all. Why it should be so I do not know and am unable to explain. But so be it. They say that I am already going astray and that, if I have already gone astray, what of the future? It's quite true: I do go astray and perhaps it will be even worse in the future. And of course I shall go astray more than once while I am discovering how to preach, to preach, that is, with both words and deeds, because that is very difficult to do. I can see all this as clear as day even now, but listen: who does not go astray? All the same, we are all going towards one and the same goal, though by different routes. That is an ancient truth. What is new is that I cannot go far astray because I have seen the truth. I have seen and know that people can be beautiful and happy without losing the capacity to live on earth. I cannot and will not believe that evil is man's normal condition. And yet they just laugh at this faith of mine. But how can I help believing? I have seen the truth – not invented it with my own mind, but seen it, seen it, and its *living image* has filled my soul for ever. I saw it in such complete wholeness that I cannot believe that other people should not experience it. So how can I go astray? Of course I shall be deflected by the words of others more than once no doubt, but not for long: the living image of what I have seen will remain with me for ever and will always set me right and direct my course.

Oh, I am cheerful and in good heart, I am setting out, setting out, if need be for a thousand years. Do you know, I wanted at first to hide the fact that I had corrupted them all, but that was a mistake – just the first mistake. But truth whispered to me that *I was lying* and preserved me and directed me. But how to build heaven I do not know because I do not know how to convey it in words. At least not the crucial words, the most essential ones. But so be it, I shall go forth and I shall say everything tirelessly, because I have at least perceived with my own eyes, even though I don't know how to relate what I have seen. But that is what those who mock do not understand: 'It's a dream, a fever, an hallucination.' Ah! Is that wisdom? And they are so proud! A dream? What is a dream? Is our life not a dream? I will say more: grant that it will never come true and heaven will never be achieved (even I understand that), I shall preach all the same. In the last analysis it is so simple: in one day, *in one hour*, it could all be arranged! The main thing is to love others as you love yourself. That is the main thing and that is all. Absolutely nothing else is required: you will find out immediately how things must be arranged. But, when all is said and done, that is an ancient truth which has been repeated and read a billion times, though it has not found acceptance. 'Consciousness of life is superior to life. Knowledge of the laws of happiness is superior to happiness' – that is what we must fight against, and I shall! If only everybody wanted it, then everything would be arranged in an instant.

I sought that little girl out, by the way . . . And I shall go forth! I shall go forth!

GARSHIN

VSEVOLOD GARSHIN's literary reputation
rests on less than two dozen short stories
which he wrote during the decade 1877–87.
He first achieved prominence in 1877 with
'Four Days', a tale reflecting his experience
of being wounded in one of the battles in the
Russo–Turkish war of that year. Most of
Garshin's stories, which were highly praised
by both Turgenev and Chekhov, are concerned with evil in one guise or another. A
typical example of his work is 'The Scarlet
Flower' (1883), which is based on the
author's own incarceration in an asylum. It
may be seen as an indictment of the contemporary treatment of mental patients, but also
as an allegory of the role to be played by
exceptional individuals in man's perpetual
struggle against evil.

THE SCARLET FLOWER

Translated by Peter Henry

To the memory of Ivan Turgenev

I

'IN the name of His Imperial Majesty, the Sovereign Emperor Peter the First, I herewith proclaim an inspection of this Lunatic Asylum!'

These words were uttered in a loud, sharp, resonant voice. The hospital clerk, who was sitting at his ink-stained desk registering the new patient in a large, tattered book, could not repress a smile. But the two young men escorting the Patient did not laugh: they could barely stand on their feet after the two days and sleepless nights that they had spent on their own with the madman whom they had just brought down to the hospital by train. At the last station but one his frenzied agitation had become worse; they got hold of a strait-jacket from somewhere and, with the assistance of the guards and a policeman whom they asked to help, they had put it on the Patient. It was in that state that they had brought him to the town, in that state they delivered him to the hospital.

He was terrifying to look at. His grey clothes had been torn to shreds during his violent outbursts, the coarse sailcloth jacket with the wide opening at the neck was laced tightly over them; the long sleeves which pressed his arms cross-wise to his chest were knotted behind his back. His dilated, bloodshot eyes – he had not slept for ten days – shone with a steady, fiery glow; the edge of his lower lip twitched nervously; his matted curly hair hung across his forehead like a mane; with rapid, heavy steps he strode from one corner of the office to the other, scrutinizing the old cupboards full of papers and the chairs covered in oil cloth, and occasionally glancing at his escorts.

'Take him to the ward. It's on the right.'

'I know, I know. I was here last year. We went over the hospital. I know everything, you'll find it hard to deceive me,' said the Patient.

He turned towards the door. An orderly opened it for him; with the same rapid, heavy and resolute steps, holding his demented head high, he walked out of the office and virtually ran off towards the right, to the mental ward. His escorts could barely keep up with him.

'Ring the bell. I can't. You've tied my arms.'

A janitor opened the door and they entered the block.

It was a large stone edifice in the style of most old-fashioned government buildings. On the ground floor there were two large rooms – one was a dining-room, the other was a common-room for the quieter patients – a wide corridor with a french window at the end overlooking a flower-bed in the hospital grounds, and a couple of dozen separate rooms where the patients slept; there were also two dark rooms, one with padded walls and the other lined with timber boards, where violent patients could be put, and a huge, gloomy, vaulted room – the bathroom. The upper storey was the women's ward. From it came a discordant noise, punctuated by howls and wailing. The hospital had been built to take eighty patients but, since it was the only one serving several adjacent provinces, there might well be as many as three hundred. There were four or five beds in each of the small rooms; in winter, when the patients were not allowed to go out into the grounds and all the windows behind their iron grilles were tightly locked, the air in the hospital became stifling beyond endurance.

The new patient was taken to the room containing the baths. Its effect would have been oppressive even to a sane person and it had an all the more oppressive effect on his deranged and agitated imagination. It was a large vaulted room with a greasy stone floor and with light entering through a solitary window in a corner; the walls and the vaults were painted in dark-red oil paint; the floor was black with filth and two stone baths had been hollowed out at floor level, like two oval-shaped pits filled with water. A huge copper stove with a cylindrical boiler for heating the water and a whole system of copper pipes and taps occupied the corner facing the window; to a disturbed mind all this looked gloomy and weirdly fantastic, and the morose expression on the face of the warder who had charge of the baths, a burly and taciturn Ukrainian, only heightened that impression.

And when they took him into this terrifying room to give him a bath and, in accordance with the chief doctor's system of treatment, to put a large mustard plaster on the nape of his neck, the Patient became terrified and enraged. Preposterous thoughts, each more monstrous than the last, crowded into his head. What was this? The Inquisition? A secret place of execution, where his enemies had taken him to finish him off? Perhaps it was Hell itself? Ultimately the idea occurred to him that this was to be some kind of Ordeal. He was undressed, despite all his desperate resistance. With his strength redoubled by his affliction, he was able to free himself again and again from the grip of the four orderlies, who fell sprawling on the floor; until finally they threw him down, grabbed him by his arms and legs and immersed him in the warm water. It seemed to him that it was boiling, and incoherent, disjointed thoughts flitted through his demented head about ordeal by boiling water and by red-hot iron rods. Jerking his arms and legs about convulsively to free them from the grasp of the orderlies, and choking with the water, he gasped for breath, shouting out an incoherent speech such as one could not imagine without actually hearing it. It was a mixture of prayers and curses. He shouted till he was exhausted and at last, as scalding tears ran down his cheeks, he quietly uttered a phrase that had no connection whatever with what he had been saying before:

'Holy martyr, Saint George! Into thy hands I commit my body. But my spirit ¬ no, oh no!'

The orderlies still held him, although he had by now calmed down. The warm water and the ice-bag they had placed on his head had done their work. But, when they took him out of the water almost unconscious and sat him on a stool to apply the mustard plaster, his remaining strength and his insane thoughts seemed to erupt again.

'Why are you doing this? Why?' he cried. 'I've not wanted to harm a soul! Why do you want to kill me? O-o-oh. Oh dear God! Oh you who were martyred before me! I beseech you, deliver me . . . !'

The searing touch of the plaster on his neck made him struggle desperately. The attendants could not cope with him and did not know what to do.

'It can't be helped,' said the old soldier performing the operation. 'It'll have to be wiped off.'

These ordinary words sent a shudder through the Patient. 'Wipe out what? Wipe out whom? Me?!' he thought and shut his eyes in mortal terror. The soldier took both ends of a rough towel and pressing down hard rubbed it briskly across his neck, thereby ripping off the plaster and the top layer of his skin, leaving a bare red wound. The pain of this operation, unbearable even for a calm and normal person, seemed to the Patient the end of everything. He gave a desperate wrench with his whole body, tore himself out of the grip of the orderlies and his naked body rolled along the flagstones. He thought his head had been cut off. He tried to cry out but could not. He was carried away and put on a bed in an unconscious state which turned into a long, deep, deathlike sleep.

It was night when he regained consciousness. All was quiet; he could hear the breathing of the patients sleeping in the larger room next door. Somewhere far off a patient who had been put in one of the dark cells for the night was talking to himself in a weird, monotonous voice; upstairs, in the women's ward, a hoarse contralto was singing some wild song. He felt an awful weakness, all his limbs felt crushed; his neck was excruciatingly painful.

'Where am I? What's happened to me?' he wondered. And suddenly the last month of his life came to his mind with extraordinary vividness and he understood that he was ill and what his illness was. He recalled his various preposterous thoughts, words and deeds, causing his whole being to shudder.

'But that's all over, thank God, it's all over!' he whispered and fell asleep again.

The open window with its iron grille overlooked a small secluded corner between the big buildings and the outer wall; nobody ever went into this area thickly overgrown with wild shrubs and lilac bushes which flowered abundantly at that time of the year . . . Behind the shrubs directly opposite the window there rose the high, dark wall and over it looked tall trees growing in the main part of the hospital grounds; they were bathed, saturated, in moonlight. To the right rose the white hospital building with its iron-barred windows, lit up from within; to the left, the white, blank wall of the mortuary, brilliant in the moonlight. Moonlight poured through the window grille into the interior of the room, spilling on to the floor, and illuminating part of a bed and the pale, exhausted face of the Patient, his eyes closed; now there was nothing insane about him. It was the deep, heavy sleep of an exhausted man, without dreams, without the slightest motion and almost without breathing. For a short while he woke fully conscious, as though he was

normal, only to rise from his bed the next morning as mad
as ever.

III

'How do you feel?' the doctor asked him the following day.

The Patient had just awoken and was still lying under his
blanket.

'Fine!' he replied, jumped up, put on his slippers and
grabbed his dressing-gown. 'Wonderful! There's just one
thing – here!'

He pointed at the back of his neck.

'I can't turn my neck without pain. But that's nothing.
Everything's all right if you understand it; and I do understand.'

'Do you know where you are?'

'Of course, Doctor! I'm in the lunatic asylum. But, once
you understand, it makes no difference. It makes absolutely
no difference.'

As he looked intently into the Patient's eyes, the doctor's
handsome, well-cared-for face, with its exquisitely groomed,
golden beard and calm blue eyes behind gold-rimmed spectacles, was immovable and impenetrable. He was observing.

'Why do you stare at me like that? You'll not be able to
read what's in my soul,' continued the Patient, 'but I can
read clearly what's in yours! Why do you do evil? Why have
you herded this unhappy crowd of people together and why
do you keep them here? It doesn't matter for me; I understand it all and I am calm; but what about them? Why all this
suffering? A person who has reached the stage where he has
a great thought in his soul, a general thought – he doesn't
mind where he lives, what he feels. Even whether to live or
not to live . . . Isn't that right?'

'Perhaps,' replied the doctor, sitting down on a chair in

the corner of the room so as to be able to watch the Patient who was rapidly striding from one corner to the other in his huge, floppy, horse-hide slippers, swinging the flaps of his cotton gown with its broad red stripes and large flowers. The medical assistant and the supervisor who accompanied the doctor stood at attention by the door.

'And I have it!' the Patient exclaimed. 'And when I found it I felt that I'd been reborn. My feelings became more acute and my brain has been functioning as never before. Things that could previously be attained only through a long process of deduction and conjecture I now comprehend intuitively. I have reached in real terms the point that has so far only been worked out in theory by philosophers. I'm experiencing in myself the great concept that Space and Time are figments. I'm living in all ages. I'm living without space, everywhere and nowhere if you like. And for this reason I don't care whether you keep me here or let me go, whether I'm free or bound. I've noticed that there are a few more like me here. But for the rest of this crowd the situation is dreadful. Why don't you set them free? Who wants . . .'

'You have said,' the doctor interrupted him, 'that you live beyond Time and Space. However, you are bound to agree that you and I are in this room and that it is now' – he took out his watch – 'half past ten, the sixth of May 18—. What do you say to that?'

'Nothing. I don't care where I live and when I live. And, if I don't care, it surely means that I am everywhere and always.'

The doctor smiled.

'That's a rare piece of logic,' he said as he got up. 'I dare say you're right. Good morning. Oh, would you like a cigar?'

'Thank you very much.' He stood still, took the cigar and quickly bit off the end. 'This helps one's thinking,' he said. 'This is the world, a microcosm. Alkalis at one end and acids at the other . . . Such, too, is the equilibrium of the universe, where opposing elements are neutralized. Good-bye, doctor!'

The doctor went off on his round. Most of the patients were standing at attention by their beds, waiting for him. No authority enjoys the kind of reverence from its subordinates that a psychiatrist gets from his mental patients.

Left on his own, the Patient continued to pace feverishly from corner to corner. They brought him some tea; without sitting down he emptied the mug in two gulps and in an instant devoured a large piece of white bread. Then he went out of the room and walked for several hours from one end of the building to the other with his rapid, heavy strides, without stopping once. It was a rainy day and the patients were not allowed into the grounds. When the medical assistant looked for the new patient, he was directed to the end of the corridor; there he stood, his face pressed against a pane in the french window, staring at the flowerbed. His attention was attracted by an unusually bright scarlet flower, belonging to the poppy family.

'Please come and be weighed,' said the medical assistant, touching him on the shoulder.

And when the Patient turned round to face him, the assistant almost recoiled with fright: so savage was the malice and hate burning in those demented eyes. But, as soon as he saw him, the Patient changed his expression and followed obediently and without uttering a word, as though sunk in deep thought. They went to the consulting-room; the Patient stood on the small weighing machine before he was told to do so; the medical assistant weighed him and recorded 109 pounds against his name in the book. The next day it was 107, on the third day 106.

'If he goes on like this, he won't live,' said the doctor and gave orders for him to be fed particularly well.

But, in spite of this and in spite of the Patient's prodigious appetite, he lost weight every day and every day the assistant

entered a smaller number of pounds in the book. The Patient
hardly slept at all and spent entire days in incessant movement.

IV

He was aware that he was in a mental hospital; he was even
aware that he was ill. Occasionally, as on the first night, he
woke up in the stillness of the night after a whole day of
turbulent movement, aching in all his limbs and with a
terrible heaviness in his head, but he would be fully conscious. Possibly it was due to the absence of sensory stimuli
in the nocturnal silence and the semi-darkness, or perhaps
the reduced functioning of his brain on waking, but at such
moments he understood his situation clearly and was more
or less normal. But with the coming of day and the wakening
of life in the hospital all those sensations would again wash
over him; his sick brain could not cope and he would be
insane again. His condition was a strange blend of correct
judgements and preposterous notions. He realized that all
those around him were sick people, yet at the same time he
saw some other person hidden or trying to hide himself in
every one of them, someone he had known before or someone he had read or heard about. The hospital was populated
by people from all times and from all lands. Here were both
the living and the dead. Here were the famous and the
mighty of the world as well as ordinary soldiers killed in the
last war and risen from the dead. He saw himself in some
magic enchanted circle that had gathered within itself all the
might of the earth, and in an ecstasy of pride he regarded
himself as the centre of that circle. All of them, his fellow
inmates, had foregathered here in order to carry out a task
which he dimly conceived of as a gigantic venture aimed at
the destruction of evil on earth. He did not know what form
this task would take, but he felt enough strength to carry it

out. He could read the thoughts of other men; he saw in objects their own history; the large elm trees in the hospital grounds told him whole legends from the past; he believed that the building, which had in fact been built quite some time ago, dated back to Peter the Great and he was certain that the Tsar had lived in it at the time of the Battle of Poltava. He could read this in the walls, in the crumbling plaster, on bits of brick and tiles that he found in the grounds; the entire history of the house and the grounds was written on them. He populated the little mortuary with dozens, hundreds, of men long dead and he would stare into the little basement window opening on to the secluded corner of the grounds, and in the light unevenly reflected in the old and dirty rainbow-coloured pane he saw familiar faces that he had once seen in life or on portraits.

Meanwhile fine, bright weather had set in; the patients were spending whole days out of doors in the grounds. Their part of the grounds was rather small but it was thickly planted with trees, and flowers grew in every possible place. The supervisor allocated gardening tasks to everybody who was at all capable of doing any work; for whole days they swept the paths and strewed sand on them, weeded and watered the flowerbeds, the cucumber, water-melon and melon patches that had all been dug and planted by their own hands. In one corner of the garden there were many cherry trees close together; alongside there was an avenue of elms; in the middle, on a small artificial mound, a flowerbed had been laid out, the most beautiful one in the whole garden; there were bright flowers around the edges of the highest part of the mound and its centre was occupied by a rare and magnificent dahlia which had large yellow petals flecked with red. It was also the centre of the garden as a whole, rising above it, and one could see that many of the patients attributed some mystical significance to it. The new patient, too, thought that it was something out of the ordinary, a Guardian Goddess of the grounds and the building. The inmates had also planted flowers along all the paths. Here were all the flowers that one would encounter in Ukrainian gardens: standard roses, bright petunias, tall tobacco plants with their small pink blossoms, mint, marigolds, nasturtiums and poppies. Not far from the porch there were three poppy plants of some special variety; they were much smaller than the ordinary ones and also differed from them by the exceptional brilliance of their scarlet colouring. It was this flower that had so struck him when on his first day at the hospital he had been looking out at the ground through the french window.

When he went into the garden for the first time he looked first at these brilliant flowers before descending the steps. There were only two of them then; it so happened that they grew apart from the other flowers on an unweeded spot, surrounded by dense goosefoot and some kind of steppe grass.

One by one the patients came through the door where the warder handed each of them a thick white knitted cap with a red cross on the forehead. These caps had been used in the war and had been bought at an auction. But, needless to say, the Patient attributed a special, mystical significance to this cross. He took off the cap, looked at the cross and then at the poppies. The flowers were brighter.

'He's winning,' said the Patient, 'but we shall see.'

And he stepped down from the porch. Though he looked round, he did not notice the orderly standing behind him, and he stepped across the flower bed and stretched his hand towards the flower, but could not bring himself to pick it. He felt a sensation of heat and stabbing in his outstretched hand and then in his whole body, as though some powerful current of a force unknown to him emanated from the red petals and permeated his entire body. He moved closer and stretched his hand quite close to the flower, but it seemed to him that the flower was defending itself by emitting a deadly, venomous breath. His head began to spin; he made one desperate, final effort and had already grasped the stalk when suddenly a heavy hand was laid on his shoulder. The orderly had caught hold of him.

'You mustn't pick the flowers,' said the old Ukrainian. 'And don't step on the flower beds. There's lots of you lunatics here: if every one of you picks a flower you'll soon have stripped the whole garden.' He spoke earnestly, still holding the Patient's shoulder.

The Patient looked him in the face, freed himself silently from his grip and walked along the path in an agitated state. 'Oh you unhappy ones!' he thought. 'You can't see, you've become so blind, that you even protect him. But I'll finish him off, come what may. If not today, then tomorrow we'll measure our strength against each other. And does it really matter if I perish . . . ?'

He walked around the garden until evening, meeting other inmates and engaging them in weird conversations, in which each speaker heard only answers to his own insane thoughts expressed in absurd, mysterious words. The Patient walked first with one inmate and then with another, and by the end of the day he was even more convinced that 'all was ready', as he said to himself. Soon, soon, the iron bars will fall asunder and all those imprisoned here will go out and rush to all the corners of the earth, and the whole world will shudder, cast off its shabby old covering and will appear in a splendid new beauty. He had all but forgotten about the flower, but as he left the garden and mounted the steps to the porch he saw what looked like two red pieces of coal in the thick grass that had already darkened and was becoming dewy. Then the Patient lingered behind the crowd, positioned himself behind the orderly and waited for a suitable moment. Nobody saw him jump across the flowerbed, seize the flower and hurriedly hide it on his chest under his shirt. When the cool, damp leaves touched his body, he turned pale as death and his eyes opened wide in terror. A cold sweat broke out on his forehead.

The lamps were lit in the hospital; most of the inmates lay down on their beds, waiting for supper, apart from a few restless ones who strode hurriedly about the corridor and the wards. Among them was the Patient with the flower. He walked about with his arms convulsively pressed crosswise over his chest: it seemed as if he wanted to crush and squash the plant that lay hidden there. When he met other inmates, he would give them a wide berth, afraid that the edge of his gown might touch them. 'Keep away, keep away!' he would shout. But in the hospital few people took any notice of such exclamations. And he walked faster and faster, making his strides bigger and bigger, and he walked for an hour, two hours, in a frenzied state.

'I'll wear you out. I'll strangle you!' he kept saying in a toneless and malicious voice.

At times he would grind his teeth.

Supper was served in the dining-hall. A thin millet gruel was served in the few wooden, painted and gilded bowls that stood on the large, bare tables; the patients took their seats on the benches; each was given a hunk of black bread. They ate with wooden spoons, about eight men eating straight from each bowl. A few who were on an improved diet were served separately. Our Patient gulped down his portion which the orderly brought to him in his room where he had been told to go; but he was not content with this and went into the dining-room.

'May I sit down here?' he asked the supervisor.

'Haven't you had your supper?' The supervisor was pouring extra helpings of gruel into the bowls.

'I'm very hungry. And I have to build up my strength as much as I can. Food is my only support; you know I don't sleep at all.'

'Help yourself, my friend, and may it do you good. Taras, give him a spoon and some bread.'

He sat near one of the bowls and ate an enormous amount of gruel.

'That will do now, surely, that will do,' said the supervisor at last when everybody had finished his supper, but our Patient was still sitting at the bowl, spooning gruel with one hand and clutching his chest with the other. 'You'll over-eat yourself.'

'Ah, if only you knew how much strength I need, how much strength! Good-bye, Nikolay Nikolaich,' said the Patient, getting up from the table and squeezing the supervisor's hand with all his strength. 'Good-bye.'

'Where are you off to?' the supervisor asked with a smile.

'Me? Nowhere. I'm staying. But maybe tomorrow we shan't be seeing each other again. Thank you for all your kindness.'

Once more he shook the supervisor's hand firmly. His voice was trembling and tears sprang to his eyes.

'Calm yourself, my friend, calm yourself,' replied the supervisor. 'Why these gloomy thoughts? You go and lie down and have a good sleep. You really ought to sleep more; once you sleep properly, you'll soon get better.'

The Patient was sobbing. The supervisor had turned away to tell the orderlies to hurry up and clear away what was left of the supper. Half an hour later all were asleep in the hospital, except for one man, who lay fully clothed on his bed in the corner room. He was shivering as in a fever and was convulsively clutching his chest which was, as he believed, impregnated by an unknown, deadly poison.

V

He did not sleep all night. He had picked that flower because he considered this to be the heroic deed which he was called upon to perform. The very moment he had first looked through the french window the scarlet petals had attracted his attention and it appeared to him that at that moment he had fully comprehended what he was required to accomplish on earth. All the evil of the world was concentrated in this scarlet flower. He knew that opium was made from poppies; it was possibly this thought, growing, ramifying and assuming monstrous shapes, that had caused him to create that weird, horrific fantasy. In his eyes the flower was the embodiment of all evil; it had absorbed all blood spilt innocently (that was why it was so red), all the tears and all the bitter gall of mankind. It was a mysterious, terrifying being, the antithesis of God – it was Ahriman, who had adopted this modest and innocuous guise. It had to be plucked and killed. But even that was not enough – it was also necessary to prevent it from pouring all its evil over the world as it expired. And that was why he kept it hidden on his chest. He hoped that by morning it would have lost all its strength. Its evil would be transferred into his breast, his soul, and there would be either defeated or victorious – then he would perish, die, but die as an honourable warrior, as the first warrior of mankind, because until then no one had yet dared to struggle with all the evil of the world at once.

'They didn't see it. But I did. How can I let it live ? Death is better.'

There he lay, his strength ebbing away in the ghostly, insubstantial fight, ebbing away in the mythical combat. In the morning the medical assistant found him barely alive. But, in spite of this, his agitation soon possessed him again, he leapt from his bed and started running about the hospital as he had done before, talking to other patients and to himself even louder and more incoherently than ever. He was not allowed to go into the grounds; seeing that he was continuing to lose weight, was still not getting any sleep and kept on walking about, the doctor ordered that he should be given a large injection of morphine. He did not resist: fortunately his insane thoughts now somehow accorded with this operation. Soon he fell asleep; his frenzied movement ended and the incessant noisy tune produced by the jerky rhythm of his footsteps vanished from his ears. He lost consciousness and stopped thinking about anything, even about the second flower that still had to be plucked.

However, he did pluck it three days later, in full view of the old orderly who did not manage to stop him in time. The orderly ran after him. With a loud triumphant howl the Patient ran into the hospital, rushed into his room and hid the plant on his chest.

'Why do you go picking flowers?' asked the orderly, running in after him. But the Patient was already lying on his bed in his customary pose with crossed arms and he started talking such gibberish that all the orderly did was silently to remove his cap with the red cross that he had forgotten to take off in his hurry, and leave him alone. And the ghostly fight began again. The Patient felt that evil came writhing out of the flower in long, creeping, serpent-like coils; they wound themselves round him, squeezing and crushing his limbs and impregnating his entire body with their horrible substance. He wept and prayed to God in between curses addressed to his Enemy. By the evening the flower had begun to wither. The Patient trampled on the blackened plant, picked up the remnants from the floor and carried them to the bathroom. He threw the shapeless little lump of vegetation on the coals in the red-hot stove and stood for a long time watching his Enemy hiss, shrivel and finally turn into a soft little heap of snowy-white ashes. He blew on it and it vanished.

The next day the Patient was worse. Dreadfully pale, with sunken cheeks, his burning eyes receding deep into their sockets, he continued his insane wanderings, tottering about and stumbling frequently, and he talked and talked unceasingly.

'I wouldn't like to resort to force,' said the chief doctor to his assistant.

'But it's vital to stop this exertion. Today his weight was only ninety-three pounds. If this goes on, he'll be dead in three days.'

The chief doctor reflected.

'Morphine? Chloral?' he said, half-questioningly.

'Yesterday the morphine ceased to have any effect.'

'Have him bound. But I doubt he'll survive.'

VI

And the Patient was bound. He lay on his bed in a strait-jacket, tightly strapped down to the iron cross-pieces of the bedstead with broad bands of canvas. But the fury of his movements did not abate, rather it increased. For many hours he made stubborn efforts to free himself from his fetters. At last, with a strong wrench he tore one of the bands, freed his legs, slipped out from under the other one and started pacing about his room with bound arms, shouting out wild, incomprehensible speeches.

'What on earth . . . ?' shouted the orderly entering the room. 'The devils must be giving you a hand! Gritsko! Ivan! Come quick, he's got loose!'

All three of them fell upon the Patient and a long fight ensued which was tiring for the attackers and agonizing for the defender, who was using up what was left of his exhausted strength. At last they threw him on the bed and tied him down even more securely than before.

'You don't realize what you're doing!' shouted the Patient, gasping for breath. 'You are done for! I saw the third one, only just beginning to flower. It's ready now. Let me finish my task! It's got to be killed! Killed! Killed! Then it'll all be over, everything will be saved. I would send you, but this is something only I can do. You would die if you even touched it.'

'Do be quiet, sir, be quiet!' said the old orderly, who had stayed behind to watch at his bedside.

Suddenly the Patient fell silent. He had resolved to trick the orderlies.

All day he was kept strapped down and was left in that position for the night. When he had given him his supper, the orderly spread a rug by his bed and lay on it. A moment later he was fast asleep, and the Patient got to work.

He bent his whole body over so as to touch the outer iron bar of his bedstead and felt for it with his wrist through the long sleeve of his strait-jacket. He started briskly and vigorously rubbing his sleeve against the iron bar. After a while the thick canvas gave way, releasing his forefinger. Then things moved more quickly. With an agility and versatility that would have been quite incredible in a normal person, he untied the knot behind his back that was holding the sleeves together, unlaced the strait-jacket and then listened to the snores of the orderly for a long time. The old man was fast asleep. The Patient took off the strait-jacket and untied the bands that held him strapped to the bed. He was free. He tried the door: it was locked from the inside and the key was presumably in the orderly's pocket. Afraid to wake him up, he dared not search his pockets and resolved to leave the room by the window.

It was a calm night, warm and dark; the window was open, stars were shining in the black sky. He looked at them, identifying familiar constellations, and felt glad that they seemed to understand him and sympathize with him. With blinking eyes he saw the endless rays that they kept sending him and his mad resolve increased. He had to bend aside a thick bar in the iron grille, climb through the narrow opening and into the deserted nook that was overgrown with shrubs, and then over the high stone wall. The last fight would be there, and then perhaps even death.

He tried to bend the thick bar with his bare hands, but the iron would not yield. Then he twisted the thick sleeves of his strait-jacket into a rope, slipped it over the spike at the top end of the iron bar and hung with his whole weight upon it. After desperate efforts that all but drained what strength he had left, the iron spike did bend; a narrow passage opened up. He forced his way through it, grazing his shoulders, elbows and bare knees, made his way through the shrubs and stopped in front of the wall. It was quiet all round; the night-lights dimly lit the windows of the building from inside; there, nobody was to be seen. Nobody would notice him; the old man, in attendance by his bedside, would still be asleep. The stars blinked affectionately, their rays penetrating right into his heart.

'I'm coming to you,' he whispered, looking up to the sky.

He lost his grip at his first attempt to climb the wall and with torn finger nails, his arms and knees covered in blood, he looked for a more suitable spot. A few bricks were missing where the garden and mortuary walls met. The Patient groped for these gaps and used them as a foothold. He scaled the wall, gripped the branches of one of the elms on the other side and quietly slipped down its trunk on to the ground. He ran to the familiar spot near the porch. The flower's head looked dark, its petals folded in, yet it stood out clearly in the grass wet with dew.

'The last one!' whispered the Patient. 'The last one! Today it's victory or death. But I don't care any more. Wait a little while,' he said, looking up to the sky: 'I'll be with you soon.'

He pulled up the plant, tore it to pieces, crushed it and, holding it in his hand, returned to his room the way he had come. The old man was still asleep. The Patient had barely reached his bed when he collapsed on it unconscious.

In the morning he was found dead. His face was calm and serene; his exhausted features, the thin lips and deeply sunken closed eyes, bore the expression of a kind of triumphant happiness. When he was placed on the stretcher, they tried to unclench his fist and take out the scarlet flower. But the hand had stiffened and he carried his trophy with him to the grave.

LESKOV

NIKOLAY LESKOV began his literary career as a journalist but turned his hand to fiction in the early 1860s. He achieved fame and popularity with his amiable novel *Cathedral Folk* (1872) but his most original work was produced during the 1880s. Leskov possessed a magnificent talent for narration: his stories – written in a highly individual style which is exceptionally difficult to translate – proceed at great speed and are packed with adventure. A good example of his gift is 'The Make-up Artist' (1883) which for all its extravagance was apparently based on real events which the writer had heard about as a child.

THE MAKE-UP ARTIST
A STORY ON A GRAVE

Translated by William Leatherbarrow

In sacred memory of the blessed day,
19 February 1861

> Amongst the righteous will their souls
> find sanctuary. (A dirge)

CHAPTER ONE

THERE are many of us in Russia who think that only
painters or sculptors can be 'artists', and then only if they
have been deemed worthy of the title by the academy. Such
people have no wish to regard any others as artists. In the
eyes of many, Sazikov and Ovchinnikov are nothing more
than 'silversmiths'. In other countries this is not the case:
Heine recalled a tailor who 'was an artist' and who 'had
ideas', and even today ladies' dresses made by Worth are
described as 'works of art'. Of one of these it was recently
written that 'a whole world of imagination is concentrated
in the cut of the bodice'.

In America art is understood in an even broader sense.
The well-known American writer Bret Harte tells of an
'artist' who gained extraordinary fame in his country for
his 'work on the dead'. He would give the faces of the
deceased various 'comforting expressions' which testified
to the more or less happy state of their departed souls.

There were several degrees of this art; I remember three:
'(1) Composure; (2) Exalted contemplation; and (3) The
bliss of direct communion with God.' The fame of the artist
corresponded to the high perfection of his work, that is, it

was tremendous, but unfortunately he died a victim of the vulgar rabble who did not respect the freedom of artistic creativity. He was stoned to death for endowing with 'the expression of blissful communion with God' the face of a certain deceased fraudulent banker who had fleeced the whole town. The rogue's delighted heirs had wished to express in this way their gratitude to their late kinsman, but their artistic executor paid with his life . . .

Once we had in Russia a master of an equally unusual art.

CHAPTER TWO

My younger brother was nursed by a tall, dried-up, but very stately old woman called Lyubov Onisimovna. She had once been one of the actresses at Count Kamensky's old theatre in Orel, and everything that I am about to relate also took place in Orel when I was a boy.

My brother is seven years younger than I. Consequently, when he was two and in the care of Lyubov Onisimovna, I was already about nine and could readily understand the stories which were told to me.

At that time Lyubov Onisimovna was still not very old, but her hair was white as snow. The features of her face were fine and gentle, her tall figure quite upright and remarkably slender, like a young girl's.

More than once my mother and aunt looked at her and remarked that she must without doubt have been a real beauty in her day.

She was utterly honest, meek and sentimental; she loved the tragic in life and . . . sometimes took a drop.

She would take us for walks to the cemetery at the Church of the Holy Trinity and always sat down there on the same simple grave with an old cross; she would frequently tell me stories.

It was there that I heard from her the tale of 'the make-up artist'.

CHAPTER THREE

He had worked with our nurse at the theatre. The difference was that she 'appeared on the stage and performed dances', whereas he was 'a make-up artist', that is to say a hairdresser and make-up man who 'painted the faces and dressed the hair' of all the count's serf actresses. But this was no ordinary, everyday expert with a comb behind his ear and a tin of powdered rouge mixed with grease; no, this was a man with *ideas*, in other words *an artist*.

Nobody could, as Lyubov Onisimovna put it, 'give a face expression' better than he.

I cannot say with any real certainty under which of the Kamensky counts these two artistic natures flourished. Three of them are remembered and all of them were described by the older inhabitants of Orel as 'unprecedented tyrants'. Fieldmarshal Mikhail Fedotovich was murdered by his serfs in 1809 for his cruelty, but he had two sons: Nikolay who died in 1811, and Sergey, who died in 1835.

I remember as a child in the 1840s seeing a massive grey wooden building that had false windows painted in with soot and ochre, and which was surrounded by an extraordinarily long, broken-down fence. This was the notorious country estate of Count Kamensky, and it was here that the theatre was situated. It was in such a position as to be seen clearly from the cemetery of the Holy Trinity Church, and for that reason whenever Lyubov Onisimovna wished to tell me a story she nearly always began with the words:

'Look over there, my dear. Do you see how dreadful it is?'

'Yes, nurse; it is dreadful.'

'Well, what I am about to relate to you is even more dreadful.'

And here is one of her tales about the hairdresser Arkady, a sensitive and bold young man who had been very dear to her heart.

CHAPTER FOUR

Arkady Ilich only 'did the hair and painted the faces' of the actresses. For the men there was another hairdresser, and if Arkady occasionally used his skills in the men's quarters he did so only if the count himself had ordered him 'to make someone up like a perfect gentleman'. The main ingredient of Arkady's artistic flair was the thought that went into it, which allowed him to give the most subtle and varied expressions to a face.

'They would send for him,' said Lyubov Onisimovna, 'and say, "This face needs such and such an expression." Arkady would step back, order the actor or actress before him to sit down or stand up, would cross his arms on his chest and ponder. At such moments he was more handsome than anyone; of medium height, but so well proportioned that I can't find words to describe it. His small nose was fine and proud, his eyes as gentle as an angel's, and thick locks of hair curled forward beautifully over his eyes, so that he seemed to be looking at you through a fluffy cloud.'

In short, the make-up artist was a fine-looking man and 'everybody liked him'. 'Even the count' was fond of him and 'treated him differently from the others, dressing him in the best, but keeping him all the same under the strictest control.' Under no circumstances did he want Arkady to shave or cut the hair of any man apart from himself, and for this reason he always kept him near his dressing-room and Arkady was never allowed out anywhere except to the theatre.

He was not even permitted to go to church for confession or to take the sacrament, since the count himself did not believe in God and had no time for ecclesiastics. One Easter he even set his hounds on priests from the St Boris and Gleb Church who were carrying the cross*.

* This tale was widely known throughout Orel. I heard it from my grandmother Alfereva and from the merchant, Ivan Ivanovich Andro-

According to Lyubov Onisimovna, the count was so terribly ugly, on account of his perpetual malice, that he looked like all the wild beasts put together. But even to this bestial countenance Arkady could, at least for a while, bring such an expression that when the count sat in his theatre box of an evening he looked more impressive than many of the others there.

To his great annoyance it was just such impressiveness and 'military bearing' above all else that the count's appearance lacked.

And so, in order that no others should enjoy the talents of such an incomparable artist, Arkady was obliged 'to spend his days indoors, and never in his life did he have money in his hand'. At that time he was already about twenty-five and Lyubov Onisimovna was nineteen. Of course they knew each other, and that which usually happens to people of their age happened to them – they fell in love. But they could not speak of their love except in veiled hints in the presence of others during the make-up sessions. A private rendezvous was absolutely impossible, indeed unthinkable . . .

'We actresses,' said Lyubov Onisimovna, 'were guarded as closely as wet nurses in distinguished houses. Elderly women with children were assigned to look after us and if – God forbid! – something had happened to one of us, the children of those women would have come in for terrible treatment at the hands of the tyrant.'

The sentence of chastity could be revoked only by the one who had imposed it.

---

sov, an old man renowned for his impeccable honesty, who *saw for himself* 'how the curs tore the clergy apart' and who himself escaped the count only by 'taking a sin upon himself'. When he was brought before the count and asked whether he felt sorry for the priests, Androsov replied: 'Not at all, your Excellency, they had it coming to them – that'll teach 'em to hang about.' For this answer Kamensky had mercy on him. (Author's note.)

CHAPTER FIVE

Lyubov Onisimovna was at that time not only in the first bloom of her maidenly beauty, but also at a most interesting stage in the development of her multi-faceted talent: she 'sang a medley in the choir', danced 'the first steps in *The Chinese Garden-maid*' and, sensing a vocation for tragedy, 'learned all the roles *simply by watching them*.'

I cannot remember precisely what year it was, but the tsar (whether it was Alexander Pavlovich or Nikolay Pavlovich I cannot say) happened to be passing through Orel. He was to spend the night there and was expected at Count Kamensky's theatre in the evening.

On this occasion the count invited all the nobility to be his guests at the theatre (you could not buy a ticket for anything), and put on the very best show. Lyubov Onisimovna was to sing her 'medley' and dance *The Chinese Garden-maid*, but suddenly during the last-minute rehearsals one of the sets fell and injured the leg of the actress who was to play 'the Duchess de Bourblianne' in the play.

I have never come across such a role anywhere, but that is exactly how Lyubov Onisimovna pronounced it.

The carpenters who had dropped the set were sent to the stables to be beaten, and the injured girl was taken to her room. But that left nobody to play the part of the Duchess de Bourblianne.

'At this point,' said Lyubov Onisimovna, 'I volunteered, since I had always loved the way the Duchess de Bourblianne begs forgiveness at her father's feet and dies with her hair untied. My own hair was strikingly long and light-brown in colour and, when Arkady dressed it, it looked a treat.'

The count was very pleased at the young girl's willingness to play the part, and on hearing assurances from the director that 'Lyuba will not ruin the part' answered:

'You will pay with your back if she does! Now take her the aquamarine earrings from me.'

From the count 'aquamarine earrings' were a gift that was both flattering and odious. They were the first sign that their recipient was about to enjoy the special favour of becoming for a while one of the master's odalisques. Soon after this, sometimes immediately, Arkady would be given instructions to dress the condemned girl after the performance 'in the virginal guise of St Cecilia,' and all in white, wearing a garland and carrying a lily in her hand as a symbol of *l'innocence*, she would then be conducted to the count's quarters.

'You cannot understand at your age,' said the nurse, 'but this was the worst thing that could befall a girl, especially me, since I dreamed of Arkady. I began to cry and flung the earrings on to the table. I wept and couldn't imagine going on stage that evening.'

CHAPTER SIX

But during these fateful hours something equally fateful and testing lay in wait for Arkady.

The count's brother arrived from his country property to present his respects to the emperor. He was even uglier than the count, and had lived for many years in the country, never dressing up and never shaving properly since 'his face was all overgrown with lumps'. For such a special occasion, however, he too had to put on his uniform, tidy himself up and acquire that 'military bearing' which propriety demanded.

And propriety demanded a lot.

'You can't imagine now just how strict things were in those days,' said our nurse. 'Uniformity was observed in everything, and there was a fixed way for gentlemen to do their hair and a prescribed facial expression. This didn't suit some people, and if they combed their hair in the accepted way with a high quiff and little curls at the temples then their whole face came out looking just like a peasant's balalaika with no strings. Important gentlemen were terribly afraid of this. So much depended on the skill with which they were shaved and their hair dressed; how the little pathways between their sidewhiskers and their moustache were shaved, how the hair was curled and combed. The slightest change could give a totally different appearance to the face.' According to our nurse, it was easier for civilians because nobody paid close attention to them – they were merely obliged to present a humble appearance. But more was demanded of the military – they had to present a look of respect before their superiors and yet cut an infinitely dashing figure for all the rest.

It was precisely this that Arkady's amazing artistry could bring to the unpleasant and unremarkable face of the count.

CHAPTER SEVEN

The brother from the country was even more unattractive than the town brother, and to make matters worse he 'had let his hair go' in the country and 'his face had grown so coarse' that he was even aware of it himself. Moreover, he had no one to tend his appearance, since he was so mean in everything that he had let his hairdresser go to work in Moscow on condition that he paid quit-rent. As a result, the face of this other count was so covered in large bumps that it was impossible to shave him without cutting one of them.

On arriving in Orel he summoned all the barbers in the town and said: 'If anyone of you can make me look like my brother, Count Kamensky, I'll give that man two gold pieces, but if anyone cuts me – well, I'm putting two pistols on the table. If you make a good job of it you can take the money and go; but, if you cut one pimple or spoil one hair of my sidewhiskers, I'll kill you on the spot.'

He was merely trying to frighten them, for the pistols were loaded with blanks.

At that time there weren't many barbers in Orel, and those that there were spent most of their time hanging about the bath-houses with their bowls, cupping and applying leeches. They had neither taste nor imagination, and were aware of this themselves, so that they all refused to undertake the 'transformation' of Kamensky. 'God keep you and your gold,' they thought to themselves, but aloud they said: 'We can't do as you wish, for we aren't worthy to touch so great a person. Also, we haven't got the right razors – ours are all plain Russian ones, and your face needs English razors. The count's man Arkady is the only man for the job.'

The count ordered the barbers to be thrown out, but they were pleased to get off so lightly. Meanwhile the count went to his elder brother and said:

'It's like this, brother: I've got a big favour to ask of you. Let me borrow your Arkady for a while before this evening so that he can fix me up properly. I haven't shaved for ages and the barbers here are no use.'

The count replied:

'It goes without saying that the local barbers are vile. I didn't even know there were any, since I even have my dogs clipped by my own serfs. But, as for your request, you must forgive me if I tell you it's out of the question. You see, I've made a vow that Arkady should barber no one but me as long as he lives. You see my point – can I break my word before a servant?'

The other answered:

'But why not? You made the vow, you can break it.'

But the host replied that that seemed a strange way of looking at things:

'Moreover, if I began to behave like that, what could I expect of my serfs? Arkady has been told of my order, everyone is aware of it, and that's why he gets better treatment than the rest. But, if he ever dared to apply his skills to anyone but me, I should have him flogged to death and sent into the army.'

'It's one thing or the other,' said his brother. 'You either flog him to death or you send him into the army. You can't do both.'

'All right,' said the count, 'have it your way. I shan't flog him to death, only half to death, and then I'll send him off.'

'And is that your last word on the matter, brother?'

'Yes, it is.'

'And that's all there is to it?'

'Yes.'

'Well, in that case, fine; but I was beginning to think that your own brother meant less to you than a serf. Well, don't break your word, but just send Arkady to me to *clip my poodle*. Then it'll be my affair what he does there.'

The count could hardly refuse his brother this.

'All right,' he said. 'I'll send him to clip your poodle.'

'That's all I want,' said the brother, and shaking the count's hand he left.

CHAPTER EIGHT

It was winter – continued Lyubov Onisimovna – at that time just before evening when dusk had fallen and the lamps were being lit.

The count summoned Arkady and told him:

'Go to my brother's and clip his poodle.'

'Is that all you want me to do?' asked Arkady.

'Nothing else,' replied the count. 'But hurry back to make up the actresses. Today Lyuba has to be made up for three different parts, and after the theatre I want you to bring her to me as St Cecilia.'

Arkady was shaken.

'What's the matter?' asked the count.

'I'm sorry, I tripped over the carpet,' answered Arkady.

'Watch out – that's a bad sign, isn't it?' remarked the count.

But Arkady's heart ached so much that he didn't care if it was a bad sign or not. He was told that I was to be made up as St Cecilia and, seeming unable any longer to see or hear, he picked up his instruments in their leather case and left.

CHAPTER NINE

Arkady presented himself before the count's brother. The candles were already lit before the mirror, and once again the two pistols lay side by side on the table, but this time there were ten gold pieces, not two, and the pistols weren't loaded with blanks, but with Circassian bullets.

'I have no poodle,' said the count's brother. 'What I want you to do is this: make me up so that I look very important, and the ten gold pieces are yours, but if you cut me – I'll kill you.'

Arkady looked at him, looked and then suddenly – God alone knows what made him do it – began to shave him and cut his hair. Within a minute he had made a good job of everything, put the gold in his pocket and said: 'Goodbye.'

'You may go,' said the count's brother, 'but I should like to know what drove you to such a desperate act?'

'What drove me?' replied Arkady. 'That's something I'm keeping to myself.'

'Perhaps you're immune to bullets and that's why you're not afraid of my pistols?'

'The pistols are neither here nor there,' replied Arkady. 'They didn't even cross my mind.'

'What! Do you really have the nerve to think that my word is not as good as your master's and that I wouldn't have shot you if you'd cut me? If you hadn't been charmed you'd be dead now!'

At the mention of the count, Arkady shuddered again and answered as if he were in a daze:

'I'm not charmed, but I've got what sense God gave me; before your hand could have raised the pistol to shoot me I'd have cut your throat from ear to ear!'

And with these words he rushed headlong from the room and arrived at the theatre just in time to make me up, even though he was shaking all over. And as he curled each ringlet and bent over me to blow on it, he kept whispering:

'Don't be afraid, I'll take you away!'

CHAPTER TEN

The performance was going well, for we were all like stone – impervious to fear and suffering. Whatever might have been in our hearts, we acted so that no one noticed anything.

From the stage we could see the count and his brother, looking just like one another. They had come behind the scenes and it was difficult to tell them apart. Only our master was extremely quiet, as if he had mellowed. This always happened before one of his particularly cruel atrocities.

We were all scared stiff and kept crossing ourselves and saying: 'Lord, have mercy on us and save us! Who will be the victim of his brutality?'

We had still not heard of the desperate thing Arkady had done, although of course Arkady himself knew he could expect no mercy and turned pale when the count's brother glanced at him and growled something quietly in the count's ear. I was very sharp of hearing and caught what he said:

'I warn you as a brother, keep an eye on him when he's shaving you with the razor.'

Our count just smiled slightly.

I think Arkady must have heard something too, because as he was making me up for the part of the Duchess in the last scene he put too much powder on my face – something he'd never done before – and the French wardrobe manager began brushing it off me, saying:

'*Trop beaucoup! Trop beaucoup!*'

CHAPTER ELEVEN

As soon as the performance was finished they took off the dress of the Duchess de Bourblianne and dressed me as Cecilia in a single white garment, a very simple affair with no sleeves and just tied at the shoulders with knots. We couldn't stand that dress. Then along came Arkady to do my hair in a chaste style, like that on the paintings of St Cecilia, and to fix a thin band on my head like a crown. As he came in he saw that six men were stationed at the door of my room.

This meant that as soon as he had finished preparing me and appeared at the door again he would immediately be seized and led away somewhere to be tortured. And such tortures were inflicted upon our people that it was a hundred times better to be sentenced to death instead. There was the rack, the cord, and a device that turned and twisted your head with a thick rope – we had the lot! Legal punishment was nothing compared to this. Under the whole house there ran secret vaults where living people were kept in chains like bears. If you happened to be going past you could sometimes hear the chains rattling and the people in fetters groaning. Probably they wanted to make their fate known in the hope that the authorities might hear of it, but the authorities didn't dare intervene. People suffered there for ages, some for as long as they lived. A man who had been imprisoned there a long time made up this verse about it:

> The serpents crawl up and suck out your eyes,
> And scorpions smear venom all over your face.

Sometimes you'd whisper those lines to yourself and be seized with terror.

Some men were even chained up with the bears so that their claws were only an inch away.

Only none of this happened to Arkady, because he'd leapt into my room, grabbed a table and smashed the whole window out . . . and that was all I remembered . . .

I began to come round because my legs felt very cold. I tried to pull my feet up, but felt that I was all trussed up in a wolfskin or bearskin. All around it was as black as pitch and a troika of gallant horses was tearing along, but I didn't know where to. Alongside me two men were sitting huddled together in the wide sledge. One was holding me – that was Arkady – the other was whipping up the horses with all his might. Snow spattered up from the horses' hoofs and the sledge lurched violently from side to side. If we hadn't been sitting on the floor in the middle, holding on with our hands, none of us would have made it in one piece.

I could hear them talking anxiously as people always do in moments of tension, but all I could make out was: 'They're after us! They're after us! Faster! Faster!' Nothing more.

As soon as Arkady saw that I'd come to he bent over me and said: 'Lyubushka, my darling! They're after us . . . Are you prepared to die if we don't make it?'

I replied that I would gladly die.

He hoped to make it to the town of Rushchuk on Turkish territory, where many of our folk had fled from Kamensky.

Suddenly we were flying across the ice of a frozen stream and ahead of us we could make out the grey shape of what looked like a dwelling, where dogs were barking. The driver whipped up the horses once more and then suddenly threw himself to one side of the sledge so that it tipped up and Arkady and I were thrown out on to the snow. Then the driver, the sledge and the horses disappeared from our sight.

'Don't be afraid!' said Arkady. 'It had to be done like

this, for I don't know the driver who brought us and he doesn't know us. He was hired for three gold pieces to get you away, but he has to look after his own skin. Now we are in God's hands. This is the village of Sukhaya Orlitsa – a brave priest lives here who marries runaway couples and who has looked after many of our folk. We'll give him something if he'll hide us till evening and marry us. Our driver will be back again by evening, and we'll get away then.'

CHAPTER TWELVE

We knocked at the door of the house and entered the hallway. The priest himself opened the door, an old, rather stocky man with one of his front teeth missing. His wife was an old, old woman who blew up the fire for us. We threw ourselves at their feet:

'Please save us! Let us warm ourselves and hide here until evening!'

The father asked us:

'Who are you, my children? Have you stolen something or are you just runaways?'

'We've not stolen anything from anyone,' said Arkady. 'We're running away from the brutality of Count Kamensky and we want to get to Turkish Rushchuk where quite a few of our folk already live. They won't find us there and we've got some money of our own. We'll give you a gold piece if you'll let us stay the night and another three if you'll marry us. Marry us if you can, but if not we'll get hitched there in Rushchuk.'

'Why shouldn't I marry you?' replied the priest. 'Of course I can. Why bother waiting till you get to Rushchuk? Let me have five gold pieces in all and I'll do you here.'

So Arkady gave him the five gold pieces, and I took the aquamarine earrings from my ears and gave them to his wife.

The priest took the money and said:

'O, my children, all this would be so easy – I've fixed up people in worse situations in my time – but the trouble is you belong to the count. Even though I'm a priest, I'm still afraid of his cruelty. But let God's will be done – give us another gold piece, a damaged one will do, and you can hide.'

Arkady gave him another coin, undamaged, and the priest turned to his wife and said:

'What are you standing there for, old woman! Give our fugitive a skirt or blouse or something to put on; I'm ashamed to look at her like that, all naked!'

Then he was about to take us to the church to hide us in the chest where he kept the robes; but no sooner had his wife begun to dress me behind the partition than we suddenly heard someone rattling the door latch.

CHAPTER THIRTEEN

Our hearts were in our mouths, but the old priest whispered to Arkady:

'Well, my son, it seems we're not going to get you into the robe chest after all, so here, quickly, crawl under the bed!'

And to me he said:

'And as for you, my child, come here!'

He seized me and pushed me into the case of a tall clock, locked it and put the key into his pocket. Then he went to see who was at the door. It sounded as though there were quite a few people there, some standing at the door and a couple of them looking in through the window.

Seven of our pursuers entered, all of them the count's huntsmen carrying bludgeons and hunting whips, and with rope leashes around their waists. With them was an eighth man, the count's butler, wearing a long wolfskin coat with a high standing collar.

The whole front half of the case in which I was hidden was fretted and latticed, with old, fine muslin stretched over it, and I could see through the muslin.

Whether the old priest lost heart and saw that things looked bad for him I don't know, but he was all a-tremble before the butler, crossing himself and speaking loudly and rapidly:

'O, my children, my dear children! I know! I know what you're after, but I am guilty of nothing before the illustrious count, nothing at all!'

But as he crossed himself he pointed over his left shoulder with his fingers to the clock case where I was hidden.

'I'm done for!' I thought, as I watched him perform this miracle.

The butler also noticed, and said:

'We know everything. Give us the key to that clock over there!'

And again the priest began to flap his arms about.

'O, my children! My dear children, forgive me! Be lenient with me! I've forgotten where I put the key, I've forgotten.'

But as he was saying this he kept stroking his pocket with his other hand.

The butler noticed this miracle too, and taking the key from the pocket he unlocked me.

'Come out, my darling,' he said, 'and I'm sure your mate will make his whereabouts known.'

But Arkady had already done so. He threw the priest's bed over on to the floor and stood up.

'It seems there's nothing to be done,' he said. 'You win. Take me away to be tortured, but she is not to blame for anything. I took her away by force.'

And then he turned to the priest, and without more ado spat in his face.

'My children,' said the priest, 'you see how he profanes my office and my loyalty. Report this to his most illustriousness, the count.'

'Of course,' replied the butler. 'Don't you worry. It'll all be taken into account.'

And then he ordered Arkady and me to be taken out.

We were split up into three sledges. Arkady was bound and put in the front one with the hunters. I had a similar escort in the rear one; and the rest of the party went in the middle one.

Whenever we came across people along the road they made way for us, thinking, perhaps, that it was a wedding.

CHAPTER FOURTEEN

We travelled at full gallop and got back very quickly. When we arrived at the count's courtyard I didn't see the sledge carrying Arkady, but was taken back to my old room and questioned time and again about how long I had spent alone with Arkady.

Each time I replied: 'Oh, not even a moment!'

It seems likely that I was fated at birth to belong to a man I despised, and not to the one I loved. And I did not escape my fate. When I got back to my room I was just about to bury my head in the pillow and weep over my sorrow, when suddenly I heard terrible groans from under the floor.

In that wooden building it was so arranged that we, the girls, had our rooms on the first floor. Below us there was a large, high-ceilinged room where we had learnt to sing and dance, and every sound carried up to us from there. And Satan, that Lord of Hell, had put it into the minds of those harsh tyrants to torture Arkady right under my room . . .

As soon as I realized it was him they were torturing I flung myself at the door in order to run to him – but the door was locked. I don't know myself what I intended to do. I fell . . . But on the floor the sounds were even louder . . . And there was no knife . . . not even a nail . . . nothing with which I could somehow or other put an end to myself. I took hold of my own plait of hair and wound it around my neck, twisting it tighter and tighter until all I could hear was the ringing in my ears, and everything started to spin before my eyes, and I passed out . . . I came to in an unfamiliar place, in a large bright shed . . . There were calves there, lots of them, a dozen or more – such lovely little calves that came up to me and nuzzled my hand with their cool lips, as if they thought they were sucking at their mother . . . That's why I woke up, they were tickling me. I let my gaze wander around the room, wondering where I was. As I looked, a woman came in. She was elderly and tall, dressed in a blue, mottled, coarse cotton smock, with a clean shawl of the same material. Her face looked kind.

The woman noticed that I had come to, and was very kind to me. She told me that I was still on the count's estate in the calf-shed. 'It used to be over there,' explained Lyubov Onisimovna, pointing towards the farthest corner of the half-ruined, grey enclosure.

CHAPTER FIFTEEN

The woman had been sent to the cattle-yard because there was some doubt about her sanity. Those who only had the wits of cattle were given a chance in the cattle-yard, because the people who worked there were middle-aged and staid and it was felt that they could keep an eye on mental cases.

The woman in the cotton shift, in whose company Lyubov Onisimovna found herself, was very kind-hearted and was called Drosida.

As she cleared up before evening – continued our nurse – the woman made me a bed out of fresh oat straw. She fluffed it up so that it was as soft as a feather bed, and said: 'I'll tell you everything, my girl. If you give me away, you give me away, but I'm another like you. I didn't always wear this smock, I also knew another kind of life. Oh, God! Don't let it all come back to me! But I'll tell you one thing: don't get upset that you've been sent out to the cattle-yard – it's better here, only you must beware the terrible bottle . . .'

And she took from the shawl around her neck a small, white, glass phial and showed it to me.

'What's that?' I asked.

'This is the terrible bottle,' she replied. 'It has the poison of oblivion in it.'

'Let me have the poison of oblivion,' I said. 'I would like to forget everything.'

'Don't drink it,' she said. 'It's vodka. I weakened once and took a drop too much – some well-meaning folk gave it to me . . . Now I can't manage without it, I need the stuff. Don't drink it if you can possibly do without it, and don't condemn me if I take a sip – I'm suffering terribly. You at least have something to comfort you – the Lord has delivered him from tyranny!'

'He's dead!' I cried, seizing my hair. But I saw that it wasn't my hair – it was white! What had happened?

But she said to me:

'Don't be frightened, don't be frightened! Your hair turned white when you were still over there and they were unwinding your plaits. But he's alive and safe from all tyranny. The count has shown him mercy such as he's never shown anyone before. When night falls I'll tell you everything, but now I'll suck at my bottle . . . I must have a good sip, my heart aches.'

And she sipped and sipped until she fell asleep.

When night had fallen and everyone was asleep Auntie Drosida quietly got up again, and without lighting a lamp went and stood by the small window, where I saw her take another sip from her phial and put it away again. Quietly she asked me:

'Does your grief sleep or not?'

'Grief does not sleep,' I replied.

She came over to my bed and told me how, after his

162

punishment, Arkady had been summoned to the count, who told him:

'You had to go through all the punishment I ordered for you, but since you used to be my favourite I now intend to show you mercy. I am sending you off to the army tomorrow as an additional conscript. But in view of the fact that you weren't afraid of my brother – a count and a landowner – nor his pistols, I'm offering you a way to honour. I wouldn't wish you to be beneath the noble spirit you have demonstrated. I am sending a letter recommending that you be posted straight to the front where you will serve, not as an ordinary private, but as a regimental sergeant, and where you'll be able to show your valour. From now on you'll be subject to the tsar's will, not mine.'

'He's better off now and has nothing more to fear,' said the old lady in the smock. 'The chance of falling in battle is the only power over him now, not the will of some tyrant master.'

I believed what she said, and every night for three years I dreamed only of Arkady in battle.

And so three years passed, and during this time God was good to me, for I was not returned to the theatre but carried on living where I was, in the cattle-shed helping Auntie Drosida. I was fine there, for I felt sorry for the old woman and loved to listen to her stories on those nights when she hadn't drunk too much. She still remembered how the old count had been killed by our people – his chief valet was amongst them – because they could no longer put up with his hellish cruelty. I still didn't drink and gladly did what I could for Drosida. The calves were like children to me: I got so used to them that when one was fattened up and taken away to be slaughtered for the table I would make the sign of the cross over it myself and cry for three days. I was no longer fit for the theatre because I now found it difficult to walk; my legs had got a bit unsteady. Before I'd had a very light step, but when Arkady carried me off unconscious in the cold I must have caught a chill in my legs, and they no longer had the strength for dancing. I became another woman in a cotton shift, like Drosida, and Lord knows how long I would have lived in such a sorry state if something hadn't suddenly happened one evening as I was sitting in our hut. The sun was going down and I was unwinding hanks of yarn by the window, when suddenly a small stone wrapped in a piece of paper flew in through the window.

CHAPTER SIXTEEN

I glanced about and looked out through the window – but there was no one there.

'Probably it was someone throwing it over the fence from outside,' I thought, 'and it didn't land where it should have, but fell near the old woman and me.' And I wondered whether I should unwrap the piece of paper or not. It seemed best to unwrap it, since there was certainly something written on it. Perhaps it was something someone needed, and if I found out I could keep the secret to myself and throw the note with a pebble in exactly the same way to whoever it was meant for.

I undid it and began to read . . . and couldn't believe my eyes . . .

CHAPTER SEVENTEEN

It said:

My faithful Lyuba! I have fought in battle, served my tsar and spilt my blood more than once; and for this I have been made an officer and a gentleman. Now I am home on leave to recover from my wounds and am staying in the village of Pushkarskoe with the innkeeper. Tomorrow I shall put on my medals and crosses and go to see the count. I'll take all the money I got for medical treatment – 500 roubles – and will ask him if I can buy your freedom, in the hope that we shall be married before the throne of the Almighty Creator.

And then – continued Lyubov Onisimovna, trying to keep her feelings under control – he wrote:

Whatever misfortune you might have suffered and whatever you've been subjected to, I shall regard it as suffering and not as sin or weakness on your part. I'll put it down to God's will, and for you I shall feel only respect.

And it was signed 'Arkady Ilin'.

Lyubov Onisimovna had immediately burned the letter in the grate, and said nothing about it to anyone, not even the old woman in the cotton shift. She just prayed to God the whole night long, asking nothing for herself only for Arkady. For, although he had written that he was now an officer with crosses and wounds, she couldn't imagine the count treating him any differently than before.

Quite simply, she was afraid he would still be flogged.

CHAPTER EIGHTEEN

Early the next morning Lyubov Onisimovna had driven the calves out into the sunlight and had begun to feed them milk from a tub with a bark ladle, when suddenly from beyond the fence, from 'the outside', she caught the sound of people rushing somewhere and talking rapidly to each other as they ran.

I couldn't catch a word of what they were saying – continued Lyubov Onisimovna – but it pierced my heart like a knife. When Phillip, the muck-spreader, came in the gate at that moment I asked him:

'Phil, dear, you didn't hear what those people were running for and what they were talking about, did you?'

'They're on their way to Pushkarskoe to look at an officer who was killed in his sleep last night by the innkeeper,' he replied. 'Cut his throat right across, he did, and stole 500 roubles. They say he was caught all covered in blood and with the money on him.'

When he said that I fell down in a dead faint . . .

But it was true: the innkeeper had murdered Arkady . . . They buried him right here in the very grave we're sitting on. He's lying under us now, under this very earth . . . I expect you've been wondering why I always bring you here on our walks, eh? It's not that I want to look at that (she pointed at the grey and gloomy ruins), but to sit here alongside him . . . and take a drop in memory of his soul . . .

CHAPTER NINETEEN

At this point Lyubov Onisimovna stopped and, considering her tale finished, took a small bottle from her pocket and 'took a drop in memory' or 'had a sip'. I asked her:

'But who buried the celebrated make-up artist here?'

'The governor, my dear, the governor himself was at the funeral. Of course he was! Arkady was an officer remember. The deacon and the priest called him "the nobleman Arkady" during the service, and as the coffin was lowered soldiers fired blanks from their rifles into the air. A year later, on St Ilya's day, the public executioner flogged the innkeeper in the town square. They gave him forty-three strokes for what he did to Arkady Ilich, and he survived. He survived and was sent away branded to penal servitude. Our menfolk, or at least those who were able, ran to watch; and the older ones, who remembered how the cruel old count's killer had been punished, said that forty-three strokes was getting off lightly, just because Arkady was born of plain folk. The count's killer had been given a hundred and one strokes. The law doesn't allow an even number of strokes to be given, you always have to give an odd number. On that occasion they say that the executioner was brought specially from Tula and was given three glasses of rum to drink before the punishment. He then flogged the man so that the first hundred lashes only caused him terrible pain without killing him. But then with the hundred and first he gave the whip such a crack that the whole of the man's backbone was shattered. They began to lift him down from the scaffold, but he was already dying ... They covered him with a rough blanket and carried him off to jail, but he died on the way. They say that the Tula executioner kept shouting: "Give me someone else to flog! I'll kill everyone in Orel." '

'What about you, did you go to Arkady's funeral?' I asked.

'Yes, I went. We all went together. The count ordered all the people from the theatre to go and see how one of our people could get on in life.'

'And did you take your leave of him?'

'Why, of course I did! Everyone went up to take their leave, and I did too. He had changed so much that I wouldn't have recognized him. Thin and very pale – they say that all his blood had drained away because he'd had his throat cut on the stroke of midnight... How much blood he'd lost...'

She stopped talking and fell into a reverie.

'And how did you manage after that?' I asked.

She seemed to recover and passed her hand over her forehead.

'At first I couldn't remember how I got home,' she said. 'We were all there together... so I expect someone brought me. That evening Drosida Fyodorovna said to me: "You can't go on like this... You don't sleep, but all the same you lie there like a stone. It's no good, you must cry to let your feelings out from your heart."

'"I can't, auntie," I replied. "My heart burns like a coal, yet I cannot let it out."

'"Well, that means you can no longer do without the bottle," said she. She poured me a drink from her little bottle and said:

'"Up till now I've kept you away from this and dissuaded you, but now there's nothing else for it: you must quench the burning coal – here, take a sip."

'"I don't want to!" I replied.

'"You're a foolish girl," she said, "who does want to at first! Why, life is bitter, but grief's poison is even more so. But if you quench the burning coal with this poison it will die down for a moment. Take a sip, quickly, take it!"

'And I drank down the whole bottle at once. It was disgusting, but I couldn't have slept without it. The next night I . . . had another drop, and now I can't get to sleep without it. I've got a little bottle of my own now and I buy vodka. But you're a good boy, don't ever tell your mummy about it, don't ever betray simple folk. You must always look after simple folk, for they are all great sufferers. And so when we're on our way home I'll knock at the window of the tavern round the corner. We won't go in ourselves, but if I give them my empty bottle they'll give me a new one.'

I was deeply moved and vowed that under no circumstances would I ever say anything about her 'little bottle'.

'Thanks, my dear. Don't say anything; I need it.'

I can see and hear her as if it were yesterday; each night, when the rest of the house was asleep, she would quietly raise herself a little in her bed, trying not to let even her bones creak. She would listen, get up and creep on her long, chilblained legs to the window. She'd stand there for a moment, looking and listening to be sure that my mother wasn't coming out of her bedroom. Then she would lift the bottle to her lips, so that its neck rattled ever so quietly against her teeth, and 'take a sip'. One swallow, two, a third . . . The burning coal was quenched and tribute paid to Arkady, so she'd go back to bed, slip under the blanket and soon she'd be quietly wheezing – whew, whew, whew . . . She was asleep!

Never in my life have I seen a more terrible and heartbreaking commemoration of the dead.

CHEKHOV

Anton Chekhov's first attempts at writing were a series of humorous sketches which he produced for comic papers while a medical student at Moscow University. In the mid-1880s, however, his work became more serious and he quickly developed into Russia's greatest master of the short story. Towards the end of his life he also became a supreme playwright. Chekhov's themes are drawn from everyday experience, his interest is focused on the emotional world of his characters, and his manner is detached but acutely sensitive. The poetic poignancy of his best work stems from the author's unvoiced awareness of the ironic gap between our modest hopes and the banal realities of life. 'The Party', first published in 1888, is a typically fine-grained story of domestic disharmony.

THE PARTY

Translated by Constance Garnett

I

AFTER the festive dinner with its eight courses and its endless conversation, Olga Mikhailovna, whose husband's
name-day was being celebrated, went out into the garden.
The duty of smiling and talking incessantly, the clatter of
the crockery, the stupidity of the servants, the long intervals
between the courses, and the stays she had put on to conceal
her condition from the visitors, wearied her to exhaustion.
She longed to get away from the house, to sit in the shade
and rest her heart with thoughts of the baby which was to be
born to her in another two months. She was used to these
thoughts coming to her as she turned to the left out of the
big avenue into the narrow path. Here in the thick shade of
the plums and cherry-trees the dry branches used to scratch
her neck and shoulders; a spider's web would settle on her
face, and there would rise up in her mind the image of a little
creature of undetermined sex and undefined features, and it
began to seem as though it were not the spider's web that
tickled her face and neck caressingly, but that little creature.
When, at the end of the path, a thin wicker hurdle came into
sight, and behind it podgy beehives with tiled roofs; when
in the motionless, stagnant air there came a smell of hay and
honey, and a soft buzzing of bees was audible, then the little
creature would take complete possession of Olga Mikhailovna. She used to sit down on a bench near the shanty
woven of branches, and fall to thinking.

This time, too, she went on as far as the seat, sat down, and
began thinking; but instead of the little creature there rose

up in her imagination the figures of the grown-up people whom she had just left. She felt dreadfully uneasy that she, the hostess, had deserted her guests, and she remembered how her husband, Pyotr Dmitrich, and her uncle, Nikolay Nikolaich, had argued at dinner about trial by jury, about the press, and about the higher education of women. Her husband, as usual, argued in order to show off his conservative ideas before his visitors – and still more in order to disagree with her uncle, whom he disliked. Her uncle contradicted him and wrangled over every word he uttered, so as to show the company that he, Uncle Nikolay Nikolaich, still retained his youthful freshness of spirit and free-thinking in spite of his fifty-nine years. And towards the end of dinner even Olga Mikhailovna herself could not resist taking part and unskilfully attempting to defend university education for women – not that that education stood in need of her defence, but simply because she wanted to annoy her husband, who to her mind was unfair. The guests were wearied by this discussion, but they all thought it necessary to take part in it, and talked a great deal, although none of them took any interest in trial by jury or the higher education of women . . .

Olga Mikhailovna was sitting on the nearest side of the hurdle near the shanty. The sun was hidden behind the clouds. The trees and the air were overcast as before rain, but in spite of that it was hot and stifling. The hay cut under the trees on the previous day was lying ungathered, looking melancholy, with here and there a patch of colour from the faded flowers, and from it came a heavy sickly scent. It was still. The other side of the hurdle there was a monotonous hum of bees . . .

Suddenly she heard footsteps and voices; someone was coming along the path towards the beehouse.

'How stifling it is!' said a feminine voice. 'What do you think – is it going to rain, or not?'

'It is going to rain, my charmer, but not before night,' a

very familiar male voice answered languidly. 'There will be a good rain.'

Olga Mikhailovna calculated that if she made haste to hide in the shanty they would pass by without seeing her, and she would not have to talk and to force herself to smile. She picked up her skirts, bent down and crept into the shanty. At once she felt upon her face, her neck, her arms, the hot air as heavy as steam. If it had not been for the stuffiness and the close smell of rye bread, fennel and brushwood, which prevented her from breathing freely, it would have been delightful to hide from her visitors here under the thatched roof in the dusk, and to think about the little creature. It was cosy and quiet.

'What a pretty spot!' said a feminine voice. 'Let us sit here, Pyotr Dmitrich.'

Olga Mikhailovna began peeping through a crack between two branches. She saw her husband, Pyotr Dmitrich, and Lyubochka Sheller, a girl of seventeen who had not long left boarding-school. Pyotr Dmitrich, with his hat on the back of his head, languid and indolent from having drunk so much at dinner, slouched by the hurdle and raked the hay into a heap with his foot; Lyubochka, pink with the heat and pretty as ever, stood with her hands behind her, watching the lazy movements of his big handsome person.

Olga Mikhailovna knew that her husband was attractive to women, and did not like to see him with them. There was nothing out of the way in Pyotr Dmitrich's lazily raking together the hay in order to sit down on it with Lyubochka and chatter to her of trivialities; there was nothing out of the way, either, in pretty Lyubochka's looking at him with her soft eyes; but yet Olga Mikhailovna felt vexed with her husband and frightened and pleased that she could listen to them.

'Sit down, enchantress,' said Pyotr Dmitrich, sinking down on the hay and stretching. 'That's right. Come, tell me something.'

'What next! If I begin telling you anything, you will go to sleep.'

'Me go to sleep? Allah forbid! Can I go to sleep while eyes like yours are watching me?'

In her husband's words, and in the fact that he was lolling with his hat on the back of his head in the presence of a lady, there was nothing out of the way either. He was spoilt by women, knew that they found him attractive, and had adopted with them a special tone which everyone said suited him. With Lyubochka he behaved as with all women. But, all the same, Olga Mikhailovna was jealous.

'Tell me, please,' said Lyubochka, after a brief silence – 'is it true that you are to be tried for something?'

'I? Yes, I am . . . numbered among the transgressors, my charmer.'

'But what for?'

'For nothing, but just . . . it's chiefly a question of politics,' yawned Pyotr Dmitrich – 'the antagonisms of Left and Right. I, an obscurantist and reactionary, ventured in an official paper to make use of an expression offensive in the eyes of such immaculate Gladstones as Vladimir Pavlovich Vladimirov and our local justice of the peace – Kuzma Grigorich Vostryakov.'

Pyotr Dmitrich yawned again and went on:

'And it is the way with us that you may express disapproval of the sun or the moon, or anything you like, but God preserve you from touching the liberals! Heaven forbid! A liberal is like the poisonous dry fungus which covers you with a cloud of dust if you accidentally touch it with your finger.'

'What happened to you?'

'Nothing particular. The whole flare-up started from the merest trifle. A teacher, a detestable person of clerical associations, hands to Vostryakov a petition against a tavern-keeper, charging him with insulting language and behaviour in a public place. Everything showed that both the teacher and the tavern-keeper were drunk as cobblers, and that they behaved equally badly. If there had been insulting behaviour the insult had anyway been mutual. Vostryakov ought to have turned them out of the court – that is all. But that's not our way of doing things. With us what stands first is not the person – not the fact itself, but the trade-mark and label. However great a rascal a teacher may be, he is always in the right because he is a teacher; a tavern-keeper is always in the wrong because he is a tavern-keeper and a money-grubber. Vostryakov placed the tavern-keeper under arrest. The man appealed to the circuit court; the circuit court triumphantly upheld Vostryakov's decision. Well, I stuck to my own opinion . . . Got a little hot . . . That was all.'

Pyotr Dmitrich spoke calmly with careless irony. In reality the trial that was hanging over him worried him extremely. Olga Mikhailovna remembered how on his return from the unfortunate session he had tried to conceal from his household how troubled he was, and how dissatisfied with himself. As an intelligent man he could not help feeling that he had gone too far in expressing his disagreement; and how much lying had been needful to conceal that feeling from himself and from others! How many unnecessary conversations there had been! How much grumbling and insincere laughter at what was not laughable! When he learned that he was to be brought up before the court, he seemed at once harassed and depressed; he began to sleep badly, stood oftener than ever at the windows, drumming on the panes with his fingers. And he was ashamed to let his wife see that he was worried, and it vexed her.

'They say you have been in the province of Poltava?' Lyubochka questioned him.

'Yes,' answered Pyotr Dmitrich. 'I came back the day before yesterday.'

'I expect it is very nice there.'

'Yes, it is very nice, very nice indeed, in fact; I arrived just in time for the haymaking, I must tell you, and in the Ukraine the haymaking is the most poetical moment of the year. Here we have a big house, a big garden, a lot of servants, and a lot going on, so that you don't see the haymaking; here it all passes unnoticed. There, at the farm, I have a meadow of forty-five acres as flat as my hand. You can see the men mowing from any window you stand at. They are mowing in the meadow, they are mowing in the garden. There are no visitors, no fuss nor hurry either, so that you can't help seeing, feeling, hearing nothing but the haymaking. There is a smell of hay indoors and outdoors. There's the sound of the scythes from sunrise to sunset. Altogether Little Russia is a charming country. Would you believe it, when I was drinking water from the rustic wells and filthy vodka in some Jew's tavern, when on quiet evenings the strains of the Little Russian fiddle and the tambourines reached me, I was tempted by a fascinating idea – to settle down on my place and live there as long as I chose, far away from circuit courts, intellectual conversations, philosophizing women, long dinners . . .'

Pyotr Dmitrich was not lying. He was unhappy and really longed to rest. And he had visited his Poltava property simply to avoid seeing his study, his servants, his acquaintances, and everything that could remind him of his wounded vanity and his mistakes.

Lyubochka suddenly jumped up and waved her hands about in horror.

'Oh! A bee, a bee!' she shrieked. 'It will sting!'

'Nonsense; it won't sting,' said Pyotr Dmitrich. 'What a coward you are!'

'No, no, no,' cried Lyubochka; and, looking round at the bees, she walked rapidly back.

Pyotr Dmitrich walked away after her, looking at her with a softened and melancholy face. He was probably thinking, as he looked at her, of his farm, of solitude, and – who knows? – perhaps he was even thinking how snug and cosy life would be at the farm if his wife had been this girl – young, pure, fresh, not corrupted by higher education, not with child ...

When the sound of their footsteps had died away, Olga Mikhailovna came out of the shanty and turned towards the house. She wanted to cry. She was by now acutely jealous. She could understand that her husband was worried, dissatisfied with himself and ashamed, and when people are ashamed they hold aloof, above all from those nearest to them, and are unreserved with strangers; she could understand, also, that she had nothing to fear from Lyubochka or from those women who were now drinking coffee indoors. But everything in general was terrible, incomprehensible, and it already seemed to Olga Mikhailovna that Pyotr Dmitrich only half belonged to her ...

'He has no right to do it!' she muttered, trying to formulate her jealousy and her vexation with her husband. 'He has no right at all. I will tell him so plainly!'

She made up her mind to find her husband at once and tell him all about it: it was disgusting, absolutely disgusting, that he was attractive to other women and sought their admiration as though it were some heavenly manna; it was unjust and dishonourable that he should give to others what belonged by right to his wife, that he should hide his soul and his conscience from his wife to reveal them to the first pretty face he came across. What harm had his wife done him? How was she to blame? Long ago she had been sickened by his lying: he was for ever posing, flirting, saying what he did not think, and trying to seem different from what he was and what he ought to be. Why this falsity? Was it seemly in a decent man? If he lied he was demeaning himself and those to whom he lied, and slighting what he lied about. Could he not understand that if he swaggered and posed at the judicial table or held forth at dinner on the prerogatives of government, that he, simply to provoke her uncle, was showing thereby that he had not a ha'p'orth of respect for the court, or himself, or any of the people who were listening and looking at him?

Coming out into the big avenue, Olga Mikhailovna assumed an expression of face as though she had just gone away to look after some domestic matter. On the veranda the gentlemen were drinking liqueur and eating strawberries; one of them, the examining magistrate – a stout elderly man, *blagueur* and wit – must have been telling some rather free anecdote, for, seeing their hostess, he suddenly clapped his hands over his fat lips, rolled his eyes, and sat down. Olga Mikhailovna did not like the local officials. She did not care for their clumsy, ceremonious wives, their scandalmongering, their frequent visits, their flattery of her husband, whom they all hated. Now, when they were drinking, were replete with food and showed no signs of going away, she felt their presence an agonizing weariness; but not to appear impolite, she smiled cordially to the magistrate, and shook her finger at him. She walked across the dining-room and drawing-room smiling, and looking as though she had gone to give some order and make some arrangement. 'God grant no one stops me,' she thought, but she forced herself to stop in the drawing-room to listen from politeness to a young man who was sitting at the piano playing; after standing for a minute, she cried, 'Bravo, bravo, M. Georges!' and, clapping her hands twice, she went on.

She found her husband in his study. He was sitting at the table, thinking of something. His face looked stern, thoughtful, and guilty. This was not the same Pyotr Dmitrich who had been arguing at dinner and whom his guests knew, but a different man – wearied, feeling guilty and dissatisfied with himself, whom nobody knew but his wife. He must have come to the study to get cigarettes. Before him lay an open cigarette-case full of cigarettes, and one of his hands was in the table drawer; he had paused and sunk into thought as he was taking the cigarettes.

Olga Mikhailovna felt sorry for him. It was as clear as day that this man was harassed, could find no rest, and was perhaps struggling with himself. Olga Mikhailovna went up to the table in silence: wanting to show that she had forgotten the argument at dinner and was not cross, she shut the cigarette-case and put it in her husband's coat pocket.

'What should I say to him?' she wondered; 'I shall say that lying is like a forest – the farther one goes into it the more difficult it is to get out of it. I will say to him, "You have been carried away by the false part you are playing; you have insulted people who were attached to you and have done you no harm. Go and apologize to them, laugh at yourself, and you will feel better. And if you want peace and solitude, let us go away together."'

Meeting his wife's gaze, Pyotr Dmitrich's face immediately assumed the expression it had worn at dinner and in the garden – indifferent and slightly ironical. He yawned and got up.

'It's past five,' he said, looking at his watch. 'If our visitors are merciful and leave us at eleven, even then we have another six hours of it. It's a cheerful prospect, there's no denying!'

And, whistling something, he walked slowly out of the study with his usual dignified gait. She could hear him with dignified firmness cross the dining-room, then the drawing-room, laugh with dignified assurance, and say to the young man who was playing, 'Bravo! bravo!' Soon his footsteps died away: he must have gone out into the garden. And now not jealousy, not vexation, but real hatred of his footsteps, his insincere laugh and voice, took possession of Olga Mikhailovna. She went to the window and looked out into the garden. Pyotr Dmitrich was already walking along the avenue. Putting one hand in his pocket and snapping the fingers of the other, he walked with confident swinging steps, throwing his head back a little, and looking as though he were very well satisfied with himself, with his dinner with his digestion, and with nature . . .

Two little schoolboys, the children of Madame Chizhen-sky, who had only just arrived, made their appearance in the avenue, accompanied by their tutor, a student wearing a white tunic and very narrow trousers. When they reached Pyotr Dmitrich, the boys and the student stopped, and probably congratulated him on his name-day. With a graceful swing of his shoulders, he patted the children on their cheeks, and carelessly offered the student his hand without looking at him. The student must have praised the weather and compared it with the climate of Petersburg, for Pyotr Dmitrich said in a loud voice, in a tone as though he were not speaking to a guest, but to an usher of the court or a witness:

'What! It's cold in Petersburg? And here, my good sir, we have a salubrious atmosphere and the fruits of the earth in abundance. Eh? What?'

And, thrusting one hand in his pocket and snapping the fingers of the other, he walked on. Till he had disappeared behind the nut bushes, Olga Mikhailovna watched the back of his head in perplexity. How had this man of thirty-four come by the dignified deportment of a general? How had he come by that impressive, elegant manner? Where had he got that vibration of authority in his voice? Where had he got these 'whats', 'to be sures', and 'my good sirs'?

Olga Mikhailovna remembered how in the first months of her marriage she had felt dreary at home alone and had driven into the town to the circuit court, at which Pyotr Dmitrich had sometimes presided in place of her godfather, Count Alexey Petrovich. In the presidential chair, wearing his uniform and a chain on his breast, he was completely changed. Stately gestures, a voice of thunder, 'what', 'to be sure', careless tones . . . Everything, all that was ordinary and human, all that was individual and personal to himself that Olga Mikhailovna was accustomed to seeing in him at home, vanished in grandeur, and in the presidential chair there sat not Pyotr Dmitrich, but another man whom everyone called Mr President. This consciousness of power prevented him from sitting still in his place, and he seized every opportunity to ring his bell, to glance sternly at the public, to shout ... Where had he got his short-sight and his deafness when he suddenly began to see and hear with difficulty, and, frowning majestically, insisted on people speaking louder and coming closer to the table? From the height of his grandeur he could hardly distinguish faces or sounds, so that it seemed that if Olga Mikhailovna herself had gone up to him he would have shouted even to her, 'Your name?' Peasant witnesses he addressed familiarly, he shouted at the public so that his voice could be heard even in the street, and behaved incredibly with the lawyers. If a lawyer had to speak to him, Pyotr Dmitrich, turning a little away from him, looked with half-closed eyes at the ceiling, meaning to signify thereby that the lawyer was utterly superfluous and that he was neither recognizing him nor listening to him; if a badly dressed lawyer spoke, Pyotr Dmitrich pricked up his ears and looked the man up and down with a sarcastic, annihilating stare as though to say: 'Queer sort of lawyers nowadays!'

'What do you mean by that?' he would interrupt.

If a would-be eloquent lawyer mispronounced a foreign word, saying, for instance, 'factitious' instead of 'fictitious', Pyotr Dmitrich brightened up at once and asked, 'What? How? Factitious? What does that mean?' and then observed impressively: 'Don't make use of words you do not understand.' And the lawyer, finishing his speech, would walk away from the table, red and perspiring, while Pyotr Dmitrich, with a self-satisfied smile, would lean back in his chair triumphant. In his manner with the lawyers he imitated Count Alexey Petrovich a little, but when the latter said, for instance, 'Counsel for the defence, you keep quiet for a while!' it sounded paternally good-natured and natural, while the same words in Pyotr Dmitrich's mouth were rude and artificial.

There were sounds of applause. The young man had finished playing. Olga Mikhailovna remembered her guests and hurried into the drawing-room.

'I have so enjoyed your playing,' she said, going up to the piano. 'I have so enjoyed it. You have a wonderful talent! But don't you think our piano's out of tune?'

At that moment the two schoolboys walked into the room, accompanied by the student.

'My goodness! Mitya and Kolya,' Olga Mikhailovna drawled joyfully, going to meet them. 'How big they have grown! One would not know you! But where is your mamma?'

'I congratulate you on the name-day,' the student began in a free-and-easy tone, 'and I wish you all happiness. Ekaterina Andreevna sends her congratulations and begs you to excuse her. She is not very well.'

'How unkind of her! I have been expecting her all day. Is it long since you left Petersburg?' Olga Mikhailovna asked the student. 'What kind of weather have you there now?' And, without waiting for an answer, she looked cordially at the schoolboys and repeated:

'How tall they have grown! It is not long since they used to come with their nurse, and they are at school already! The old grow older while the young grow up . . . Have you had dinner?'

'Oh, please don't trouble!' said the student.

'Why, you have not had dinner?'

'For goodness' sake, don't trouble!'

'But I suppose you are hungry?' Olga Mikhailovna said it in a harsh, rude voice, with impatience and vexation – it escaped her unawares, but at once she coughed, smiled, and flushed crimson. 'How tall they have grown!' she said softly.

'Please don't trouble!' the student said once more.

The student begged her not to trouble; the boys said nothing; obviously all three of them were hungry. Olga Mikhailovna took them into the dining-room and told Vassily to lay the table.

'How unkind of your mamma!' she said as she made them sit down. 'She has quite forgotten me. Unkind, unkind, unkind . . . you must tell her so. What are you studying?' she asked the student.

'Medicine.'

'Well, I have a weakness for doctors, only fancy. I am very sorry my husband is not a doctor. What courage anyone must have to perform an operation or dissect a corpse, for instance! Horrible! Aren't you frightened? I believe I should die of terror! Of course, you drink vodka?'

'Please don't trouble.'

'After your journey you must have something to drink. Though I am a woman, even I drink sometimes. And Mitya and Kolya will drink Malaga. It's not a strong wine; you need not be afraid of it. What fine fellows they are, really! They'll be thinking of getting married next.'

Olga Mikhailovna talked without ceasing; she knew by experience that when she had guests to entertain it was far easier and more comfortable to talk than to listen. When you talk there is no need to strain your attention to think of answers to questions, and to change your expression of face. But unawares she asked the student a serious question; the student began a lengthy speech and she was forced to listen. The student knew that she had once been at the university, and so tried to seem a serious person as he talked to her.

'What subject are you studying?' she asked, forgetting that she had already put that question to him.

'Medicine.'

Olga Mikhailovna now remembered that she had been away from the ladies for a long while.

'Yes? Then I suppose you are going to be a doctor?' she said, getting up. 'That's splendid. I am sorry I did not go in for medicine myself. So you will finish your dinner here, gentlemen, and then come into the garden. I will introduce you to the young ladies.'

She went out and glanced at her watch: it was five minutes to six. And she wondered that the time had gone so slowly, and thought with horror that there were six more hours before midnight, when the party would break up. How could she get through those six hours? What phrases could she utter? How should she behave to her husband?

There was not a soul in the drawing-room or on the veranda. All the guests were sauntering about the garden.

'I shall have to suggest a walk in the birch wood before tea, or else a row in the boats,' thought Olga Mikhailovna, hurrying to the croquet ground, from which came the sounds of voices and laughter. 'And sit the old people down to vint . . .' She met Grigory the footman coming from the croquet ground with empty bottles.

'Where are the ladies?' she asked.

'Among the raspberry bushes. The master's there, too.'

'Oh, good heavens!' someone on the croquet lawn shouted with exasperation. 'I have told you a thousand times over! To know the Bulgarians you must see them! You can't judge from the papers!'

Either because of the outburst or for some other reason, Olga Mikhailovna was suddenly aware of a terrible weakness all over, especially in her legs and in her shoulders. She felt she could not bear to speak, to listen, or to move.

'Grigory,' she said faintly and with an effort, 'when you have to serve tea or anything, please don't appeal to me, don't ask me anything, don't speak of anything . . . Do it all yourself, and . . . and don't make a noise with your feet, I entreat you . . . I can't, because . . .'

Without finishing, she walked on towards the croquet lawn, but on the way she thought of the ladies, and turned towards the raspberry bushes. The sky, the air and the trees looked gloomy again and threatened rain; it was hot and stifling. An immense flock of crows, foreseeing a storm, flew cawing over the garden. The paths were more overgrown, darker, and narrower as they got nearer the kitchen garden. In one of them, buried in a thick tangle of wild pear, crab-apple, sorrel, young oaks, and hopbine, clouds of tiny black flies swarmed round Olga Mikhailovna. She covered her face with her hands and began forcing herself to think of the little creature . . . There floated through her imagination the figures of Grigory, Mitya, Kolya, the faces of the peasants who had come in the morning to present their congratulations . . .

She heard footsteps, and she opened her eyes. Uncle Nikolay Nikolaich was coming rapidly towards her.

'It's you, dear? I am very glad . . .' he began, breathless. 'A couple of words . . .' He mopped with his handkerchief his red shaven chin, then suddenly stepped back a pace, flung up his hands and opened his eyes wide. 'My dear girl, how long is this going on?' he said rapidly, spluttering. 'I ask you: is there no limit to it? I say nothing of the demoralizing effect of his martinet views on all around him, of the way he insults all that is sacred and best in me and in every honest thinking man – I will say nothing about that, but he might at least behave decently! Why, he shouts, he bellows, gives himself airs, poses as a sort of Bonaparte, does not let one say a word . . . I don't know what the devil's the matter with him! These lordly gestures, this condescending tone; and laughing like a general! Who is he, allow me to ask you? I ask you, who is he? The husband of his wife, with a few paltry acres and the rank of a titular who has had the luck to marry an heiress! An upstart and a *junker*, like so many others! A type out of Shchedrin! Upon my word, it's either that he's suffering from megalomania, or that old rat in his dotage, Count Alexey Petrovich, is right when he says that children and young people are a long time growing up nowadays, and go on playing they are cabmen and generals till they are forty!'

'That's true, that's true,' Olga Mikhailovna assented. 'Let me pass.'

'Now just consider: what is it leading to?' her uncle went on, barring her way. 'How will this playing at being a general and a conservative end? Already he has got into trouble! Yes, to stand his trial! I am very glad of it! That's what his noise and shouting has brought him to – to stand in the prisoner's dock. And it's not as though it were the circuit court or something: it's the central court! Nothing worse could be imagined, I think! And then he has quarrelled with everyone! He is celebrating his name-day, and look, Vostryakov's not here, nor Yakhontov, nor Vladimirov, nor Shevud, nor the count . . . There is no one, I imagine, more conservative than Count Alexey Petrovich, yet even he has not come. And he never will come again. He won't come, you will see!'

'My God! but what has it to do with me?' asked Olga Mikhailovna.

'What has it to do with you? Why, you are his wife! You are clever, you have had a university education, and it was in your power to make him an honest worker!'

'At the lectures I went to they did not teach us how to influence tiresome people. It seems as though I should have to apologize to all of you for having been at the university,' said Olga Mikhailovna sharply. 'Listen, Uncle. If people played the same scales over and over again the whole day long in your hearing, you wouldn't be able to sit still and listen, but would run away. I hear the same thing over again for days together all the year round. You must have pity on me at last.'

Her uncle pulled a very long face, then looked at her searchingly and twisted his lips into a mocking smile.

'So that's how it is,' he piped in a voice like an old woman's. 'I beg your pardon!' he said, and made a ceremonious bow. 'If you have fallen under his influence yourself, and have abandoned your convictions, you should have said so before. I beg your pardon!'

'Yes, I have abandoned my convictions,' she cried. 'There; make the most of it!'

'I beg your pardon!'

Her uncle for the last time made her a ceremonious bow, a little on one side, and, shrinking into himself, made a scrape with his foot and walked back.

'Idiot!' thought Olga Mikhailovna. 'I hope he will go home.'

She found the ladies and the young people among the raspberries in the kitchen garden. Some were eating raspberries; others, tired of eating raspberries, were strolling about the strawberry beds or foraging among the sugar-peas. A little on one side of the raspberry bed, near a branching apple tree propped up by posts which had been pulled out of an old fence, Pyotr Dmitrich was mowing the grass. His hair was falling over his forehead, his cravat was untied. His watch-chain was hanging loose. Every step and every swing of the scythe showed skill and the possession of immense physical strength. Near him were standing Lyubochka and the daughters of a neighbour, Colonel Bukreev – two anaemic and unhealthily stout fair girls, Natalya and Valentina, or, as they were always called, Nata and Vata, both wearing white frocks and strikingly like each other. Pyotr Dmitrich was teaching them to mow.

'It's very simple,' he said. 'You have only to know how to hold the scythe and not to get too hot over it – that is, not to use more force than is necessary! Like this . . . Wouldn't you like to try?' he said, offering the scythe to Lyubochka. 'Come!'

Lyubochka took the scythe clumsily, blushed crimson, and laughed.

'Don't be afraid, Lyubov Alexandrovna!' cried Olga Mikhailovna, loud enough for all the ladies to hear that she was with them. 'Don't be afraid! You must learn! If you marry a Tolstoyan he will make you mow.'

Lyubochka raised the scythe, but began laughing again, and, helpless with laughter, let go of it at once. She was ashamed and pleased at being talked to as though grown up. Nata, with a cold, serious face, with no trace of smiling or shyness, took the scythe, swung it and caught it in the grass; Vata, also without a smile, as cold and serious as her sister, took the scythe and silently thrust it into the earth. Having done this, the two sisters linked arms and walked in silence to the raspberries.

Pyotr Dmitrich laughed and played about like a boy, and this childish, frolicsome mood in which he became exceedingly good-natured suited him far better than any other. Olga Mikhailovna loved him when he was like that. But his boyishness did not usually last long. It did not this time; after playing with the scythe, he for some reason thought it necessary to take a serious tone about it.

'When I am mowing, I feel, do you know, healthier and more normal,' he said. 'If I were forced to confine myself to an intellectual life I believe I should go out of my mind. I feel that I was not born to be a man of culture! I ought to mow, plough, sow, drive out the horses.'

And Pyotr Dmitrich began a conversation with the ladies about the advantages of physical labour, about culture, and then about the pernicious effects of money, of property. Listening to her husband, Olga Mikhailovna, for some reason, thought of her dowry.

'And the time will come, I suppose,' she thought, 'when he will not forgive me for being richer than he. He is proud and vain. Maybe he will hate me because he owes so much to me.'

She stopped near Colonel Bukreev, who was eating raspberries and also taking part in the conversation.

'Come,' he said, making room for Olga Mikhailovna and Pyotr Dmitrich. 'The ripest are here . . . And so, according to Proudhon,' he went on, raising his voice, 'property is robbery. But I must confess I don't believe in Proudhon, and don't consider him a philosopher. The French are not authorities, to my thinking – God bless them!'

'Well, as for Proudhons and Buckles and the rest of them, I am weak in that department,' said Pyotr Dmitrich. 'For philosophy you must apply to my wife. She has been at university lectures and knows all your Schopenhauers and Proudhons by heart . . .'

Olga Mikhailovna felt bored again. She walked again along a little path by apple and pear trees, and looked again as though she was on some very important errand. She reached the gardener's cottage. In the doorway the gardener's wife, Varvara, was sitting together with her four little children with big shaven heads. Varvara, too, was with child and expecting to be confined on Elijah's Day. After greeting her, Olga Mikhailovna looked at her and the children in silence and asked:

'Well, how do you feel?'

'Oh, all right . . '

A silence followed. The two women seemed to understand each other without words.

'It's dreadful having one's first baby,' said Olga Mikhailovna after a moment's thought. 'I keep feeling as though I shall not get through it, as though I shall die.'

'I fancied that, too, but here I am alive . . . One has all sorts of fancies.'

Varvara, who was just going to have her fifth, looked down a little on her mistress from the height of her experience and spoke in a rather didactic tone, and Olga Mikhailovna could not help feeling her authority; she would have liked to have talked of her fears, of the child, of her sensations, but she was afraid it might strike Varvara as naïve and trivial. And she waited in silence for Varvara to say something herself.

'Olya, we are going indoors,' Pyotr Dmitrich called from the raspberries.

Olga Mikhailovna liked being silent, waiting and watching Varvara. She would have been ready to stay like that till night without speaking or having any duty to perform. But she had to go. She had hardly left the cottage when Lyubochka, Nata and Vata came running to meet her. The sisters stopped short abruptly a couple of yards away; Lyubochka ran right up to her and flung herself on her neck.

'You dear, darling, precious,' she said, kissing her face and her neck. 'Let us go and have tea on the island!'

'On the island, on the island!' said the precisely similar Nata and Vata, both at once, without a smile.

'But it's going to rain, my dears.'

'It's not, it's not,' cried Lyubochka with a woebegone face. 'They've all agreed to go. Dear! darling!'

'They are all getting ready to have tea on the island,' said Pyotr Dmitrich, coming up. 'See to arranging things ... We will all go in the boats, and the samovars and all the rest of it must be sent in the carriage with the servants.'

He walked beside his wife and gave her his arm. Olga Mikhailovna had a desire to say something disagreeable to her husband, something biting, even about her dowry perhaps – the crueller the better, she felt. She thought a little, and said:

'Why is it Count Alexey Petrovich hasn't come? What a pity!'

'I am very glad he hasn't come,' said Pyotr Dmitrich, lying. 'I'm sick to death of that old lunatic.'

'But yet before dinner you were expecting him so eagerly!'

III

Half an hour later all the guests were crowding on the bank near the pile to which the boats were fastened. They were all talking and laughing, and were in such excitement and commotion that they could hardly get into the boats. Three boats were crammed with passengers, while two stood empty. The keys for unfastening these two boats had been some-

how mislaid, and messengers were continually running from
the river to the house to look for them. Some said Grigory
had the keys, others that the bailiff had them, while others
suggested sending for a blacksmith and breaking the pad-
locks. And all talked at once, interrupting and shouting one
another down. Pyotr Dmitrich paced impatiently to and fro
on the bank, shouting:

'What the devil's the meaning of it! The keys ought always to be lying in the hall window! Who has dared to take
them away? The bailiff can get a boat of his own if he wants
one!'

At last the keys were found. Then it appeared that two
oars were missing. Again there was a great hullabaloo.
Pyotr Dmitrich, who was weary of pacing about the bank,
jumped into a long, narrow boat hollowed out of the trunk
of a poplar, and, lurching from side to side and almost falling
into the water, pushed off from the bank. The other boats
followed him one after another, amid loud laughter and the
shrieks of the young ladies.

The white cloudy sky, the trees on the riverside, the boats
with the people in them, and the oars, were reflected in the
water as in a mirror; under the boats, far away below in the
bottomless depths, was a second sky with the birds flying
across it. The bank on which the house and gardens stood
was high, steep, and covered with trees; on the other, which
was sloping, stretched broad green water-meadows with
sheets of water glistening in them. The boats had floated a
hundred yards when, behind the mournfully drooping
willows on the sloping banks, huts and a herd of cows came
into sight; they began to hear songs, drunken shouts, and
the strains of a concertina.

Here and there on the river fishing-boats were scattered
about, setting their nets for the night. In one of these boats
was the festive party, playing on home-made violins and
violoncellos.

Olga Mikhailovna was sitting at the rudder; she was

smiling affably and talking a great deal to entertain her visitors, while she glanced stealthily at her husband. He was ahead of them all, standing up punting with one oar. The light sharp-nosed canoe, which all the guests called the 'death-trap' – while Pyotr Dmitrich, for some reason, called it Penderaklia – flew along quickly; it had a brisk, crafty expression, as though it hated its heavy occupant and was looking out for a favourable moment to glide away from under his feet. Olga Mikhailovna kept looking at her husband, and she loathed his good looks which attracted everyone, the back of his head, his attitude, his familiar manner with women; she hated all the women sitting in the boat with her, was jealous, and at the same time was trembling every minute in terror that the frail craft would upset and cause an accident.

'Take care, Pyotr!' she cried, while her heart fluttered with terror. 'Sit down! We believe in your courage without all that!'

She was worried, too, by the people who were in the boat with her. They were all ordinary good sort of people like thousands of others, but now each one of them struck her as exceptional and evil. In each one of them she saw nothing but falsity. 'That young man,' she thought, 'rowing, in gold-rimmed spectacles, with chestnut hair and a nice-looking beard: he is a mamma's darling, rich, and well fed, and always fortunate, and everyone considers him an honourable, free-thinking, advanced man. It's not a year since he left the university and came to live in the district, but he already talks of himself as "we active members of the Zemstvo". But in another year he will be bored like so many others and go off to Petersburg and, to justify running away, will tell everyone that the Zemstvos are good-for-nothing, and that he has been deceived in them. While from the other boat his young wife keeps her eyes fixed on him, and believes that he is "an active member of the Zemstvo", just as in a year she will believe that the Zemstvo is good-for-nothing. And that stout, carefully shaven gentleman in the straw hat with the broad ribbon, with an expensive cigar in his mouth: he is fond of saying, "It is time to put away dreams and set to work!" He has Yorkshire pigs, Butler's hives, rape-seed, pineapples, a dairy, a cheese factory, Italian book-keeping by double entry; but every summer he sells his timber and mortgages part of his land to spend the autumn with his mistress in the Crimea. And there's Uncle Nikolay Nikolaich, who has quarrelled with Pyotr Dmitrich, and yet for some reason does not go home.'

Olga Mikhailovna looked at the other boats, and there, too, she saw only uninteresting, queer creatures, affected or stupid people. She thought of all the people she knew in the district, and could not remember one person of whom one could say or think anything good. They all seemed to her mediocre, insipid, unintelligent, narrow, false, heartless; they all said what they did not think, and did what they did not want to. Dreariness and despair were stifling her; she longed to leave off smiling, to leap up and cry out. 'I am sick of you,' and then jump out and swim to the bank.

'I say, let's take Pyotr Dmitrich in tow!' someone shouted.

'In tow, in tow!' the others chimed in. 'Olga Mikhailovna, take your husband in tow.'

To take him in tow, Olga Mikhailovna, who was steering, had to seize the right moment and to catch hold of his boat by the chain at the beak. When she bent over to the chain Pyotr Dmitrich frowned and looked at her in alarm.

'I hope you won't catch cold,' he said.

'If you are uneasy about me and the child, why do you torment me?' thought Olga Mikhailovna.

Pyotr Dmitrich acknowledged himself vanquished, and, not caring to be towed, jumped from Penderaklia into the boat which was overfull already, and jumped so carelessly that the boat lurched violently, and everyone cried out in terror.

'He did that to please the ladies,' thought Olga Mikhailovna; 'he knows it's charming.' Her hands and feet began trembling, as she supposed, from boredom, vexation from the strain of smiling and the discomfort she felt all over her body. And, to conceal this trembling from her guests, she tried to talk more loudly, to laugh, to move.

'If I suddenly begin to cry,' she thought, 'I shall say I have toothache . . .'

But at last the boats reached the 'Island of Good Hope', as they called the peninsula formed by a bend in the river at an acute angle, covered with a copse of old birch trees, oaks, willows and poplars. The tables were already laid under the trees; the samovars were smoking, and Vassily and Grigory, in their swallow-tails and white knitted gloves, were already busy with the tea things. On the other bank, opposite the 'Island of Good Hope', there stood the carriages which had come with the provisions. The baskets and parcels of provisions were carried across to the island in a little boat like the Penderaklia. The footmen, the coachmen, and even the peasant who was sitting in the boat, had the solemn expression befitting a name-day such as one only sees in children and servants.

While Olga Mikhailovna was making the tea and pouring out the first glasses, the visitors were busy with the liqueurs and sweet things. Then there was the general commotion usual at picnics over drinking tea, very wearisome and exhausting for the hostess. Grigory and Vassily had hardly had time to take the glasses round before hands were being stretched out to Olga Mikhailovna with empty glasses. One asked for no sugar, another wanted it stronger, another weak, a fourth declined another glass. And all this Olga Mikhailovna had to remember, and then to call, 'Ivan Petrovich, is it without sugar for you?' or, 'Gentlemen, which of you wanted it weak?' But the guest who had asked for weak tea, or no sugar, had by now forgotten it, and, absorbed in agreeable conversation, took the first glass that came. Depressed-looking figures wandered like shadows at a little distance from the table, pretending to look for mushrooms in the grass, or reading the labels on the boxes – these were those for whom there were not glasses enough. 'Have you had tea?' Olga Mikhailovna kept asking, and the guest so addressed begged her not to trouble, and said, 'I will wait,' though it would have suited her better for the visitors not to wait but to make haste.

Some, absorbed in conversation, drank their tea slowly, keeping their glasses for half an hour; others, especially some who had drunk a good deal at dinner, would not leave the table, and kept on drinking glass after glass, so that Olga Mikhailovna scarcely had time to fill them. One jocular young man sipped his tea through a lump of sugar, and kept saying, 'Sinful man that I am, I love to indulge myself with the Chinese herb.' He kept asking with a heavy sigh: 'Another tiny dish of tea more, if you please.' He drank a great deal, nibbled his sugar, and thought it all very amusing and original, and imagined that he was doing a clever imitation of a Russian merchant. None of them understood that these trifles were agonizing to their hostess, and, indeed, it was hard to understand it, as Olga Mikhailovna went on all the time smiling affably and talking nonsense.

But she felt ill . . . She was irritated by the crowd of people, the laughter, the questions, the jocular young man, the footmen harassed and run off their legs, the children who hung round the table; she was irritated at Vata's being like Nata, at Kolya's being like Mitya, so that one could not tell which of them had had tea and which of them had not. She felt that her smile of forced affability was passing into an expression of anger, and she felt every minute as though she would burst into tears.

'Rain, my friends,' cried someone.

Everyone looked at the sky.

'Yes, it really is rain . . .' Pyotr Dmitrich assented, and wiped his cheek.

Only a few drops were falling from the sky – the real rain had not begun yet; but the company abandoned their tea and made haste to get off. At first they all wanted to drive home in the carriages, but changed their minds and made for the boats. On the pretext that she had to hasten home to give directions about the supper, Olga Mikhailovna asked to be excused for leaving the others, and went home in the carriage.

When she got into the carriage, she first of all let her face rest from smiling. With an angry face she drove through the village, and with an angry face acknowledged the bows of the peasants she met. When she got home, she went to her bedroom by the back way and lay down on her husband's bed.

'Merciful God!' she whispered. 'What is all this hard labour for? Why do all these people hustle each other here and pretend that they are enjoying themselves? Why do I smile and lie? I don't understand it.'

She heard steps and voices. The visitors had come back.

'Let them come,' thought Olga Mikhailovna; 'I shall lie a little longer.'

But a maid-servant came and said:

'Marya Grigorevna is going, Madam.'

Olga Mikhailovna jumped up, tidied her hair and hurried out of the room.

'Marya Grigorevna, what is the meaning of this?' she began in an injured voice, going to meet Marya Grigorevna. 'Why are you in such a hurry?'

'I can't help it, darling! I've stayed too long as it is; my children are expecting me home.'

'It's too bad of you! Why didn't you bring your children with you?'

'If you will let me, dear, I will bring them on some ordinary day, but today . . .'

'Oh, please do,' Olga Mikhailovna interrupted; 'I shall be delighted! Your children are so sweet! Kiss them all for me . . . But, really, I am offended with you! I don't understand why you are in such a hurry!'

'I really must, I really must ... Good-bye, dear. Take care of yourself. In your condition, you know ...'

And the ladies kissed each other. After seeing the departing guest to her carriage, Olga Mikhailovna went in to the ladies in the drawing-room. There the lamps were already lighted and the gentlemen were sitting down to cards.

IV

The party broke up after supper about a quarter past twelve. Seeing her visitors off, Olga Mikhailovna stood at the door and said:

'You really ought to take a shawl! It's turning a little chilly. Please God, you don't catch cold!'

'Don't trouble, Olga Mikhailovna,' the ladies answered as they got into the carriage. 'Well, good-bye. Mind now, we are expecting you; don't play us false!'

'Wo-o-o!' the coachman checked the horses.

'Ready, Denis! Good-bye, Olga Mikhailovna!'

'Kiss the children for me!'

The carriage started and immediately disappeared into the darkness. In the red circle of light cast by the lamp in the road, a fresh pair or trio of impatient horses, and the silhouette of a coachman with his hands held out stiffly before him, would come into view. Again there began kisses, reproaches, and entreaties to come again or to take a shawl. Pyotr Dmitrich kept running out and helping the ladies into their carriages.

'You go now by Efremovshchina,' he directed the coachman; 'it's nearer through Mankino, but the road is worse that way. You might have an upset ... Good-bye, my charmer. *Mille compliments* to your artist!'

'Good-bye, Olga Mikhailovna, darling! Go indoors, or you will catch cold! It's damp!'

'Wo-o-o! you rascal!'

'What horses have you got here?' Pyotr Dmitrich asked.

'They were bought from Khaidarov, in Lent,' answered the coachman.

'Capital horses . . .'

And Pyotr Dmitrich patted the trace horse on the haunch. 'Well, you can start! God give you good luck!'

The last visitor was gone at last; the red circle on the road quivered, moved aside, contracted and went out, as Vassily carried away the lamp from the entrance. On previous occasions when they had seen off their visitors, Pyotr Dmitrich and Olga Mikhailovna had begun dancing about the drawing-room, facing each other, clapping their hands and singing: 'They've gone! They've gone!' But now Olga Mikhailovna was not equal to that. She went to her bedroom, undressed and got into bed.

She fancied she would fall asleep at once and sleep soundly. Her legs and her shoulders ached painfully, her head was heavy from the strain of talking, and she was conscious, as before, of discomfort all over her body. Covering her head over, she lay still for three or four minutes, then peeped out from under the bedclothes at the lamp before the ikon, listened to the silence, and smiled.

'It's nice, it's nice,' she whispered, curling up her legs, which felt as if they had grown longer from so much walking 'Sleep, sleep . . .'

Her legs would not get into a comfortable position; she felt uneasy all over, and she turned on the other side. A big fly flew buzzing about the bedroom and thumped against the ceiling. She could hear, too, Grigory and Vassily stepping cautiously about the drawing-room, putting the chairs back in their places; it seemed to Olga Mikhailovna that she could not go to sleep, nor be comfortable till those sounds were hushed. And again she turned over on the other side impatiently.

She heard her husband's voice in the drawing-room. Someone must be staying the night, as Pyotr Dmitrich was addressing someone and speaking loudly:

'I don't say that Count Alexey Petrovich is an impostor. But he can't help seeming to be one, because all of you gentlemen attempt to see in him something different from what he really is. His craziness is looked upon as originality, his familiar manners as good-nature, and his complete absence of opinions as conservatism. Even granted that he is a conservative of the stamp of eighty-four, what after all is conservatism?'

Pyotr Dmitrich, angry with Count Alexey Petrovich, his visitors and himself, was relieving his heart. He abused both the count and his visitors, and in his vexation with himself was ready to speak out and to hold forth upon anything. After seeing his guest to his room, he walked up and down the drawing-room, walked through the dining-room, down the corridor, then into his study, then again went into the drawing-room, and came into the bedroom. Olga Mikhailovna was lying on her back, with the bedclothes only to her waist (by now she felt hot), and with an angry face, watched the fly that was thumping against the ceiling.

'Is someone staying the night?' she asked.

'Egorov.'

Pyotr Dmitrich undressed and got into his bed. Without speaking, he lighted a cigarette, and he, too, fell to watching the fly. There was an uneasy and forbidding look in his eyes. Olga Mikhailovna looked at his handsome profile for five minutes in silence. It seemed to her for some reason that if her husband were suddenly to turn facing her, and to say, 'Olya, I am unhappy,' she would cry or laugh, and she would be at ease. She fancied that her legs were aching and her body was uncomfortable all over because of the strain on her feelings.

'Pyotr, what are you thinking of?' she said.

'Oh, nothing . . .' her husband answered.

'You have taken to having secrets from me of late; that's not right.'

'Why is it not right?' answered Pyotr Dmitrich drily and

not at once. 'We all have our personal life, every one of us, and we are bound to have our secrets.'

'Personal life, our secrets ... that's all words! Understand you are wounding me!' said Olga Mikhailovna, sitting up in bed. 'If you have a load on your heart, why do you hide it from me? And why do you find it more suitable to open your heart to women who are nothing to you, instead of to your wife? I overheard your outpourings to Lyubochka by the beehouse today.'

'Well, I congratulate you. I am glad you did overhear it.'

This meant 'Leave me alone and let me think.' Olga Mikhailovna was indignant. Vexation, hatred, and wrath, which had been accumulating within her during the whole day, suddenly boiled over; she wanted at once to speak out, to hurt her husband without putting it off till tomorrow, to wound him, to punish him ... Making an effort to control herself and not to scream, she said:

'Let me tell you, then, that it's all loathsome, loathsome, loathsome! I've been hating you all day; you see what you've done.'

Pyotr Dmitrich, too, got up and sat on the bed.

'It's loathsome, loathsome, loathsome,' Olga Mikhailovna went on, beginning to tremble all over. 'There's no need to congratulate me; you had better congratulate yourself! It's a shame, a disgrace. You have wrapped yourself in lies till you are ashamed to be alone in the room with your wife! You are a deceitful man! I see through you and understand every step you take!'

'Olya, I wish you would please warn me when you are out of humour. Then I will sleep in the study.'

Saying this, Pyotr Dmitrich picked up his pillow and walked out of the bedroom. Olga Mikhailovna had not foreseen this. For some minutes she remained silent with her mouth open, trembling all over and looking at the door by which her husband had gone out, and trying to understand what it meant. Was this one of the devices to which deceitful people have recourse when they are in the wrong, or was it a deliberate insult aimed at her pride? How was she to take it? Olga Mikhailovna remembered her cousin, a lively young officer, who often used to tell her, laughing, that when 'his spouse nagged at him' at night, he usually picked up his pillow and went whistling to spend the night in his study, leaving his wife in a foolish and ridiculous position. This officer was married to a rich, capricious and foolish woman whom he did not respect but simply put up with.

Olga Mikhailovna jumped out of bed. To her mind there was only one thing left for her to do now; to dress with all possible haste and to leave the house for ever. The house was her own, but so much the worse for Pyotr Dmitrich. Without pausing to consider whether this was necessary or not, she went quickly to the study to inform her husband of her intention ('Feminine logic!' flashed through her mind), and to say something wounding and sarcastic at parting . . .

Pyotr Dmitrich was lying on the sofa and pretending to read a newspaper. There was a candle burning on a chair near him. His face could not be seen behind the newspaper.

'Be so kind as to tell me what this means? I am asking you.'

'Be so kind . . .' Pyotr Dmitrich mimicked her, not showing his face. 'It's sickening, Olga! Upon my honour, I am exhausted and not up to it . . . Let us do our quarrelling tomorrow.'

'No, I understand you perfectly!' Olga Mikhailovna went on. 'You hate me! Yes, yes! You hate me because I am richer than you! You will never forgive me for that, and will always be lying to me!' ('Feminine logic!' flashed through her mind again.) 'You are laughing at me now . . . I am convinced, in fact, that you only married me in order to have property qualifications and those wretched horses . . . Oh, I am miserable!'

Pyotr Dmitrich dropped the newspaper and got up. The unexpected insult overwhelmed him. With a childishly helpless smile he looked desperately at his wife and, holding out his hands to her as though to ward off blows, he said imploringly:

'Olya!'

And, expecting her to say something else awful, he leaned back in his chair, and his huge figure seemed as helplessly childish as his smile.

'Olya, how could you say it?' he whispered.

Olga Mikhailovna came to herself. She was suddenly aware of her passionate love for this man, remembered that he was her husband, Pyotr Dmitrich, without whom she could not live for a day, and who loved her passionately, too. She burst into loud sobs that sounded strange and unlike her, and ran back to her bedroom.

She fell on the bed, and short hysterical sobs, choking her and making her arms and legs twitch, filled the bedroom. Remembering there was a visitor sleeping three or four rooms away, she buried her head under the pillow to stifle her sobs, but the pillow rolled on to the floor, and she almost fell on the floor herself when she stooped to pick it up. She pulled the quilt up to her face, but her hands would not obey her, but tore convulsively at everything she clutched.

She thought that everything was lost, that the falsehood she had told to wound her husband had shattered her life into fragments. Her husband would not forgive her. The insult she had hurled at him was not one that could be effaced by any caresses, by any vows ... How could she convince her husband that she did not believe what she had said?

'It's all over, it's all over!' she cried, not noticing that the pillow had slipped on to the floor again. 'For God's sake, for God's sake!'

Probably roused by her cries, the guest and the servants were now awake; next day all the neighbourhood would know that she had been in hysterics and would blame Pyotr Dmitrich. She made an effort to restrain herself, but her sobs grew louder and louder every minute.

'For God's sake,' she cried in a voice not like her own, and not knowing why she cried it. 'For God's sake!'

She felt as though the bed were heaving under her and her feet were entangled in the bedclothes. Pyotr Dmitrich, in his dressing-gown, with a candle in his hand, came into the bedroom.

'Olya, hush!' he said.

She raised herself and, kneeling up in bed, screwing up her eyes at the light, articulated through her sobs:

'Understand ... understand! ...'

She wanted to tell him that she was tired to death by the party, by his falsity, by her own falsity, that it had all worked together, but she could only articulate:

'Understand ... understand!'

'Come, drink!' he said, handing her some water.

She took the glass obediently and began drinking, but the water splashed over and was spilt on her arms, her throat and knees.

'I must look horribly unseemly,' she thought.

Pyotr Dmitrich put her back in bed without a word, and covered her with the quilt, then he took the candle and went out.

'For God's sake!' Olga Mikhailovna cried again. 'Pyotr, understand, understand!'

Suddenly something gripped her in the lower part of her body and back with such violence that her wailing was cut short, and she bit the pillow from the pain. But the pain let her go again at once, and she began sobbing again.

The maid came in and, arranging the quilt over her, asked in alarm:

'Mistress, darling, what is the matter?'

'Go out of the room,' said Pyotr Dmitrich sternly, going up to the bed.

'Understand ... understand! ...' Olga Mikhailovna began.

'Olga, I entreat you, calm yourself,' he said. 'I did not

mean to hurt you. I would not have gone out of the room if I had known it would have hurt you so much; I simply felt depressed. I tell you, on my honour . . .'

'Understand! . . . You were lying, I was lying . . .'

'I understand . . . Come, come, that's enough! I understand,' said Pyotr Dmitrich tenderly, sitting down on her bed. 'You said that in anger; I quite understand. I swear to God I love you beyond anything on earth, and when I married you I never once thought of your being rich. I loved you immensely, and that's all . . . I assure you. I have never been in want of money or felt the value of it, and so I cannot feel the difference between your fortune and mine. It always seemed to me we were equally well off. And that I have been deceitful in little things, that . . . of course, is true. My life has hitherto been arranged in such a frivolous way that it has somehow been impossible to get on without paltry lying. It weighs on me, too, now . . . Let us leave off talking about it, for goodness sake!'

Olga Mikhailovna again felt an acute pain, and clutched her husband by the sleeve.

'I am in pain, in pain, in pain . . .' she said rapidly. 'Oh, what pain!'

'Damnation take those visitors!' muttered Pyotr Dmitrich getting up. 'You ought not to have gone to the island to-day!' he cried. 'What an idiot I was not to prevent you! Oh, my God!'

He scratched his head in vexation, and, with a wave of his hand, walked out of the room.

Then he came into the room several times, sat down on the bed beside her, and talked a great deal, sometimes tenderly, sometimes angrily, but she hardly heard him. Her sobs were continually interrupted by fearful attacks of pain, and each time the pain was more acute and prolonged. At first she held her breath and bit the pillow during the pain, but then she began screaming on an unseemly piercing note. Once, seeing her husband near her, she remembered that she had insulted him and, without pausing to think whether it were really Pyotr Dmitrich or whether she were in delirium, clutched his hand in both hers and began kissing it.

'You were lying, I was lying . . .' she began justifying herself. 'Understand, understand . . . They have exhausted me, driven me out of all patience.'

'Olya, we are not alone,' said Pyotr Dmitrich.

Olga Mikhailovna raised her head and saw Varvara, who was kneeling by the chest of drawers and pulling out the bottom drawer. The top drawers were already open. Then Varvara got up, red from the strained position, and with a cold, solemn face began trying to unlock a box.

'Marya, I can't unlock it!' she said in a whisper. 'You unlock it, won't you?'

Marya, the maid, was digging a candle end out of the candlestick with a pair of scissors, so as to put in a new candle; she went up to Varvara and helped her to unlock the box.

'There should be nothing locked . . .' whispered Varvara. 'Unlock this basket, too, my good girl. Master,' she said, 'you should send to Father Mikhail to unlock the holy gates! You must!'

'Do what you like,' said Pyotr Dmitrich, breathing hard, 'only, for God's sake, make haste and fetch the doctor or the midwife! Has Vassily gone? Send someone else. Send your husband!'

'It's the birth,' Olga Mikhailovna thought. 'Varvara,' she moaned, 'but he won't be born alive!'

'It's all right, it's all right, Mistress,' whispered Varvara. 'Please God, he will be alive! he will be alive!'

When Olga Mikhailovna came to herself again after a pain she was no longer sobbing nor tossing from side to side, but moaning. She could not refrain from moaning even in the intervals between the pains. The candles were still burning, but the morning light was coming through the blinds. It was probably about five o'clock in the morning.

At the round table there was sitting some unknown woman with a very discreet air, wearing a white apron. From her whole appearance it was evident she had been sitting there a long time. Olga Mikhailovna guessed that she was the midwife.

'Will it soon be over?' she asked, and in her voice she heard a peculiar and unfamiliar note which had never been there before. 'I must be dying in childbirth,' she thought.

Pyotr Dmitrich came cautiously into the bedroom, dressed for the day, and stood at the window with his back to his wife. He lifted the blind and looked out of the window.

'What rain!' he said.

'What time is it?' asked Olga Mikhailovna, in order to hear the unfamiliar note in her voice again.

'A quarter to six,' answered the midwife.

'And what if I really am dying?' thought Olga Mikhailovna, looking at her husband's head and the window-panes on which the rain was beating. 'How will he live without me? With whom will he have tea and dinner, talk in the evenings, sleep?'

And he seemed to her like a forlorn child; she felt sorry for him and wanted to say something nice, caressing and consolatory. She remembered how in the spring he had meant to buy himself some harriers, and she, thinking it a cruel and dangerous sport, had prevented him from doing it.

'Pyotr, buy yourself harriers,' she moaned.

He dropped the blind and went up to the bed, and would have said something; but at that moment the pain came back, and Olga Mikhailovna uttered an unseemly, piercing scream.

The pain and the constant screaming and moaning stupefied her. She heard, saw, and sometimes spoke, but hardly understood anything, and was only conscious that she was in pain or was just going to be in pain. It seemed to her that the name-day party had been long, long ago – not yesterday, but a year ago perhaps; and that her new life of agony had lasted longer than her childhood, her schooldays, her time at the university and her marriage, and would go on for a long, long time, endlessly. She saw them bring tea to the midwife, and summon her at midday to lunch and afterwards to dinner; she saw Pyotr Dmitrich grow used to coming in, standing for long intervals by the window, and going out again; saw strange men, the maid, Varvara, come in as though they were at home . . . Varvara said nothing but, 'He will, he will,' and was angry when anyone closed the drawers and the chest. Olga Mikhailovna saw the light change in the room and in the windows: at one time it was twilight, then thick like fog, then bright daylight as it had been at dinner-time the day before, then again twilight . . . and each of these changes lasted as long as her childhood, her schooldays, her life at the university . . .

In the evening two doctors – one bony, bald, with a big red beard; the other with a swarthy Jewish face and cheap spectacles – performed some sort of operation on Olga Mikhailovna. To these unknown men touching her body she felt utterly indifferent. By now she had no feeling of shame, no will, and anyone might do what he would with her. If anyone had rushed at her with a knife, or had insulted Pyotr Dmitrich, or had robbed her of her right to the little creature, she would not have said a word.

They gave her chloroform during the operation. When she came to again, the pain was still there and insufferable. It was night. And Olga Mikhailovna remembered that there had been just such a night with the stillness, the lamp, with the midwife sitting motionless by the bed, with the drawers of the chest pulled out, with Pyotr Dmitrich standing by the window, but some time very, very long ago . . .

v

'I am not dead . . .' thought Olga Mikhailovna when she began to understand her surroundings again, and when the pain was over.

A bright summer day looked in at the widely open windows; in the garden below the windows, the sparrows and the magpies never ceased chattering for one instant.

The drawers were shut now, her husband's bed had been made. There was no sign of the midwife or of the maid, or of Varvara in the room, only Pyotr Dmitrich was standing, as before, motionless by the window looking into the garden. There was no sound of a child's crying, no one was congratulating her or rejoicing, it was evident that the little creature had not been born alive.

'Pyotr!'

Olga Mikhailovna called to her husband.

Pyotr Dmitrich looked round. It seemed as though a long time must have passed since the last guest had departed and Olga Mikhailovna had insulted her husband, for Pyotr Dmitrich was perceptibly thinner and hollow-eyed.

'What is it?' he asked, coming up to the bed.

He looked away, moved his lips and smiled with childlike helplessness.

'Is it all over?' asked Olga Mikhailovna.

Pyotr Dmitrich tried to make some answer, but his lip quivered and his mouth worked like a toothless old man's, like Uncle Nikolay Nikolaich's.

'Olya,' he said, wringing his hands; big tears suddenly dropping from his eyes. 'Olya, I don't care about your property qualifications, nor the circuit courts . . .' (he gave a sob) 'nor particular views, nor those visitors, nor your fortune . . . I don't care about anything! Why didn't we take care of our child? Oh, it's no good talking!'

With a despairing gesture he went out of the bedroom.

But nothing mattered to Olga Mikhailovna now, there was a mistiness in her brain from the chloroform, an emptiness in her soul . . . The dull indifference to life which had overcome her when the two doctors were performing the operation still had possession of her.

GORKY

MAXIM GORKY (the Russian word '*gorky*' means 'bitter') was the pen-name of Alexey Peshkov. Gorky, who had no formal education and as a young man spent several years wandering through Russia, achieved sudden literary fame in the early 1890s with stories about the lives of the poor. In 1917 he welcomed the Bolshevik Revolution but then emigrated to spend the years 1921 to 1928 abroad; when he returned home at the end of that period he became a highly revered and influential Soviet literary figure. Gorky produced short stories, novels and plays, but his most successful works are an autobiographical trilogy and his superb reminiscences of Tolstoy, both of which reflect the writer's talent for robust portraiture combined with a sensitive evocation of atmosphere. The same qualities are manifest in 'Twenty-six Men and a Girl', a short story of 1899 which is Gorky's fictional masterpiece.

TWENTY-SIX MEN AND A GIRL
A NARRATIVE POEM

Translated by Roger Cockrell

THERE were twenty-six of us – twenty-six living machines – incarcerated from morning to night in a damp basement-room, making dough for pretzels and cracknels. The windows of this room gave out on to a large pit sunk into the ground and lined with bricks which had grown green from mould; the window frames were barred on the outside with close-meshed metal grilles and the sunlight was unable to penetrate the flour-covered glass. Our boss had barred off the windows to prevent us giving any of his bread to the beggars and those comrades of ours who were unemployed and starving. He called us crooks and gave us putrid offal instead of meat for dinner.

Life in this stone box with its low, heavy ceiling, covered in cobwebs and blackened from smoke, was stifling and cramped. Within these thick, dirt-stained walls, rotten with mildew, we led a wretched and miserable existence. We got up at five in the morning, still tired, and by six o'clock, dulled and indifferent, we were sitting at the table making pretzels from dough which others had been preparing while we were asleep. And the whole day, until ten in the evening, some of us sat at the table untwisting the soft dough and swaying backwards and forwards to prevent stiffness, while the others mixed the flour and water. All day long the boiling water in the cauldron where the pretzels were cooked bubbled away to itself in sorrowful meditation, and the baker's shovel rasped in hasty anger against the bottom of the oven, as he tossed the slippery pieces of boiled dough on to the hot bricks. From morning till night the wood burnt in one section of the oven, the red flames casting a flickering shadow onto the wall of the bakery, as if in silent mockery of its inhabitants. The huge oven was like the misshapen head of some mythical monster, seemingly rising out of the floor and opening its huge fiery jaws, exhaling flames and viewing our endless toil through the two sunken air-vents in its forehead. These two deep hollows were like eyes – a monster's pitiless, dispassionate eyes with a persistently veiled expression, as if they had grown tired of looking at slaves, despising them with the cold scorn of wisdom and expecting nothing human from them.

Day in, day out, covered with flour dust and the dirt which we brought in on our boots, in the fetid, suffocating atmosphere we untwisted dough and made pretzels, moistening them with the sweat of our brows, and we hated our work with a deep loathing. We never ate anything that we ourselves had made, preferring black bread to the pretzels. Sitting at a long table opposite each other – nine against nine – we worked mechanically away with our fingers and hands for hours on end, and we had grown so used to our work that we no longer even watched what we were doing. We knew each other's faces so well that every wrinkle was familiar. There was nothing to talk about and we had become accustomed to the silence, broken only by the sound of cursing, for you can always find a reason to curse someone, especially if he is a mate. But this didn't happen very often; how can someone be to blame if he's half-dead, turned to stone, his feelings crushed by the burden of work? But silence is painful and terrifying only for those who have already said everything and who have nothing left to say; but to those who have not yet begun to talk, silence comes easily and simply.

Sometimes, however, we would sing, and our singing would generally start in the following way: as we sat there working, one of us would suddenly sigh deeply like a weary horse, and start quietly to sing one of those long-drawn-out songs whose plaintively caressing melody always has the effect of lightening the singer's heart. At first we would listen in silence to his solitary voice, and his song would melt and die away in the heavy basement ceiling, like the flickering of a bonfire in the steppes on a raw autumn evening when the grey sky hangs over the earth like a leaden roof. Then someone else would take up the song and the two voices would hover wistfully and gently in the suffocating air of our crowded dungeon. Suddenly several voices would join in all at once and the song would roar and foam like an ocean wave, increasing in volume until it seemed that it would tear asunder the damp, thick walls of our stone prison.

All twenty-six of us would sing and the room would be filled with the sound of loud, confident voices. The room was too small to contain such a sound: it crashed against the stone walls, its cries and groans evoking a dull, throbbing anguish in our hearts, and re-opening old wounds. The singers would sigh, deeply and heavily. Every so often someone would abruptly stop singing and sit for a long time listening to the rest and then his voice would once more merge into the general wave of sound. Some would sing with their eyes closed, interspersing their singing with loud, anguished exclamations, imagining perhaps this broad and dense wave of sound to be a sunlit road leading into the distance, a wide road along which they were walking . . .

And all the time the stove crackled, the baker's shovel rasped against the bricks, the water bubbled in the boiler and the reflection of the fire played on the wall in silent mockery . . . and we would use the words of the song to express our dulled feeling of despair, the overbearing anguish of living people who have been deprived of the sun, the anguish of slaves. Thus the twenty-six of us lived, in the basement of a large stone house, and our lives were so oppressed that it seemed as if we were carrying all three storeys of this house on our shoulders.

But there was something else that brought joy into our lives, apart from the singing, something that we had come to love and look forward to and which perhaps took the place of the sun in our hearts. On the second floor of the house there was a workshop where gold-lined silk threads were made. Here, among the girls who worked there, lived a sixteen-year-old girl who did the cleaning and tidying, called Tanya. Every morning a small pink face with laughing blue eyes would press up against the little window let into the door of our room and a ringing, affectionate voice would call out:

'Hey, convicts, let's have the pretzels then!'

At the sound of this clear voice we would all turn round and look happily and good-naturedly at the innocent face of the young girl, smiling so sweetly at us. We used to love seeing her nose, pressed up against the glass and her small, white teeth showing between her pink, smiling lips. We would rush to open the door for her, jostling each other, and she would come in looking so sweet and happy, holding up her apron, and stand in front of us, her head a little to one side and smiling all the while. Her long, thick, chestnut-coloured hair fell in a plait over her shoulder and lay on her breast. Ugly, dirty, ignorant, we would stand there and look up at her – the doorway was four steps higher than the floor of our room – we would look at her, our heads turned upwards, saying good morning to her and using words which came to us only when we talked to her. Our voices became more gentle, our jokes less harsh. We were quite different when she was with us. The baker would take a shovelful of newly baked, especially crunchy pretzels and skilfully toss them into Tanya's apron.

'Watch out for the boss!' we would warn her. She would give a sly little laugh and, bidding us good-bye, would vanish as quickly as a mouse.

And that was all . . . But long after she had gone, we would talk happily about her amongst ourselves, saying the same things as the day before and the day before that, because both she and we, and everything around us, were just the same as they had always been. Life for those whose circumstances never change is agonizing and very difficult: the longer they live, the more agonizing such circumstances become, if their spirits are not broken altogether. When we spoke about women, the coarse and indecent expressions we used would sometimes revolt even us; the women we knew, of course, perhaps deserved no better. But we never spoke in this way about Tanya and not only did we never touch her, but we never made any suggestive remarks in her presence. Perhaps this may have been because she never stayed with us for long: she would appear fleetingly before our eyes like a falling star and then disappear. Or perhaps it was because she was small and very beautiful and anything beautiful always commands the respect of even uncultured people. And also, even although our forced labour had reduced us to the level of beasts of the field, we nonetheless were still human beings and, like all human beings, we were unable to live without worshipping at least something. We had nobody who was better than she was, nobody, apart from her, who paid any attention to us living down in the basement, although the house was inhabited by scores of people. And finally, probably most importantly, we all considered her to be ours, someone who existed only because of our pretzels; we considered it our duty to provide her with pretzels hot from the oven, and this became for us an act of daily sacrifice to our idol, an almost sacred ritual which bound us more closely to her with each passing day. Apart from the pretzels we would also give Tanya a lot of advice, telling her to dress more warmly, not to run down the stairs too fast or to carry bundles of wood which were too heavy for her. She would listen to our advice with a smile and laughed in reply, but she never obeyed us and we were not in the least offended; we wanted only to show that we cared about her.

Often she would ask us to do something for her, such as to open the heavy door into the cellar for her, or to chop some wood. We would do these things for her, and anything else she wanted, eagerly and with a sense even of pride.

But when one day one of us asked her to darn his shirt, the only one he had, she snorted scornfully, saying:

'I'm not doing that! Whatever next!'

We burst out laughing at the naïve fellow and never asked her to do anything for us again. We loved her, and that's all there is to be said. People always need somebody to love, even though sometimes such a love can oppress, sully or poison a fellow human being's life, for they can love someone without respecting him. We loved Tanya, we had to love her, because there was no one else to love.

Sometimes one of us would suddenly begin to ask:

'What do we want to pay the girl so much attention for? What's so special about her? We fuss over her too much!'

But anybody who took it into his head to say such things we cut quickly and sharply down to size, for we needed an object for our love. We had found something, which for each of us had to remain for ever sacred, and anybody who denied us this was our enemy. Perhaps we loved something that was not truly good, but there were after all twenty-six of us and so we always wanted to see that the rest of us held sacred what was most precious to each of our hearts.

Our love is no less oppressive than hatred, and this is perhaps precisely why some proud souls among us maintain that our hatred is more flattering than love . . . But, if that is so, why do they not run away from us?

Apart from the pretzel bakehouse our boss also owned an ordinary bakery. It was situated in the same house, separated from our dungeon only by a wall; but the bakers there, of which there were four, kept apart from us, considering their work purer than ours and therefore considering themselves better than us. They never visited us in our room and would laugh disdainfully at us whenever they met us outside. Neither would we go into their room: the boss had forbidden us to do so in case we should start stealing the buns. We had no love for those bakers because we envied them: their work was easier than ours, they were paid better, fed better, their room was spacious and light and we found them all repulsively clean and healthy. We all had yellowish-grey faces, three of us had syphilis, some had skin disease, and one was completely crippled with rheumatism. At holidays and in their free time the bakers would dress up in jackets and squeaky boots, a couple of them owned accordions, and they would all go for a walk in the municipal park, whereas we wore filthy rags, with down-at-heel shoes or bast-sandals on our feet, and the police would not allow us in the park – how then could we like them?

One day we learnt that one of them had gone on the bottle, for which the boss had sacked him and taken on someone else – a soldier who went around in a satin waist-coat with a watch on a gold chain. We were very anxious to catch sight of this splendid fellow and we started to take turns to run out into the yard in the hope of seeing him.

But he came to our room himself. Kicking the door open, he stood in the doorway, saying with a smile:

'God bless you! Greetings, lads!'

The frosty air, rushing into the room in thick, billowing clouds, swirled about his feet while he stood there in the doorway looking down at us, his large, yellow teeth gleaming under his fair, smartly twirled moustache. His waistcoat was indeed something out of the ordinary – dark blue, embroidered with flowers, it seemed to shine all over. Its buttons were of little red stones, and there was a watch-chain too . . .

He was handsome, this soldier, tall, healthy-looking with ruddy cheeks and a friendly cheerful expression in his large, clear eyes. On his head he wore a white starched cap and from under his spotlessly clean apron peeped the pointed toes of a pair of fashionable, highly polished boots. Our baker politely asked him to close the door; he did so unhurriedly and started to question us about the boss. Interrupting each other, we informed him that our boss was a cunning rogue, a crook, a scoundrel and a tyrant – and anything else that could and should have been said about him, but which is impossible to repeat here. The soldier listened to us, twirling his moustache, and looking at us with a friendly, open expression.

'You've got a lot of girls here,' he suddenly said.

Some of us laughed deferentially, others put on honeyed expressions and someone told him that there were nine girls altogether.

'Do you make use of them?' the soldier asked with a wink.

Once again we laughed, but this time rather quietly and sheepishly. Many of us would like to have shown the soldier that we too shared his devil-may-care attitude, but not one of us was able to do so. Someone confessed as much:

'That's not really our line . . .' he said.

'Hm, yes, I see: it can't be easy for you!' said the soldier confidently, examining us carefully. 'You're a bit . . . well . . . I mean, you haven't got the right manner or look, as it were. And women like the way a man looks, above all! They like a man with a real body, with everything in its place. And they respect strength, too, men with arms like this . . .!'

The soldier drew his right hand out of his pocket and showed us his bare arm, with his shirt-sleeve rolled up to the elbow. It was a white, strong arm, covered in glistening, golden hair.

'Legs, chest – everything should be firm and strong. And then again, a man should be well dressed, as the fashion demands. Women go for me in a big way. I don't have to egg them on at all; I have them hanging on my neck, five at a time, of their own accord.'

He sat down on a bag of flour where he stayed for a long

time, telling us how much the women loved him and how royally he treated them. Then he left and when the door had creaked shut behind him we remained silent for a long while thinking about him and what he had told us. And then we all suddenly began to talk, and it became clear at once that he had made a good impression on all of us. Such an unassuming, splendid fellow – he had simply come in, sat down and started talking. Nobody came in to see us, nobody talked with us in such a friendly way. And so we continued to talk about him and discuss his future exploits with the sewing girls. Whenever these girls met us in the yard they would either haughtily purse their lips and deliberately avoid us or walk directly at us as if we were not there at all. But we always continued to admire them, whether we saw them in the yard or walking past our windows, dressed, in winter, in their best hats and fur coats and, in summer, in flowery hats and carrying gaily coloured parasols. And yet, amongst ourselves, we always referred to these girls in terms which, had they heard us, would have infuriated them with a sense of shame and outrage.

'Let's hope he doesn't get his hands on our Tanya!' the baker suddenly said anxiously.

We all fell silent, struck by these words. We had somehow forgotten about Tanya: it was as if the soldier's well-set, handsome figure had quite driven her out of our minds. Then a noisy argument developed, some of us saying that Tanya would never allow it to happen, others that she would not be able to resist the soldier's advances, and still others maintaining that they would break the soldier's ribs if he began to force his attentions on her. In the end we all decided to watch both of them and to warn Tanya to be wary of him. On this note the argument ended.

About a month passed; the soldier baked his rolls, went about with the sewing girls and frequently dropped in to see us, but said nothing about any conquests, simply twirling his moustache and smacking his lips.

Each morning Tanya came for her pretzels, as happy, sweet and kind to us as ever. We tried to start talking to her about the soldier, but she called him a 'goggle-eyed calf' and other such funny nicknames, which set our minds at rest. We were proud of our Tanya when we saw the other girls crowding round the soldier. Her attitude towards him lifted all our hearts somehow, and, as if guided by this attitude, we ourselves began to adopt a rather disparaging approach to him. But we loved her all the more and greeted her every morning even more happily and good-naturedly than before.

But one day the soldier came to see us somewhat the worse for drink. He sat down and began to laugh, and when we asked him what was so funny he said:

'A couple of them have been fighting over me – Lida and Grushka. You should have seen them clawing at each other! Ha, ha! One got the other by the hair, threw her down on the floor of the passage and sat on her! Ha, ha, ha! They scratched and tore at each other's faces ... what a laugh! Why can't women fight fairly, without scratching each other, eh?'

He sat there on the bench, radiating health, freshness and happiness, and roaring with laughter. We were silent. This time he made an unpleasant impression on us.

'I don't half have luck with the girls, eh? What a laugh! One wink and they're ready, by God!'

He raised his white hands glistening with hair and then slapped them down on his knees. Then he looked at us with an expression of surprised pleasure on his face as if he were genuinely puzzled at his own success with women. His plump, red face gleamed with happiness and self-satisfaction and all the time he smacked his lips in enjoyment.

Suddenly our baker thrust his shovel noisily and angrily along the bottom of the oven and remarked ironically:

'It doesn't take very much strength to chop down a

tiny fir tree, but just try chopping down a full-grown pine.'
'What do you mean? Are you talking to me?' asked the
soldier.
'Yes, I am . . .'
'What about me?'
'It's nothing . . . just a slip of the tongue.'
'Hey, no, hold on! What are you talking about? What
pine?'

Our baker did not reply but just went on shovelling away,
tossing the half-cooked pretzels into the stove, fishing out
the ones that were done and tossing them noisily onto the
floor where the young lads threaded them on to bast strings.
He seemed to have forgotten about the soldier and what he
had been saying to him. But the soldier suddenly became
very agitated. He stood up and went to the oven, risking a
collision with the end of the shovel, which was flashing
feverishly through the air.

'Now tell me who she is. You've offended me, insulted
me with what you've just said. I could get any one of them I
wanted to!'

It was true; he did seem genuinely put out. It seemed that
it was only from his prowess as a seducer of women that he
derived his self-respect; this was perhaps the only vital
quality he possessed and without it he could not consider
himself a living person.

For there are people whose sickness of mind or body is the
most precious trait they possess. They spend their whole
lives nurturing it and live only for it. They suffer terribly
because of it and complain about it to other people and so
draw attention to themselves. And in this way they elicit
other people's sympathy but, apart from this, they have
nothing. If you were to deprive them of this illness by curing
it, they would be unhappy because they would have lost
their one resource in life and would be left quite empty. A
man's life can sometimes become so wretched that he can be

driven against his will to cherish his particular vice and to
live by it alone; it could be said, too, that it is often boredom
which turns people to depravity.

Anyway the soldier took umbrage, went up to our baker
and started shouting at him.

'You just tell me who you mean?'

'You want me to tell you?' said the baker, suddenly turning to face him.

'Well?'

'You know Tanya?'

'Well?'

'Well, that's the one! Just try her . . .'

'Me?'

'Yes, you!'

'Tanya! Pah, that's nothing!'

'We'll see!'

'You'll see, all right! Ha!'

'She'll . . .'

'Give me a month!'

'You're just a windbag, soldier!'

'A fortnight! I'll show you! Tanya, you say? Pah!'

'Go on, get out. You're in my way!'

'A fortnight, that's all! You . . .'

'Get out, I say!'

And our baker, in a fit of fury, suddenly started brandishing his shovel. The soldier stepped back in astonishment,
looked at us for a moment in silence, quietly and menacingly
said, 'Right, then!' and left the room.

During all this time we had stayed silent, engrossed in the
argument. But when the soldier had gone there was an
outburst of noise and animated conversation.

'You shouldn't have done that, Pavel!' someone shouted
at the baker.

'You get on with your work!' the baker answered
savagely.

We sensed that the soldier had been deeply wounded and

that danger threatened Tanya, and yet at the same time we were all seized by a burning and pleasurable feeling of curiosity: what would happen? Would she be able to resist him? And almost everyone shouted with certainty:

'Our Tanya? She'll hold out! You can't get her just like that!'

We had a terrible longing to test the strength of our idol; we repeatedly assured ourselves that our idol would stand firm and emerge the victor from this encounter. And, finally, we began to feel that we had not incited the soldier enough, that he would forget about the argument and that we should wound his pride properly. From that day onwards our way of life changed into something we had never experienced before. We became especially tense and nervous, argued amongst ourselves for days on end, gaining, as it were, in intelligence and talking better and at greater length. It seemed to us that we were somehow gambling with the devil and that our stake was Tanya. And when we learnt from the bakers next door that the soldier had begun to 'go after our Tanya' we experienced a sort of delighted terror and we became so fascinated by it all that we did not even notice when our boss, taking advantage of our state, added an extra 500 pounds of dough to our day's quota. Our work, it seemed, no longer even tired us. Tanya's name was constantly on our lips, and we used to wait for her each morning with particular impatience. Sometimes we imagined that she would come, and that it wouldn't be the girl we knew, but a different Tanya.

However, we said nothing to her about the argument we had had. We put no questions to her and treated her as well and as affectionately as ever. But now our attitude contained a hint of something new, something which we had not felt before towards her, and this was a sharp curiosity, as sharp and as cold as a steel knife.

'The two weeks are up today, mates!' the baker announced one morning, as he set to work.

We were well aware of this, without being reminded, but a thrill ran through us nonetheless.

'Look at her, when she comes,' said the baker. 'She'll be here in a minute.'

'Yes, but we won't know just by looking at her, surely,' someone exclaimed regretfully.

And once again a noisy, lively argument flared up among us. Today, at last, we would find out just how pure and chaste the vessel was into which we had poured all that was good in us. It was that morning for the first time we suddenly realized that we were indeed playing for high stakes and that this test of our idol's purity might destroy it in our eyes. Throughout the two weeks we had heard that the soldier had been persistently and relentlessly chasing Tanya, but why then had one of us not asked her what she thought of him? And she had continued coming to us punctually each morning for her pretzels and had been just the same as ever.

That morning, too, we soon heard her voice:

'Hey, convicts! Here I am!'

We rushed to let her in, and when she came into the room met her in unaccustomed silence. Our eyes fixed on her, we did not know what to say to her or what to ask her, but just stood before her in a dark, silent mass. She was clearly astonished by this unusual greeting and, as we watched, we suddenly saw her face grow pale and agitated. She started fidgeting and then asked in a subdued voice:

'What's the matter with you all?'

'What about you?' the baker snapped morosely, not taking his eyes off her.

'Me? What do you mean?'

'Ah, forget it . . .'

'Well, come on, be quick, let's have the pretzels.'

Never before had she tried to hasten us.

'What's the hurry?' asked the baker, standing quite motionless, his eyes still fixed on her.

She suddenly turned and disappeared through the door.

The baker took up his shovel and, turning to the oven, said calmly:

'Well, that's it, then. That soldier, the bastard!'

Jostling each other like a flock of sheep, we went to the table, silently sat down and apathetically started working. Soon one of us said:

'Maybe, after all, she didn't . . .'

'Tell us another one!' shouted the baker.

We all knew that he was a clever man, cleverer than the rest of us. And we all took this response as an indication of his certainty that the soldier had won . . . We felt an uneasy sadness.

The soldier came at twelve o'clock when we were eating. As always he had a clean, smart appearance and, as always, he looked us straight in the eyes. But we were too embarrassed to look at him.

'Well then, my dear sirs,' he said with an arrogant smirk. 'Would you like me to show you the stuff a soldier's made of? Come out into the passage then and look through the cracks, all right?'

We went out and, crowding together, squeezed up against the cracks in the wooden walls of the passage which led out into the yard. We did not have to wait long. Soon Tanya came into the yard walking quickly with an anxious expression, jumping over the puddles of melting snow and mud. She disappeared into the door leading down into the cellar. Then we saw the soldier strolling unhurriedly along, whistling, his hands in his pockets and his moustache quivering; he too disappeared into the cellar doorway.

It was raining and we watched the rain drops wrinkling the surface of the puddles. It was a raw, grey and extremely dreary day. Snow still lay on the rooftops, but on the ground dark patches of mud were beginning to appear, and even the snow on the roofs was stained a dark, muddy brown colour. The rain was falling slowly with a melancholy sound. For us, waiting there, it was cold and unpleasant.

First to emerge from the cellar was the soldier. He walked slowly across the yard, his moustache quivering, his hands in his pockets – just the same as ever.

And then Tanya appeared. Her eyes – her eyes were radiant with joy and happiness and her lips were smiling. She walked as though in a dream, swaying unsteadily.

Unable to restrain ourselves, we rushed at once to the door, dashed out into the yard and began to whistle and jeer at her loudly and viciously, like wild beasts.

She started when she saw us and stood as though rooted to the mud under her feet. We surrounded her and reviled her maliciously, without restraint, heaping obscenities on her.

We did this quietly and unhurriedly, seeing that she could not escape us, that we surrounded her and that we could jeer at her as much as we liked. She stood in the middle of us, turning her head from side to side, as she listened to our insults. And with ever increasing violence we bombarded her with the filth and venom of our words.

The colour drained from her face. Her blue eyes, which had a minute before been so happy, were now wide open, her breathing was laboured and her lips trembled.

But we stood in a ring round her and exacted our revenge, for she had robbed us. She had belonged to us, we had poured all that was good in us into her and, although this may well have been the crumbs of mere beggars, nevertheless there was only one of her while we were twenty-six, and so there was no pain we could inflict on her which was equal to her guilt! How we insulted her! She did not say a word, but just looked at us with wild eyes and trembled all over.

We laughed, roared and yelled . . . Other people ran over to join us, and one of us tugged at the sleeve of her jacket.

Suddenly her eyes flashed; she slowly raised her hands to her head and, smoothing her hair, said loudly but calmly straight to our faces:

'Ah, you miserable little convicts!'

And she walked straight at us, just like that, as if we were not there blocking her way. And, because of this, we made way for her.

When she had got out of our ring she, without turning round, said just as loudly but with an added note of contemptuous pride:

'You pigs . . . you brutes!'

And upright, beautiful, proud, she walked away.

And we were left standing in the middle of the yard, in the mud and the rain under the grey, sunless sky.

Then we too went silently back into our damp stone pit. As before, the sun never shone into our windows – and Tanya never came to us again!

ANDREEV

DURING the early years of this century Leonid Andreev was one of the most popular writers in Russia. He graduated in law from Moscow University in 1897, but soon turned from the legal profession to writing. Andreev's first stories, welcomed by Gorky, were realistic in manner, but his work subsequently became more sensational (and more lucrative) and then somewhat recondite. One of the most satisfying stories from his early, relatively straightforward period is 'The Grand Slam' (1899) which among other things reflects pre-revolutionary Russia's passion for card-playing – though the author introduces a typically mysterious final twist. The work also contains echoes of Tolstoy's 'The Death of Ivan Ilich' and some of Chekhov's tales of provincial social routine.

THE GRAND SLAM

Translated by Josephine Forsyth

They played vint* three times a week, on Tuesdays, Thursdays and Saturdays. Sunday was a very good day for cards but they had to keep it free for all sorts of chance events such as the arrival of guests and visits to the theatre. As a result they considered Sunday the most boring day of the week. Of course in the summer, out at their country villa, they played on Sundays as well. They always sat round the card table in the same order. Mr Maslennikov, fat and irascible, played with Yakov Ivanovich, and Euphemia Vasilevna partnered her morose brother Prokopy Vasilevich. This arrangement had been agreed six years ago, and Euphemia Vasilevna made them stick to it. If she and her brother had played against each other, it would have been totally uninteresting because the winnings of the one would have been the losses of the other and at the end of the evening they would have been all square. Although the stakes were extremely low and neither Euphemia Vasilevna nor her brother were short of money, playing for its own sake did not give her pleasure and she liked to win. She put her winnings aside into a money box, and the coins seemed much more significant and valuable to her than the large bank notes with which she paid for the housekeeping and the rent of their expensive flat. The players always met at

* Vint or Siberian whist was introduced into Russia in the 1870s and became very popular. It is like contract bridge with some differences in scoring. A special feature of vint is the 'box', formed from four cards which the dealer puts aside during the deal. The highest bidder picks up the box and chooses a card or cards to strengthen his hand. He then gives the other players a card each so that everyone has thirteen cards (Translator's note.)

Prokopy Vasilevich's as he and his sister lived alone in the spacious flat, apart from a large white cat which was always asleep in an armchair, and quietness, essential for the game, pervaded every room. Euphemia Vasilevna's brother was a widower. His wife had died in the second year of their marriage and he had spent the two months following her death in a mental hospital. Euphemia Vasilevna had never married, although at one time she had been in love with a student. No one knew, and she herself had apparently forgotten, why she had never happened to marry her student, but every year, when the usual appeal was made for aid to needy students, she sent off a neatly folded one-hundred-rouble note 'from an anonymous donor'. At forty-three she was the youngest of the players.

When the partnerships had first been chosen, Mr Maslennikov, the oldest player, objected most strongly to the arrangement. He was annoyed that he always had to play with Yakov Ivanovich because this meant that he had to give up his dream of making a grand slam in no trumps. The two partners were really quite ill-matched. Yakov Ivanovich was a short, wizened old man, quiet and humourless, who wore a quilted frock-coat and trousers, summer and winter alike. He always arrived punctually at eight o'clock, not a minute earlier or later, and straight away picked up a piece of chalk in his thin fingers, on one of which he wore a big loose diamond ring. Mr Maslennikov objected most to the fact that his partner never bid higher than four tricks, even when he had been dealt a very good safe hand. It happened once that Yakov Ivanovich led with the two and went right through to the ace taking all thirteen tricks. Mr Maslennikov angrily threw his cards on the table, but the white-haired old man just gathered them up calmly and wrote down the number of game points scored by a bid of four tricks.

'Why on earth didn't you bid a grand slam?' shouted Nikolay Dmitrievich. (The others addressed Mr Maslennikov by his name and patronymic.) 'I never bid more than four,' drily replied the old man, adding sagely, 'You never know what might happen.'

Nikolay Dmitrievich could not make him change his mind. Nikolay Dmitrievich himself always took risks and, as he was unlucky with cards, continually lost but never despaired, believing that he would recoup his losses the next time. Gradually the partners got used to the situation and did not interfere with one another. Nikolay Dmitrievich took risks and the old man calmly went on writing down the losses and making bids of four tricks.

So they played summer and winter, spring and autumn. The decrepit old world went on meekly bearing its heavy yoke, sometimes reddened by blood, sometimes bathed in tears, proclaiming its path through space with the groans of sick, hungry and oppressed mankind. Nikolay Dmitrievich used to bring in faint echoes of this disturbing and alien life. Occasionally he was late and arrived when the table had been set up and everyone was already sitting with their cards spread out in red fans on the green surface.

Nikolay Dmitrievich, rosy-cheeked and smelling of fresh air, would hastily take up his place opposite Yakov Ivanovich, apologize and say, 'There were so many people out on the boulevard. They kept streaming past.'

Euphemia Vasilevna as the hostess felt obliged not to pay any attention to the idiosyncrasies of her guests. She was the only one to answer, while the old man silently and punctiliously got the chalk ready and her brother saw to the tea.

'Yes of course. The weather's fine today. Shouldn't we start?'

And they would start. Total silence descended in the high-ceilinged room with its soft furnishings and carpets which absorbed all sound. The maid Annushka walked silently over the deep carpet serving glasses of strong tea. There was only the rustling of her starched petticoats, the squeaking of chalk and Nikolay Dmitrievich's sighs when he had to pay a large penalty. He drank his tea rather weak and he was given a special little table because he liked to drink from his saucer and eat toffees at the same time.

In the winter Nikolay Dmitrievich would announce that the daytime temperature had been minus ten degrees, and by now it had fallen to minus twenty. In summertime he used to say, 'Crowds of people have gone to the forest today. They've all taken baskets.' Euphemia Vasilevna then politely looked at the sky, for they played on the terrace in summer, and, although it was a clear day and the tops of the pine trees were golden in the sunlight, she would remark, 'I do hope it won't rain.'

Meanwhile old Yakov Ivanovich was dealing out the cards, looking severe. He picked up the two of hearts, and thought how frivolous and incorrigible Nikolay Dmitrievich was. At one time Mr Maslennikov seriously disturbed the other players. Every time he arrived he began to say something about Dreyfus. He would put on a serious expression and say, 'Things aren't going well for our Dreyfus.' Or he would laugh, delighted to tell them that the unjust sentence would probably be changed. Then he began to bring in newspapers and read out anything concerning Dreyfus.

'You've read us that already,' Yakov Ivanovich said drily, but his partner paid no attention and went on reading through everything which he considered interesting and important. One day he drew the others into an argument which became very heated because Euphemia Vasilevna didn't want to recognize the due process of justice and demanded that Dreyfus should be freed at once. Yakov Ivanovich and her brother insisted that it was necessary to observe certain formalities before Dreyfus could be released. Yakov Ivanovich was the first to get back to reality. He pointed at the table and said, 'Isn't it time to start?'

They sat down to play and from then on whenever Nikolay Dmitrievich talked about Dreyfus no one replied.

So they played summer and winter, spring and autumn.
Events sometimes took place, but they were usually rather
comic. From time to time something went wrong with
Euphemia Vasilevna's brother. He forgot what the others
had bid and with a safe contract of five went one down. Then
Nikolay Dmitrievich laughed loudly and exaggerated the
significance of the loss, while the old man smiled and said,
'If you'd bid four, you'd have been all square.'

All the players felt especially agitated whenever Euphemia
Vasilevna made a high bid. Flushed and confused, she
wouldn't know which card to play and looked pleadingly at
her taciturn brother, while the other two players with a
chivalrous sympathy for her feminine weakness encouraged
her with indulgent smiles and waited patiently. Yet in
general they took the game seriously and thoughtfully. In
their eyes the cards had long since lost their inanimate
quality and each suit, each separate card in a suit, was strictly
individual, living its own independent life. They liked or
disliked particular suits and regarded them as lucky or
unlucky. The cards fell into an infinite number of combinations. You couldn't analyse or make rules for this variety,
but all the same there was some pattern in it. The life of the
cards was contained in this pattern, a life quite different
from that of the players. Human beings wanted to achieve
their own ends from the cards, but the cards did as they
pleased, as if they had their own will, tastes, sympathies and
caprices. Yakov Ivanovich very often got hearts, while
Euphemia Vasilevna's hands were always full of spades, a
suit she detested. Sometimes the cards were unpredictable;
Yakov Ivanovich was inundated with spades while Euphemia Vasilevna happily finding hearts in her hand made
high bids and went down. Then the cards seemed to be
laughing at the players. Nikolay Dmitrievich used to get
cards from all suits, none remaining very long in his hand.
His cards were like hotel guests who come and go, indifferent
to the place where they happen to have spent a few days.

Sometimes for several evenings running he was dealt only twos and threes which seemed to have an insolent, mocking expression. Nikolay Dmitrievich was sure that because of this he could never make a grand slam, for the cards knew about his wish and deliberately gave him bad hands to irritate him. He pretended that he was quite indifferent to his hands and tried to avoid turning up the box as long as possible. On the rare occasion he could deceive the cards this way, but usually they guessed and, when he did resort to opening the box, three sixes grinned at him and the king of spades, brought along for company, smiled sullenly.

Euphemia Vasilevna entered into the secret life of the cards less than any of the others. Old Yakov Ivanovich had long ago worked out a purely philosophical attitude and was neither surprised nor disappointed. His trusty weapon against fate was his bid of four tricks. Nikolay Dmitrievich alone could not come to terms with the capricious nature of the cards, their mockery and inconstancy. Before he went to sleep he used to imagine making a grand slam in no trumps, and it seemed easy and quite possible. You get an ace, followed by a king and then another ace. Yet when he sat down at the card table full of hope the confounded sixes flashed their big white teeth at him again. He felt there was something fated and malicious in this. Gradually a grand slam in no trumps became Nikolay Dmitrievich's strongest desire and dream.

Other things did happen apart from card-playing. Euphemia Vasilevna's cat died of old age and, with the landlord's permission, was buried in the garden under a lime tree. Then Nikolay Dmitrievich disappeared once for two whole weeks. The others did not know what to think or do, as three-handed vint broke all their established habits and seemed boring. The cards themselves seemed conscious of this and came out in unaccustomed combinations. When Nikolay Dmitrievich reappeared, his rosy cheeks which in the past had contrasted sharply with his unruly white hair, had turned grey and he had become smaller and shorter. He explained that his eldest son had been arrested for something and taken to St Petersburg. They were all surprised, as no one knew that Mr Maslennikov had a son. Perhaps he had talked about him once, but they had all forgotten. Soon after that he was absent again, and as if on purpose on a Saturday when play could go on longer than usual. Again they were surprised to learn that he had been suffering from heart trouble for a long time and that on Saturday he had experienced a severe attack. Then everything went back to normal and card-playing became even more serious and interesting because Nikolay Dmitrievich was less inclined to talk about outside matters. The only sounds were the rustling of the maid's starched petticoats and the satin-finished cards slipping from the players' hands. The cards continued to live their own secret, silent lives, quite apart from the lives of the people who played with them. They were indifferent as ever to Nikolay Dmitrievich, even malicious at times, and this seemed ominous and predestined.

On Thursday, 26 November a curious change came over the cards. As soon as play began Nikolay Dmitrievich was dealt a 'coronet' of three aces and made not only the five tricks he had bid but a little slam because Yakov Ivanovich had not indicated that he had the remaining ace. After that he was dealt sixes again for a while, but they soon disappeared and whole suits started to turn up, in strict order of rotation as if they wanted to see how pleased Nikolay Dmitrievich would be. He won game after game and everyone was amazed, even the placid Yakov Ivanovich. Nikolay Dmitrievich's fat fingers with their dimpled knuckles were sweating and the cards slipped out of them. His excitement infected the other players.

'You're in luck today,' said Euphemia Vasilevna's brother gloomily. He profoundly distrusted too much good fortune, because great unhappiness always follows. Euphemia Vasilevna was pleased that Nikolay Dmitrievich had finally got some good cards. To ward off misfortune she spat over her shoulder three times after her brother had spoken. 'Don't be silly. There's nothing special about it. You're getting one good hand after another and with God's help there'll be more.'

For a moment the cards seemed to hesitate and a few twos with embarrassed expressions turned up. Then aces, kings and queens started to appear again with greater frequency. Nikolay Dmitrievich could hardly manage to sort out his cards and make his bids. He misdealt twice, so that there had to be a fresh deal. He kept on winning even though Yakov Ivanovich stubbornly kept quiet about his aces. By now Yakov Ivanovich's surprise had changed to distrust of the sudden change of luck, and he repeated yet again his unalterable maxim, 'Never bid higher than four.'

This irritated Nikolay Dmitrievich; his face was flushed and he was puffing and panting. He was no longer thinking out his play, and boldly made high bids, certain that he would find the card he wanted in the box. When Mr Maslennikov looked at his cards after Prokopy Vasilevich had solemnly dealt them his heart pounded and then was still, his eyes went dim and he winced. He had twelve tricks in his hand; clubs and hearts from ace to ten, the ace and king of diamonds. If he were to find the ace of spades in the box, he would have a grand slam in no trumps.

'Two no trumps,' he began, controlling his voice with difficulty.

'Three spades,' answered Euphemia Vasilevna. She was also very excited as she had all the spades, from the king downwards.

'Four hearts,' drily countered Yakov Ivanovich.

Nikolay Dmitrievich immediately raised his bid to a little slam in no trumps, but Euphemia Vasilevna was too excited to give in and, although she realized that she could not make it, bid a grand slam in spades. Nikolay Dmitrievich thought for a moment and, with a solemnity which concealed fear, slowly announced, 'A grand slam in no trumps!'

Nikolay Dmitrievich had bid a grand slam in no trumps! Everyone was astonished, and Prokopy Vasilevich grunted out, 'Well, well!'

Nikolay Dmitrievich stretched out his hand towards the box, gave a lurch and knocked over a candle. Euphemia Vasilevna caught it while Nikolay Dmitrievich, laying his cards down on the table, sat motionless and erect for a moment. Then he raised his hands and began to roll over slowly to the left. In falling he overturned the little table on which stood his saucer of tea and broke a fragile table-leg with the weight of his body.

When the doctor arrived, he said that Nikolay Dmitrievich had died of paralysis of the heart, and to comfort the living explained that such a death was painless. The body was laid out on the Turkish divan in the room where they had been playing. Covered by a sheet, it seemed bulky and frightening. One foot with the toes turned inwards was uncovered and it seemed alien, as if it belonged to another person. A toffee-paper was sticking to the sole of the boot, the instep of which was still new and black. The card table had not yet been tidied up and cards were untidily scattered over it face up, apart from Nikolay Dmitrievich's hand which lay in a slim, neat pile just as he had placed it.

Yakov Ivanovich paced round the room with small, uncertain steps, trying not to look at the body and not to walk off the carpet onto the polished parquet where his high heels made a sharp, staccato rap. When he had passed the table several times, he stopped and carefully took up Nikolay Dmitrievich's cards, inspected them, and replaced them carefully as they were. Then he looked at the box. There was the ace of spades, the very card that Nikolay Dmitrievich needed to make a grand slam. Yakov Ivanovich walked up and down a few more times, went into the next room, buttoned up his quilted frock-coat more tightly and began to weep because he felt pity for the dead man. With his eyes closed he tried to recall Nikolay Dmitrievich's face as it had been when he was alive, winning and laughing. He was particularly sad to remember Nikolay Dmitrievich's frivolity and his desire to make a grand slam in no trumps. He went over the whole evening in his mind, starting with the five tricks in diamonds which the dead man had made and ending with the flood of good cards, which was somehow frightening. Then Nikolay Dmitrievich had died just at the point when he would have made a grand slam.

One terrifyingly simple thought shook Yakov Ivanovich's thin body and made him jump out of his armchair. Looking about him as if the thought had not come to him on its own but someone had whispered it in his ear, Yakov Ivanovich said out loud, 'So he will never know that the ace was in the box and that he had a safe grand slam in his hand. Never!'

It seemed to Yakov Ivanovich that up till then he had not understood what death meant. Now he understood and the reality was so senseless, horrible and irreparable. He would never know! Even if Yakov Ivanovich were to shout right in his ear, were to weep and show him the cards, Nikolay Dmitrievich would never hear, never know because he no longer existed. If only there could have been another movement, a second more of what is called life, then Nikolay Dmitrievich would have seen the ace and understood that he had his grand slam. Now it was all over, he did not know and would never know.

'Ne–ver,' Yakov Ivanovich said slowly, separating the syllables to convince himself that such a word existed and made sense.

Such a word indeed existed and made sense, but it was so monstrous and bitter that Yakov Ivanovich sank back into the chair again and wept helplessly out of pity for the man who would never know, and pity for himself and all mankind because this dreadful, senselessly cruel thing would

happen to them all. He wept and played Nikolay Dmitrievich's cards for him, taking tricks, one after the other, up
to the complete thirteen. What a huge score could be written
down, but Nikolay Dmitrievich would never know about it.
For the first and last time in his life Yakov Ivanovich
ignored his rule of four tricks and in the name of friendship
bid a grand slam in no trumps.

'You're in here, Yakov Ivanovich?' said Euphemia
Vasilevna as she entered the room. She sat down on a
chair beside him and burst into tears. 'Oh, how awful.'

They did not look at each other, and wept quietly, aware
that a dead body, cold, heavy and silent lay on the divan in
the next room.

'Have you told his relatives?' asked Yakov Ivanovich,
blowing his nose loudly and earnestly.

'Yes. My brother has gone with Annushka. I don't know
how they'll find his flat because we don't have his address.'

'Surely he's at the same address as last year?' asked
Yakov Ivanovich absently.

'No, he moved. Annushka says he used to take a cab to
somewhere on Novinsky Boulevard.'

'The police will trace him,' the old man reassured her.
'He's married, isn't he?'

Euphemia Vasilevna looked at Yakov Ivanovich thoughtfully and didn't reply. Her eyes expressed the thought which
had just occurred to Yakov Ivanovich. He blew his nose
again, put his handkerchief in the pocket of his frock-coat
and, his brows arching over his reddened eyes, said:

'Where shall we find a fourth now?'

Euphemia Vasilevna did not hear what he said because
she was preoccupied by thoughts of a domestic nature.
After a silence she asked:

'You're still living in the same flat, aren't you, Yakov
Ivanovich?'

TOLSTOY

THE complex and contradictory Lev Tolstoy was the greatest of the Russian novelists. In his private life he developed from intellectual rake through hard-working family man to tetchy sage, striving unsuccessfully to mortify both flesh and mind; as a writer he achieved almost Homeric stature only to renounce as harmful the bulk of his own literary work along with many of the beliefs and values of educated European civilization. Throughout his tergiversations, however, he remained a supreme artist, and even at the age of seventy-five he could produce a masterpiece like 'After the Ball', which is not only a didactic work about the reanimation of a man's conscience but also a wonderfully balanced story resting on a series of contrasts, some obvious but others very subtle. 'After the Ball' was not published until 1911, a year after the author's death.

AFTER THE BALL

A SHORT STORY

Translated by Lesley Chamberlain

'So you would say that by himself a man cannot tell good from evil, that it's all a question of environment, that we are prey to our environment. But for my part I think it's all a matter of chance. Take my own case . . .'

This was how our highly respected friend, Ivan Vasilevich began talking. We had been having a conversation to the effect that if ever the individual man were to be improved one would have first of all to change the conditions in which people live. Now no one had actually said that it wasn't possible for a man by himself to tell good from evil, but Ivan Vasilevich had a way of responding to his own ideas as they were prompted by conversations and of using them as a pretext to relate episodes from his own life. Often, because he used to tell his story with such frankness and honesty, he would become quite engrossed in it and forget completely what had moved him to begin. This is what happened this time too.

'I'll tell you about my own case. My whole life was shaped the way it is, rather than any other, not by environment, but by something quite different.'

'By what then?' we asked.

'Well, it's a long story. I'll need some time to make you understand.'

'Go ahead, we're listening.'

Ivan Vasilevich thought for a moment, then shook his head.

'Yes,' he said. 'From that one night, or rather that one morning onwards my whole life changed.'

'So what happened then?'

'It happened that I was very much in love. I had fallen in love many times, but this was my greatest love. It's all over now; her daughters are already married. It was Varenka, yes, Varenka B.' (Ivan Vasilevich gave her surname.) 'Even at the age of fifty she was a remarkably beautiful woman. But in her youth, at eighteen, she was captivating: tall, slim, graceful and regal, quite regal. She always carried herself extraordinarily erect, as if this were the only way possible for her, and her beauty and height, along with her habit of tilting her head back slightly, gave her an air of majesty, in spite of her thinness, or rather skinniness. This would have frightened people away from her, had it not been for the tender, invariably merry smile on her lips and in her brilliant, captivating eyes, and in the whole of her lovely young being.'

'Just listen to how he describes her!'

'Yes, and however I describe her, I'll never be able to make you understand what she was like. But that doesn't matter. What I want to tell you about happened in the forties. At that time I was a student at a provincial university. I don't know whether it was a good or bad thing, but in our university at that time there were no philosophical circles and no theories, we were simply young, and we lived as young people do: we worked and we had a good time. I was a high-spirited and very lively young fellow, and rich into the bargain. I owned a fine thoroughbred, and I used to go tobogganing down the hills with the girls – skates were not yet in fashion; and I lived it up with my friends – we drank nothing but champagne at that time; if we didn't have any money, we drank nothing, but we didn't drink vodka like they do now. I enjoyed most of all going to *soirées* and balls. I could dance very well and was quite good-looking.'

'Come now, there's no need to be modest,' interrupted one of the women present. 'We all know your picture, don't we? You were not just quite good-looking, you were very handsome.'

'Handsome or not, that's not important. What is important, though, is that during the time my love for her was at its height, just before the beginning of Lent, I was at a ball given by the marshal of our province. He was a kindly old man, a generous host, and he held a position at court. His wife was equally kindly and, standing to receive her guests in a low-cut, brown velvet dress which left her plump, elderly white shoulders bare and wearing a diamond frontlet in her hair, she looked like portraits one sees of the Empress Elizabeth. The ball was wonderful. There was a splendid room where the musicians – the then highly acclaimed serf-orchestra of a local landowner-patron – had a gallery to themselves and where there was a magnificent buffet and an overflowing sea of champagne. Although I was a devotee of champagne, I didn't drink, because even without wine I was drunk with love, but to make up for it I danced until I was dropping – quadrilles, waltzes, and polkas – and of course as many of them as possible with Varenka. She was wearing a white dress with a pink sash, white kid gloves reaching almost to her thin pointed elbows and white satin shoes. I was robbed of the mazurka: a quite repulsive engineer, Anisimov – I haven't yet been able to forgive him for what he did – had asked her for the dance as soon as she came into the room, whilst I had called in at my barber's for a pair of gloves and was late. So I didn't dance the mazurka with her, but with a German girl in whom I had taken some interest previously. But I fear on that evening I was very impolite to her, I didn't talk to her and didn't look at her; I had eyes only for that tall, slim figure in the white dress with its pink sash, for Varenka's radiant, flushed face and her lovely tender eyes. Not only I, but everyone else was looking at her and admiring her, men and women alike, even though she put them all in the shade. It was impossible not to admire her.

'According to the rules, so to speak, I shouldn't have danced the mazurka with her, but in fact I danced with her almost the whole time. She would come boldly forward across the whole length of the room straight to me, and I would jump up without waiting for an invitation, and she would thank me with a smile for my quick-wittedness. Whenever our row was led up to hers, and she miscalculated my position in the set, she would give her hand to one of the other men, shrugging her thin little shoulders, and smile at me as a token of regret and consolation. Whenever there was a waltz figure in the mazurka, I waltzed with her for a long time. Breathing fast, she would smile and say *"Encore"*. And I waltzed with her over and over again and could not feel my body.'

'What do you mean, you couldn't feel it? When you put your arms around her waist I think you must have felt a lot, not only your own body, but hers too,' said one of the guests.

Ivan Vasilevich suddenly blushed, and almost shouted in anger:

'Yes, that's just like you young people nowadays. You see nothing apart from a woman's body. It was not like that in our day. The more passionately I was in love, the less physical she became for me. Today you see legs, and ankles, and things like that, you undress the women you love, for me, though, as Alphonse Karr said – and what a fine writer he was – the object of my love was always clad in bronze. Far from undressing those we loved, we strove, like the good son of Noah, to cover up their nakedness. But you wouldn't understand any of that.'

'Take no notice of him. Did anything happen after that?' one of us asked.

'Yes. So I went on dancing with her and didn't notice the time passing. The musicians struck up the same old mazurka tune over and over again with the sort of despairing weariness you often see at the end of a ball – you know the kind of thing – and in the drawing-room the mamas and papas had already got up from their card tables ready for supper. The servants were more frequently hurrying through the room with various things. It was after two o'clock. I had to take advantage of these last minutes. I asked her to dance again, and for the hundredth time we glided down the room.

'"So, is the quadrille after supper mine?" I said to her, taking her back to her place.

'"Of course," she said smiling, "unless I have to go."

'"I won't let that happen," I said.

'"Give me my fan a moment," she said.

'"I'm reluctant to part with it," I said, handing her the cheap little white fan.

'"Well here you are then, so that you don't grieve," she said, and she plucked a little feather from the fan and gave it to me. I took the feather and only my eyes were able to express the rapturous gratitude I felt inside. I was not only cheerful and contented, I was happy, I was blissful, I was good, I was not myself, but some otherworldly being, ignorant of evil and capable only of good. I concealed the feather in my glove, and stood up, not having the strength to walk away from her.

'"Look, they're asking papa to dance," she said to me, pointing to the tall, imposing figure of her father, a colonel with silver epaulettes on his jacket, who was standing in the doorway with our hostess and some other women.

'The loud voice of our hostess with her diamond frontlet and her shoulders like the Empress Elizabeth's called over in our direction, "Varenka, come here." Varenka went over to the door and I followed her. "*Ma chère*, do persuade your father to take the floor with you. Now please, Pyotr Vladislavich," said our hostess, turning to the colonel.

'Varenka's father was a very handsome, elderly man, tall, stately and well preserved. He had a ruddy face, a white upswept moustache *à la* Nicholas I, white whiskers which came to meet the moustache and hair combed forward over his temples; and the same tender, merry smile as radiated from his daughter sparkled in his eyes and on his lips. He was superbly built, with a broad chest protruding in military fashion and modestly decorated with medals. His shoulders were strong and his legs long and slender. He was a military commander with the highly disciplined manner of an old campaigner under Nicholas.

'When we approached him the colonel tried to refuse, saying that he had forgotten how to dance, but eventually he smiled, swung his right arm to the left, and took his sword out of its sheath and handed it to an obliging young man standing near by. Then, pulling a suede glove onto his right hand, he said with a smile, "Everything according to the rules," took his daughter's hand and stood one quarter turned, waiting for the music.

'When the mazurka began he tapped one foot with gusto, and struck out with the other, his tall, solid figure moving first of all gently, then noisily and spiritedly about the room, his soles stamping on the floor and his feet clicking together. Varenka's graceful figure glided beside him almost unnoticed as she shortened or lengthened the steps of her little white satin feet at just the right moment. The whole room followed their every moment. For myself I not only admired them, but felt an ecstatic tenderness as I watched them. I was especially moved by his boots with footstraps round them – they were fine calfskin boots, not the latest pointed type, but old-fashioned, with square toes and without heels. Obviously they had been made for him by the regimental cobbler. "He doesn't buy fashionable boots, but wears home-made ones," I thought. "That's so he can bring his favourite daughter out in society and buy clothes for her." And I found the square toes of his boots particularly touching. One could see that at one time he had been a superb dancer, but now he was heavy, and his legs had not sufficient spring for all those elegant and rapid steps he tried to execute. Nevertheless he still managed two circles round the room with agility. And on one occasion, when he quickly brought his legs together and – even though somewhat heavily – went down onto one knee, while she, smiling and straightening her skirt, glided smoothly around him, there was a loud burst of applause from everyone in the room. Raising himself with some effort, he gently and tenderly drew his daughter's face towards him and kissed her forehead, then he brought her over to me, thinking that I was dancing with her. I said that I was not her partner. "Well, never mind, you dance with her now," he said, smiling affectionately and replacing his sword in its sheath.

'Just as once one drop has been poured from a bottle its whole content bursts forth, in a great stream, so in my heart my love for Varenka released all that heart's latent capacity for love. At that moment I embraced the whole world with my love. I loved the hostess with her diamond frontlet and her Elizabethan neckline, and her husband, and her guests, and her servants, and even Anisimov, the engineer, who was sulking because of me. And looking at her father, with his home-made boots and his tender smile – the same smile that Varenka had – I experienced an emotion of rapturous affection.

'The mazurka ended, and the hosts asked their guests into supper, but Colonel B. declined, saying that he had to get up early next morning, and took his leave of the host and his wife. I was afraid he might take her away too, but she stayed with her mother.

'After supper I danced the promised quadrille with her and, even though I seemed to be infinitely happy, my happiness continued to grow. We said nothing of love. I asked neither her nor even myself whether she loved me. It was enough for me to love her. And I was afraid of only one thing – that something might spoil my happiness.

'When I arrived home, undressed and began to think of sleep, I realized that that was quite impossible. In my hand I held the little feather from her fan and also one of her gloves which she had given me as she was leaving, when I had helped first her mother and then her into their carriage. I looked at these things and without closing my eyes I could see her again before me. I saw her faced with a choice between two partners and trying to guess aright where I would be standing in the set; I saw her saying in her lovely voice, "Pride? That's it, isn't it?" and joyfully giving me her hand; I saw her at supper lifting a glass of champagne to her lips and looking at me shyly with her soft eyes. But most vividly of all I saw her partnering her father, dancing smoothly round him and, with pride and delight for both her father and herself, looking at the admiring crowd around her. And I couldn't help uniting the two of them in a single overwhelming feeling of affection.

'At that time I was living with my late brother. In general my brother didn't like society and didn't go to balls, and now he was working for his examinations at the university and leading a highly proper life. He was asleep. I looked at his face, buried in the pillow and half-covered by a flannel blanket, and I felt lovingly sorry for him, sorry that he didn't know and couldn't share the happiness I was experiencing. Our servant Petrushka came to meet me with a candle and wanted to help me undress, but I sent him away. The sight of his sleepy face and his dishevelled hair seemed to me intensely moving. Trying not to make a noise, I went on tip-toe to my room and sat down on the bed. No, I was too happy, I couldn't sleep. On top of that I was hot in our heated rooms and, without taking off my uniform, I crept quietly into the hall, put on my overcoat, opened the outside door and went into the street.

'I had left the ball between four and five o'clock, then I had come home and sat there for a while, so that about two more hours had gone by, and when I went out it was already light. The weather was typical for that time of year. There was a fog, and slushy snow was melting on the paths and dripping from every roof. At that time Varenka's family was living at the far end of the town, just past a large open space, on one side of which there was a parade ground and on the other a girls' boarding school. I went along our deserted side-street and out on to the main road, where pedestrians and carters with firewood on their sledges were beginning to appear. As the sledges moved, their runners grated against the surface of the road. The horses, rhythmically nodding their damp heads beneath their gleaming harnesses, and the draymen, splashing along in huge boots beside their carts, their shoulders covered with bast mats, and the houses along the road, which in the fog seemed to be towering above me – all these things I found especially pleasing and significant.

'As I came to the open space where their house stood, I could see at the other end of it, in the direction of the parade ground, some large black object, and from the same direction came the sound of pipe and drum. My heart still sang, and now and again I could still hear the tune of the mazurka. But this was some other kind of music, cruel and harsh. "What on earth can that be?" I thought, and set off along the slippery path running through the middle of the open space in the direction of the noise. I had gone only a hundred yards or so when through the fog I was able to make out a large number of black figures. They were obviously soldiers. "That's it, they're out training," I thought and, together with a blacksmith in a short, greasy fur coat and an apron who was walking in front of me carrying something, I went closer. Soldiers in black uniforms were standing in two lines opposite each other, all with their rifles at ease, and motionless. Behind them stood a drummer and a piper, incessantly playing the same shrill, unpleasant tune. "What's that they're doing?" I asked the blacksmith, who had stopped alongside me. "They're making the Tatar run the gauntlet for trying to desert," answered the blacksmith angrily, as he looked to the far end of the lines.

'I began to look in that direction too and caught sight of

something terrible coming towards me between the two rows of soldiers. What was coming towards me was a man stripped to the waist, and bound to the soldiers who were leading him forward. Alongside him was a tall officer in a greatcoat and a peaked cap, a figure who seemed familiar to me. With blows being showered upon him from both sides and dragging his feet through the slushy snow, the prisoner was moving towards me, his whole body twitching; sometimes he would fall backwards, whereupon the corporals who were leading him on with their rifles would push him forwards; and sometimes he would lurch forwards, whereupon they would pull him up and stop him falling over. And all the time the tall resolute officer strode firmly beside him. It was her father, with his ruddy face, white moustache and whiskers.

'Every time he was hit the prisoner screwed up his face with pain and turned it, as if in surprise, to the side from which the blow came, and, gritting his white teeth, he repeated over and over again the same words. Only when he drew quite close to me could I hear these words. He sobbed rather than spoke them: "Brothers, have mercy; brothers, have mercy." But his brothers had no mercy, and when the column drew level with me I saw the soldier standing opposite me take a resolute step forward and, swishing his stick through the air, bring it down hard across the Tatar's back. The Tatar lurched forwards, but the corporals held him up, and a similar blow fell upon him from the other side, and then again from my side, and then again from the other side. The colonel strode alongside, looking now at his feet, now at the prisoner, inhaling deeply, as he blew out his cheeks and then slowly releasing the air through his pursed lips. Once the column had passed where I was standing I caught a glimpse through the ranks of the prisoner's back. It was something so bloody, so glaringly red and unreal, I couldn't believe it was the body of a man. "Lord forgive them," said the blacksmith alongside me out loud.

'The column disappeared into the distance, and all the time they continued to beat the stumbling, writhing man from both sides, and all the time the drum and the pipe went on playing, and the tall, imposing figure of the colonel strode with the same resolute step alongside the prisoner. Suddenly the colonel stopped and went quickly up to one of the soldiers. "I'll teach you to be soft," I heard his angry voice shout. "So you're going to pat him like that, are you?" And I saw him with his strong, gloved fist punch a frightened, undersized, puny soldier in the face because he was not bringing his stick down hard enough on the red back of the Tatar. "Bring fresh rods!" he shouted, looking round, and caught sight of me. Pretending he didn't know me, he turned away hastily, with a menacing, ill-tempered frown on his face. I was so ashamed I didn't know where to look; it was as if I had been caught committing the most despicable crime, and I lowered my eyes and hurried home. The roll of the drum and the whistling of the pipe rang in my ears the whole way, and I could hear the words, "Brothers, have mercy," and then the self-assured and angry voice of the colonel crying, "So you're going to be soft with him, are you?" And in the meantime my heart had become so full with an almost physical anguish, bordering on nausea, that I stopped still several times, and it seemed as if my stomach were about to heave and purge itself of all the horror which had entered into me at that sight. I don't remember how I got home and into my bed. But, as soon as I started to fall asleep, I began to see and hear everything again, and leapt up. "Obviously he knows something that I don't," I said to myself, thinking of the colonel. "If I knew what he knows, I would understand what I saw and it wouldn't torment me." But, however much I thought, I couldn't grasp what the colonel knew, and when eventually, towards evening, I fell asleep, it was only after I had visited a friend and drunk myself silly with him.

'Well, do you think I decided there and then that what I

had seen was evil? Not at all. "If it was done with such certainty, and was recognized by everyone as being inevitable, then it follows they must have known something I didn't," I kept thinking, and tried to realize what that something was. But, hard as I tried, I couldn't understand. And without this understanding I was unable to go into the army, as I had wanted to do previously, and not only did I not serve as a soldier, I didn't take up a government position at all and, as you can see, I haven't made anything of my life.'

'Oh, come, we know all about your not having made anything of your life,' said one of us. 'How many other people would have made nothing of their lives, if it hadn't been for you. That's what you really ought to say.'

'Really! That's quite ridiculous,' said Ivan Vasilevich with genuine annoyance.

'And what about your love?' we asked.

'Love? My love began to wane that very day. Whenever she fell into a thoughtful mood – and that used to happen quite a lot – a smile would appear on her face, and I would immediately recall the colonel on the parade ground and feel somehow awkward and uncomfortable; I stopped meeting her so often and my love just faded away. You see then what can happen, and how a man's entire life can be changed and redirected. And yet you say . . .' he concluded.

BUNIN

IVAN BUNIN, who in 1933 became the first
Russian to be awarded the Nobel Prize for
Literature, is regarded by his fellow-country-
men as the last of the classics. Like Pushkin,
he was an aristocratic individualist and an
aesthetic hedonist rather than a thinker or
moralist. Bunin's first published works were
in verse, but he soon became more celebrated as a writer of highly polished, realistic
but lyrical prose – mostly short stories. In
1920 he emigrated to Western Europe, but
continued to write about the Russia of his
youth. 'Ida', first published in 1926, is a
charmingly nostalgic story from this second
half of the writer's long literary career. The
structure of the work – a reminiscence within
a reminiscence – is one Bunin often used.

IDA

Translated by David Richards

ONE Christmas four of us – three old friends and a certain
Georgy Ivanovich – were lunching together in the restaurant of the Grand Moscow Hotel.

Because of the holiday the Grand Moscow was empty and
cool. We walked through the old dining-room, which was
dully illuminated by the grey frosty afternoon, and paused in
the doorway of the new one, looking for the most comfortable place to sit and running our eyes over the tables
with their freshly spread, stiff, snow-white tablecloths. The
manager, all neatness and affability, made a modest but
elegant gesture towards a far corner, to a round table
standing in front of a semi-circular sofa. We went there.

'Gentlemen,' said the composer, going round to the sofa
and lowering his stocky frame onto it. 'Gentlemen, for some
reason I am entertaining today and I want to feast magnificently.

'Spread out for us then, servitor, your most lavish magic
cloth,' he said, turning his broad peasant face with its
narrow little eyes towards one of the waiters. 'You know my
regal ways.'

'Certainly we do; by now we should have learnt them by
heart,' replied the wise old waiter who had a little beard of
pure silver, and, smiling gently, he placed an ashtray in
front of him. 'Rest assured, Pavel Nikolaevich, we shall do
our best.'

And a minute later there appeared before us large and
small glasses, bottles of different-coloured spirits, some pink
salmon, some dark fillet of sturgeon, a dish with open shells
on chippings of ice, an orange wedge of Cheshire cheese, a
black gleaming block of pressed caviar and a white cham-

pagne bucket, smoking from the cold. We began with a
pepper-brandy. The composer liked to pour out. He filled
three glasses and then jokingly hesitated.

'Most reverend Georgy Ivanovich, will you permit me to
pour you some too?'

Georgy Ivanovich, a very quiet and invariably good-
humoured man, whose sole and highly bizarre occupation
was to be a friend of famous writers, artists and theatre
people, blushed slightly – he always blushed before saying
anything – and answered in a somewhat reckless and
familiar tone:

'Indeed, very much so, most sinful Pavel Nikolaevich!'

And the composer poured some pepper-brandy into his
glass too, gently clinked glasses with us, tossed the spirit
back into his mouth, saying 'God speed!' and then, blowing
into his moustache, turned his attention to the *hors d'oeuvres*.
We also turned our attention in that direction and busied
ourselves with them for a fair time. Then we ordered some
fish soup and lit our cigarettes. In the old dining-room a
reproachful growl was heard and a gramophone suddenly
started up a sad song. The composer, who was sitting with
his head thrown back against the sofa, puffing his cigarette
and, as was his custom, drawing air into his thrust-out
chest, began to speak:

'Dear friends, in spite of my inner delight I feel rather sad
today. And I feel sad because today as soon as I woke up I
recalled a little adventure which happened to a friend of
mine – a real fool as it later proved – exactly three years ago,
on the second day of Christmas.'

'A little adventure, but doubtless an amorous one,' said
Georgy Ivanovich with his girlish smile.

The composer cast a sidelong glance at him.

'Amorous?' he said, coldly and sarcastically. 'Oh,
Georgy Ivanovich, Georgy Ivanovich, how are you going
to account for all your depravity and your wicked mind at
the last judgment? Well, let it pass.'

And, raising his eyebrows, he began to sing in accompaniment to the gramophone which was playing *Faust*:

> *'Je veux un trésor qui les contient tous,*
> *Je veux la jeunesse!'*

Then, turning to us, he continued:

'My friends, this was the adventure. Once upon a time there used to visit a certain gentleman's house a maiden, a friend of his wife's from college, who was so modest and sweet that the gentleman called her simply Ida, that is just by her first name. Ida, yes, Ida – he wasn't even sure of her second name. He knew simply that she came from a decent but impecunious family, was the daughter of a musician who had once been a famous conductor, was living with her parents and waiting, as one must, for a husband – and that was all.

'How should I describe this Ida to you? The gentleman was very favourably disposed towards her, but he paid her, I repeat, frankly no attention at all. When she arrived he would say, "Ah, Ida, my dear. Hullo, hullo, I'm so glad to see you." But she would only smile, hide her handkerchief in her muff, look serene and girlish (and a little foolish) and reply "Is Masha at home?" – "Yes, she's at home, do come in." – "May I go to her room?" And she would go calmly through the dining-room to Masha's door. "Masha, may I come in?" A low, reverberating voice, and to the voice add all this: the freshness of youth and health, the fragrance of a girl who has just come indoors from the frost outside; then, she was quite tall and slim and moved with an exceptional grace and naturalness. Her face too was exceptional – at first glance it seemed quite ordinary but, if you looked carefully, you began to marvel at it: at the even, warm texture of the skin, like the texture of a first-class apple, and at the bright and strong colour of her violet eyes . . .

'Yes, if you looked carefully you began to marvel. And

this blockhead, that is the hero of our tale, would look, go into foolish raptures and say, "Oh, Ida, Ida, you don't know what you're worth!" He would see her answering smile, sweet, but somehow slightly inattentive, and he would go off into his room, into his study, and again busy himself with some nonsensical so-called creative work or other, damn it. And so, time went by, and our gentleman never gave even one slightly serious thought to this Ida and – can you believe it? – completely failed to notice that one fine day she had disappeared. There's no Ida, no Ida, yet he doesn't even think of asking his wife, "Tell me, what's happened to our Ida?" Now and again he would remember her and sense that he was missing something; he would imagine the sweet torment he might feel if she were to put his arm round her waist; he would see in his mind's eye her little white muff, her complexion, her violet eyes, her exquisite hand and her English skirt; he would feel a momentary heartache – and then forget her again. And in this way a year went by, and another. Then suddenly one day he had to make a journey to one of the western provinces.

'It was Christmas, but nevertheless he had to go. And so, bidding farewell to his menservants and his maidservants, our hero mounted his fiery steed and set off. He travels all day, he travels all night, and arrives at last at a great junction where he has to change. But he arrives, you must note, very behind schedule, and for this reason, as soon as the train begins to slow down alongside the platform, he jumps out of the carriage, seizes the first passing porter by the lapels and shouts, "Has the such-and-such express left yet?" But the porter smiles politely and responds, "It's just gone, sir. You were a whole hour and a half late you know." – "What, you wretch? Are you having me on? What am I supposed to do now? I'll have you sent to Siberia, to hard labour, to the block!" – "My fault, my fault," answers the porter. "But a sin confessed is half forgiven, Your Excellency.

Please be good enough to wait for the ordinary train." And our noble traveller hung his head and humbly made his way to the station buildings.

'Inside the station, however, there were lots of people and the atmosphere was pleasant, cosy and warm. A snowstorm had been raging for almost a week and the whole railway system was in confusion, all the schedules had gone awry, and all the large junctions were chock-a-block. Of course, here too it was just the same. People and luggage everywhere, all day the refreshment rooms open, all day the smell of food and samovars – which as you know is no bad thing in frost and snowstorm. And, on top of this, the station was luxurious and extensive so that the traveller immediately realized that it wouldn't be a great misfortune even if he had to stop there for several days. "I'll tidy myself up and then have something decent to eat and drink," he thought with delight as he went into the passenger hall and immediately set about putting his plan into action. He had a shave, washed his hands and face and put on a clean shirt; a quarter of an hour later he emerged from the wash-room looking twenty years younger and made his way to the buffet. There he had a drink, then another one, nibbled first some paté, then some pike, and was just about to have another drink when suddenly behind him he heard a familiar voice, the most wonderful feminine voice in the world. Immediately he of course "whirled round" and can you imagine who he saw in front of him? Ida!

'For joy and astonishment he was at first unable to utter a single word and just stared at her, like a ram at a new gate. And she – and that, my friends, shows a real woman! – didn't even raise an eyebrow. Naturally she too couldn't help being surprised and her face even expressed a certain pleasure, but she preserved, I tell you, a perfect composure. "My dear," she says, "what has brought you here? What a pleasant meeting!" And her eyes tell you that she's speaking the truth, but she speaks somehow with an exaggerated simplicity and with a quite, quite different manner from the way she used to speak, but the main thing was she spoke with a slightly mocking tone, you see. But our gentleman was still completely dumbfounded, partly because in all other respects too Ida had changed beyond recognition: she had blossomed out, as a magnificent flower sometimes blossoms in the purest water, in a crystal goblet; and she was also dressed accordingly: she wore an immensely modest but immensely flirtatious little winter hat which must have cost a fortune, and on her shoulders was a hugely expensive sable cape. When the gentleman awkwardly and meekly kissed her hand with its sparkling rings she glanced back over her shoulder to indicate someone with her little hat and said casually, "By the way, meet my husband," and immediately a student stepped out quickly from behind her and modestly, but with a touch of military dash, introduced himself.'

'The impudent fellow!' exclaimed Georgy Ivanovich. 'An ordinary student?'

'No, that's just the point, dear Georgy Ivanovich, he was no ordinary student,' said the composer with a sad smile. 'I believe, in his whole life, our gentleman had never seen such a – what shall we say? – noble, such a marvellous, marble-like young face. He was dressed like a dandy, with a perfectly fitting short jacket of that finest light grey cloth which is worn only by the very greatest beaux, trousers with foot-straps, a dark-green, Prussian-style cap and a luxurious Nikolaevan beaver-trimmed overcoat. And with all that he was also exceptionally likable and modest. Ida muttered one of the most celebrated Russian surnames and he quickly took off his cap with a hand cased in a white suede glove – the cap was of course lined with red moiré – quickly unsheathed his other hand, which was slender, bluishly-white and flecked with flour-like specks from the glove's lining, clicked his heels and politely dropped onto his chest his small, carefully groomed head. "Well, there's something!"

thought our hero in even greater astonishment, looked blankly again at Ida – and by the way she ran her gaze over the student he instantly recognized that she was the queen and he her slave, not a simple slave, however, but one who bore his enslavement with the greatest pleasure and even pride. "I am very, very glad to make your acquaintance," said the slave with complete sincerity and, giving a cheerful and pleasant smile, he raised his bowed head. "I am both a long-standing admirer of yours and have heard much about you from Ida," he said with an amicable expression and was just about to launch into further conversation suitable for the occasion when he was unexpectedly interrupted. "Be quiet, Peter, don't embarrass me," said Ida hastily and turned to the gentleman. "My dear, I haven't seen you for a thousand years. I'd like to talk to you for ages, but I've no desire to talk in his presence. Our recollections will be of no interest to him, he will simply be bored and feel awkward, so let's go, let's walk along the platform . . ." And, saying this, she put her arm through our traveller's and led him out onto the platform; and down the platform she went with him almost half a mile, to where the snow was almost knee-deep and there, quite unexpectedly, declared her love for him.'

'What do you mean, her love?' we asked as one man.

Instead of answering, the composer again drew air into his lungs, swelling his chest and raising his shoulders. He lowered his eyes and, getting up heavily, pulled the bottle out of the silver ice-bucket, out of the crackling ice, and filled the largest wine-glass for himself. His cheekbones had grown red and his short neck was flushed. Hunched up in an attempt to conceal his embarrassment, he drained the glass to the bottom and was just about to start accompanying the gramophone in the aria '*Laisse-moi, laisse-moi contempler ton visage*', quickly broke off and, resolutely raising his eyes which had grown even narrower, he said:

'Yes, I mean her love. And her declaration was unfortunately very real and very serious. Stupid, absurd, unexpected, implausible? Yes, of course, but it's a fact. It was exactly as I report it to you. They set out along the platform, and straight away quickly and with feigned animation she began to question him about Masha, about how she was getting on and how their various Moscow acquaintances were getting on, about what was new in Moscow in general, and so on, and then she informed him that she was in the second year of her marriage, that she and her husband had been living partly in St Petersburg, partly abroad and partly on their estate near Vitebsk. The gentleman, however, simply walked quickly after her and was already beginning to sense that there was something wrong, that something idiotic and implausible was about to happen, and was staring as hard as he could at the whiteness of the drifts which had piled up and covered everything round about with an incredible quantity of snow – all the platforms, the tracks, the roofs of the buildings and the tops of the red and green carriages thrown into confusion on every track – he stared and with an awesome sinking in his heart he could grasp only one thing, that is, as was becoming clear, that he had for years been madly in love with this very Ida. And so, you can imagine what happened next; what happened was that on a very distant side-platform Ida went up to some crates, brushed the snow off one of them with her muff, sat down and, raising towards our hero her slightly pale face and her violet eyes, said to him with mind-shattering abruptness, and with no pause for breath, "And now, my dear, answer me one more question: did you know and do you know now that I was in love with you for five whole years and have been in love with you right up to this moment?"'

The gramophone, which until then had been growling indistinctly and faintly in the distance, suddenly crashed out heroically, triumphantly and threateningly. The composer fell silent and looked up at us with eyes which seemed frightened and astonished. Then he said quietly:

'Yes, that's what she said to him. And now, let me ask, how can all that scene be described in stupid human words? What can I say to you beyond banalities about the face looking up, palely illuminated by that special snow you have after blizzards and about the exquisitely tender and ineffable texture of the face which was also like that snow, and what can I say in general about the face of a ravishing young woman breathing in the snowy air as she walks along and suddenly declaring her love for you and awaiting your response to that declaration? How did I describe her eyes? Violet? No, that's not right, not right of course. And her half-opened lips? And the expression, the expression of all that at once all together, that is, her face, her eyes and her lips? And the long sable muff in which she kept her hands, and her knees, outlined under some sort of blue and green checked Scottish material? My God, can one even begin to touch all that with words? But the main thing, the main thing was what on earth could you say in response to this staggeringly unexpected, awesome and happy declaration, in response to the expectant expression on that face, trustingly uplifted, pale and distorted by both embarrassment and a semblance of a smile?'

We all remained silent, also not knowing what to say, or how to respond to all those questions, and stared in astonishment at our friend's sparkling narrow eyes and red face. And he himself answered his own questions:

'Nothing, nothing, absolutely nothing. There are moments when one mustn't utter a single sound and fortunately, to the great credit of our traveller, he said precisely nothing. And she understood his stupefaction; she saw his face. After waiting a while, standing motionless in that absurd and awe-inspiring silence which followed her terrible question, she got up and, taking her warm hand out of her warm perfumed muff, she put her arm round his neck and kissed him, tenderly and firmly, with one of those kisses which you remember not only all your life but even as you lie in your grave. Yes, that's all there was – she kissed him and walked away. And with that the whole adventure ended . . .

'And now, that's enough of that,' said the composer suddenly, sharply changing his tone, and with affected jollity he added loudly:

'And let us for this reason drink ourselves silly! Drink to all those who have loved us, to all those whom we, idiots that we are, failed to appreciate, to all those with whom we were happy, blissfully happy, but whom we left and lost in life for ever and ever, but to whom we are eternally bound by the most awesome bond in the world. And let us agree on this – if anyone adds one single word to the foregoing I'll crack his skull with this very champagne bottle.'

'Servitor!' he shouted in a voice which filled the whole dining-room. 'Bring us the fish soup. And some sherry, some sherry, a cask of sherry, so that I can plunge my stupid face into it, horns and all!'

We lunched that day until eleven o'clock at night. And then we went to Yar's Restaurant, and from Yar's to the Strelna, where just before dawn we ate pancakes, ordered a red-capped bottle of the roughest vodka and all in all behaved quite disgracefully – singing, shouting and even dancing the *kazachok*. The composer danced in silence, but with a ferocious exuberance and lightness extraordinary for one of his build. When we rode home in the troika it was already morning, terrifyingly pink and frosty. As we went past the Strastroi Convent an icy red sun suddenly appeared over the rooftops and the bell-tower sent forth its first particularly heavy and magnificent boom, which shook the whole of frost-bound Moscow, and the composer suddenly tore off his cap and with tears in his eyes shouted with all his might in a voice which filled the whole square:

'Sun of my life! My beloved! Hurrah!'

BABEL

ISAAC BABEL, a master of terse, precise Russian prose, is celebrated for two cycles of short stories, *Red Cavalry* (1926) and *Odessa Tales* (1931). The former are based on his experiences as a political commissar with Budyonny's forces in the Civil War; the latter reflect the pre-revolutionary Jewish ghetto of the author's childhood. In both sets of stories the irony and the apparently cool indifference of the narrator mask powerful feelings. 'Guy de Maupassant' (1932), a later story set in St Petersburg, exhibits a similar complex mélange of detachment and involvement, irony and emotion. During the purges of the late 1930s Babel was arrested and shortly afterwards died in one of Stalin's concentration camps.

GUY DE MAUPASSANT

Translated by Raymond Rosenthal and Waclaw Solski

IN the winter of 1916 I found myself in St Petersburg with a forged passport and not a cent to my name. Alexey Kazantsev, a teacher of Russian literature, took me into his house.

He lived on a yellow, frozen, evil-smelling street in the Peski district. The miserable salary he received was padded out a bit by doing translations from the Spanish. Blasco Ibáñez was just becoming famous at that time.

Kazantsev had never so much as passed through Spain, but his love for that country filled his whole being. He knew every castle, every garden, and every river in Spain. There were many other people huddling around Kazantsev, all of them, like myself, flung out of the round of ordinary life. We were half-starved. From time to time the yellow press would publish, in the smallest print, unimportant news-items we had written.

I spent my mornings hanging around the morgues and police stations.

Kazantsev was happier than any of us, for he had a country of his own – Spain.

In November I was given the chance to become a clerk at the Obukhov Mills. It was a rather good position, and would have exempted me from military service.

I refused to become a clerk.

Even in those days, when I was twenty years old, I had told myself: better starve, go to jail, or become a tramp than spend ten hours every day behind a desk in an office.

There was nothing particularly laudable in my resolve, but I have never broken it and I never will. The wisdom of my ancestors was firmly lodged in my head: we are born to

enjoy our work, our fights, and our love; we are born for
that and for nothing else.

Listening to my bragging, Kazantsev ruffled the short
yellow fluff on the top of his head. The horror in his stare was
mixed with admiration.

At Christmas-time we had luck. Bendersky the lawyer,
who owned a publishing house called 'Halcyon', decided to
publish a new edition of Maupassant's works. His wife Raïsa
tried her hand at the translation, but nothing came of her
lofty ambition.

Kazantsev, who was known as a translator of Spanish, had
been asked whether he could recommend someone to assist
Raïsa Mikhailovna. He told them of me.

The next day, in someone else's coat, I made my way to
the Benderskys'. They lived at the corner of the Nevsky and
the Moyka, in a house of Finland granite adorned with pink
columns, crenellations, and coats-of-arms worked in stone.

Bankers without a history and catapulted out of nowhere,
converted Jews who had grown rich selling materials to the
army, they put up these pretentious mansions in St Petersburg before the war.

There was a red carpet on the stairs. On the landings, upon
their hind legs, stood plush bears. Crystal lamps burned in
their open mouths.

The Benderskys lived on the second floor. A high-breasted
maid with a white cap on her head opened the door. She led
me into a drawing-room decorated in the old Slav style. Blue
paintings by Roerich depicting prehistoric stones and
monsters hung on the walls. On stands in the corners stood
ancestral icons.

The high-breasted maid moved smoothly and majestically.
She had an excellent figure, was near-sighted and rather
haughty. In her open grey eyes one saw a petrified lewdness.
She moved slowly. I thought: when she makes love she
must move with unheard-of agility. The brocade portière
over the doorway suddenly swayed, and a black-haired

woman with pink eyes and a wide bosom entered the room. It was easy to recognize in Raïsa Bendersky one of those charming Jewesses who have come to us from Kiev and Poltava, from the opulent steppe-towns full of chestnut trees and acacias. The money made by their clever husbands is transformed by these women into a pink layer of fat on the belly, the back of the neck and the well-rounded shoulders. Their subtle sleepy smiles drive officers from the local garrisons crazy.

'Maupassant,' Raïsa said to me, 'is the only passion of my life.'

Trying to keep the swaying of her great hips under control, she left the room and returned with a translation of 'Miss Harriet'. In her translation not even a trace was left of Maupassant's free-flowing sentences with their fragrance of passion. Raïsa Bendersky took pains to write correctly and precisely, and all that resulted was something loose and lifeless, the way Jews wrote Russian in the old days.

I took the manuscript with me, and in Kazantsev's attic, among my sleeping friends, spent the night cutting my way through the tangled undergrowth of her prose. It was not such dull work as it might seem. A phrase is born into the world both good and bad at the same time. The secret lies in a slight, an almost invisible twist. The lever should rest in your hand, getting warm, and you can only turn it once, not twice.

Next morning I took back the corrected manuscript. Raïsa wasn't lying when she told me that Maupassant was her sole passion. She sat motionless, her hands clasped, as I read it to her. Her satin hands drooped to the floor, her forehead paled, and the lace between her constricted breasts danced and heaved.

'How did you do it?'

I began to speak of style, of the army of words, of the army in which all kinds of weapons may come into play. No iron can stab the heart with such force as a full stop put just at the right place. She listened with her head down and her painted lips half open. In her hair, pressed smooth, divided by a parting and looking like patent leather, shone a dark gleam. Her legs in tight-fitting stockings, with their strong soft calves, were planted wide apart on the carpet.

The maid, glancing to the side with her petrified wanton eyes, brought in breakfast on a tray.

The glassy rays of the Petersburg sun lay on the pale and uneven carpet. Twenty-nine volumes of Maupassant stood on the shelf above the desk. The sun with its fingers of melting dissolution touched the morocco backs of the books – the magnificent grave of a human heart.

Coffee was served in blue cups, and we started translating 'Idyll'. Everyone remembers the story of the youthful, hungry carpenter who sucked the breast of the stout nursing-mother to relieve her of the milk with which she was over-laden. It happened in a train going from Nice to Marseilles, at noon on a very hot day, in the land of roses, the birthplace of roses, where beds of flowers flow down to the seashore.

I left the Benderskys with a twenty-five rouble advance. That night our crowd at Peski got as drunk as a flock of drugged geese. Between drinks we spooned up the best caviare, and then changed over to liver sausage. Half-soused, I began to berate Tolstoy.

'He turned yellow, your count; he was afraid. His religion was all fear. He was frightened by the cold, by old age, by death; and he made himself a warm coat out of his faith.'

'Go on, go on,' Kazantsev urged, swaying his birdlike head.

We fell asleep on the floor beside our beds. I dreamed of Katya, a forty-year-old washerwoman who lived a floor below us. We went to her every morning for our hot water. I had never seen her face distinctly, but in my dream we did god-awful things together. We almost destroyed each other with kisses. The very next morning I couldn't restrain myself from going to her for hot water.

I saw a wan woman, a shawl across her chest, with ash-grey hair and labour-worn, withered hands.

From then on I took my breakfast at the Benderskys' every day. A new stove, herrings, and chocolate appeared in our attic. Twice Raïsa took me out in her carriage for drives to the islands. I couldn't prevent myself from telling her all about my childhood. To my amazement the story turned out to be quite sordid. From under her moleskin cowl her gleaming, frightened eyes stared at me. The rusty fringe of her eyelashes quivered with pity.

I met Raïsa's husband, a yellow-faced Jew with a bald skull and a flat, powerful body that seemed always poised obliquely, ready for flight.

There were rumours about his being close to Rasputin. The enormous profits he made from war supplies drove him almost crazy, giving him the expression of a person with a fixed hallucination. His eyes never remained still: it seemed that reality was lost to him for ever. Raïsa was embarrassed whenever she had to introduce him to new acquaintances. Because of my youth I noticed this a full week later than I should have.

After the New Year Raïsa's two sisters arrived from Kiev. One day I took along the manuscript of 'L'Aveu' and, not finding Raïsa at home, returned that evening. They were at dinner. Silvery, neighing laughter and excited male voices came from the dining-room. In rich houses without tradition dinners are always noisy. It was a Jewish noise, rolling and tripping and ending up on a melodious, singsong note. Raïsa came out to me in evening dress, her back bare. Her feet stepped awkwardly in wavering patent-leather slippers.

'I'm drunk, darling,' she said, and held out her arms, loaded with chains of platinum and emerald stars.

Her body swayed like a snake's dancing to music. She tossed her marcelled hair about, and suddenly, with a tinkle of rings, slumped into a chair with ancient Russian carvings. Scars glowed on her powdered back.

Women's laughter again came from the dining-room. Raïsa's sisters, with delicate moustaches and as full-bosomed and round-bodied as Raïsa herself, entered the room. Their busts jutted out and their black hair fluttered. Both of them had their own Benderskys for husbands. The room was filled with disjointed, chaotic feminine merriment, the hilarity of ripe women. The husbands wrapped the sisters in their sealskins and Orenburg shawls and shod them in black boots. Beneath the snowy visors of their shawls only painted glowing cheeks, marble noses, and eyes with their myopic Jewish glitter could be seen. After making some more happy noise they left for the theatre, where Chaliapin was singing *Judith*.

'I want to work,' Raïsa lisped, stretching her bare arms to me; 'we've skipped a whole week.'

She brought a bottle and two glasses from the dining-room. Her breasts swung free beneath the sacklike gown, the nipples rose beneath the clinging silk.

'It's very valuable,' said Raïsa, pouring out the wine. 'Muscatel '83. My husband will kill me when he finds out.'

I had never drunk Muscatel '83, and tossed off three glasses one after the other without thinking. They carried me swiftly away into alleys where an orange flame danced and sounds of music could be heard.

'I'm drunk, darling. What are we doing today?'

'Today it's "*L'Aveu*". *The Confession*, then. The sun is the hero of this story, *le soleil de France*. Molten drops of it pattering on the red-haired Céleste changed into freckles. The sun's direct rays and wine and apple-cider burnished the face of the coachman Polyte. Twice a week Céleste drove into town to sell cream, eggs, and chickens. She gave Polyte ten sous for herself and four for her basket. And every time Polyte would wink at the red-haired Céleste and ask: "When are we going to have some fun, *ma belle*?"—"What do you mean, Monsieur Polyte?" Jogging up and down on the box, the coachman explained: "To have some fun means

. . . why, what the hell, to have some fun! A lad with a lass; no music necessary . . ."

'"I do not care for such jokes, Monsieur Polyte," replied Céleste, moving farther away the skirts that hung over her mighty calves in red stockings.

'But that devil Polyte kept right on guffawing and coughing: "Ah, but one day we shall have our bit of fun, *ma belle*," while tears of delight rolled down a face the colour of brick-red wine and blood.'

I downed another glass of the rare muscatel. Raïsa touched glasses with me. The maid with the stony eyes crossed the room and disappeared.

'*Ce diable de Polyte* . . . In the course of two years Céleste had paid him forty-eight francs; that is, two francs short of fifty! At the end of the second year, when they were alone in the carriage, Polyte, who had had some cider before setting out, asked her his usual question: "What about having some fun today, Mamselle Céleste?" And she replied, lowering her eyes: "I am at your disposal, Monsieur Polyte."'

Raïsa flung herself down on the table, laughing. '*Ce diable de Polyte* . . .'

'A white spavined mare was harnessed to the carriage. The white hack, its lips pink with age, went forward at a walking-pace. The gay sun of France poured down on the ancient coach, screened from the world by a weatherbeaten hood. A lad with a lass; no music necessary . . .'

Raïsa held out a glass to me. It was the fifth.

'*Mon vieux*, to Maupassant!'

'And what about having some fun today, *ma belle*?'

I reached over to Raïsa and kissed her on the lips. They quivered and swelled.

'You're funny,' she mumbled through her teeth, recoiling.

She pressed herself against the wall, stretching out her bare arms. Spots began to glow on her arms and shoulders.

Of all the gods ever put on the crucifix, this was the most ravishing.

'Be so kind as to sit down, Monsieur Polyte.'

She pointed to an oblique blue armchair done in Slavonic style. Its back was constructed of carved interlacing bands with colourful pendants. I groped my way to it, stumbling as I went.

Night had blocked the path of my famished youth with a bottle of Muscatel '83 and twenty-nine books, twenty-nine bombs stuffed with pity, genius, and passion. I sprang up, knocking over the chair and banging against the shelf. The twenty-nine volumes crashed to the floor, their pages flew open, they fell on their edges . . . and the white mare of my fate went on at a walking-pace.

'You are funny,' moaned Raïsa.

I left the granite house on the Moyka between eleven and twelve, before the sisters and the husbands returned from the theatre. I was sober and could have walked a chalk-line, but it was pleasanter to stagger, so I swayed from side to side, singing in a language I had just invented. Through the tunnels of the streets bounded by lines of street-lights the steamy fog billowed. Monsters roared behind the boiling walls. The roads amputated the legs of those walking on them.

Kazantsev was asleep when I got home. He slept sitting up, his thin legs extended in their felt boots. The canary fluff rose on his head. He had fallen asleep by the stove bending over a volume of *Don Quixote*, the edition of 1624. On the title-page of the book was a dedication to the Duc de Broglie. I got into bed quietly, so as not to wake Kazantsev; moved the lamp close to me and began to read a book by Edouard Maynial on Guy de Maupassant's life and work.

Kazantsev's lips moved; his head kept keeling over.

That night I learned from Edouard Maynial that Maupassant was born in 1850, the child of a Normandy gentleman and Laure Le Poittevin, Flaubert's cousin. He was twenty-five when he was first attacked by congenital syphilis. His productivity and *joie de vivre* withstood the onsets of the disease. At first he suffered from headaches and fits of hypochondria. Then the spectre of blindness arose before him. His sight weakened. He became suspicious of everyone, unsociable, and pettily quarrelsome. He struggled furiously, dashed about the Mediterranean in a yacht, fled to Tunis, Morocco, Central Africa . . . and wrote ceaselessly. He attained fame, and at forty years of age cut his throat, lost a great deal of blood, yet lived through it. He was then put away in a madhouse. There he crawled about on his hands and knees, devouring his own excrement. The last line in his hospital report read: *Monsieur de Maupassant va s'animaliser*. He died at the age of forty-two, his mother surviving him.

I read the book to the end and got out of bed. The fog came close to the window, the world was hidden from me. My heart contracted as the foreboding of some essential truth touched me with light fingers.

ZAMYATIN

Evgeny Zamyatin's most famous work is undoubtedly his brilliant anti-utopian novel *We* (1920) but he also wrote plays, some incisive literary criticism and a number of highly individual short stories. At one time a supporter of the Bolsheviks, Zamyatin soon became disillusioned and in 1931 emigrated to Western Europe, which he had visited during the First World War, working as a naval architect. A good example of Zamyatin's art is 'The Lion' in which simplicity of language, a gentle irony, some delicate repetitions and a subtle interplay of dream and reality combine to form a beautifully balanced whole. 'The Lion' appeared first in a French translation in 1935 and was published in Russian only in 1939, two years after the writer's death.

THE LION

Translated by David Richards

I⟨T⟩ all began with a most bizarre incident: the lion, great king of the beasts, was found hopelessly drunk. He kept tripping over all four paws and rolling onto his side. It was an utter catastrophe.

The lion was a student at Leningrad University and at the same time worked as an extra in the theatre. In that day's performance, dressed in a lionskin, he was to have stood on a rock, waiting to be struck down by a spear hurled at him by the heroine of the ballet; thereupon he was to fall onto a mattress in the wings. At rehearsals everything had gone off splendidly, but now suddenly, only half an hour before the curtain was due to go up for the première, the lion had taken it into his head to behave like a pig. No spare extras were available, but the performance couldn't be postponed since a cabinet minister from Moscow was expected to be there. An emergency conference was in session in the office of the theatre's Red director.

There was a knock on the door and the theatre fireman, Petya Zherebyakin, came in. The Red director (now he really was red – with anger) rounded on him.

'Well, what is it? What do you want? I've no time. Get out!'

'I. .I . . . I've come about the lion, Comrade Director,' said the fireman.

'Well, what about the lion?'

'Seeing, I mean, as our lion is drunk, that is, I'd like to play the lion, Comrade Director.'

I don't know if bears ever have blue eyes and freckles but, if they do, then the enormous Zherebyakin in his iron-soled boots was much more like a bear than a lion. But suppose by

273

some miracle they could make a lion out of him? He swore that they could: he had watched all the rehearsals from backstage, and when he was in the army he had taken part in *Tsar Maximillian*. So, to spite the producer, who was grinning sarcastically, the director ordered Zherebyakin to put the costume on and have a try.

A few minutes later the orchestra was already playing, *con sordini*, the 'March of the Lion' and Petya Zherebyakin was performing in his lion costume as if he had been born in the Libyan desert rather than in a village near Ryazan. But at the last moment, when he was supposed to fall off the rock, he glanced down and hesitated.

'Fall, damn you, fall!' whispered the producer fiercely.

The lion obediently plumped down, landed heavily on his back and lay there, unable to get up. Surely he was going to get up? Surely there was not to be another catastrophe at the last moment?

He was helped to his feet. He got out of the costume and stood there, pale, holding his back and giving an embarrassed smile. One of his upper front teeth was missing and this made the smile somewhat rueful and childlike (incidentally, there is always something rather childlike about bears, isn't there?).

Fortunately he appeared not to be seriously hurt. He asked for a glass of water, but the director insisted that a cup of tea be brought from his own office. Once Petya had drunk the tea the director began to chivvy him.

'Well, Comrade, you've appointed yourself lion, you'd better get into the costume. Come on, come on, lad, we'll soon be starting!'

Someone obligingly sprang forward with the costume, but the lion refused to put it on. He declare that he had to slip out of the theatre for a moment. What this unforeseen exigency was he wouldn't explain; he simply gave his embarrassed smile. The director flared up. He tried to order Zherebyakin to stay and reminded him that he was a candidate-member of the Party and a shockworker, but the shockworker-lion obstinately stood his ground. They had to give in, and with a radiant, gap-toothed smile Zherebyakin hurried off out of the theatre.

'Where the devil's he off to?' asked the director, red with anger again. 'And what are all these secrets of his?'

Nobody could answer the Red director. The secret was known only to Petya Zherebyakin – and of course to the author of this story. And, as Zherebyakin runs through the autumnal St Petersburg rain, we can move for a while to that July night when his secret was born.

There was no night that night: it was the day lightly dozing off for a second, like a marching soldier who keeps in step but cannot distinguish dream from reality. In the rosy glass of the canals doze inverted trees, windows and columns – St Petersburg. Then suddenly, at the lightest of breezes, St Petersburg disappears and in its place is Leningrad. A red flag on the Winter Palace stirs in the wind, and by the railings of the Alexandrovsky Park stands a policeman armed with a rifle.

The policeman is surrounded by a tight group of night tramworkers. Over their shoulders Petya Zherebyakin can see only the policeman's face, round as a Ryazan honey-apple. Then a very strange thing happens: somebody seizes the policeman's hands and shoulders, and one of the workers, thrusting his lips forward in the shape of a trumpet, plants an affectionate smacking kiss on his cheek. The policeman turns crimson and blows a loud blast on his whistle; the workers run away. Zherebyakin is left face to face with the policeman – and the policeman disappears, just as suddenly as the reflection of St Petersburg in the canal, puffed away by the breeze: in front of Zherebyakin stands a girl in a policeman's cap and tunic – the first policewoman to be stationed by the Revolution on Nevsky Prospekt. Her dark eyebrows met angrily over the bridge of her nose and her eyes flashed fire.

'You ought to be ashamed of yourself, Comrade,' was all she said – but it was the way she said it! Zherebyakin became confused and muttered guiltily:

'But it wasn't me, honestly. I was just walking home.'

'Come off it, and you a worker too!' The policewoman looked at him – but what a look!

If there had been a trapdoor in the roadway, as there is in the theatre, Zherebyakin would have fallen straight through it and been saved; but he had to walk away slowly, feeling her eyes burning into his back.

The next day brought another white night, and again Comrade Zherebyakin was walking home after his duty-turn in the theatre, and again the policewoman was standing by the railings of the Alexandrovsky Park. Zherebyakin wanted to slip past, but he noticed she was looking at him, so he gave a guilty, embarrassed nod. She nodded back. The twilight glinted on the glossy black steel of her rifle, turning it pink; and in the face of this pink rifle Zherebyakin felt more cowardly than before all the rifles which for five years had been fired at him on various fronts.

Not until a week later did he risk starting up a conversation with the policewoman. It turned out that she too was from Ryazan, just like Zherebyakin, and moreover she too remembered their Ryazan honey-apples – you know, the sweet ones with a slightly bitter taste; you can't get them here ...

Every day on his way home Zherebyakin would stop by the Alexandrovsky Park. The white nights had gone quite mad: the green, pink and copper-coloured sky did not grow dark for a single second. The courting couples in the park had to look for shady spots to hide in just as if it were daytime.

One such night Zherebyakin, with bear-like awkwardness, suddenly asked the policewoman:

'Er, are you, that is, are policewomen allowed to get married like in the course of duty? I mean, not in the course of duty, but in general, seeing as your work is sort of military . . . ?'

'Married?' said policewoman Katya, leaning on her rifle. 'We're like men now: if we take a fancy to someone, we have him.'

Her rifle shone pink. The policewoman lifted her face towards the feverishly blazing sky and then looked past Zherebyakin into the distance and completed her thought:

'If there was a man who wrote poetry like . . . or perhaps an actor who came out onto the stage and the whole audience started clapping . . .'

It was like the honey-apple – sweet and yet bitter at the same time. Petya Zherebyakin saw that he'd better be off and not come back there again, his cause was done for . . .

But no! Wonders haven't ceased! When there occurred that bizarre incident of the lion, thank the Lord, drinking himself silly, an idea flashed into Petya Zherebyakin's head and he flew into the director's room . . .

However, that is all in the past. Now he was hurrying through the autumn rain to Glinka Street. Luckily it wasn't far from the theatre and luckily he found policewoman Katya at home. She wasn't a policewoman now, but simply Katya. With her sleeves rolled up, she was washing a white blouse in a basin. Dewdrops hung on her nose and forehead. She had never looked sweeter than like this, in her domestic setting.

When Zherebyakin placed a free ticket in front of her and told her he had a part in the ballet that evening she didn't believe him at first; then she grew interested; then for some reason she became embarrassed and rolled her sleeves down; finally she looked at him (but what a look!) and said she would definitely come.

The bells were already ringing in the theatre smoking-room, in the corridors and in the foyer. The bald cabinet minister was in his box, squinting through a pince-nez. On the stage behind the curtain, which was still down, the ballerinas were smoothing their skirts with the movement swans use to clean their wings under the water. Behind the rock the producer and the director were both fussing round Zherebyakin.

'Don't forget, you're a shockworker. Mind you don't ruin everything!' whispered the director into the lion's ear.

The curtain rose, and behind the bright line of the footlights the lion suddenly saw the dark auditorium, packed to the roof with white faces. Long ago, when he was simply Zherebyakin, and had to climb out of trenches with grenades exploding in front of him, he used to shudder and automatically cross himself, but still run forward. Now, however, he felt unable to take a single step, but the producer gave him a shove and, somehow moving arms and legs which seemed not to belong to him, he slowly climbed up onto the rock.

On top of the rock, the lion raised his head and saw, right next to him, policewoman Katya, leaning over the front barrier of one of the second-row boxes. She was looking straight at him. The leonine heart thumped once, twice, and then stopped. He was trembling all over. His fate was about to be decided. Already the spear was flying towards him . . . Ouch! – it struck him in the side. Now he had to fall. But suppose he again fell the wrong way and ruined everything? He had never felt so terrified in all his life – it was far worse than when he used to climb out of the trenches . . .

The audience had already noticed that something wasn't right: the mortally wounded lion was standing stock-still on top of the rock and gazing down. The front rows heard the producer's terrible whisper:

'Fall, damn you, fall!'

Then they all saw a most bizarre thing: the lion raised its right paw, quickly crossed itself, and plumped down off the rock like a stone . . .

There was a moment of numbed silence, then a roar of laughter exploded in the auditorium like a grenade. Policewoman Katya was laughing so hard that she was in tears. The slain lion buried its muzzle in its paws and sobbed.

PLATONOV

ANDREY PLATONOV, who had fought on
the Bolshevik side in the Civil War, issued his
first collection of stories, entitled *The Epifan
Sluices* in 1927. This was well received, but
some later satires directed against Soviet
bureaucracy incurred the displeasure of the
authorities and ensured that for many years
very little of his work was published.
Platonov writes for the most part about
day-to-day events and the psychology of
ordinary working people trying to make
sense of their lives. His style is laconic, and
his principal concern is for moral values.
'The Third Son' (1937), which earned the
praise of Ernest Hemingway for its taut
psychological realism, is a good example of
Platonov's art.

THE THIRD SON

Translated by David Richards

IN the provincial capital an old woman died. Her husband, a seventy-year-old workman on a pension, went to the telegraph office and sent off to various parts of the country six identical telegrams: 'MOTHER DEAD COME HOME FATHER'. The elderly assistant in the telegraph office took a long time to count the money, making mistakes in the addition; she wrote out the receipts, and stamped them with trembling hands. Through the wooden hatch the old man meekly watched her with his red eyes and vacantly thought of other things, hoping to lighten the grief in his heart. He felt that the elderly assistant also had a broken heart and a constantly troubled soul – perhaps she was a widow, or a cruelly abandoned wife.

And here she was, working slowly, muddling the money, and losing her memory and concentration; even for ordinary, straightforward work we need inner contentment.

After sending the telegrams the old father returned home; he sat down on a stool by the long table, at the cold feet of his late wife; he smoked, whispered sorrowful words, watched the solitary antics of his grey bird as it hopped along the little perches in its cage; from time to time he would weep quietly, then compose himself; he'd wind up his pocket watch and glance towards the window, through which he could see the changing weather – now leaves falling, together with flakes of wet, tired snow, now rain, and now the evening sun which shone as cold as a star. And the old man waited for his sons.

The first, the eldest son, arrived by plane the very next day. The other five gathered during the course of the following forty-eight hours.

One of them, the third oldest, arrived with his daughter, a little six-year-old girl who'd never seen her grandfather.

The mother had been lying on the table for over three days, but there was no smell of death about her body, so cleansed had it been by illness and withering emaciation; having given her sons abundant, healthy life, the old woman had left herself with only a frugal, small, spare body, which she had striven to preserve – even in its most pitiable state, so as to love her children and take pride in them – right up to her death.

The huge men, ranging in age from twenty to forty, stood in silence round the coffin on the table. There were six of them; the seventh was their father, who was shorter and weaker even than his youngest son. In his arms the grand-father held his granddaughter, who screwed up her eyes in terror at the sight of the dead, unknown old woman whose white, unblinking eyes almost seemed to be looking at her from beneath their half-closed lids.

The sons wept infrequent, suppressed tears, contorting their faces in order to bear their grief without making any sound. Their father was no longer crying; he'd cried himself out alone earlier than all the others and now, with a covert excitement and an inopportune joy, he was looking at his half dozen powerful sons. Two of them were sailors, ships' captains; one was a Moscow actor; one, the son with the little daughter, was a physicist and a communist; the youngest was studying to become an agronomist, while the eldest son was a section-head in an aircraft factory and wore a ribbon on his breast denoting his achievements as a worker. All six together with their father stood in silence round the dead mother and mourned her without a word, concealing from each other their despair, their memories of childhood and the lost happiness of that love which had continuously risen up in their mother's heart without expecting any reward and always reached out to them – even across thous-ands of miles; they'd sensed it constantly and instinctively, and their knowledge of it had given them strength and enabled them to make more confident progress in life. Now their mother had become a corpse; she could no longer love anyone and lay there like a disinterested stranger.

Each of her sons now felt alone and afraid. It was as if out in a dark stretch of countryside a lamp had been burning on the window-sill of an old house and had lit up the night, the flying insects, the bluish grass and the swarm of midges in the air – that entire childhood world which used to surround the old house, abandoned by those who were born there; the doors of that house had never been shut, so that those who left it could always return, but no one had come back. And now it was as if the light in the dark window had suddenly gone out and reality had become a memory.

As she lay dying, the old woman had instructed her husband to find a clergyman to conduct a funeral service over her while her body was still at home; then she could be carried out and buried without any priest, her sons wouldn't be offended and they could walk behind her coffin. It was not so much that the old woman believed in God, as that she wanted her husband, whom she'd loved all her life, to pine for her and grieve for her all the more at the chanting of the prayers and with the light of the wax candles on her lifeless face; she didn't want to say farewell to life without some solemnity and remembrance. After his children's arrival the old man spent a long time looking for a priest and at last towards evening he brought home a man as little and old as himself, dressed in ordinary civilian clothes, pink from a vegetarian diet and with bright eyes which darted quick, purposeful glances. The priest came with an army officer's leather bag on his hip; in it he carried his ecclesiastical accoutrements – incense, some slender candles, a book, his stole, and a small censer on a chain. He quickly set the candles up round the coffin and lit them; he fanned the incense in the censer and, as he walked round the coffin, suddenly, without any warning, he began to mumble from the book. The sons who were all in the room got to their feet, they felt uncomfortable and somehow ashamed. One behind the other, they stood motionless before the coffin, looking at the floor. In front of them the elderly priest chanted and mumbled hurriedly, almost ironically, all the while throwing glances at the old woman's guarding offspring with his tiny, knowing eyes. Part of him feared them a little, and part of him respected them and would clearly not have minded entering into conversation with them or even expressing enthusiasm over the building of socialism. But the sons remained silent; no one, not even the old woman's husband, crossed himself: they were keeping a vigil at the coffin, not attending divine service.

When he had completed the hurried office, the priest quickly gathered his things, then extinguished the candles which were burning by the coffin and packed all his goods back into his army officer's bag. The father of the sons pressed some money into his hand, and the priest immediately made his way through the line of six men who did not look at him, and apprehensively disappeared through the door. He would really have liked to stay in the house for the funeral supper, chat about the likelihood of wars and revolutions and take lasting comfort from meeting representatives of this new world which he secretly admired but which he was unable to enter; when alone, he would dream of one day performing some heroic feat, so as to burst into the bright future and join the ranks of the new generations; to this end he'd even applied to the local aerodrome to be taken up as high as possible and then dropped by parachute without an oxygen mask, but they hadn't replied.

That evening the father made up six beds in the spare room and put his little granddaughter to bed next to him, where his late wife had slept for the past forty years. This bed stood in the same large room as the coffin; the sons went into the other room. The father stood in the doorway until his children had undressed and got into bed, then he shut the door and stepped away to sleep next to his grand-daughter, having first extinguished all the lights. The granddaughter was already asleep, alone in the wide bed, with the blanket pulled up over her head.

The old man stood over her for a moment in the twilight, the snow in the street gathered the meagre, scattered light from the sky and through the window lightened the darkness in the room. The old man went over to the open coffin, kissed his wife's hands, forehead and lips and said to her, 'Now lie in peace.' He carefully lay down beside his grand-daughter and shut his eyes, hoping that his heart would forget everything. He dozed off, but suddenly woke up again. Under the door of his sons' room a light was shining: they'd switched the electricity on, and the noise of laughter and loud conversation resounded. The noise made the little girl stir; perhaps she too couldn't sleep, but was simply afraid to poke her head out from under the blanket, for fear of the night and the dead old woman.

The eldest son spoke with the animation, the rapture even, of conviction about hollow metal propellors, and his voice sounded complacent and authoritative; you could sense his stong, well-preserved teeth and his red, deep larynx. The two sailor-brothers related their various adventures in foreign ports and then chortled over their father's giving them the same old blankets which they used to have on their beds when they were boys. Both sides of these blankets had sewn on them white strips of calico labelled 'Head' and 'Feet', so that the blankets would be put on the beds the right way round and the dirty, sweaty ends meant for their feet would not touch their faces. Then one of the sailors seized the actor and they began to roll about the floor as in their childhood when they all used to live together. And the youngest son egged them on and promised to fight them both with just his left hand. It was evident that the brothers all loved each other and were overjoyed at meeting. They hadn't gathered together for many years, and no one knew when they'd gather again in the future. Perhaps only for their father's funeral? Reaching a peak of excitement, the two brothers who were wrestling on the floor suddenly knocked over a chair; at that they grew quiet for a moment but then, remembering that their mother was dead and couldn't hear anything, they started fighting again. Shortly after this the eldest son asked the actor to sing something quietly to them – after all, he must know some fine Moscow songs. But the actor said he found it difficult to start just like that, and without his words. 'But put something over me,' he said. They put something over his face, and he began to sing under the cover which stopped him feeling embarrassed. While he was singing, the youngest son did something which made one of the other brothers fall off his bed onto a third brother who was lying on the floor. Everyone burst out laughing and challenged the youngest brother to pick up the one who had fallen with just his left hand and put him back onto the bed. The youngest son made some quiet reply, and two of his brothers chortled so loudly that the little granddaughter poked her head out from under the blanket and called out in the dark room:

'Grandfather, grandfather! Are you asleep?'

'No, I'm not asleep; I'm just lying here,' said the old man and coughed diffidently.

The little girl couldn't hold back her tears and began to sob. The old man stroked her face; it was wet.

'Why are you crying?' whispered the old man.

'I feel sorry for grandmother,' said the granddaughter. 'They're alive and laughing, but she died all alone.'

The old man didn't say anything. From time to time he snuffled or coughed. The little girl began to feel frightened and sat up to see her grandfather more clearly and make sure that he wasn't asleep. She examined his face closely and asked:

'But why are you crying too? I've stopped.'

The grandfather stroked her head and whispered back:

'There, I'm not crying; I'm only sweating.'

The little girl sat on the bed by the old man's pillow. 'Do you miss the old woman?' she asked. 'Please don't cry; you're old; you'll be dead soon; you won't cry then in any case.'

'No, I won't,' the old man answered quietly.

In the noisy room next door silence suddenly set in. Just before that one of the sons had said something which made them all quieten down. One son again said something quite softly. The old man recognized the voice of his third son, the physicist and father of the little girl. Up to then no sound had been heard from him; he hadn't been saying anything or laughing. Somehow he made all his brothers calm down, and they even stopped talking.

Shortly afterwards the bedroom door opened and the third son came out, fully dressed. He went up to his mother in her coffin and leant over her shadowy face in which there was no longer any feeling for anyone.

The silence of deep night had fallen. No one was driving past or walking about in the street outside. The five brothers were not stirring in the next room. The old man and his granddaughter watched their son and father, hardly breathing with their concentration.

The third son suddenly straightened himself up, stretched out his hand in the darkness and clutched at the side of the coffin but missed his hold on it and simply pulled it a little to one side across the table, and then fell onto the floor. His head struck the floorboards like some inanimate object, but the son uttered no sound – only his daughter gave a shout.

The other five brothers came running out in their underwear and carried him back into their room in order to bring him round and soothe him. Shortly afterwards, when the third son regained consciousness, all the other sons were already dressed in their uniforms or day clothes, even though it wasn't yet 2 a.m. One by one and secretly they walked round the rooms, round the yard and out into the night which enveloped the house where they had spent their childhood, and there they wept, whispering disconnected words and lamenting, just as though their mother were standing over each one of them, listening to him and grieving that she had died and made her children pine for her: if she could, she would have stayed alive for ever, so that no one need worry over her and waste on her that heart and body to which she had given birth. But the mother hadn't had the strength to live a long life.

The next morning the six sons lifted the coffin onto their shoulders and carried it out to be buried, while the old man took his granddaughter into his arms and walked after them; by now he was used to pining for the old woman and was contented and proud that he too would be buried by these six powerful men – and equally well.

NABOKOV

VLADIMIR NABOKOV, born in St Petersburg into a celebrated Russian family, abandoned his homeland after the revolution and settled in Western Europe. Here he acquired an enviable literary reputation in Russian émigré circles with works published under his pen-name, Sirin. In 1940 he moved to the U.S.A., where he taught Russian literature and began writing in English. World-wide renown came to him in 1958 with the appearance of *Lolita*. This was followed by new fictional works in English and by his English translations of stories originally written by him in Russian. 'Spring in Fialta' which first appeared in Russian in 1938 was one of the latter. Nabokov's work is characterized by brilliant verbal dexterity and a sharp wit, his fictional worlds are bizarrely individual and instantly recognizable as products of his finely tuned, cosmopolitan, ostentatiously self-confident and quite un-Russian mind.

SPRING IN FIALTA

Translated by Vladimir Nabokov

SPRING in Fialta is cloudy and dull. Everything is damp: the piebald trunks of the plane trees, the juniper shrubs, the railings, the gravel. Far away, in a watery vista between the jagged edges of pale bluish houses, which tottered up from their knees to climb the slope (a cypress indicating the way), the blurred Mount St George is more than ever remote from its likeness on the picture postcards which since 1910, say, (those straw hats, those youthful cabmen), have been courting the tourist from the sorry-go-round of their prop, among amethyst-toothed lumps of rock and the mantelpiece dreams of sea-shells. The air is windless and warm, with a faint tang of burning. The sea, its salt drowned in a solution of rain, is less glaucous than grey with waves too sluggish to break into foam.

It was on such a day in the early thirties that I found myself, all my senses wide open, on one of Fialta's steep little streets, taking in everything at once, that marine rococo on the stand, and the coral crucifixes in a shop window, and the dejected poster of a visiting circus, one corner of its drenched paper detached from the wall, and a yellow bit of unripe orange peel on the old, slate-blue sidewalk, which retained here and there a fading memory of ancient mosaic design. I am fond of Fialta; I am fond of it because I feel in the hollow of those violaceous syllables the sweet dark dampness of the most rumpled of small flowers, and because the alto-like name of a lovely Crimean town is echoed by its viola; and also because there is something in the very somnolence of its humid Lent that especially anoints one's soul. So I was happy to be there again, to trudge uphill in inverse direction to the rivulet of the gutter, hatless, my head wet, my skin already suffused with warmth, although I wore only a light macintosh over my shirt.

I had come on the Capparabella express, which, with that reckless gusto peculiar to trains in mountainous country, had done its thundering best to collect throughout the night as many tunnels as possible. A day or two, just as long as a breathing spell in the midst of a business trip would allow me, was all I expected to stay. I had left my wife and children at home, and that was an island of happiness always present in the clear north of my being, always floating beside me, and even through me, I dare say, but yet keeping on the outside of me most of the time.

A pantless infant of the male sex, with a taut mud-grey little belly, jerkily stepped down from a doorstep and waddled off, bow-legged, trying to carry three oranges at once, but continuously dropping the variable third, until he fell himself, and then a girl of twelve or so, with a string of heavy beads around her dusky neck and wearing a skirt as long as that of a gipsy, promptly took away the whole lot with her more nimble and more numerous hands. Near by, on the wet terrace of a café, a waiter was wiping the slabs of tables; a melancholy brigand hawking local lollipops, elaborate-looking things with a lunar gloss, had placed a hopelessly full basket on the cracked balustrade, over which the two were conversing. Either the drizzle had stopped or Fialta had got so used to it that she herself did not know whether she was breathing moist air or warm rain. Thumb-filling his pipe from a rubber pouch as he walked, a plus-foured Englishman of the solid exportable sort came from under an arch and entered a pharmacy, where large pale sponges in a blue vase were dying a thirsty death behind their glass. What luscious elation I felt rippling through my veins, how gratefully my whole being responded to the flutters and effluvia of that grey day saturated with a vernal essence which itself it seemed slow in perceiving! My nerves were unusually receptive after a sleepless night; I assimilated everything; the whistling of a thrush in the almond trees beyond the chapel, the peace of the crumbling houses, the pulse of the distant sea, panting in the mist, all this together with the jealous green of bottle glass bristling along the top of a wall and the fast colours of a circus advertisement featuring a feathered Indian on a rearing horse in the act of lassoing a boldly endemic zebra, while some thoroughly fooled elephants sat brooding upon their star-spangled thrones.

Presently the same Englishman overtook me. As I absorbed him along with the rest, I happened to notice the sudden side roll of his big blue eye straining at its crimson canthus, and the way he rapidly moistened his lips – because of the dryness of those sponges, I thought; but then I followed the direction of his glance, and saw Nina.

Every time I had met her during the fifteen years of our – well, I fail to find the precise term for our kind of relationship – she had not seemed to recognize me at once; and this time too she remained quite still for a moment, on the opposite sidewalk, half turning towards me in sympathetic incertitude mixed with curiosity, only her yellow scarf already on the move like those dogs that recognize you before their owners do – and then she uttered a cry, her hands up, all her ten fingers dancing, and in the middle of the street, with merely the frank impulsiveness of an old friendship (just as she would rapidly make the sign of the cross over me every time we parted), she kissed me thrice with more mouth than meaning, and then walked beside me, hanging on to me, adjusting her stride to mine, hampered by her narrow brown skirt perfunctorily slit down the side.

'Oh yes, Ferdie is here too,' she replied and immediately in her turn inquired nicely after Elena.

'Must be loafing somewhere around with Segur,' she went on in reference to her husband. 'And I have some shopping to do; we leave after lunch. Wait a moment, where are you leading me, Victor dear?'

Back into the past, back into the past, as I did every time I met her, repeating the whole accumulation of the plot from the very beginning up to the last increment – thus in Russian fairytales the already told is bunched up again at every new turn of the story. This time we had met in warm and misty Fialta, and I could not have celebrated the occasion with greater art, could not have adorned with bright vignettes the list of fate's former services, even if I had known that this was to be the last one; the last one, I maintain, for I cannot imagine any heavenly firm of brokers that might consent to arrange me a meeting with her beyond the grave.

My introductory scene with Nina had been laid in Russia quite a long time ago, around 1917 I should say, judging by certain left-wing theatre rumblings back-stage. It was at some birthday party at my aunt's on her country estate, near Luga, in the deepest folds of winter (how well I remember the first sign of nearing the place: a red barn in a white wilderness). I had just graduated from the Imperial Lyceum; Nina was already engaged: although she was of my age and of that of the century, she looked twenty at least, and this in spite or perhaps because of her neat slender build, whereas at thirty-two that very slightness of hers made her look younger. Her fiancé was a guardsman on leave from the front, a handsome heavy fellow, incredibly well-bred and stolid, who weighed every word on the scales of the most exact common sense and spoke in a velvety baritone, which grew even smoother when he addressed her; his decency and devotion probably got on her nerves; and he is now a successful if somewhat lonesome engineer in a most distant tropical country.

Windows light up and stretch their luminous lengths upon the dark billowy snow, making room for the reflection of the fan-shaped light above the front door between them. Each of the two side-pillars is fluffily fringed with white, which rather spoils the lines of what might have been a perfect ex-libris for the book of our two lives. I cannot recall why we had all wandered out of the sonorous hall into the still darkness, peopled only with firs, snow-swollen to twice their size; did the watchmen invite us to look at a sullen red glow in the sky, portent of nearing arson? Possibly. Did we go to admire an equestrian statue of ice sculptured near the pond by the Swiss tutor of my cousins? Quite as likely. My memory revives only on the way back to the brightly symmetrical mansion towards which we tramped in single file along a narrow furrow between snow-banks, with that crunch-crunch-crunch which is the only comment that taciturn winter night makes upon humans. I walked last; three singing steps ahead of me walked a small bent shape; the firs gravely showed their burdened paws. I slipped and dropped the dead flashlight someone had forced upon me; it was devilishly hard to retrieve; and instantly attracted by my curses, with an eager, low laugh in anticipation of fun, Nina dimly veered towards me. I call her Nina, but I could hardly have known her name yet, hardly could we have had time, she and I, for any preliminary. 'Who's that?' she asked with interest – and I was already kissing her neck, smooth and quite fiery hot from the long fox fur of her coat-collar, which kept getting into my way until she clasped my shoulder, and with the candour so peculiar to her gently fitted her generous, dutiful lips to mine.

But suddenly parting us by its explosion of gaiety, the theme of a snowball fight started in the dark, and someone, fleeing, falling, crunching, laughing, and panting, climbed a drift, tried to run, and uttered a horrible groan: deep snow had performed the amputation of an Arctic. And soon after, we all dispersed to our respective homes, without my having talked with Nina, nor made any plans about the future, about those fifteen itinerant years that had already set out towards the dim horizon, loaded with the parts of our unassembled meetings; and as I watched her in the maze of gestures and shadows of gestures of which the rest of that evening consisted (probably parlour games – with

Nina persistently in the other camp), I was astonished, I remember, not so much by her inattention to me after that warmth in the snow as by the innocent naturalness of that inattention, for I did not yet know that had I said a word it would have changed at once into a wonderful sunburst of kindness, a cheerful, compassionate attitude with all possible cooperation, as if woman's love were spring water containing salubrious salts which at the least notice she ever so willingly gave anyone to drink.

'Let me see, where did we last meet,' I began (addressing the Fialta version of Nina) in order to bring to her small face with prominent cheek-bones and dark-red lips a certain expression I knew; and sure enough, the shake of her head and the puckered brow seemed less to imply forgetfulness than to deplore the flatness of an old joke; or to be more exact, it was as if all those cities where fate had fixed our various rendezvous without ever attending them personally, all those platforms and stairs and three-walled rooms and dark back alleys, were trite settings remaining after some other lives all brought to a close long before and were so little related to the acting out of our own aimless destiny that it was almost bad taste to mention them.

I accompanied her into a shop under the arcades; there, in the twilight beyond a beaded curtain, she fingered some red leather purses stuffed with tissue paper, peering at the price tags, as if wishing to learn their museum names. She wanted, she said, exactly that shape but in fawn, and when after ten minutes of frantic rustling the old Dalmatian found such a freak by a miracle that has puzzled me ever since, Nina, who was about to pick some money out of my hand, changed her mind and went through the streaming beads without having bought anything.

Outside it was just as milky dull as before; the same smell of burning, stirring my Tatar memories, drifted from the bare windows of the pale houses; a small swarm of gnats was busy darning the air above a mimosa, which bloomed

listlessly, her sleeves trailing to the very ground; two work
men in broad-brimmed hats were lunching on cheese an
garlic, their backs against a circus billboard, which depicte
a red hussar and an orange tiger of sorts; curious – in hi
effort to make the beast as ferocious as possible, the artis
had gone so far that he had come back from the other side
for the tiger's face looked positively human.

'*Au fond*, I wanted a comb,' said Nina with belated regret
How familiar to me were her hesitations, second thoughts
third thoughts mirroring first ones, ephemeral worrie:
between trains. She had always either just arrived or wa:
about to leave, and of this I find it hard to think withou:
feeling humiliated by the variety of intricate routes on€
feverishly follows in order to keep that final appointmen!
which the most confirmed dawdler knows to be unavoid-
able. Had I to submit before judges of our earthly existence a
specimen of her average pose, I would have perhaps
placed her leaning upon a counter at Cook's, left calf crossing
right shin, left toe tapping floor, sharp elbows and coin-
spilling bag on the counter, while the employee, pencil in
hand, pondered with her over the plan of an eternal sleeping
car.

After the exodus from Russia, I saw her – and that was the
second time – in Berlin at the house of some friends. I was
about to get married; she had just broken with her fiancé.
As I entered the room I caught sight of her at once and,
having glanced at the other guests, I instinctively determined
which of the men knew more about her than I. She was
sitting in the corner of a couch, her feet pulled up, her small
comfortable body folded in the form of a Z; an ash-tray
stood aslant on the couch near one of her heels; and, having
squinted at me and listened to my name, she removed her
stalk-like cigarette holder from her lips and proceeded to
utter slowly and joyfully, 'Well, of all people –' and at once
it became clear to everyone, beginning with her, that we had
long been on intimate terms; unquestionably, she had for-

gotten all about the actual kiss, but somehow because of that trivial occurrence she found herself recollecting a vague stretch of warm, pleasant friendship, which in reality had never existed between us. Thus the whole cast of our relationship was fraudulently based upon an imaginary amity – which had nothing to do with her random goodwill. Our meeting proved quite insignificant in regard to the words we said, but already no barriers divided us; and when that night I happened to be seated beside her at supper, I shamelessly tested the extent of her secret patience.

Then she vanished again; and a year later my wife and I were seeing my brother off to Posen, and when the train had gone, and we were moving towards the exit along the other side of the platform, suddenly near a car of the Paris express I saw Nina, her face buried in the bouquet she held, in the midst of a group of people whom she had befriended without my knowledge and who stood in a circle gaping at her as idlers gape at a street row, a lost child, or the victim of an accident. Brightly she signalled to me with her flowers; I introduced her to Elena, and in that life-quickening atmosphere of a big railway station where everything is something trembling on the brink of something else, thus to be clutched and cherished, the exchange of a few words was enough to enable two totally dissimilar women to start calling each other by their pet names the very next time they met. That day, in the blue shade of the Paris car, Ferdinand was first mentioned: I learned with a ridiculous pang that she was about to marry him. Doors were beginning to slam; she quickly but piously kissed her friends, climbed into the vestibule, disappeared; and then I saw her through the glass settling herself in her compartment, having suddenly forgotten about us or passed into another world, and we all, our hands in our pockets, seemed to be spying upon an utterly unsuspecting life moving in that aquarium dimness, until she grew aware of us and drummed on the window-pane, then raised her eyes, fumbling at the frame as if hanging a picture, but nothing happened; some fellow-passenger helped her, and she leaned out, audible and real, beaming with pleasure; one of us, keeping up with the stealthily gliding car, handed her a magazine and a Tauchnitz (she read English only when travelling); all was slipping away with beautiful smoothness, and I held a platform ticket crumpled beyond recognition, while a song of the last century (connected, it has been rumoured, with some Parisian drama of love) kept ringing in my head, having emerged, God knows why, from the music-box of memory, a sobbing ballad which often used to be sung by an old maiden aunt of mine, with a face as yellow as Russian church wax, but whom nature had given such a powerful, ecstatically full voice that it seemed to swallow her up in the glory of a fiery cloud as soon as she would begin:

> *On dit que tu te maries,*
> *tu sais que j'en vais mourir,*

and that melody, the pain, the offence, the link between hymen and death evoked by the rhythm, and the voice itself of the dead singer, which accompanied the recollection as the sole owner of the song, gave me no rest for several hours after Nina's departure and even later arose at increasing intervals like the last flat little waves sent to the beach by a passing ship, lapping ever more frequently and dreamily, or like the bronze agony of a vibrating belfry after the bell-ringer had already reseated himself in the cheerful circle of his family. And another year or two later, I was in Paris on business; and one morning on the landing of a hotel where I had been looking up a film-actor fellow, there she was again, clad in a grey tailored suit, waiting for the elevator to take her down, a key dangling from her fingers. 'Ferdinand has gone fencing,' she said conversationally; her eyes rested on the lower part of my face as if she were lip-reading, and after a moment of reflection (her amatory comprehension was matchless), she turned and rapidly swaying on slender

ankles led me along the sea-blue carpeted passage. A chair
at the door of her room supported a tray with the remains of
breakfast – a honey-stained knife, crumbs on the grey
porcelain; but the room had already been done, and because of our sudden draught a wave of muslin embroidered
with white dahlias got sucked in, with a shudder and knock,
between the responsive halves of the french window, and
only when the door had been locked did they let go that
curtain with something like a blissful sigh; and a little later
I stepped out on the diminutive cast-iron balcony beyond to
inhale a combined smell of dry maple leaves and gasoline –
the dregs of the hazy blue morning street; and as I did not
yet realize the presence of that growing morbid pathos which
was to embitter so my subsequent meetings with Nina, I was
probably quite as collected and carefree as she was, when
from the hotel I accompanied her to some office or other to
trace a suitcase she had lost, and thence to the café where her
husband was holding session with his court of the moment.

I will not mention the name (and what bits of it I happen
to give here appear in decorous disguise) of that man, that
Franco-Hungarian writer . . . I would rather not dwell upon
him at all, but I cannot help it – he is surging up from under
my pen. Today one does not hear much about him; and this
is good, for it proves that I was right in resisting his evil
spell, right in experiencing a creepy chill down my spine
whenever this or that new book of his touched my hand.
The fame of his like circulates briskly but soon grows heavy
and stale; and as for history it will limit his life story to the
dash between two dates. Lean and arrogant, with some
poisonous pun ever ready to fork out and quiver at you, and
with a strange look of expectancy in his dull brown veiled
eyes, this false wag had, I daresay, an irresistible effect on
small rodents. Having mastered the art of verbal invention
to perfection, he particularly prided himself on being a
weaver of words, a title he valued higher than that of a
writer; personally, I never could understand what was the

good of thinking up books, of penning things that had not really happened in some way or other; and I remember once saying to him as I braved the mockery of his encouraging nods that, were I a writer, I should allow only my heart to have imagination, and for the rest rely upon memory, that long-drawn sunset shadow of one's personal truth.

I had known his books before I knew him; a faint disgust was already replacing the aesthetic pleasure which I had suffered his first novel to give me. At the beginning of his career, it had been possible perhaps to distinguish some human landscape, some old garden, some dream-familiar disposition of trees through the stained glass of his prodigious prose ... but with every new book the tints grew still more dense, the gules and purpure still more ominous; and today one can no longer see anything at all through that blazoned, ghastly rich glass, and it seems that were one to break it, nothing but a perfectly black void would face one's shivering soul. But how dangerous he was in his prime, what venom he squirted, with what whips he lashed when provoked! The tornado of his passing satire left a barren waste where felled oaks lay in a row, and the dust still twisted, and the unfortunate author of some adverse review, howling with pain, spun like a top in the dust.

At the time we met, his *Passage à niveau* was being acclaimed in Paris; he was, as they say, 'surrounded', and Nina (whose adaptability was an amazing substitute for the culture she lacked) had already assumed if not the part of a muse at least that of a soul mate and subtle adviser, following Ferdinand's creative convolutions and loyally sharing his artistic tastes; for although it is wildly improbable that she had ever waded through a single volume of his, she had a magic knack of gleaning all the best passages from the shop talk of literary friends.

An orchestra of women was playing when we entered the café; first I noted the ostrich thigh of a harp reflected in one of the mirror-faced pillars, and then I saw the composite table (small ones drawn together to form a long one) at which, with his back to the plush wall, Ferdinand was presiding; and for a moment his whole attitude, the position of his parted hands, and the faces of his table companions all turned towards him reminded me in a grotesque, nightmarish way of something I did not quite grasp, but when I did so in retrospect, the suggested comparison struck me as hardly less sacrilegious than the nature of his art itself. He wore a white turtle-neck sweater under a tweed coat; his glossy hair was combed back from the temples, and above it cigarette smoke hung like a halo; his bony, pharoah-like face was motionless: the eyes alone roved this way and that, full of dim satisfaction. Having forsaken the two or three obvious haunts where naïve amateurs of Montparnassian life would have expected to find him, he had started patronizing this perfectly bourgeois establishment because of his peculiar sense of humour, which made him derive ghoulish fun from the pitiful *spécialité de la maison* – this orchestra composed of half a dozen weary-looking, self-conscious ladies interlacing mild harmonies on a crammed platform and not knowing, as he put it, what to do with their motherly bosoms, quite superfluous in the world of music. After each number he would be convulsed by a fit of epileptic applause, which the ladies had stopped acknowledging and which was already arousing, I thought, certain doubts in the minds of the proprietor of the café and its fundamental customers, but which seemed highly diverting to Ferdinand's friends. Among these I recall: an artist with an impeccably bald though slightly chipped head, which under various pretexts he constantly painted into his eye-and-guitar canvases; a poet, whose special gag was the ability to represent, if you asked him, Adam's Fall by means of five matches; a humble business man who financed surrealist ventures (and paid for the *apéritifs*) if permitted to print in a corner eulogistic allusions to the actress he kept; a pianist, presentable in so far as the face was concerned, but with a dreadful expression of the fingers; a jaunty but linguistically impotent Soviet writer fresh from Moscow, with an old pipe and a new wrist watch, who was completely and ridiculously unaware of the sort of company he was in; there were several other gentlemen present who have become confused in my memory, and doubtless two or three of the lot had been intimate with Nina. She was the only woman at the table; there she stooped, eagerly sucking at a straw, the level of her lemonade sinking with a kind of childish celerity, and only when the last drop had gurgled and squeaked, and she had pushed away the straw with her tongue, only then did I finally catch her eye, which I had been obstinately seeking, still not being able to cope with the fact that she had had time to forget what had occurred earlier in the morning – to forget it so thoroughly that upon meeting my glance, she replied with a blank questioning smile, and only after peering more closely did she remember suddenly what kind of answering smile I was expecting. Meanwhile, Ferdinand (the ladies having temporarily left the platform after pushing away their instruments like so many pieces of furniture) was juicily drawing his cronies' attention to the figure of an elderly luncher in a far corner of the café, who had, as some Frenchmen for some reason or other have, a little red ribbon or something on his coat lapel and whose grey beard combined with his moustaches to form a cosy yellowish nest for his sloppily munching mouth. Somehow the trappings of old age always amused Ferdie.

I did not stay long in Paris, but that week proved sufficient to engender between him and me that fake chumminess the imposing of which he had such a talent for. Subsequently I even turned out to be of some use to him: my firm acquired the film rights of one of his more intelligible stories, and then he had a good time pestering me with telegrams. As the years passed, we found ourselves every now and then beaming at each other in some place, but I never felt at ease in his presence, and that day in Fialta, too, I experienced a familiar depression upon learning that he was on the prowl near by; one thing, however, considerably cheered me up: the flop of his recent play.

And there he was coming towards us, garbed in an absolutely waterproof coat with belt and pocket flaps, a camera across his shoulder, double rubber soles to his shoes, sucking with an imperturbability that was meant to be funny a long stick of moonstone candy, that speciality of Fialta's. Beside him walked the dapper, doll-like, rosy Segur, a lover of art and a perfect fool; I never could discover for what purpose Ferdinand needed him; and I still hear Nina exclaiming with a moaning tenderness that did not commit her to anything: 'Oh, he is such a darling, Segur!' They approached; Ferdinand and I greeted each other lustily, trying to crowd into handshake and backslap as much fervour as possible, knowing by experience that actually that was all but pretending it was only a preface; and it always happened like that: after every separation we met to the accompaniment of strings being excitedly tuned, in a bustle of geniality, in the hubbub of sentiments taking their seats; but the ushers would close the doors, and after that no one·was admitted.

Segur complained to me about the weather, and at first I did not understand what he was talking about; even if the moist, grey, greenhouse essence of Fialta might be called 'weather', it was just as much outside of anything that could serve us as a topic of conversation as was, for instance, Nina's slender elbow, which I was holding between finger and thumb, or a bit of tin-foil someone had dropped, shining in the middle of the cobbled street in the distance.

We four moved on, vague purchases still looming ahead. 'God, what an Indian!' Ferdinand suddenly exclaimed with fierce relish, violently nudging me and pointing at a poster. Farther on, near a fountain, he gave his stick of candy to a native child, a swarthy girl with beads round her pretty neck; we stopped to wait for him: he crouched saying something to her, addressing her sooty-black lowered eyelashes, and then he caught up with us, grinning and making one of those remarks with which he loved to spice his speech. Then his attention was drawn by an unfortunate object exhibited in a souvenir shop: a dreadful marble imitation of Mount St George showing a black tunnel at its base, which turned out to be the mouth of an inkwell, and with a compartment for pens in the semblance of railroad tracks. Openmouthed, quivering, all agog with sardonic triumph, he turned that dusty, cumbersome, and perfectly irresponsible thing in his hands, paid without bargaining, and with his mouth still open came out carrying the monster. Like some autocrat who surrounds himself with hunchbacks and dwarfs, he would become attached to this or that hideous object; this infatuation might last from five minutes to several days or even longer if the thing happened to be animate.

Nina wistfully alluded to lunch, and seizing the opportunity when Ferdinand and Segur stopped at a post office, I hastened to lead her away. I still wonder what exactly she meant to me, that small dark woman of the narrow shoulders and 'lyrical limbs' (to quote the expression of a mincing émigré poet, one of the few men who had sighed platonically after her), and still less do I understand what was the purpose of fate in bringing us constantly together. I did not see her for quite a long while after my sojourn in Paris, and then one day when I came home from my office I found her having tea with my wife and examining on her silk-hosed hand, with her wedding ring gleaming through, the texture of some stockings bought cheap in Tauentzienstrasse. Once I was shown her photograph in a fashion magazine full of autumn leaves and gloves and windswept golf links. On a certain Christmas she sent me a picture postcard with snow and stars. On a Riviera beach she almost escaped my notice behind her dark glasses and terracotta tan. Another day, having dropped in on an ill-timed errand at the house of some strangers where a party was in progress, I saw her scarf and fur coat among alien scarecrows on a coat rack. In a bookshop she nodded to me from a page of one of her husband's stories, a page referring to an episodic servant girl, but smuggling in Nina in spite of the author's intention: 'Her face,' he wrote, 'was rather nature's snapshot than a meticulous portrait, so that when ... tried to imagine it, all he could visualize were fleeting glimpses of disconnected features: the downy outline of her pommettes in the sun, the amber-tinted brown darkness of quick eyes, lips shaped into a friendly smile which was always ready to change into an ardent kiss.'

Again and again she hurriedly appeared in the margins of my life, without influencing in the least its basic text. One summer morning (Friday – because housemaids were thumping out carpets in the sun-dusted yard), my family was away in the country and I was lolling and smoking in bed when I heard the bell ring with tremendous violence – and there she was in the hall having burst in to leave (incidentally) a hairpin and (mainly) a trunk illuminated with hotel labels, which a fortnight later was retrieved for her by a nice Austrian boy, who (according to intangible but sure symptoms) belonged to the same very cosmopolitan association of which I was a member. Occasionally, in the middle of a conversation her name would be mentioned, and she would run down the steps of a chance sentence, without turning her head. While travelling in the Pyrénées, I spent a week at the château belonging to people with whom she and Ferdinand happened to be staying, and I shall never forget my first night there: how I waited, how certain I was that without my having to tell her she would steal to my room, how she did not come, and the din thousands of crickets made in the delirious depth of the rocky garden dripping with moonlight, the mad bubbling brooks, and my struggle between blissful southern fatigue after a long day of hunting on the screes and the wild thirst for her stealthy coming, low laugh, pink ankles above the swan's-down trimming of high-heeled slippers; but the night raved on, and she did not come, and when next day, in the course of a general ramble in the mountains, I told her of my waiting, she clasped her hands in dismay – and at once with a rapid glance estimated whether the backs of the gesticulating Ferd and his friend had sufficiently receded. I remember talking to her on the telephone across half of Europe (on her husband's business) and not recognizing at first her eager barking voice; and I remember once dreaming of her: I dreamt that my eldest girl had run in to tell me the doorman was sorely in trouble – and when I had gone down to him, I saw lying on a trunk, a roll of burlap under her head, pale-lipped and wrapped in a woollen kerchief, Nina fast asleep, as miserable refugees sleep in God-forsaken railway stations. And regardless of what happened to me or to her, in between, we never discussed anything, as we never thought of each other during the intervals in our destiny, so that when we met the pace of life altered at once, all its atoms were re-combined, and we lived in another, lighter time-medium, which was measured not by the lengthy separations but by those few meetings of which a short, supposedly frivolous life was thus artificially formed. And with each new meeting I grew more and more apprehensive; no – I did not experience any inner emotional lapse, the shadow of tragedy did not haunt our revels, my married life remained unimpaired, while on the other hand her eclectic husband ignored her casual affairs although deriving some profit from them in the way of pleasant and useful connections. I grew apprehensive because something lovely, delicate, and unrepeatable was being wasted, something which I abused by snapping off poor bright bits in gross haste while neglecting the modest but true core which perhaps it kept offering me in a pitiful whisper. I was apprehensive because, in the long run, I was somehow accepting Nina's life, the lies, the futility, the gibberish of that life.

Even in the absence of any sentimental discord, I felt myself bound to seek for a rational, if not moral, interpretation of my existence, and this meant choosing between the world in which I sat for my portrait, with my wife, my young daughters, the Doberman pinscher (idyllic garlands, a signet ring, a slender cane), between that happy, wise, and good world . . . and what? Was there any practical chance of life together with Nina, life I could barely imagine, for it would be penetrated, I knew, with a passionate, intolerable bitterness and every moment of it would be aware of a past, teeming with protean partners. No, the thing was absurd. And moreover was she not chained to her husband by something stronger than love – the staunch friendship between two convicts? Absurd! But then what should I have done with you, Nina, how should I have disposed of the store of sadness that had gradually accumulated as a result of our seemingly carefree, but really hopeless meetings?

Fialta consists of the old town and of the new one; here and there, past and present are interlaced, struggling either to disentangle themselves or to thrust each other out; each one has its own methods: the newcomer fights honestly – importing palm trees, setting up smart tourist agencies, painting with creamy lines the red smoothness of tennis courts; whereas the sneaky old-timer creeps out from behind a corner in the shape of some little street on crutches or the steps of stairs leading nowhere. On our way to the hotel, we passed a half-built white villa, full of litter within, on a wall of which again the same elephants, their monstrous baby knees wide apart, sat on huge, gaudy drums; in ethereal bundles the equestrienne (already with a pencilled moustache) was resting on a broad-backed steed; and a tomato-nosed clown was walking a tight-rope, balancing an umbrella ornamented with those recurrent stars – a vague symbolic recollection of the heavenly fatherland of circus performers. Here, in the Riviera part of Fialta, the wet gravel crunched in a more luxurious manner, and the lazy sighing of the sea was more audible. In the back yard of the hotel, a kitchen boy armed with a knife was pursuing a hen which was clucking madly as it raced for its life. A boot-black offered me his ancient throne with a toothless smile. Under the plane trees stood a motor-cycle of German make, a mud-bespattered limousine, and a yellow long-bodied Icarus that looked like a giant scarab: ('That's ours – Segur's, I mean,' said Nina, adding: 'Why don't you come with us, Victor?' although she knew very well that I could not come); in the lacquer of its elytra a gouache of sky and branches was engulfed; in the metal of one of the bomb-shaped lamps we ourselves were momentarily reflected, lean film-land pedestrians passing along the convex surface; and then, after a few steps, I glanced back and foresaw, in an almost optical sense, as it were, what really happened an hour or so later: the three of them wearing motoring helmets, getting in, smiling and waving to me, transparent to me like ghosts, with the colour of the world shining through them, and then they were moving, receding, diminishing (Nina's last ten-fingered farewell); but actually the automobile was still standing quite motionless, smooth and whole like an egg, and Nina under my outstretched arm was entering a laurel-flanked doorway, and as we sat down we could see through the window Ferdinand and Segur, who had come by another way, slowly approaching.

There was no one on the veranda where we lunched except the Englishman I had recently observed; in front of him, a long glass containing a bright crimson drink threw an oval reflection on the tablecloth. In his eyes, I noticed the same bloodshot desire, but now it was in no sense related to Nina; that avid look was not directed at her at all, but was fixed on the upper right-hand corner of the broad window near which he was sitting.

Having pulled the gloves off her small thin hands, Nina, for the last time in her life, was eating the shellfish of which she was so fond. Ferdinand also busied himself with food, and I took advantage of his hunger to begin a conversation which gave me the semblance of power over him: to be specific, I mentioned his recent failure. After a brief period of fashionable religious conversion, during which grace descended upon him and he undertook some rather ambiguous pilgrimages, which ended in a decidedly scandalous adventure, he had turned his dull eyes towards barbarous Moscow. Now, frankly speaking, I have always been irritated by the complacent conviction that a ripple of stream consciousness, a few healthy obscenities, and a dash of communism in any old slop-pail will alchemically and automatically produce ultra-modern literature; and I will contend until I am shot that art as soon as it is brought into contact with politics inevitably sinks to the level of any ideological trash. In Ferdinand's case, it is true, all this was rather irrelevant: the muscles of his muse were exceptionally strong, to say nothing of the fact that he didn't care a damn for the plight of the underdog; but because of certain obscurely mischievous undercurrents of that sort, his art had become still more repulsive. Except for a few snobs none had understood the play; I had not seen it myself, but could well imagine that elaborate Kremlinesque night along the impossible spirals of which he spun various wheels of dismembered symbols; and now, not without pleasure, I asked him whether he had read a recent bit of criticism about himself.

'Criticism!' he exclaimed. 'Fine criticism! Every slick jackanapes sees fit to read me a lecture. Ignorance of my work is their bliss. My books are touched gingerly, as one touches something that may go bang. Criticism! They are examined from every point of view except the essential one. It is as if a naturalist in describing the equine genus, started to jaw about saddles or Mme de V.' (He named a well-known literary hostess, who indeed strongly resembled a grinning horse.) 'I would like some of that pigeon's blood, too,' he continued in the same loud, ripping voice, addressing the waiter, who understood his desire only after he had looked in the direction of the long-nailed finger which unceremoniously pointed at the Englishman's glass. For some reason or other, Segur mentioned Ruby Rose, the lady who painted flowers on her breast, and the conversation took on a less insulting character. Meanwhile the big Englishman suddenly made up his mind, got up on a chair, stepped from there on to the window-sill, and stretched up till he reached that coveted corner of the frame where rested a compact furry moth, which he deftly slipped into a pill-box.

'... rather like Wouwerman's white horse,' said Ferdinand, in regard to something he was discussing with Segur.

'*Tu es très hippique ce matin,*' remarked the latter.

Soon they both left to telephone. Ferdinand was particularly fond of long-distance calls, and particularly good at endowing them, no matter what the distance, with a friendly warmth when it was necessary, as for instance now, to make sure of free lodgings.

From afar came the sounds of music – a trumpet, a zither. Nina and I set out to wander again. The circus on its way to Fialta had apparently sent out runners: an advertising pageant was tramping by; but we did not catch its head, as it had turned uphill into a side alley: the gilded back of some carriage was receding, a man in a burnous led a camel, a file of four mediocre Indians carried placards on poles, and behind them, by special permission, a tourist's small son in a sailor suit sat reverently on a tiny pony.

We wandered by a café where the tables were now almost dry but still empty; the waiter was examining (I hope he adopted it later) a horrible foundling, the absurd inkstand affair, stowed by Ferdinand on the banisters in passing. At the next corner we were attracted by an old stone stairway, and we climbed up, and I kept looking at the sharp angle of Nina's step as she ascended, raising her skirt, its narrowness requiring the same gesture as formerly length had done; she diffused a familiar warmth, and going up beside her, I recalled the last time we had come together. It had been in a Paris house, with many people around, and my dear friend Jules Darboux, wishing to do me a refined aesthetic favour, had touched my sleeve and said, 'I want you to meet –' and led me to Nina, who sat in the corner of a couch, her body folded Z-wise, with an ashtray at her heel, and she took a long turquoise cigarette-holder from her lips and joyfully, slowly exclaimed, 'Well, of all people –' and then all the evening my heart felt like breaking, as I passed from group to group with a sticky glass in my fist, now and then looking at her from a distance (she did not look), and listened to scraps of conversation, and overheard one man saying to another, 'Funny, how they all smell alike, burnt leaf through whatever perfume they use, those angular dark-haired girls,' and as it often happens, a trivial remark related to some unknown topic coiled and clung to one's own intimate recollection, a parasite of its sadness.

At the top of the steps, we found ourselves on a rough kind of terrace. From here one could see the delicate outline of the dove-coloured Mount St George with a cluster of bone-white flecks (some hamlet) on one of its slopes; the smoke of an indiscernible train undulated along its rounded base – and suddenly disappeared; still lower, above the jumble of roofs, one could perceive a solitary cypress, resembling the moist-twirled black tip of a water-colour brush; to the right, one caught a glimpse of the sea, which was grey, with silver wrinkles. At our feet lay a rusty old key, and on the wall of the half-ruined house adjoining the terrace, the ends of some wire still remained hanging . . . I reflected that formerly there had been life here, a family had enjoyed the coolness at nightfall, clumsy children had coloured pictures by the light of a lamp . . . We lingered there as if listening to something; Nina, who stood on higher ground, put a hand on my shoulder and smiled, and carefully, so as not to crumple her smile, kissed me. With an unbearable force, I relived (or so it now seems to me) all that had ever been between us beginning with a similar kiss; and I said (substituting for our cheap, formal 'thou' that strangely full and expressive 'you' to which the circumnavigator, enriched all round, returns), 'Look here – what if I love you?' Nina glanced at me, I repeated those words, I wanted to add . . .but something like a bat passed swiftly across her face, a quick, queer, almost ugly expression, and she, who would utter coarse words with perfect simplicity, became embarrassed; I also felt awkward ... 'Never mind, I was only joking,' I hastened to say, lightly encircling her waist. From somewhere a firm bouquet of small dark, unselfishly smelling violets appeared in her hands, and before she returned to her husband and car, we stood for a little longer by the stone parapet, and our romance was even more hopeless than it had ever been. But the stone was as warm as flesh, and suddenly I understood something I had been seeing without understanding – why a piece of tin-foil had sparkled so on the pavement, why the gleam of a glass had trembled on a tablecloth, why the sea was a-shimmer: somehow, by imperceptible degrees, the white sky above Fialta had got saturated with sunshine, and now it was sun-pervaded throughout, and this brimming white radiance grew broader and broader, all dissolved in it, all vanished, all passed, and I stood on the station platform of Mlech with a freshly bought newspaper, which told me that the yellow car I had seen under the plane trees had suffered a crash beyond Fialta, having run at full speed into the truck of a travelling circus entering the town, a crash from which Ferdinand and his friend, those invulnerable rogues, those salamanders of fate, those basilisks of good fortune, had escaped with local and temporary injury to their scales, while Nina, in spite of her long-standing, faithful imitation of them, had turned out after all to be mortal.

PAUSTOVSKY

KONSTANTIN PAUSTOVSKY's first story was published in 1911, but he did not become a professional writer until 1925. Best known in the Soviet Union for his lyrical descriptions of nature, Paustovsky was a great admirer of Bunin's art, but while sharing the latter's sensitivity he completely lacked his austere vitality. The English reader – who may well enjoy Paustovsky's autobiographical cycle, *The Tale of Life* – often finds his fiction somewhat vapid. A good example of Paustovsky's manner as a short-story writer is 'Streams Where Trout Play' (1941) with its fairytale atmosphere and gentle musing about romantic love. In his later years Paustovsky served as a literary mentor to many younger Soviet writers and is remembered with great affection.

STREAMS WHERE TROUT PLAY

Translated by David Richards

THE fate which befell one of Napoleon's marshals – we shan't mention his name so as not to irritate historians and pedants – is worth relating to you, since you deplore the poverty of human emotions.

The marshal was still young. A touch of grey in his hair and a scar on his cheek lent a certain allure to his face, which had darkened from deprivations and campaigns.

His soldiers loved the marshal because he shared with them the burdens of war. He often slept in the open air by the camp fire, wrapped in his cloak, and woke up at the raucous note of the trumpet. He would drink out of the same mess-tin as the soldiers and wore a threadbare uniform which was covered in dust.

He neither saw nor knew anything apart from exhausting marches and combat. It never occurred to him to lean down from his saddle and casually ask a peasant the name of the herbage which his horse was trampling down or to ascertain the achievements of the cities captured by his soldiers to the glory of France. Continuous warfare had taught him to keep silent and to forget his personal life.

One winter the marshal's cavalry corps, which was stationed in Lombardy, received orders to leave immediately for Germany and join forces with *La Grande Armée*.

Twelve days later the corps halted for the night in a little German town. Snow-capped mountains gleamed white in the darkness. A forest of beeches stretched for miles all round, and only the stars twinkled in the sky amid the universal stillness.

The marshal lodged at the inn. After a modest supper he sat down by the stove in the little reception-room and dismissed his subordinates. He was tired and wanted to be alone. The silence of the little town, up to its eyes in snow, reminded him of something between his childhood and some recent dream which perhaps he had only imagined. The marshal knew that any day now the emperor would join a decisive engagement and he reassured himself that this unaccustomed desire for tranquility was necessary for him, the marshal, as a last respite before the violent charge into battle.

Fire can induce a trance-like state in people. The marshal, with his eyes fixed on the logs blazing in the stove, did not notice an elderly man with a thin, bird-like face come into the room. The stranger was wearing a blue, patched tail-coat. He came over to the stove and began to warm his numbed hands. The marshal raised his head and asked peevishly:

'Who are you, sir? Why have you appeared here so silently?'

'I am Baumweiss, the musician,' the stranger replied. 'I came in cautiously because on this winter night one naturally wants to move without making any noise.'

The face and voice of the musician were engaging, and after a moment's thought the marshal said:

'Sit down by the fire, sir. I must confess, such peaceful evenings rarely come my way, and I am glad to talk a while with you.'

'I thank you,' answered the musician, 'but, if you will permit me, I shall rather sit at the piano and play. For two hours a certain tune has been haunting me. I must play it through, and in my room upstairs there is no piano.'

'Very well,' replied the marshal, 'though the quiet of this night is incomparably more agreeable than the most divine sounds.'

Baumweiss sat down at the piano and began to play, almost inaudibly. Suddenly it seemed to the marshal that he could hear the deep, light snows around the little town, it seemed

that the winter and all the snow-laden branches of the beech
trees were singing, and that even the fire in the stove was
jingling. The marshal frowned, glanced at the logs and saw
that it wasn't the fire jingling, but the spur on his jack-boot.

'I'm already imagining all manner of strange things,' said
the marshal. 'You must be a wonderful musician?'

'No,' replied Baumweiss and stopped playing. 'I play at
weddings and at evening parties for minor princes and
landowners.'

The crunch of sleigh-runners was suddenly heard at the
porch. Horses neighed.

'Well,' Baumweiss stood up. 'They've come for me.
Permit me to take my leave of you.'

'Where are you going?' asked the marshal.

'In the mountains, two leagues from here, lives a forester,'
answered Baumweiss. 'At the moment our charming songstress, Maria Czerny, is staying in his home. She is sheltering
here from the vicissitudes of war. Today Maria Czerny is
twenty-three years old and she is organizing a small celebration. And what celebration is complete without old party-pianist Baumweiss?!'

The marshal got up out of his chair.

'Sir,' he said, 'my corps is leaving here tomorrow morning. Would it be discourteous on my part if I were to join
you and spend this night at the forester's house?'

'As you please,' answered Baumweiss and gave a restrained bow, but he was noticeably surprised at the marshal's
words.

'But,' said the marshal, 'not a word of this to anyone. I
shall leave by the back porch and join the sleigh by the well.'

'As you please,' Baumweiss repeated, bowed again and
went out.

The marshal began to laugh. He had drunk no wine that
evening, but a carefree intoxication had seized him with
extraordinary force.

'Into the winter!' he said to himself. 'To the devil, into

the forest, into the nocturnal mountains! Wonderful!'

He threw on his cloak and slipped unnoticed out of the inn through the garden. By the well stood the sleigh – Baumweiss was already waiting for the marshal. The horses, snorting, rushed past the sentry at the town gate. The sentry sloped his rifle in the customary manner, though a little belatedly, and saluted the marshal. For a long time he listened to the tinkling of the sleigh-bells as they retreated into the distance and shook his head:

'What a night! O for just one mouthful of hot wine!'

The horses raced over the silver-shod earth. The snow melted on their hot noses. The hard frost had cast a spell over the forest. Black ivy firmly entwined the trunks of the beech trees, as if it were trying to warm the life-giving sap in them.

Suddenly the horses halted by a stream. It was not frozen but foamed fiercely and splashed over stones as it ran down from the mountain caves and from the virgin forest which was packed with congealed foliage and with trees blown down by gales.

As the horses drank from the stream, something darted through the water under their hooves like a gleaming arrow. The horses shied and galloped off along the narrow track.

'A trout,' said the driver. 'A merry fish!'

The marshal smiled. His intoxication had not passed. Nor had it passed when the horses drew the sleigh out into a mountain glade and up to an old house with a high roof.

There were lights in the windows. The driver jumped down and folded back the travelling rug.

The door was thrown open and, shedding his cloak, the marshal, arm in arm with Baumweiss, entered a low, candle-lit room and paused just inside the door. In the room sat a number of elegantly dressed men and women.

One of the women rose. The marshal looked at her and guessed that she must be Maria Czerny.

'Forgive me,' said the marshal, blushing slightly.

'Forgive this intrusion. But we soldiers know neither family, nor celebrations, nor peaceful merriment. Permit me then to warm myself a little at your fire.'

The old forester bowed to the marshal, but Maria Czerny came across the room, looked into the marshal's eyes and offered her hand. The marshal kissed her hand and it felt to him as cold as a fragment of ice. Everyone remained silent.

Maria Czerny cautiously touched the marshal's cheek, drew her finger along the deep scar and asked:

'Was that very painful?'

'Yes,' answered the marshal in confusion, 'it was a powerful sabre cut.'

Then she took his arm and led him over to her guests. Embarrassed and radiant, she introduced him to them as though she were presenting her bridegroom. A whisper of bewilderment ran through the guests.

I don't know whether I must describe Maria Czerny's appearance to you. If, like me, you were a contemporary of hers, then you would surely have heard of this woman's pure beauty, of her light step and her wayward, but enchanting disposition. There was no man who dared to hope for the love of Maria Czerny. Perhaps only such men as Schiller could be worthy of her love.

What happened after this? The marshal spent two days in the forester's house. We shall not speak about love, because to this day we do not know what it is. Perhaps it is the thick snow falling all night, or the wintry streams where trout play. Or perhaps it is laughter and singing and the smell of old pitch just before dawn when the candles burn down and the stars press against the window-pane to shine in Maria Czerny's eyes. Who knows? Perhaps it is a bare arm on a rough epaulette, fingers stroking cold hair, or Baumweiss's patched tail-coat. It is masculine tears over what the heart never expected, over tenderness, caresses and incoherent whispers amid the forest nights. Perhaps it is the return of childhood. Who knows? And perhaps it is despair at parting, when the heart sinks and Maria Czerny convulsively strokes the wallpaper, the tables and the doors of the room which had been a witness to her love. And perhaps finally it is a woman's cry and her swoon when outside in the smoke of torches Napoleon's police jump down from their saddles at sharp shouts of command and come into the house to arrest the marshal on the personal order of the emperor.

There are occurrences which fly by and disappear like birds, but always remain in the memories of those who chanced to witness them.

Everything around remained as before. Just as before, the forest rustled in the wind, and the stream made the dark leaves spin in little whirlpools. Just as before, the echo of an axe resounded in the mountains, and the women chattered in the little town as they gathered round the well.

But for some reason the forest and the slowly falling snow and the gleam of trout in the stream would cause Baumweiss to take an old but snow-white handkerchief from the back pocket of his tail-coat, press it to his eyes and whisper disconnected, sad words about the brief love of Maria Czerny and about how at times life becomes like music.

But, Baumweiss would whisper, in spite of the ache in his heart he was glad to have been a participant in this incident and to have experienced emotions which rarely fall to the lot of an old and needy party-pianist.

NAGIBIN

YURY NAGIBIN's first story was published in 1940, but he did not achieve prominence as a writer until the mid-1950s when he became recognized as one of the leaders of his literary generation. Like Kazakov, with whom he is often grouped, Nagibin describes the private inner lives of his heroes and extols simple human goodness. His stories are always realistic, but also subtly lyrical; he writes with especial charm about childhood – often with autobiographical motifs – and about nature, which is for him always full of magic and wisdom. 'The Winter Oak' (1953) is both typical of the writer and one of his masterpieces.

THE WINTER OAK

Translated by Olive Stevens

THE snow that fell during the night had covered the narrow
path leading from Uvarovka to the school, and it was only
the intermittent shadows on the blindingly snowy surface
that gave an indication of its direction. The schoolmistress
took each step carefully, ready to draw back her foot in its
small, fur-trimmed boot, should the snow prove treacherous.

It was only half a kilometre to the school, and the schoolmistress had merely flung a short fur coat over her shoulders
and tied a light woollen scarf over her head. It was freezing
hard, and in addition a wind was rising, whirling fresh
snowflakes up from the thin icy crust that had formed over
the snow and bespattering her with them from head to foot.
But everything delighted this twenty-four-year-old schoolmistress. She was delighted that the frost nipped her nose
and cheeks, and that the wind blew in under her coat,
continually lashing her body. Turning away from the wind,
she saw behind her the regular track of her pointed little
boots; it looked like the track of some small animal, and this
too delighted her.

The fresh January day, suffused with light, gave rise to
happy thoughts about herself and her life. Only two years
ago she had come here straight from college, and already
she had achieved a reputation as an able and experienced
Russian-language teacher. Everywhere – in Uvarovka, in
Kuzminki, in Black Yar, in the peat-mining village and at
the horse-breeding centre – she was known and appreciated,
and addressed respectfully as Anna Vasilevna.

A man was coming towards her across the field. 'And
what if he doesn't want to step aside for me?' Anna Vasilevna thought, amused by her fear. 'We cannot pass each

other on the path and, if one steps off it, one immediately
sinks into the snow.' But she knew very well that there was
not a man in the neighbourhood who would not have given
way to the Uvarovka schoolmistress.

They came up to each other. It was Frolov, the horse-
breaker at the horse-breeding centre.

'Good morning, Anna Vasilevna,' said Frolov, raising
the round fur hat off his strong, close-cropped head.

'Don't you do that! Put your hat on at once. It's so
cold!'

Frolov must surely have wanted to pull his hat well down
over his head as soon as possible, but he showed no hurry
in order to prove that he did not mind the frost. His fur
jacket fitted his elegant, slim figure closely, and he carried a
thin snake-like little whip, with which he tapped his white
knee-length felt boot.

'How is my Lyosha getting on? Not fooling about?'
Frolov inquired respectfully.

'Of course he fools about. All normal children do. They
just mustn't go too far,' Anna Vasilevna replied, conscious
of her experience as a teacher.

Frolov grinned.

'My Leshka is a good boy. He takes after his father!'

He stepped aside, and sank up to his knees in the snow;
like that he was no taller than a twelve-year-old.

Anna Vasilevna nodded to him condescendingly, and
went her way.

The two-storeyed school building, with wide windows
patterned by the frost, stood close to the road behind a
low fence. The snow was all pink right up to the road from
the reflection of the red school walls. The school had been
built on the road away from Uvarovka, because it catered for
children from the whole district – the neighbouring villages,
the horse-breeding settlement, the oil-industry workers'
sanatorium and the distant peat-mining village. And now
children in peaked caps and in caps with ear flaps, in bonnets

and in hoods, streamed along the road on either side of the school.

'Good morning, Anna Vasilevna' could be heard every second either in clear, ringing tones, or muffled and scarcely audible through the scarves and shawls that were wound round and round up to the eyes.

Anna Vasilevna's first lesson was with the fifth A*. The piercing bell that announced the beginning of the school day had hardly died down when Anna Vasilevna came into the class-room. The children stood up in a friendly way to greet her, and then settled down in their places. Quiet was not immediately established. There was a banging of desk lids and a squeaking of benches, and someone sighed noisily, apparently bidding farewell to the serenity of the morning atmosphere.

'Today we are going to continue learning about parts of speech.'

The class quietened down, and a heavy lorry with a trailer could be heard crawling along the road.

Anna Vasilevna remembered how last year she used to worry before a lesson, and would repeat to herself like a schoolgirl at an examination, 'The noun is that part of speech ... the noun is that part of speech ...' And she remembered too how she used to be tormented by a ridiculous fear that perhaps they would not understand her.

Anna Vasilevna smiled at this memory, pushed a hairpin back into her heavy knot of hair, and, conscious of the self-control which spread like warmth through her whole body, began in a calm voice:

'The word *noun* is used for that part of speech which is the subject. In grammar the subject is what we call everything about which we can ask, who is this, or what is this. For

---

*In the USSR children start school at the age of seven in the first form, and there are ten forms. Children in the fifth form should therefore be eleven. (Translator's note.)

instance: "Who is this?" – "A pupil." Or: "What is this?"
– "A book."'

'May I come in?' A small figure in worn felt boots and
covered in sparklets of frost that were thawing and losing
their brightness stood by the half-open door. The round
face was burning and as red from the frost as if it had been
rubbed with beetroot, while the eyebrows were grey with
rime.

'Late again, Savushkin?' Like most young teachers,
Anna Vasilevna enjoyed being stern, but on this occasion
her question sounded plaintive.

Assuming that the schoolmistress's words gave him
permission to enter the class-room, Savushkin quickly
slipped into his place. Anna Vasilevna saw the boy push his
oil-cloth bag into his desk, and, without turning his head,
say something to his neighbour, presumably asking what
she was explaining.

Anna Vasilevna was disappointed by Savushkin's late-
ness; it was an unfortunate mishap spoiling a day that had
begun well. She had had complaints about Savushkin being
late from the geography mistress, a shrivelled little old
woman who looked like a moth. Actually she often complained – of noisy classes and inattentive pupils. 'The first
lesson is so difficult,' the old woman would sigh. 'It is, for
those who cannot control the children and make the lesson
interesting,' Anna Vasilevna thought to herself with self-
assurance, and offered to exchange periods. She now felt
guilty towards the old lady, who was sufficiently perceptive
to recognize the challenge and rebuke in Anna Vasilevna's
amicable suggestion.

'Do you all understand?' Anna Vasilevna asked, addressing herself to the class.

'Yes, yes,' chorused the children.

'Good. Now give me some examples.'

There was absolute silence for some seconds, and then
someone said uncertainly:

'Cat.'

'Right,' said Anna Vasilevna, immediately remembering that last year the first example had also been 'cat'. And then there was an outburst.

'Window! Table! House! Road!'

'Right,' Anna Vasilevna went on saying.

The class bubbled happily. Anna Vasilevna was surprised by the delight with which the children named familiar objects, recognizing, as it were, their new and unaccustomed significance. The range of examples went on widening, but in the first minutes the children stuck to what was closest to them, to tangible objects – wheel, tractor, well, starling-house.

From a desk at the back where fat Vasyata sat there came a high, persistent voice:

'Nail ... nail ... nail.'

Then someone said timidly:

'Town.'

'Town, that's good,' said Anna Vasilevna approvingly. And then the words began to fly:

'Street, metro, tram, film.'

'That's enough,' said Anna Vasilevna. 'I see you understand.'

Rather unwillingly the voices fell silent; only fat Vasyata went on muttering his unacknowledged 'nail'. Suddenly, just as if he had woken up out of a dream, Savushkin stood up in his desk, and shouted out in a ringing tone:

'Winter oak.'

The children began to laugh.

'Quiet,' said Anna Vasilevna, banging the table with her hand.

'Winter oak,' Savushkin repeated, noticing neither the laughter of his schoolfellows, nor the teacher's admonishment. He did not speak as the other children had. The words were torn out of his soul, like a confession, or a joyful secret which he could not keep from spilling out of his heart.

Not understanding his strange excitement, Anna Vasilevna hid her irritation with difficulty, and said:

'Why winter? Just oak.'

'No, not just oak. Winter oak, that's the noun!'

'Sit down, Savushkin; this is what happens when you are late. "Oak" is a noun, and we have not yet come to what "winter" would be. Kindly come and see me in the staff-room during break.'

'There's winter oak for you,' someone sniggered from a back desk.

Savushkin sat down, smiling at his own thoughts, and not in the least perturbed by the teacher's threatening words. 'A difficult boy,' thought Anna Vasilevna.

The lesson continued.

'Sit down,' said Anna Vasilevna when Savushkin came in to the staff-room.

The boy sank into an armchair with pleasure, and bounced up and down on the springs a few times.

'Kindly explain why you are consistently late.'

'I really don't know, Anna Vasilevna,' he said, spreading out his hands in a grown-up way. 'I leave home an hour beforehand.'

How difficult it is to get at the truth in the very simplest matter! Many of the children lived much farther away than Savushkin, and yet none of them spent more than an hour getting to school.

'You live at Kuzminki?'

'No, by the sanatorium.'

'Are you not ashamed to say that you leave home an hour before school starts? It takes fifteen minutes to get from the sanatorium to the road, and then not more than half an hour to walk along the road.'

'I don't go along the road. I go the short way, straighting

through the forest,' said Savushkin, as if this circumstance surprised him.

'Not straighting, straight,' Anna Vasilevna corrected automatically.

She felt sad and confused as she always did when faced with a child telling lies. She was silent, hoping that Savushkin would say, 'I'm sorry, Anna Vasilevna, I was snowballing with some boys,' or something equally simple and innocent, but he only looked at her with big grey eyes, and his expression seemed to be saying, 'There now, it has all been explained. What else do you want of me?'

'It's a pity, Savushkin, a great pity! I shall have to speak to your parents.'

'I've only got a mother,' said Savushkin smiling.

Anna Vasilevna blushed slightly. She remembered Savushkin's mother, the 'shower-bath nurse', as her son called her. She worked at the hydropathic baths in the sanatorium, and was a thin, tired woman, with hands that were white and looked like cloth, through constant immersion in hot water. She was on her own, as her husband had been killed in the war, and she had three other children to feed and bring up besides Kolya.

Obviously Savushkina already had enough worries. Nevertheless Anna Vasilevna had to go and see her.

'I'll have to call on your mother.'

'Do come and see her, Anna Vasilevna. My mother will be pleased.'

'Unfortunately, I have nothing to say that will give her any pleasure. Does your mother work in the mornings?'

'No, she's on the second shift, from three o'clock.'

'Well, that's good. I am free at two. When lessons are over, you will take me home.'

The path along which Savushkin led Anna Vasilevna began just behind the school building. As soon as they stepped into the forest and the fir branches that looked like paws heavily laden with snow closed behind them, they were immediately transported into another world, an enchanted world of peace and silence. Magpies and crows flew from tree to tree, shaking the branches, knocking off the fir cones, and sometimes their wings caught on the dry, brittle twigs, and broke them. Yet not a sound could be heard.

All around everything was white. Only high up the wind had blown on the tops of the soaring weeping birches, so that they showed up black, and their delicate little branches looked as if they had been etched in Indian ink on the blue surface of the sky.

The path ran by the stream, sometimes alongside it, submissively following its twisting course, sometimes rising high up and winding along a steep bank.

Now and again the trees would part and reveal sunny, joyful glades, criss-crossed with hare tracks that looked like watch-chains. There would also be heavier tracks shaped like a trefoil, and they must have been made by a larger beast. These tracks ran right into the thicket, in among tree-trunks that had fallen to the wind.

'An elk has been here,' said Savushkin, as if talking about a close friend, when he saw that Anna Vasilevna was interested in the tracks. 'But don't be afraid,' he added in response to the glance the schoolmistress threw towards the depths of the forest, 'the deer is gentle.'

'Have you seen one?' asked Anna Vasilevna excitedly.

'No,' – Savushkin sighed. 'I haven't actually seen one, not alive. But I've seen his pellets.'

'Pellets?'

'Droppings,' Savushkin explained shyly.

Slipping under an archway of bent branches, the path again ran down to the stream. In some places the stream was covered with a thick white blanket of snow, while in others it was imprisoned in an armour of clear ice, and sometimes living water would gleam through the ice, looking like a dark, malevolent eye.

'Why has it not all frozen up?' asked Anna Vasilevna.

'There's a warm spring which rises up in it. Look! See that little jet?'

Bending over an unfrozen patch in the middle of the ice, Anna Vasilevna could see a thin little thread rising up from the bottom; by the time it reached the surface it had broken into tiny bubbles. This minute stem with the little bubbles on it looked like a spray of lily of the valley.

'There are loads of springs like that here,' said Savushkin enthusiastically. 'The stream is alive even under the snow.'

He brushed away the snow, and they saw the coal-black but transparent water.

Anna Vasilevna noticed that, when the snow fell into the water, it did not melt away, but immediately turned into slush, a greenish jelly suspended in the water as if it were algae. She was so pleased with this that she began to kick snow into the water with the toe of her boot, and was enraptured when a particularly intricate figure emerged from a large lump of snow. She was so enthralled that she did not at once notice that Savushkin had gone on, and was waiting for her, sitting high up in the fork of a bough overhanging the stream. Anna Vasilevna caught him up. Here the action of the warm springs came to an end, and the stream was covered with a thin film of ice. Light shadows darted rapidly over the marble surface.

'Look, the ice is so thin that we can even see the current!'

'No, Anna Vasilevna, I'm swaying this branch, and that's its shadow moving.'

Anna Vasilevna bit her tongue. Clearly here in the forest she had better keep quiet.

Savushkin strode on again in front of the schoolmistress, bending down slightly and looking around him.

And the forest led them on still farther along its intricate, tangled paths. It seemed as if there was no end to the trees, the snowdrifts and the silence of the sun-dappled twilight.

Suddenly, in the distance, a smoky-blue chink appeared.

The trees began to thin out, there was more space and it was fresher. Soon there was no longer a chink, but a broad shaft of sunlight appeared before them, and in it something glistened and sparkled, swarming with frosty stars.

The path went round a hazel bush, and straightaway the forest fell away on either side. In the middle of the glade, clothed in glittering white raiment, huge and majestic as a cathedral, stood an oak. It seemed as if the trees had respectfully stood aside to give their older brother room to display himself in all his strength. The lower branches spread out over the glade like a canopy.

Snow was packed into the deep corrugations of the bark, and the trunk, three times the normal girth, seemed to be embroidered with silver thread. Few of the leaves that had withered in the autumn had fallen, and the oak was covered right up to the top with leaves encased in snow.

'There it is, the winter oak!'

Anna Vasilevna approached the oak timidly, and the mighty, magnanimous guardian of the forest quietly waved a branch in greeting to her.

Savushkin had no idea what was going on in the schoolmistress's heart, and he busied himself at the foot of the oak, as if approaching an old acquaintance.

'Look, Anna Vasilevna!'

He had managed to drag away a lump of snow that had stuck to the ground and was covered with the remains of dead grass. There, in a little hollow, lay a ball wrapped in rotted leaves as thin as spiders' webs. Sharp-tipped quills stuck out through the leaves. Anna Vasilevna guessed that this was a hedgehog.

'See how he has muffled himself up!'

Savushkin carefully covered the hedgehog up with his unpretentious blanket. Then he scraped away the snow from another root to reveal a tiny grotto, with a bunch of icicles hanging from its roof. A brown frog was sitting inside; it could have been made of cardboard, and its skin, tightly drawn over its bone structure, might have been lacquered. Savushkin touched the frog, but it did not move.

'It's pretending to be dead,' said Savushkin laughing. 'But just let the sun warm it, and you'll see how it hops about!'

He went on showing Anna Vasilevna his own small world. A number of other lodgers – beetles, lizards and small insects – had taken refuge at the foot of the oak. Some had buried themselves under the roots, others had wriggled into crevices in the bark; emaciated, practically hollow inside, they were surviving the winter in a sleep from which they could not be woken. The mighty tree, laden with life, had gathered so much living warmth round itself that the poor creatures could not have found a better lodging. Anna Vasilevna was gazing with delighted interest at this secret forest life, hitherto unknown to her, when she heard Savushkin exclaim in concern:

'Oh, we'll miss mother now!'

Anna Vasilevna hurriedly looked at her watch – it was a quarter past three. She felt as if she had walked into a trap. Privately asking the oak to forgive her for being human and slightly cunning, she said:

'Well, Savushkin, this just shows that the short cut is not always the surest. You'll have to go by the road.'

Savushkin did not say anything; he just hung his head.

'Heavens,' thought Anna Vasilevna painfully, 'could one have shown one's incompetence more clearly?' She remembered the lesson that day, and all her other lessons: how inadequately, drily and coldly she had spoken of words and language, without which man is dumb and powerless to express his feelings before the world, when all the time her own native tongue was as fresh, beautiful and rich as life is generous and beautiful.

And she had considered herself an able teacher! Quite possibly she had not yet taken the first step along that road which takes more than a whole life to traverse. And how can one find that road? It is no more easy and simple to discover it than to find the key to Koschey's* casket. But perhaps the first signpost was dimly visible in the delight, incomprehensible to her at the time, with which the children shouted out 'tractor,' 'well,' 'starling-house.'

'Well, Savushkin, thank you for the walk. Of course you can come this way.'

'Thank you, Anna Vasilevna.'

Savushkin blushed; he very much wanted to say to the schoolmistress that he would never be late again, but he was afraid of telling a lie. He turned up the collar of his jacket and pulled down his cap with the ear flaps.

'I'll see you home.'

'You needn't, Savushkin. I'll go by myself.'

He looked at the schoolmistress doubtfully, and then he picked up a stick from the ground, broke off its crooked end and gave the stick to Anna Vasilevna.

'If the elk comes near you, hit him on the back, and he'll run away. Or better still, just wave the stick at him, and that will be enough. Otherwise he might take offence and leave the forest altogether.'

'All right, Savushkin, I won't hit him.'

When she had gone a little way, Anna Vasilevna turned round to have a last look at the oak, rosy white in the setting sun, and at its foot she saw a small, dark figure. Savushkin had not gone home. He was guarding his teacher from afar. And suddenly Anna Vasilevna understood that the most amazing thing in the forest was not the winter oak, but the small human being in the worn felt boots and the poor, patched clothes, the son of the soldier who had been killed in the war and the 'shower-bath nurse', a mysterious and wonderful future citizen.

She waved to him and quietly went off along the twisting path.

* Koshchey is a mysterious spirit in Russian folklore. (Translator's note.)

KAZAKOV

LIKE many contemporary Soviet writers, Yury Kazakov graduated from the Gorky Literary Institute. His first collection of stories, *At the Railway Halt,* earned unanimous praise when it was published in 1958 and established its author's reputation as a master of Russian prose. Kazakov's stories concentrate on the emotional experiences of sensitive, often isolated individuals and are strongly reminiscent of Chekhov's work, for which Kazakov has expressed great admiration. A fine example of his art is 'On the Island' (1958) wherein the questions which run through so much nineteenth-century Russian literature – What is happiness? What is love? What shall we do? – are debated in a modern setting.

ON THE ISLAND

Translated by Roger Cockrell

THE steamer which had brought Zabavin gave a deep, sonorous blast on its siren, turned, heeling over to starboard, and set off for the remote northerly stations. But Zabavin was so fed up after three days on this dirty white boat, with the clatter of its winches when mooring, the hum of its engines, the short-legged captain, the first officer with his insolent, dissolute face, the ill-mannered waitresses and the non-stop drunkenness down in the third-class buffet that he didn't even look round.

The more Zabavin travelled in the north in his position as factory inspector, the more humdrum and monotonous it seemed. He no longer even noticed the forbidding grandeur of the cliffs, the beauty of the sea and the northern landscape, although he had at one time been very impressed by it all. And now, as he sat in the boat taking him ashore, irritated, bad-tempered and unshaven, he paid no attention either to the strange outline of the island, crouching before him in the water like some hump-backed monster, or to the dark-green rocks on the sea-bed, or to the happy chatter of his fellow-passengers, but just wanted to get as quickly as possible onto dry land and into a warm room.

When the boat had pushed its way through the mass of launches, motor-boats and other small craft and tied up to the wooden jetty, Zabavin was the first to clamber out on shore, where he stopped and stretched his legs, relishing the feel of firm land under his feet.

The jetty was cluttered with huge bales of dried bluish and brown seaweed, barrels of cement, pipes, and stacks of rails rusting against the sides of a low warehouse. There was a strong intoxicatingly sweet aroma of seaweed, mingled with the fainter smell of fish, ropes, oil, planks, hay and the sea – all the smells in fact of a typical landing-stage.

Zabavin yawned and wearily set off along the trampled-down slag covering the jetty, past the workshops from which came the faint rumble of machinery, past the boiler-room, its heat momentarily warming the cold, morning air. All around him the forlorn-looking earth was covered with a whitish moss and with outcrops of grey rocks. Solitary horses and cows wandered aimlessly about the moss; emaciated, cast away on this wild, remote island to which they were utterly irrelevant and unnecessary, they were a pitiful sight. He grimaced, sighed, asked some workmen the way to the office and went straight there without looking at anything else, thinking only of how soon he could get some sleep; his last night on the steamer he had hardly slept at all.

He was shown a room where he slept soundly. On waking, he shaved, dabbed some eau-de-cologne onto his hair which he carefully combed until it shone. Then he brewed himself some strong hot tea which he drank out of a thick glass and enjoyed a cigarette. He then put on his tie, picked up his folder of documents and, delighting in the sense of well-being and cleanliness, glad that for a few days at least he had escaped the revolting smell of salt cod which he had grown so tired of on the steamer, smartly dressed, refreshed and in good humour, smelling of eau-de-cologne and expensive tobacco, he set off for the office to get down at last to what he had come here to do.

Zabavin spent the whole of that day and the two succeeding ones on routine work, checking the documents which were brought in thick folders to his office, performing complex calculations, examining vats of gelatine, crushers, warehouses and laboratories. And all the time he maintained a cold, formal and business-like air, while the manager, delighted to see a fresh face, bustled around him, chatting and eagerly asking about Archangel. The manager, in a skull-cap, with bulging eyes, protruding eyelids and thick folds on his dove-grey fleshy cheeks, followed Zabavin everywhere, heaving from side to side and lumbering about on his heavy legs, perspiring and suffering from asthma. Next to this huge, obscenely stout figure Zabavin, with his lean frame, dark hair and fashionable narrow trousers, looked a young man. The manager, who more than once informed Zabavin that he would shortly be retiring on a pension, would recite Fet's poetry in a quavering voice gazing out to sea, and, with tears in his eyes, invite Zabavin to join him in partaking of whatever 'heaven has provided'. But Zabavin, who could sense the openly avid glances of the girls in the office, simply became increasingly colder and more polite.

II

One day Zabavin had to go to the weather station to send a telegram to Archangel. He found it without any difficulty from its tall radio mast, radiating a web of taut steel cables down into the ground. He climbed up to the entrance and knocked. When there was no reply, he opened the door and went into the building. Immediately he found himself in a large, warm room with a varnished floor, a table by the window and an aneroid barometer in a thin wooden case. On the table lay a chronometer with a velvet cover, a pair of binoculars and several open journals. From the room led three or four other doors, one of which suddenly burst open. A radio-operator stood there, looking into the room. He was a self-possessed young man with a thick neck, a prominent Adam's apple, large ears and hair brushed down over his forehead. Seeing Zabavin, he made a threatening face.

'Who are you, then?' he asked timidly, trying to speak more gruffly and not knowing what to do with his large hands. Without waiting for Zabavin to finish his reply, he rudely interrupted him, frowning and blushing, saying that the director of the station was not there at the moment, that without her he could not accept anything for transmission and that there would be no radio communication with Archangel until the evening.

Zabavin smiled and said that he would call in again that evening. Feeling the operator's frightened and suspicious look on the back of his neck, he went out onto the entrance porch and, taking advantage of the fine weather and his temporary freedom, set off to wander around the island.

He climbed up to the white tower of the lighthouse from where, looking back, he noticed for the first time the beauty of the sea as it shimmered in the heat of the sun. Next to the lighthouse he came across a small wooden chapel, its windows and doors boarded up, and, a little farther down, an old cemetery. Breathing in the fresh air, he began to walk in amongst the sunken mounds and dark gravestones. On one of them he was just able to make out this inscription:

BENEATH THIS STONE LIE THE REMAINS
OF VASILY IVANOV PRUDNIKOV
SERVANT OF GOD
LIEUTENANT AND KEEPER
OF THE LIGHTHOUSE
FROM BELAYA SMOLENSK PROVINCE
ENDED THIS LIFE AT THE AGE OF 56
THE 6TH DAY OF SEPTEMBER 1858
AFTER A VISIT TO SOLOVETSKY MONASTERY
MAY THE LORD RECEIVE HIS SOUL IN PEACE

'So . . .' mused Zabavin sadly, 'a hundred years ago . . . one hundred years.' He tried to read some of the inscriptions on the other stones, but these were even older, completely covered in moss and impossible to make out. Then he sat down on one of the stones, facing the sea, where he stayed for a long time without moving, immersed in the melancholy beauty of autumn and the abandoned cemetery, pondering on the people who must have lived here perhaps more than a hundred years ago. Then slowly, engrossed in deep and pleasant thoughts, he walked back down to his room for a sleep.

He slept badly, however, and soon woke up and went to sit by the window. While he had been asleep fog had set in and covered the island. It was very thick, obscuring everything around – the radio mast, the lighthouse, the long, dark line of hills, the workshops and the factory chimneys. Under the window some goats were huddled together, standing quite still. It seemed that life on the island had ceased; the fog absorbed all sounds, except for the plaintive and ominous bellow of a foghorn somewhere to the north.

Zabavin's visit to the cemetery had awakened in him strange feelings towards the island, and he was unable to rid himself of the thought of the lighthouse-keeper who had lived and died one hundred years ago, when everything here had very probably been even more depressing. The fog, the outlandish cries of the foghorn and the motionless goats all dispirited him and he began to crave conversation, company and music. He quickly got ready and set out for the weather station, looking around him anxiously, finding his way in the fog and the approaching early autumn dusk only with difficulty.

The director of the weather station was a young woman of about twenty-six with the uncommon name of Augusta. She was small, with slender legs and close-cropped hair, and this, together with the remarkably soft and frail line of her neck, the dark oval of her face and the large eyes framed by thick eyelashes, lent her whole face a strikingly animated appearance. She was known throughout the island simply as Gustya. When she smiled her cheeks became suffused with a warm glow which spread immediately to her small ears. Looking at her, Zabavin felt strangely moved and excited and wanted to embrace her, to stroke her short, downy hair and to feel her faint, warm breath on his neck...

Having given the text of his telegram to the radio

operator, he fixed Gustya with his dark, shining eyes, and asked her if he could sit for a while and listen to the radio. Gustya quickly, willingly and, it seemed to Zabavin, eagerly led him to her own little room, turned on the table lamp and went to put on some tea.

Becoming more and more flustered, she fetched the cups, setting them on the table with her small slender hands, rattling the teaspoons, and pouring sugar into the sugar-basin, while Zabavin sat, tugging down the bottoms of his narrow trousers and crossing his legs, as was his custom. He switched on the radio, which shone with a dark-red glow, tuned in to some near-by Norwegian station, lit a cigarette and set his lips in a happy expression.

With an unaccustomed attentiveness he suddenly began to scrutinize this enchanting woman and her tiny room with its single south-facing window, the dozen or so books on the little bookcase, the rug on the floor and the narrow, tidily made and evidently hard bed ... He remembered the avid expressions of the women at the factory and, to stop himself smiling, began to think of the island, the cemetery and the darkness and fog outside. But, strangely, such thoughts now no longer troubled or depressed him; on the contrary, he listened to the transparently clear music and the crackling from the stove in the other room, and stealthily watched the woman's movements with an ever-increasing sense of enjoyment.

'Astonishing! I had no idea that an evening like this lay ahead of me!' he exclaimed happily. 'You know what it's like; you travel and travel, and everywhere it's the same – the tea, the stale grey rolls, the loneliness – even if your wife is with you! But luck like today comes once in a blue moon ...'

'Ah!' said Gustya, lowering her eyes. 'You're married? Have you been married for long?'

'Yes,' Zabavin answered somewhat dejectedly. 'And we have two children ... Terrible! I still can't get used to the fact that I'm married, that I'm thirty-five years old – time passes so quickly. When you travel alone, or find yourself sitting in the evening in some waiting-room or other, you keep on thinking to yourself that for ages now you've been dreaming of love, or of some extraordinary happiness, but nothing happens and you rush about the place doing your job and growing apart from your family . . . But my wife is a fine person; there are others who are worse off.'

Zabavin suddenly saw Gustya looking at him in a strange way, and he recollected himself and blushed.

'Forgive me . . .' he mumbled, experiencing a sudden self-dissatisfaction. 'What am I thinking of? All this is very boring for you and I just got carried away. I've been silent all week and this is such a wonderful evening . . .'

'Please don't apologize!' replied Gustya hastily and gave a melancholy smile. 'At least, you're not complaining . . .'

'What do you mean?'

'Husbands on business trips generally don't love their wives,' said Gustya, this time mockingly, pouring Zabavin a cup of tea. 'Come on, have your tea.'

Zabavin laughed and picked up his cup. As they talked, he soon learnt that she had worked there for a long time, was already contracted onto a higher salary, that she was bored and wanted to go to Archangel or Leningrad. They talked for a bit about boredom, referring to mutual acquaintances, and, when the conversation turned to love and happiness, they both became even livelier.

'There you are talking about conscious love,' said Zabavin thoughtfully and bitterly, although Gustya had not been talking about conscious love at all. 'Everyone discusses love, deciding and judging who should love whom. Writers write about love, and readers sit round and debate whether he's worthy of her or she of him, which of them is the better, purer and more aware person, who is more suited to this socialist age of ours. But in the meantime not one of us can define what love really is! And, the more

I think about it, the more I become convinced that such qualities as intelligence, talent, honour and so on play a very minor part in love and that the most important thing is something else, something which is not talked about and not understood at all. You don't have to look very far! I know one fellow, for instance, who's an idiot, an insolent drunkard, a man without a conscience or a sense of honour. And just imagine it! Women are mad about him, clever, intelligent women moreover. And he knows that they love him, borrows money from them, drinks, and treats them abominably, reducing them to tears. I've seen it myself. Why?'

'You obviously don't see in him what these women do,' said Gustya seriously.

'Ah, yes, but what is it they see in him? Wit? Talent? Depth? No, of course not, he's an insolent, lazy fool. With his ugly fat face, he's not even good-looking! I can't for the life of me understand why!'

In the radio-room a chair squeaked, there was a rattle of keys and, after a moment's silence, the sound of footsteps. 'Well, it's all finished . . . The reports are on the table!' the operator shouted and slammed the outside door. 'Tomorrow's forecast is for fine weather! I'm off to the club now!' he yelled from outside, stamping in the entrance. Everything inside became quiet.

The expression on Gustya's face immediately changed. She seemed to be frightened of something and glanced back out of the window. She looked for a moment directly at Zabavin and then lowered her gaze, blushing. And Zabavin, as if he were no longer thirty-five, no longer had behind him either the army, or his wife and children, or his job, suddenly felt a keen, tingling excitement and dryness in his mouth, precisely what he used to feel as a boy when he fell in love with schoolgirls and kissed them on quiet, summer evenings.

'And then there is happiness, too . . .' began Zabavin

quietly, and from the way he said it Gustya realized that he was going to say something serious and important. She grew calm and smiled at him, her beautiful velvety eyes widening and coming to rest on his face.

'Generally people look forward to the future,' he went on quickly, gulping down his tea and sensing the darkness outside and the chill breath of the sea. 'They look forward to the future and lead lives which are trivial, fussy and boring ... They live, without seeing or noticing anything good around them, cursing their existence, certain that one day happiness will come. Everyone's the same, you're the same and so am I ... And yet there is happiness in everything, everywhere, happiness in the fact that you and I are sitting here together and drinking tea, in the fact that I like you and you know that I do ...'

Zabavin faltered, sighed, and smiled as if to himself, and Gustya who had grown quite crimson could not bring herself to raise her eyes.

'I would like some strong, wise person to come and force us all to take a good look at ourselves. For, the longer we live, the less happiness there is. Mankind is always young but we ... we get older ... I am now thirty-five, and you are ...'

'Twenty-six,' whispered Gustya, willing herself to lift her shining face and to look directly into his eyes.

'There you are, you see! In a year's time, I will be thirty-six and you will be twenty-seven. Both of us, like everyone else, will have grown a year older, we shall have lost something, some essential particle of vitality, a certain number of cells will have died for ever, and so it will go on, from year to year ... And, most important of all, it will not be just our bodies that will grow old, it's not just that we shall grow grey and bald and that we shall have various illnesses which we don't have now, but it's that our inner selves will grow older too, gradually, imperceptibly but inevitably. Where's the happiness in that? No, there isn't

any, and I can't understand those people who keep waiting
and saying to themselves: "When summer comes, I shall be
happy," and, when summer does come and they're not
happy, they think: "When winter comes, I shall be
happy . . ." It's not worth talking about even!'

'Where is happiness to be found then?' she asked
quietly.

'Where? I ask myself that too. Take you, for example.
Here you are wanting to escape from this island, waiting
and thinking: "In a year or so I shall be happy." No! It is
precisely now that you are happy, immeasurably and hugely
happy, because you are young and healthy, you have
beautiful eyes, because now, when you are twenty-six, it is
pure joy to look into your eyes, and you have an important
job, and the sea, and this island . . . Just think!'

'It's easy to talk!' Gustya said, smiling uncertainly.

'Yes! It's a big world, of course, with plenty of beautiful
places; why this island, if it comes to that? Certainly
Archangel is a far more interesting place. When you think,
as I am thinking now, of Archangel or Moscow or Leningrad, we can both imagine the theatres, lights, museums,
exhibitions, noise, traffic and so on . . . Life, in a word! I'm
right, aren't I? And yet when I'm there, at home, I don't
notice any of these things but begin to think of them only
when I'm far away. And when I arrive in Archangel I
suddenly learn that my son is ill, that I've got a conference
at work that evening, that there's a report urgently needed
. . . and immediately you're caught up in life's endless round
and you don't get to see any theatres or anything of the
sort. In what way then am I better off than you? In some
higher sense, as it were? No, not at all, you're far happier
than I am: you're twenty-six, whereas I'm thirty-five!

'Sooner or later of course you'll leave here and go to
Leningrad, you'll see the Neva, the bridges, St Isaac's
Cathedral. But, believe me, once you've left here, you will
certainly remember this island, its inhabitants, the sea, the

smell of seaweed, the fleecy clouds, the sun, the thunderstorms, the Northern Lights, the storms; and in years to come you'll realize that it was precisely here that you were happy.'

'Perhaps, I don't know,' said Gustya pensively. 'I haven't really thought about it much . . .'

'Yes, it's almost always like that. We regret the past – everything always looks better from a distance.'

Zabavin had grown quite agitated and, looking at Gustya, he thought how wonderful it would be to be married to her. He tried to rid himself of such thoughts, realizing their futility and his total inability to change his life in any way, but he could not stop having these thoughts and was quite unable to leave, although it was already late.

He got up to go only when they heard the radio operator return from the club, go to his room, find some jazz on the radio and start to whistle. Gustya went out with Zabavin onto the porch where they stood for a long time, getting used to the darkness.

'I'll go with you a little way because of the cables,' she said and took his hand. Her hand felt rough and hot in his; it was trembling. 'You sweet, kind person,' thought Zabavin in silent gratitude and at once began disconsolately to think about himself.

The fog had cleared and the foghorn long since fallen silent. Overhead small stars twinkled piercingly, and across the sky ran the forked river of the Milky Way, broken in places but clearly visible. Quickly accustoming herself to the darkness, Gustya went on ahead and Zabavin could only just make out her pale headscarf. Gingerly he felt his way along the stone path through the moss. They walked for a few minutes in silence, then Gustya stopped and he immediately saw the scattered yellow lights of the settlement beneath them.

'There you are,' Gustya said. 'You'll be able to make it yourself now without losing your way. Good-bye'

'Wait a little longer,' he begged. 'I'll have a cigarette.'

'All right,' Gustya answered, after a moment's thought. She took his hand once more, went a few paces and stopped by a fence, leaning up against it and turning to face him. Zabavin lit a cigarette, trying in vain to see the expression on her face by the light of the match.

From down below came the measured pounding of the breakers; the tide was coming in. There was a cool breeze, bringing with it the peculiarly melancholy smell of the autumnal sea. The sea itself was deep, shrouded in mysterious blackness.

Zabavin suddenly noticed that every so often Gustya's face shone palely in the darkness. He glanced round and after a few seconds saw the tall star on top of the lighthouse shining out radiantly for a moment and then disappearing. Once again it flashed, followed by darkness, and so it continued all the time, and the sight of this fleeting, silent light awoke in him a strange sensation of pleasure.

He turned to Gustya once more.

'You're a wonderful girl,' he whispered tenderly and sorrowfully and, feeling a sense of shame as if he were standing to one side in self-condemnation, he bent down and kissed her firmly on her still, cold lips.

Gustya silently turned away from him; the sight of her sweet, small, lonely figure brought a lump to Zabavin's throat. He put his arm round her thin shoulders and led her into the darkness over the soft moss through which the hard rocky ground could be felt, to some bushes, rustling in the wind, and low trees giving off the harsh astringent smell of autumn. Finally they stopped, farther away from the lighthouse; in front lay the impenetrable dark and the roar of the sea.

'Why, why?' she said unhappily. 'You don't know me at all. But why, though?'

But he began once more to kiss her face and hands,

knowing now that this was the happiness and the love which they had so recently been discussing.

'Please stop; let's go back,' she asked quietly.

'Don't be angry,' he said just as quietly, and meekly followed her. At the fence where they had first kissed Gustya suddenly stopped, sobbing and pressing her face into his cold raincoat.

'Until tomorrow,' she said, finally, wiping her tears and sighing. 'I shan't be able to sleep at all now . . . Why, why must it be like this?'

Pushing him away, she set off quickly home, almost at a run, but Zabavin stayed for a long time, looking now at the flashing of the lighthouse, now at the distant warm light in Gustya's window. His face burned, there was a tickling in his throat and he stood there coughing a little, unable to move; his heart beat in slow, heavy strokes.

III

The steamer on which Zabavin was intending to go to Archangel was due to arrive in a week's time. Ahead lay seven impossibly wonderful, happy days. But the following morning the radio operator from the weather station came to the office where Zabavin worked and silently handed him a radio message. On it were the following irregularly written lines: 'EXPECTED ARCHANGEL SOONEST STOP DON'T WAIT FOR STEAMER STOP TODAY OR TOMORROW SCHOONER SUVOI ARRIVES ISLAND STOP MAXIMOV'

Zabavin grew cold. The radio operator went away. Zabavin wanted to continue working but was now quite unable to understand anything that was said to him or remember any figures. Having somehow or other got through the work and signed the last documents, he completed the final formalities with the manager and went home.

That evening, after he had shaved more carefully than usual, combed his hair and tied his tie with cold fingers, and got ready to go to Gustya for the last time, a schooner came in to the island. It appeared suddenly, like fate, announcing its arrival with a short blast on its siren, by the green and white lights on its masts and by the radio message which was received first at the lighthouse and then at the weather station. Zabavin agitatedly sent off a reply, and the schooner dropped anchor until morning.

Zabavin and Gustya walked around the island until two in the morning, disturbing the ptarmigans which rose up, fluttering their wings in a strangely subdued manner. They sat on rough stones, holding each other tightly, and feeling for each other a love that grew stronger and more painful, while all the time the lights on the schooner shone as a constant reminder of their impending separation.

Then they went to the weather station where once again there was the red glow of the radio, the faint sound of music and the murmuring of announcers. Once again they drank tea and talked, unable to take their eyes off each other . . .

'Is this happiness, then?' she asked. 'Tell me!'

'Yes . . . this is happiness!' he answered ruefully.

'My God!' she said, her eyes filling with tears.

And Zabavin would now quite willingly have given up everything, his family, his job, and stayed there for ever. But he knew that this was impossible. Gustya knew this too, and their hearts became even heavier. And in this way passed their first and last night together.

Dawn came, reluctantly and hesitantly. The window grew light. Zabavin got up, glanced in the mirror, where he saw his pale, drawn, frightened, unhappy and suffering face, went to the window and wiped the condensation off the glass. The sky was light-blue and transparently empty; the sea was huge, graphically vivid and quite calm. The black schooner, as if from some evil dream, lay at anchor a couple of hundred yards offshore; the lights on its masts still showed faintly. Everything, as far as the eye could see, on land and out to sea, was deathly quiet and still. Not a single person was visible. Suddenly a large dark dog appeared from behind some rocks and ran purposively past the window, holding its tail erect. Its appearance was so unexpected that Zabavin was momentarily quite startled.

He turned from the window and looked at Gustya. She was sitting by the table, her arms pressed to her breasts, across her heart. Her eyes were closed and the small, pale oval of her face was calm, as if she were asleep. Zabavin carefully got dressed, his waterproof crackling and rustling as he put it on. Then, after a moment's thought, he took a bottle of eau-de-cologne out of his case, poured some into his hand, spilling a little on the floor, and smeared it into his face.

'Gustya, it's time to go,' he said hoarsely, and lit a cigarette.

'What, already? Wait a moment . . . I'll come with you and see you off,' she said hastily.

Zabavin turned back to the window, and hunched his shoulders, listening to Gustya's hurried breathing as she moved about the room.

They went out together onto the porch. Zabavin breathed in the sharp, cold morning air, huddling up against it; in front of him he could see the brightening dawn and the grey moss, encrusted with hoarfrost. They walked together, not along the path, but straight down to the sea. The moss crunched underfoot. The dog reappeared and started to run behind them.

It was low tide and the rowing boat lay on wooden rollers some distance from the water. They had to drag it a long way, growing red and puffing from the exertion, until at last they were able to climb in and push off from the shore. Zabavin took the oars and began slowly to row out to the schooner. The dog stood on the beach long after they had gone, its muzzle raised attentively, sniffing the air, and then it suddenly started to whine faintly, shuffling its wet paws in the sand. Gustya sat in the stern, looking over the top of Zabavin's head, and worked the scull.

The water was unusually clear. Rocks, sand, seaweed like horses' tails, and fronds of sea-kale drifted quietly along beneath them. From time to time Zabavin would stop rowing and peer at the darkly pink jellyfish hanging motionless in the water, amazed that anything could absorb his interest at such a time.

The boat hit the side of the schooner with a muffled thud. The captain, wearing a dark-blue padded jacket and boots, came up on deck immediately. He had no cap, long fair hair, and high cheekbones; his youthful face was puffy from sleep.

'Comrade Zabavin?' he asked in a strong northern accent, leaning over the side. 'Pass me the end of your line.'

Zabavin handed him his suitcase and threw the rope. Then he turned to Gustya and, swaying from side to side, took three steps to the stern. She stood up and looked into his face through the veil of tears filling her eyes.

For a long time they stood, kissing each other with painful intensity. Then Zabavin, choking, turned and climbed on board the schooner. The captain, who had been watching them thoughtfully, gave him a hand and then quickly vanished down into the crew's quarters at the bows of the ship.

A minute later sleepy-looking sailors emerged from their quarters, tugging on their jackets, and the schooner came to life. The dark imprints of boots covered the frosty deck, the engine started, the anchor chain rattled. An almost imperceptible breeze arose, ruffling the smooth surface of the water. A lock of hair fell over Gustya's forehead but she sat motionless, not smoothing it back.

The captain took the wheel himself and, with a glance at

Zabavin, ordered slow ahead. The schooner began to move away from the rowing boat. An unkempt sailor stood on the bows throwing a weighted line into the water and shouting the mark in a raucous voice.

'Eight metres!'

'Seven!'

'Seven and a half!'

In the water greenish rocks, dark clumps of seaweed and jellyfish were visible, just as before.

Zabavin stood at the side and watched the land and the rowing boat recede. Gustya still sat there, not stirring, in the stern of the boat. Its black bows, raised high out of the water, were being pushed gently towards the shore by the wind. Zabavin watched the boat and the island with a dry, prickling sensation in his eyes, and a strange, empty ringing in his ears.

Emerging from the dangerous shallows into the open sea, the schooner picked up speed. The captain handed the wheel over to a sailor, left the wheelhouse and came to stand beside Zabavin.

'By tomorrow evening we shall be in Archangel,' he said quietly.

The island was now only a thin, bluish line; all that could be picked out clearly was the white tower of the lighthouse. A fair-sized swell had got up and the schooner's hull was shuddering from the diesel engine. Then even the line of the island disappeared, leaving nothing but water all around – the smooth, steep-sided waves running as far as the horizon. The sun was rising but there were clouds approaching from the east, and the sky was getting no lighter.

'There's going to be a bit of a blow,' said the captain, yawning. 'Hey, you there, clear the decks! Look lively!' he suddenly shouted harshly. 'Why don't you come below, into the crew's quarters,' he invited Zabavin.

Once down below, they sat down opposite each other at a narrow table and began to smoke.

'Was that your wife?' asked the captain, after a few moments' silence.

'No,' answered Zabavin faintly, his lips shaking.

'Lie down and have a rest,' the captain suggested. 'There's a spare bunk over there.'

Zabavin obediently took his things off and lay down on the hard, narrow bunk; at its head a lifebelt was fixed. The cabin almost imperceptibly rose and fell with the waves. The water gurgled merrily along the sides. 'So that's happiness,' thought Zabavin and immediately saw in front of him the image of Gustya's face. 'So that's love! How strange . . . love!'

As he lay there, his lips pressed together in anguish, he could not stop thinking of Gustya or of the island, and all the while he could see her face and eyes and hear her voice until he no longer knew whether he was awake or dreaming. Outside the water gurgled along, like the cheerful rushing of an ever-flowing stream.

SOLZHENITSYN

In 1962 Alexander Solzhenitsyn achieved fame almost overnight with the publication in the Soviet Union of his *One Day in the Life of Ivan Denisovich*. This was followed by the novels *Cancer Ward*, *The First Circle* and *August 1914* and by his powerful indictment of the Soviet concentration camps, *The Gulag Archipelago*. In 1974 Solzhenitsyn, who had been awarded the Nobel Prize for Literature four years earlier, was expelled from the Soviet Union; he settled in Western Europe – and found there almost as much to censure as in his homeland. Seeing literature as a vehicle for enlightenment, Solzhenitsyn writes in a blunt style and is usually moralistic. He has produced very few short stories inasmuch as that delicate genre is clearly not his most natural medium. The modest 'Zakhar-the-Pouch' was first published in 1966.

ZAKHAR-THE-POUCH

Translated by Michael Glenny

You asked me to tell you something about my cycling holiday last summer. Well, if it's not too boring, listen to this one about Kulikovo Field.

We had been meaning to go there for a long time, but it was somehow a difficult place to reach. There are no brightly painted notices or signposts to show you the way, and you won't find it on a single map, even though this battle cost more Russian lives in the fourteenth century than Borodino did in the nineteenth. There has only been one such encounter for fifteen hundred years, not only in Russia but in all Europe. It was a battle not merely between principalities or nation-states, but between continents.

Perhaps we chose a rather roundabout way to get there: from Epiphania through Kazanovka and Monastyrshchina. It was only because there had been no rain till then that we were able to ride instead of pushing our bikes; to cross the Don, which was not yet in full spate, and its tributary, the Nepryadva, we wheeled them over narrow, two-plank footbridges.

After a long trek, we stood on a hill and caught sight of what looked like a needle pointing into the sky from a distant flat-topped rise. We went downhill and lost sight of it. Then, we started to climb again, and the grey needle reappeared, this time more distinct, and next to it we saw what looked like a church. There seemed to be something uniquely strange about its design, something never seen except in fairytales: its domes looked transparent and fluid; they shimmered deceptively in the cascading sunlight of the hot August day – one minute they were there and the next they were gone.

We guessed rightly that we would be able to quench our

thirst and fill our water-bottles at the well in the valley, which proved to be invaluable later on. But the peasant who handed us the bucket, in reply to our question: 'Where's Kulikovo Field?' just stared at us as if we were idiots.

'You don't say Kulikóvo, you say Kulíkovo. The village of Kulíkovka is right next to the battlefield, but Kulikóvka's over there, on the other side of the Don.'

After our meeting with this man we travelled along deserted country lanes, and until we reached the monument several kilometres away we did not come across a single person. It must have been because no one happened to be around on that particular day, for we could see the wheel of a combine harvester flailing somewhere in the distance. People obviously frequented this place and would do so again, because all the land had been planted with crops as far as the eye could see, and the harvest was almost ready – buckwheat, clover, sugar-beet, rye and peas (we had shelled some of those young peas); yet we saw no one that day and we passed through what seemed like the blessed calm of a nature reserve. Nothing disturbed us from musing on the fate of those fair-haired warriors, nine out of every ten of whom lay seven feet beneath the present topsoil, and whose bones had now dissolved into the earth, in order that Holy Russia might rid herself of the heathen Mussulman.

The features of the land – this wide slope gradually ascending to Mamai Hill – could not have greatly changed over six centuries, except that the forest had disappeared. Spread out before us was the very place where they had crossed the Don in the evening and the night of 7 September, then settled down to feed their horses (though the majority were foot-soldiers), sharpen their swords, restore their morale, pray and hope – almost a quarter of a million Russians, certainly more than two hundred thousand. The population of Russia then was barely a seventh of what it is now, so that an army of that size staggers the imagination.

And for nine out of every ten warriors that was to be their last morning on earth.

On that occasion our men had not crossed the Don from choice, for what army would want to stand and fight with its retreat blocked by a river? The truth of history is bitter but it is better to admit it: Mamai had as allies not only Circassians, Genoese and Lithuanians but also Prince Oleg of Ryazan. (One must also understand Oleg's motives: he had no other way of protecting his territory from the Tatars, as it lay right across their path. His land had been ravaged by fire three times in the preceding seven years.) That is why the Russians had crossed the Don – to protect their rear from their own people, the men of Ryazan: in any other circumstances Orthodox Christians would not have attacked them.

The needle loomed up in front of us, though it was no longer a needle but an imposing tower, unlike anything I had ever seen. We could not reach it directly: the tracks had come to an end and we were confronted by standing crops. We wheeled our bicycles round the edges of the fields and, finally, starting nowhere in particular, there emerged from the ground an old, neglected, abandoned road, overgrown with weeds, which grew more distinct as it drew nearer to the monument and even had ditches on either side of it

Suddenly the crops came to an end and the hillside became even more like a nature reserve, a piece of fallow land overgrown with tough rye-grass instead of the usual feather-grass. We paid homage to this ancient place in the best way possible – just by breathing in the pure air. One look around, and behold! – there in the light of sunrise the Mongol chief Telebei is engaged in single combat with Prince Peresvet, the two leaning against each other like two sheaves of wheat; the Mongolian cavalry are shooting their arrows and brandishing their spears; with faces contorted with blood-lust they trample on the Russian infantry, breaking through the core of their formation and driving them back to where a milky cloud of mist has risen from the Nepryadva and the Don.

Our men were mown down like wheat, and we were trampled to death beneath their hoofs.

Here (provided that the person who guessed the spot did so correctly) at the very pivot of the bloody carnage, are the monument and the church with the unearthly domes which had so amazed us from afar. There turned out to be a simple solution to the puzzle: the local inhabitants have ripped off the metal from all five domes for their own requirements, so the domes have become transparent; their delicate structure is still intact, except that it now consists of nothing but the framework, and from a distance it looks like a mirage.

The monument, too, is remarkable at close quarters. Unless you go right up to it and touch it you will not understand how it was made. Although it was built in the last century, in fact well over a hundred years ago, the idea – of piecing the monument together from sections of cast iron – is entirely modern, except that nowadays it would not be cast in iron. It is made up of two square platforms, one on top of another, then a twelve-sided structure which gradually becomes round; the lower part is decorated in relief with iron shields, swords, helmets and Slavonic inscriptions. Farther up it rises in the shape of a fourfold cylinder, cast so that it looks like four massive organ-pipes welded together. Then comes a capping-piece with an incised pattern, and above it all a gilded cross triumphing over a crescent. The whole tower – fully thirty metres high – is made up of figured slabs tightly bolted together, just as if the monument had been cast in a single piece, so that not a single rivet or seam is visible, at least until time, or more likely the sons and grandsons of the men who put it up, had begun to knock holes in it.

After the long route to the monument through empty fields, we had assumed that the place would be deserted. As we walked along we were wondering why it was in this

state. This was, after all, a historic spot. What happened
here was a turning point in the fate of Russia. For our in-
vaders have not always come from the West . . . Yet this
place is spurned, forgotten.

How glad we were to be mistaken! At once, not far from
the monument, we caught sight of a grey-haired old man
and two young boys. They had thrown down their rucksacks
and were lying in the grass, writing something in a large
book the size of a class register. When we approached we
found that he was a literature teacher who had met the boys
somewhere near by, and that the book was not a school
exercise-book, but none other than the visitors' comments-
book. But there was no museum here; where, then, in all
this wild field was the book kept?

Suddenly a massive shadow blotted out the sun. We
turned around. It was the keeper of Kulikovo Field – the
man whose duty it was to guard our glorious heritage.

We did not have time to focus the camera, and in any case
it was impossible to take a snap into the sun. What is more,
the keeper would have refused to be photographed (he
knew what he was worth and refused all day to let himself
be photographed). How shall I set about describing him?
Should I begin with the man himself? Or start with his
sack? (He was carrying an ordinary peasant's sack, only
half-full and evidently not very heavy since he was holding
it without effort.)

The keeper was a hot-tempered muzhik, who looked
something of a ruffian. His arms and legs were hefty, and his
shirt was dashingly unbuttoned. Red hair stuck out from
under the cap planted sideways on his head, and, although
it was obviously a week since he had shaved, a fresh reddish
scratch ran right across his cheek.

'Ah!' he greeted us in a disapproving voice as he loomed
over us. 'You've just arrived, have you? How did you get
here?'

He seemed puzzled, as if the place were completely fenced

in and we had found a hole to crawl through. We nodded towards the bicycles which we had propped up in the bushes. Although he was holding the sack as though about to board a train, he looked as if he would demand to see our passports. His face was haggard, with a pointed chin and a determined expression.

'I'm warning you! Don't damage the grass with your bicycles!'

With this, he let us know immediately that here, on Kulikovo Field, you were not free to do as you liked.

The keeper's unbuttoned coat was long-skirted and enveloped him like a parka: it was patched in a few places and was the colour you read about in folktales – somewhere between grey, brown, red and purple. A star glinted in the lapel of his jacket; at first we thought it was a medal, but then we realized it was just the ordinary little badge, with Lenin's head in a circle, that everyone buys on Revolution Day. A long blue and white striped linen shirt, obviously home-made, was hanging out from underneath his jacket and gathered at the waist by an army belt with a five-pointed star on the buckle. His second-hand officer's breeches were tucked into the frayed tops of his canvas boots.

'Well?' he asked the teacher in a much gentler tone of voice. 'How's the writing going?'

'Fine, Zakhar Dmitrich,' he replied, calling him by name. 'We've nearly finished.'

'Will you' (more sternly again) 'be writing too?'

'Later on.' We tried to escape from his insistent questions by cutting in: 'Do you know when this monument was built?'

'Of course I do!' he snapped, offended, coughing and spluttering at the insult. 'What do you think I'm here for?'

And carefully lowering his sack (which clinked with what sounded like bottles), the keeper pulled a document out of his pocket and unfolded it; it was a page of an exercise-book on which was written, in capital letters and in complete disregard of the ruled lines, a copy of the monument's dedication to Dmitry Donskoy and the year – 1848.

'What is that?'

'Well, comrades,' sighed Zakhar Dmitrich, revealing by his frankness that he was not quite the tyrant that he had at first pretended to be, 'it's like this. I copied it myself from the plaque because everyone asks when it was built. I'll show you where the plaque was, if you like.'

'What became of it?'

'Some rogue from our village pinched it – and we can't do anything about it.'

'Do you know who it was?'

'Of course I know. I scared off some of his gang of louts. I dealt with them all right, but he and the rest got away. I'd like to lay my hands on all those vandals, I'd show 'em.'

'But why did he steal the plaque?'

'For his house.'

'Can't you take it back?'

'Ha, ha!' Zakhar threw back his head in reply to our foolish question. 'That's the problem! I don't have any authority. They won't give me a gun. I need a machine-gun in a job like this.'

Looking at the scratch across his cheek, we thought to ourselves it was just as well they didn't give him a gun.

Then the teacher finished what he was writing and handed back the comments-book. We thought that Zakhar Dmitrich would put it under his arm or into his sack, but we were wrong. He opened the flap of his dirty jacket and revealed, sewn inside, a sort of pocket or bag made of sacking (in fact, it was more like a pouch than anything else) the exact size of the comments-book, which fitted neatly into it. Also attached to the pouch was a slot for the blunt indelible pencil which he lent to visitors.

Convinced that we were now suitably intimidated, Zakhar-the-Pouch picked up his sack (the clinking was glass) and went off with his long, loping stride into the bushes. Here the brusque forcefulness with which he had first met us vanished. Hunching himself miserably, he sat down, lit a cigarette, and smoked with such unalleviated grief, with such despair, that one might have thought that all those who had perished on this battlefield had died only yesterday and had been his closest relatives, and that now he did not know how to go on living.

We decided to spend the whole day and night here, to see whether night-time at Kulikovo really was as Blok described it in his poem. Without hurrying we walked over to the monument, inspected the abandoned church and wandered over the field, trying to imagine the dispositions of the battlefield on that eighth of September; then we clambered up on to the iron surface of the monument.

Plenty of people had been here before us. It would be quite wrong to say that the monument had been forgotten. People had been busy carving the iron surface of the monument with chisels and scratching it with nails, whilst those with less energy had written more faintly on the church walls with charcoal: 'Maria Polyneeva and Nikolay Lazarev were here from 8/5/50 to 24/5 . . .', 'Delegates of the regional conference were here . . .', 'Workers from the Kimovskaya Postal Administration were here 23/6/52 . . .' and so on and so on.

Then three young working lads from Novomoskovsk drove up on motor-bikes. Jumping off lightly on to the iron surface, they started to examine the warm, grey-black body of the monument and to slap it affectionately; they were surprised at how well made it was and explained to us how it had been done. In return, from the top platform we pointed out everything we knew about the battle.

But who can nowadays know exactly where and how it took place? According to the manuscripts, the Mongol-Tatar cavalry cut into our infantry regiments, decimated them and drove them back towards the crossings over the Don, thus turning the Don from a protective moat against

Oleg into a possible death-trap. If the worst had happened, Dmitry would have been called 'Donskoy' for the opposite reason. But he had taken everything into careful account and stood his ground, something of which not every grand duke was capable. He left a boyar dressed in his, Dmitry's, attire, fighting beneath his flag, while he himself fought as an ordinary foot-soldier, and he was once seen taking on four Tatars at once. But the grand-ducal standard was chopped down and Dmitry, his armour severely battered, barely managed to crawl to the wood when the Mongols broke through the Russian lines and drove them back. But then another Dmitry, Volynsky-Bobrok, the governor of Moscow, who had been lying in ambush with his army, attacked the ferocious Tatars from the rear. He drove them back, harrying them as they galloped away, then he wheeled sharply and forced them into the river Nepryadva. From that moment the Russians took heart: they re-formed and turned on the Tatars, rose from the ground and drove all the khans, the enemy commanders, even Mamai himself, forty versts away across the river Ptan as far as Krasivaya Mech. (But here one legend contradicts another; an old man from the neighbouring village of Ivanovka had his own version: the mist, he said, had not lifted, and in the mist Mamai, thinking a broad oak tree beside him was a Russian warrior, took fright – 'Ah, mighty is the Christian god!' – and so fled.)

Afterwards the Russians cleared the field of battle and buried the dead: it took them eight days.

'There's one they didn't pick up – they left him behind!' a cheerful fitter from Novomoskovsk said accusingly.

We turned around and could not help bursting out laughing. Yes! – one fallen warrior was lying there this very day, not far from the monument, face down on mother-earth, his native land. His bold head had dropped to the ground and his valiant limbs were spreadeagled; he was without his shield or sword, in place of his helmet wore a threadbare cap, and near his hand lay a sack. (All the same, he was careful not to crush the edge of his jacket with the pouch in it, where he kept the comments-book; he had pulled it out from underneath his stomach and it was lying on the grass beside him.) Perhaps he was just lying there in a drunken stupor, but if he was sleeping or thinking, then the way he was sprawled across the ground was very touching. He went perfectly with the field. They should cast an iron figure like that and place it here.

However, for all his height, Zakhar was too skinny to be a warrior.

'He doesn't want to work on the *kolkhoz*, so he found himself a soft government job where he can get a suntan,' one of the lads growled.

What we disliked most of all was the way Zakhar flew at all the new arrivals, especially those who looked as if they might cause him trouble. During the day a few more people arrived; when he heard their cars he would get up, shake himself and immediately pounce on them with threats, as if they, not he, were responsible for the monument. Before they had time to be annoyed, Zakhar himself would give vent to such violent indignation about the desolation of the place that it seemed incredible that he could harbour such passion.

'Don't you think it's a disgrace?' he said, waving his arms aggressively to four people who got out of a Zaporozhets car. 'I'll bide my time, then I'll walk right through the regional department of culture.' (With those long legs he could easily have done it.) 'I'll take leave and I'll go to Moscow, right to Furtseva, the minister of culture herself. I'll tell her everything.'

But as soon as he noticed that the visitors were intimidated and were not standing up to him, he picked up his sack with an air of importance, as an official picks up his briefcase, and went off to have a smoke and a nap.

Wandering here and there, we met Zakhar several times

during the day. We noticed that when he walked he limped
in one leg, and we asked him what had caused it. He replied
proudly:

'It's a souvenir from the war!'

Again we did not believe him: he was just a practised liar.

We had drunk our water-bottles dry, so we went up to
Zakhar and asked him where we could get some water.
Wa-ater? The whole trouble was, he explained, that there
was no well here and they wouldn't allocate any money to
dig one. The only source of drinking water in the whole
field was the puddles. The well was in the village.

After that, he no longer bothered to get up to talk to us,
as if we were old friends.

When we complained about the inscriptions having been
hacked away or scratched over, Zakhar retorted:

'Have a look and see if you can read any of the dates. If you
find any new damage, then you can blame me. All this
vandalism was done before my time, they don't dare try it on
when I'm around! Well, perhaps some scoundrel hid in the
church and then scribbled on the walls – I've only got one
pair of legs, you know!'

The church, dedicated to St Sergey of Radonezh, who
united the Russian forces and brought them to battle, and
soon afterwards effected the reconciliation between Dmitry
Donskoy and Oleg of Ryazan, was a sturdy fortress-like
building with tightly interlocking limbs: the squat rectangle
of the nave, a cloister surmounted by a watch-tower, and
two round castellated towers. There were a few windows
like loopholes.

Inside it everything had been stripped and there wasn't
even a floor – you walked over sand. We asked Zakhar about
it.

'Ha, ha, ha! It was all pinched!' He gloated over us. 'It
was during the war. Our people in Kulikovo tore up all the
slabs from the floors and paved their yards so they wouldn't
have to walk in the muck. I made a list of who took the

slabs . . . Then the war ended, but they still went on pinching the stuff. Even before that our troops had used all the ikon-screens to put round the edges of dug-outs and for heating their stoves.'

As the hours passed and he got used to us, Zakhar was no longer embarrassed to delve into his sack in front of us, and we gradually found out exactly what was inside it. It contained empty bottles (twelve kopecks) and jam-jars (five kopecks) left behind by visitors, which he picked up in the bushes after their picnics, and also a full bottle of water because he had no other access to drinking water during the day. He carried two loaves of rye bread, which he broke off now and again and chewed for his frugal meals.

'People come here in crowds all day long. I don't have any time to go off to the village for a meal.'

On some days he carried a precious half-bottle of vodka in there or some canned fish; then he would clutch the sack tightly, afraid to leave it anywhere. That day, when the sun had already begun to set, a friend on a motor-bike came to see him; they sat in the bushes for an hour and a half, then the friend went away and Zakhar came back without his sack. He talked rather more loudly, waved his arms more vigorously, and, noticing that I was writing something, warned us:

'I'm in charge here, let me tell you! In '57 they decided to put a building up here. See those posts over there, planted round the monument? They've been here since then. They were cast in Tula. They were supposed to join up the posts with chains, but the chains never came. So they gave me this job and they pay me for it. Without me the whole place would be in ruins!'

'How much do you get paid, Zakhar Dmitrich?'

With a sigh like a blacksmith's bellows, he was speechless for a moment. He mumbled something, then said quietly:

'Twenty-seven roubles.'

'What? The minimum's thirty.'

'Well, maybe it is . . . And I don't get any days off either. Morning to night I'm on the job without a break, and I even have to come back at night too.'

What an incorrigible old liar he is, we thought.

'Why do you have to be here at night?'

'Why d'you think?' he said in an offended voice. 'How can I leave the place at night? Someone's got to watch it all the time. If a car comes I have to make a note of its number.'

'Why the number?'

'Well, they won't let me have a gun. They say I might shoot the visitors. The only authority I've got is to take their number. And supposing they do some damage?'

'What do you do with the number afterwards?'

'Nothing. I just keep it . . . Now they've built a house for tourists, have you seen it? I have to guard that too.'

We had, of course, seen the house. Single-storey, with several rooms, it was near completion but was still kept locked. The windows had already been put in, though several of them were already broken; the floors were laid, but the plastering was not yet finished.

'Will you let us stay the night there?' (Towards sunset it had begun to get cold – it was going to be a bitter night.)

'In the tourist house? No, it's impossible.'

'Then who's it for?'

'No, it can't be done. Anyway, I haven't got the keys. So you needn't bother to ask. You can sleep in my shed.'

His low shed with its sloping roof was designed for half a dozen sheep. Bending down, we peered inside. Broken, trampled straw was scattered around, on the floor there was a cooking-pot with some left-overs in it, a few more empty bottles and a desiccated piece of bread. However, there was room for our bikes, and we could lie down and still leave enough space for Zakhar to stretch out.

He made use of our stay to take some time off.

'I'm off to Kulikovo to have supper at home. Grab a bite of something hot. Leave the door on the hook.'

'Knock when you want to come in,' we said laughingly.
'OK.'

Zakhar-the-Pouch turned back the other flap of his miraculous jacket to reveal two loops sewn into it. Out of his inexhaustible sack he drew an axe with a shortened handle and placed it firmly in the loops.

'Well,' he said gloomily, 'that's all I have for protection. They won't allow me anything else.'

He said this in a tone of the deepest doom, as if he were expecting a horde of infidels to gallop up one of these nights and overthrow the monument, and he would have to face them alone with his little hatchet. We even shuddered at his voice as we sat there in the half-light. Perhaps he wasn't a buffoon at all? Perhaps he really believed that if he didn't stand guard every night the battlefield and the monument were doomed?

Weakened by drink and a day of noisy activity, stooping and barely managing to hobble, Zakhar went off to his village and we laughed at him once more.

As had been our wish, we were left alone on Kulikovo Field. Night set in with a full moon. The tower of the monument and the fortress-like church were silhouetted against it like great black screens. The distant lights of Kulikovo and Ivanovka competed faintly with the light of the moon. Not one aeroplane flew overhead, no motor-car rumbled by, no train rattled past in the distance. By moonlight the pattern of the near-by fields was no longer visible. Earth, grass and moonlit solitude were as they had been in 1380. The centuries stood still and as we wandered over the Field we could evoke the whole scene – the camp-fires and the troops of dark horses. From the river Nepryadva came the sound of swans, just as Blok had described.

We wanted to understand the battle of Kulikovo in its entirety, grasp its inevitability, ignore the infuriating ambiguities of the chronicles: nothing had been as simple or as straightforward as it seemed; history had repeated itself after a long time-lag and when it did the result was disastrous. After the victory the warriors of Russia faded away; Tokhtamysh immediately replaced Mamai and two years after Kulikovo he crushed the power of Muscovy; Dmitry Donskoy fled to Kostroma, while Tokhtamysh again destroyed both Ryazan and Moscow, took the Kremlin by a ruse, plundered it, set it on fire, chopped off heads and dragged his prisoners back in chains to the Golden Horde, the Tatar capital.

Centuries pass and the devious path of history is simplified for the distant spectator until it looks as straight as a road drawn by a cartographer.

The night turned bitterly cold, but we shut ourselves in the shed and slept soundly right through it. We had decided to leave early in the morning. It was hardly light when we pushed our bicycles out and, with chattering teeth, started to load them up.

The grass was white with hoarfrost; wisps of fog stretched from the hollow in which Kulikovka village lay and across the fields, dotted with haycocks. Just as we emerged from the shed to mount our bicycles and leave, we heard a loud, ferocious bark coming from one of the haycocks and a shaggy grey dog ran out and made straight for us. As it bounded out, the haycock collapsed behind it; wakened by the barking, a tall figure arose from beneath it, called for the dog and began to shake off the hay. It was already light enough for us to recognize him as our Zakhar-the-Pouch, still wearing his curious short-sleeved overcoat.

He had spent the night in the haycock, in the bone-chilling cold. Why? Was it anxiety or was it devotion to the place that had made him do it?

Immediately our previous attitude of amused condescension vanished. Rising out of the haycock on that frosty morning, he was no longer the ridiculous 'keeper', but rather the Spirit of the Field, a kind of guardian angel who never left the place.

He came towards us, still shaking himself and rubbing his hands together, and with his cap pushed back on his head he seemed like a dear old friend.

'Why didn't you knock, Zakhar Dmitrich?'

'I didn't want to disturb you.' He shrugged his shoulders and yawned. He was covered all over in hay and fluff. As he unbuttoned his coat to shake himself, we caught sight of both the comments-book and his sole legal weapon, the hatchet, in their respective places.

The grey dog by his side was baring its teeth.

We said good-bye warmly and were already pedalling off when, with his long arm raised, he called out:

'Don't worry! I'll see to it! I'll go right to Furtseva! To Furtseva herself!'

That was two years ago. Perhaps the place is tidier now and better cared for. I have been a bit slow about writing this article, but I haven't forgotten the Field of Kulikovo, nor its keeper, its red-haired tutelary spirit.

And let it be said that we Russians would be very foolish to neglect that place.